HIS ACCIDENTAL DADDY

LUNA DAVID

WARNINGS

Childhood trauma/neglect, alcoholism, mental health, anxiety disorder

To anyone who's had someone important come into their lives accidentally. Sometimes fate has a way of helping us when we need it most.

CHAPTER ONE

Asher

"How are you guys doing today? Hmm? You're looking healthy and hearty. Almost time for harvest. A few more days, I think." Asher moved from one aquaponics grouping of plants to the next, tracking their growth cycles on his tablet. He kept a constant conversation going with the plants, knowing it probably made no difference but hoping it helped them in some small way. Regardless, it felt right. They were his babies, after all.

He checked the water pumps and the timers and then scanned his pH data gathered from the last twenty-four hours and went down the row of ponds, adjusting the pH levels depending on their data set. He spent the last couple of hours of every shift performing these tasks, talking all the while and tracking everything on his tablet. He liked to chart growth patterns for every plant in the greenhouse, the numbers fascinating him, educating him, and giving him a clearer understanding of what to expect and when to expect it.

His boss and the owner of The Glasshouse, Jennifer Cook, who had taught him nearly everything he knew over the last four years of his employment, called to him from across a sea of aquaponics ponds growing all sorts of plants, vegetables, and flowers, their most profitable of which was cannabis. The

Glasshouse was the biggest provider of medical marijuana in four counties, and it was what made Jenn's greenhouse a very lucrative business and provided him with health insurance and a pretty good salary.

He held up a hand, asking her to wait a moment until he'd gathered his current reading, put down his equipment, and made his way towards her. She was a statuesque woman, taller than him by at least six inches, and who, at fifty-five, was still a stunner. She met him halfway and patted him on the shoulder. "I've already spoken to Madi but wanted to ask if you had time to come in an hour early tomorrow. We'll have enough staff for you both to take a couple of hours for lunch, if you're willing to stay until the end of the day."

His brow furrowed in confusion. "I thought the supply delivery wasn't until Friday."

She gave him a sad smile, which pinged his anxiety as she shook her head. "This is a management meeting to discuss some changes coming up."

Yeah, that was more than just a ping. That was a full-fledged uppercut to his stress levels, and she must have seen it on his face. "Asher, it's all right. I don't want you worrying about this. We'll get things sorted out tomorrow. It could be a really great thing for you both, okay?"

Well, that was cryptic. He crossed his arms over his chest but didn't want to make her feel guilty, so he gave her what he hoped was a smile but was probably more like a grimace. "All right. Sure. If she's okay with it, I'm fine with it as well. I'm catching a ride with her, so that works."

She gave him a gentle smile and rubbed his back. "Great. I'll bring coffee and bagels."

A real smile graced his face, and he chuckled. "You're the best."

She winked at him. "I'm gonna finish up with the financials, but I'll be ready to go when you are."

He started to walk backwards towards his next testing pond as he replied, "Sounds good. See you in about an hour."

As he watched her leave the greenhouse, dread pooled in his belly. His heart started to beat in earnest when he realized he was so close to the end of his workday. The stress he'd been able to push back once he'd arrived hit him full force. Driving. Driving anywhere was so stress-inducing for him, it was almost painful physically. He knew where the fear came from. He knew it was all in his head. He knew he gave it too much credence over his day-to-day existence. None of that mattered when his body was cold and clammy from panic.

He made fists of his hands, imagining the calm he knew he could force on himself. He had another hour's worth of work to do. He visualized relaxation and forced the vision of it, starting at his hands and moving up his arms to his head and his mind, and down from there to the rest of his body. It wasn't a magic pill. It didn't make the feelings go away, but every Tuesday evening, an hour before work was over, it allowed him to finish what needed to be done.

Turning, he made his way back to where he'd left off and continued making adjustments. It was monotonous work, but he didn't mind that. In fact, monotony worked in his favor. His job rarely stressed him out, and he loved what he did. He couldn't imagine doing anything else and hoped like hell he wouldn't have to, regardless of what Jenn had to say the following morning.

When he was finished, he made his way to the back where there was an employee bathroom, a breakroom, the stockroom, and two offices. All the other employees had gone home an hour prior. Taking his apron off, he stowed it in his locker and pulled out his wallet and his cell phone, grabbing his coat off the hook as he walked out the door. He approached Jenn's office and knocked on the doorjamb, only stepping in when she glanced up from her desk and took off her reading glasses.

"Did an hour go by already?"

He smirked at her surprise. "In the zone, huh?"

"This is the only part of the business I don't enjoy. I should have hired a business manager long ago. They could have taken care of all the accounting for me."

"Why not do it now?"

She glanced at her desk again and shut down her computer. He couldn't help but feel she was avoiding meeting his eyes, which made his heart beat a little faster. "We'll have to see. I'm good at it. It's just not fun for me, so I'm just feeling whiney."

He chuckled. "Well, I wouldn't want to do it either. My best work is done with the plants."

She gave him a beaming smile that lit up her face. "Which is why you're the greenhouse manager. I can't believe how lucky I was when you walked in that door asking for an application."

He blushed, unable to help himself, and looked down at his shoes for a moment or two before gazing back up. "Thanks. Um, are you ready to go?"

"Yeah, I am. I'll finish the rest tomorrow."

She picked up her jacket and put it on, pulled her purse from the lower drawer of her desk, and walked his way. He gestured her through the door and followed her out to the front, where she unlocked the front door and held it open for him to walk through. "See you bright and early tomorrow morning."

"Yup. I'll be here. Have a good night."

"You too, dear," she said as they both headed to their cars.

Jenn finally pulled out of the parking lot, waving jauntily. He always had to make himself look busy when she left at the same time as he did. He didn't want her to know how bad his anxiety got. So, when she was gone, he sat in the driver's seat and took several deep breaths, repeating his mantra, trying to convince himself everything was fine. "You can do this. You can do this. You can do this." It didn't work. It never did. He dreaded the days he had to drive. Dreaded going to bed the night before, dreaded waking up the next morning, and dreaded heading home after his shift.

The ball of anxiety in the pit of his stomach that had, more than once, caused stress ulcers, never truly went away. However, his deep breathing exercises, coupled with his relaxation music mix and his ridiculous mantra, usually helped him function long enough to get the job done.

Panic attacks were a part of his daily life, and there were way too many things that triggered them. He'd bought several self-help books, read lots of blogs from others who dealt with the same thing, and focused on helping himself, rather than expecting others to help him, because if his past was anything to go by, he knew the only person he could truly count on was himself.

Obviously, the books only helped so much because getting in the car and having to drive, something simple millions of people did every day, triggered panic. Every. Single. Damn. Time. It was exhausting. He thanked his lucky stars his best friend, Madison Girand, worked every other day of the week with him and lived in an apartment complex not too far from his own, which she had to pass on her way to work every day.

He still got nervous being driven, but it was much more manageable. But Tuesdays. Fuck. Tuesdays were his worst days. That was the day Madi had all her labs for her night classes, and she never worked. Hence his current predicament of driving-induced panic. He'd made it to work, and he knew he'd make it home, now that his day was over. That didn't make his stress dissipate in the least. It never did.

The car was on. He'd learned long ago that turning the car on after he calmed himself down ratcheted up his panic, and he was back where he'd started. So, every time he had to drive, he forced himself to get in the car and turn it on immediately, and only then would he start his deep breathing and mantra exercises, such as they were.

Feeling sick to his stomach, he put the car in reverse and backed ever so slowly out of his parking space, being hyper vigilant of what was around him, even though he knew everyone was gone and his was the only car left in the parking lot. As he turned onto the street, he flicked on his stereo, soaking up the sound of Enya's "Watermark," increasing the volume to drown out some of the road noise he knew he'd be hearing. It was a fifteen-minute drive, which, in the grand scheme of things, wasn't too bad. Mentally, he knew this. Emotionally, it felt like hours.

Not only was he stressed about the meeting the next morning, but it had been drizzling when he'd left. That had increased his stress levels, making everything that much harder. But halfway through his drive home, some fucked up, monsoon-type rain started attacking his windshield like he'd personally pissed it off.

His body was still locked up with tension, and sheets of rain battered his car, causing him to slow down and focus on the road right in front of him so he didn't lose track of the lines and move into another lane accidentally. The streets seemed strangely empty, which made him feel a little more at ease that he didn't have to be worried about too many drivers around him as he drove into town.

He pulled to a stop at a red light, taking a deep breath and shaking his hands out to relieve the ache in his fingertips caused by his brutal grip on the wheel. Not much longer and he'd be home. The rain fucking sucked, but he'd be all right. Taking a few deep breaths to calm himself down, he glanced up to see the light turning from red to green and slowly pulled out into the intersection. Visibility was absolute shit, but when he glanced both ways down the street, the glow of a pair of headlights rushing towards him gave him only a second to suck in a breath.

His heart rate shot through the roof, and he pushed his foot down on the gas in a futile attempt to take some action to avoid the inevitable, but he knew it wouldn't help. He could only close his eyes, his muscles locking up, before the car slammed into his passenger side. The seat belt wasn't enough to keep him from harm; his head collided with the car door's window, and everything went black.

CHAPTER TWO

Thornton

I t was Taco Tuesday, so Thornton was visiting Mama's Chimichangas, the best Tex-Mex food truck in town. He was there every Tuesday at some point during the day. It also happened to be one of the businesses he'd invested in. He hadn't regretted it for a second. He'd never tasted better. Business was good.

Polishing off the trio of steak soft tacos he favored, he tossed his plate and napkins in the trash can Mama Hernandez kept under the counter, folded his arms over his chest, and smiled down at the tiny lady he'd grown to care a lot about over the last couple of years of their business dealings together. "So, you were able to survive the lunch rush without me?"

He'd texted her earlier, asking if she was still working and had enough steak for his favorite tacos. She'd kept the truck open for an extra thirty minutes just for him, and his stomach was blissfully happy about it. As soon as he'd arrived, she'd closed the truck for other business and had gone about making him the best dinner he could think of for a Tuesday evening.

She snorted and continued wiping down the counters and cleaning up for the day. "It was nearly impossible, but Sofia tried her best to put her feet in your big shoes."

My big shoes? Why would she… Oh!

He chuckled when he realized that was her take on "big shoes to fill." That and her sarcasm about needing his help amused him. He knew full well that he was lacking in the skills it took to take care of her customers and that her daughter would have had no trouble handling any rush that came through. He always tried to lend a hand when he showed up and the truck was busy, which it was more often than not. But he often just did his best to help clean up, deal with the trash if it was full, bring them things they needed, and refill the ice box with drinks.

He'd thought Mama was joking when she told him at the very beginning of their business dealings that Taco Tuesdays really were her busiest days. He found the fact that such a thing could impact her business in that way so amusing. But he'd seen it proven on a weekly basis and usually tried to stop by to help out, occasionally bringing her extra food if she ran out during the lunch rush.

They usually had their business meetings once a month, and this was not that day, so he'd really only stopped by to say hello, visit one of his favorite people, and grab one of his favorite meals on the way home after a long day. He gathered up the trash bag, tied it off, and did the same for the one outside, bringing it in so she could throw it in the dumpster at the commissary.

"Gracias, mijo. You are good to me."

He smiled. "I could say the same about you. Where else can I get the world's best steak tacos? Why don't we run away together? We were obviously meant to be."

Her eyes were filled with mirth as she shooed him towards the door. "Go find someone else to flirt with. I'm much too old for you and don't have the right parts."

He threw his head back and laughed. "That's true, but if you did, your age wouldn't matter."

She shook her head, trying not to laugh with him, face mock serious. "Andale. Get out of here, mijo. You need to find a sexy man to keep you occupied."

He clutched his heart as if in pain. "You wound me, Mama! And you know you'd miss me if I wasn't here to harass you on a weekly basis."

She snapped a towel at him, but he'd never admit to yelping before he wiggled his eyebrows. "Feisty! I like that!" Another towel snap. "Okay, okay. Jesus, woman!"

She smiled and approached, leaning in to receive his usual cheek kiss of goodbye. He opened the back door of the food truck, stepped out, and waved. "See you next week. Don't work too hard."

"Bah! Then we'd both be penniless."

He chuckled at that ridiculous statement and shut the door, jogging to his car to escape the drizzling rain. Once he'd pulled on his seat belt, he turned the car on and asked Alexa to play some Creedence. He hummed, tapping his fingers on the steering wheel, unable to keep himself from singing along. "Someone told me long ago there's a calm before the storm. I know it's been coming for some time."

He continued singing, nodding along to the classic beat, when the rain went from drizzle to downpour. Unprepared for it, he slowed a bit and jumped in his seat at the shrill sound of his phone ringing. Fumbling with the volume, he found the button on his steering wheel and clicked it.

"Hello?"

One of his closest friends, Damon, asked, "Hey, you get your steak soft tacos?"

He scoffed. "You don't know me!"

"Pffft. Keep telling yourself that. Listen, Sir and I are having a few people over on Saturday, and we expect you to be there."

"I dunno. I have plans this weekend with Jimmy."

There was a beat of silence on the other end before Damon replied, "Well, bring him if you have to, but I know you hate mixing real life with all your many littles."

He shook his head, knowing Damon was just trying to get a rise out of him. "You make it sound like I have boys just surrounding me at all times."

His friend snorted. "You could."

"Hardly. You know I've been dating Jimmy for a several weeks, and before that I was with Charly for a couple of months. I'm not a player."

"Mmhmm, and you'll drop Jimmy just like you did Charly, before he gets any ideas."

It wasn't like that. He knew what he wanted, and so did Jimmy. They'd been scratching an itch, and it had run its course. "You act like I'm just breaking hearts all over the place. The boys I see are great, but when we're both feeling like it's not working, I don't want to drag it out for either of us."

"And Jimmy knows?"

"Yeah. He does. We've both talked about it. I've got a playdate with him this weekend. He said he wants to have little time once more, and I want to give that to him. He's a good boy, and it's not easy finding Daddies who enjoy age regression."

"Yeah, it's rare around here."

"And that makes it hard to find what I'm looking for. We've been over this. I'm not going to be a celibate monk until the right boy comes along, but I also don't want to play too long with a boy who isn't the one. We'd both end up settling, and that's not what I want to do."

His friend sighed, and he could practically see his exasperated expression. "I get it. So, you'll come then, yeah?"

"I'll see what I can do. What time?"

He heard Damon ask his husband, who was also his Dom, before coming back on the line to answer. "Around five-thirty, give or take."

"All right. I'll try to juggle things around."

"See that you do, or I'll have Sir torture you the next time you're in to see him."

The thought of Damon trying to convince his *very* professional husband, Syed, who just happened to be Thornton's doctor, to do anything unprofessional to him at his next physical was completely ludicrous. He laughed, rolling his eyes and shaking his head.

He turned the wipers as high as they would go barely able to see ahead of him, let alone use his side mirrors. Glancing behind him to check for cars, he switched lanes to prepare for his turn on the next block. He heard Damon talking in the background when he turned to face the road in front of him again. But before he could reply, panic seized his whole body when he saw a car drive into the intersection. At the same time, he could barely make out his light had turned red. "Fuck!"

He saw what was coming in hundreds of little snapshots, like a photographer's shutter speed was rapidly capturing the horror of the moment. Everything happened so fast, it was like his car was moving at the speed of light when he knew he was driving under the speed limit. He didn't even have time to slam on his brakes or brace himself before he was colliding with the little gray hatchback.

The screech of metal, the breaking of glass, and the eerie silence that followed had his head spinning and his body shocked into immobility. The impact was so jarring he knew he'd be feeling it for a long while afterwards and quite possibly have a bad case of whiplash. He took several deep breaths, trying to calm himself, finally beginning to hear the world around him again, the pouring rain on the roof of the car, and a tic tic tic of his engine, letting him know it wasn't happy with him. He took mental stock of his body to ensure nothing was broken. Thank fuck for the seat belt.

He glanced up at the car his SUV had slammed into and didn't see any movement. Not that he'd see much in the downpour, but no movement at all scared him to death. Seeing movement to his left, he glanced and saw another car had stopped just shy of the car he'd hit, the driver a young girl who had her hands over her mouth in shock as the rain drenched her from head to toe.

He finally registered that Damon was yelling his name. "Thorn, what happened? Are you okay?"

"Fuck. Yeah. But I just fucking t-boned someone. Jesus. Call 911. I'm at the intersection of Thirty-first and Vine. I gotta go check on the driver I hit. There's no movement in the car."

"Calling now. Let me know as soon as possible if everyone is all right and if you need anything."

Glad his friend would take care of a task that would have slowed him down, he launched himself out of his car, slamming the door closed behind him. He rounded the tiny car, a rainbow Human Rights Campaign sticker catching his eye. He yelled to the teenage girl, not wanting anyone else hurt with visibility so low. "Get back in your car and pull over to the side of the street and wait there. The police are on their way, and they'll need you to be a witness."

She looked relieved he'd taken charge and turned to run to her car as he approached the driver's side and was nearly sick to his stomach at the amount of blood on the window. "Jesus Christ. Oh, fuck."

Thornton tried the door, and when it opened, he breathed a sigh of relief. The boy inside looked tiny and so very vulnerable. His body was leaning heavily against the seat belt strap. It looked to be the only thing that was keeping him upright in his unconscious state. And the blood. Oh, god, the blood was everywhere and just kept coming. When he'd opened the door, the rain landed on the boy's skin, the blood being diluted and traveling faster down his cheek.

Fucking head wounds. "Fuck, fuck, fuck. Kid, can you hear me? You're gonna be all right. An ambulance is on its way."

Goddammit. All of his instincts urged him to unbuckle the boy and cradle him in his arms, but he didn't trust that it wouldn't do more harm than good. He had no idea if his neck and back were damaged and didn't want to make anything worse. But he had to know if the boy was alive, as he couldn't even see if he was breathing or not. He reached in and placed his fingers on his carotid artery, not wanting to put too much pressure but needing to know.

Thornton thanked whatever deity would listen when he felt a steady pulse beneath his fingers. He needed to reassure the young man somehow with touch, so he knew he wasn't alone. He glanced down and saw his fingers twitching where his hand rested on the seat of the car. Thornton sat down gingerly on the narrow ledge of the door and gathered the young man's hand in his. "You're going to be okay. I'm here with you. You're not alone. The ambulance is on its way."

The rain let up a bit, causing him to look towards the street. His heart thrummed more rapidly when he felt the boy squeeze his hand in a barely there acknowledgment of his words. He glanced back and was stunned speechless when he was met with a pair of the most gorgeous eyes he'd ever seen with tiny chips of blues, greens, and ambers—eyes that gripped him, made his heart beat faster, sent goosebumps skittering over his skin. Something indefinable shifted inside of him, and he couldn't look away. They were eyes that were world-weary and more than likely older than his years.

And as much as he felt something strange was happening between them, right then and there, he shook himself back into the present. Focusing on his face and wincing at the blood that just kept coming out of the wound on his temple, Thornton spoke softly so he didn't spook him. "I'm here with you. You're going to be all right. Do you understand me?"

The boy nodded, then winced at the pain the movement had caused, and Thornton winced in sympathy. "Don't try to move. I don't know the extent of your injuries, so I think it's better if you don't." The kid whispered what Thornton thought was an affirmative response and, thankfully, didn't move again.

He couldn't wait for the ambulance, though. The amount of blood he was losing from his head wound had Thornton in a panic. He looked down at himself, trying to figure out what he could use to staunch the blood. He might have to use

12

the cotton lining of his coat. Moving to take it off, his hand brushed past the pocket, and he remembered the napkins he'd stuck in there when Mama had given him the tacos.

Reaching in, he pulled the wad of napkins out and scooted a little closer. He had to steady the boy's head on the opposite side with his other hand, so he didn't get hurt by moving it. Placing the napkins against the wound, he applied as much pressure as he dared, not wanting to hurt the boy any more than he already was. He heard the far-off sound of an ambulance and turned to face the direction he thought it was coming from. Jesus, he'd never been more grateful to hear that sound in his life.

Thornton's heart broke when he turned back and saw tears gather in the boy's lashes and nearly shattered in two when he heard pain and regret in the sweetest voice he'd ever heard. "I'm so sorry."

God.

"Don't apologize. None of this was your fault." Thornton glanced over when the sirens became deafening and squinted at the bright lights of the oncoming emergency vehicles, realizing the rain had lessened even more. Only a drizzle now. "The ambulance is here. You're gonna be…" When he glanced back at the young man, his eyes were closed again. "Shit… okay, you're gonna be okay."

Those startling eyes slowly opened again, and before Thornton knew what was coming out of his mouth, he asked, "Can you tell me your name?"

The man's eyes closed again, and Thornton figured he wouldn't answer, but when he finally said, "Asher," Thornton breathed a sigh of relief. He knew Asher was falling in and out of consciousness and only wanted to soothe him. "All right, Asher. My name is Thornton. It'll be just a few more moments, all right?"

Panic bled through the pain in Asher's eyes, and Thornton's heart gave a jerk in his chest when the boy said, "Don't leave me. Please."

The anguish in his voice and the tears he saw slip down Asher's face broke Thornton's heart. He felt something and glanced down and saw the boy's hand gripping his coat in a death grip, desperation making the boy's hand shake.

"I won't. I'm right here. I'll stay with you until they ask me to move so they can help you."

Asher opened his eyes, and stark fear showed in their depths. "Arrhythmia. Tell them…"

Horror lanced through his body as he realized what the boy was saying. A heart condition? Fuck, fuck, fuck. The boy lifted his right wrist and waved it a bit. Thornton saw the bracelet there and clasped Asher's arm, gently pulling it closer to him so he could read what it said. Asher Simmons, a phone number, Atrial Fibrillation, Coumadin.

He stood up, needing to do something to help and panicked that Asher's heart was giving out as he sat there doing his best to comfort him and stop the blood. He glanced back down, feeling helpless, and grew more worried when he realized Asher had lost consciousness again. He heard doors slamming and feet pounding on wet pavement. Two men, one older than Thornton and one younger, were suddenly there before him.

The older man placed his hand on Thornton's shoulder. "Sir, you need to back away so we can help the victim."

The pressure of the man's hand startled him out of his panicked state, and he rushed to speak. "He's been in and out of consciousness. His name is Asher Simmons. He managed to tell me he has an arrhythmia. His bracelet says atrial fibrillation and coumadin." He moved out of their way and watched as they set their equipment down.

The older EMT nodded and thanked him, and they began checking if Asher was conscious. When he didn't answer them, they moved fast, wrapping a huge, plastic neck brace on him and placing a board behind his back. Thornton knew he was no longer needed. But hell if he could force himself to move away. He watched as they carefully maneuvered Asher out of the car and placed him on a stretcher another EMT brought them. He glanced around and saw two ambulances had arrived, not just one. A firetruck and several cop cars. Jesus.

He stood, watching them roll Asher away, unsure what to do. He wanted to get in his car and follow them to the hospital, but he knew that was ridiculous. Wasn't it? He turned and started around Asher's car to do just that and was stopped by a police officer. "Sir, is that your car?"

He realized he was more shaken than he thought he was when he remembered he had to stay and deal with the mess he'd made. Fuck.

The cop pointed at his BMW with its crushed front end. Yeah, he wasn't going anywhere. He turned to face the cop, and another EMT approached him. This was going to be a long fucking night. The EMT looked him over to make sure he was truly all right. When the EMT suggested the ER to get him checked, he refused, and then the cop began peppering him with questions. After explaining everything and handing over his driver's license, he turned to get his registration from the car, when he finally realized he hadn't checked back in with the girl.

"The girl. Did she stay to talk to you?" He turned around, looking for her.

"Yeah, she's answering questions now. How are you feeling?"

"Physically, I'm fine. A little sore. I'm just feeling awful for running into the young man."

The policeman nodded. "Yeah. I understand that. He's in good hands, though. You'll be bruised in more places than you can imagine, and your neck is gonna hurt for a while. Like the EMT said, if you're refusing to go to the ER to get checked, make an appointment with your primary care doctor right away just to make sure everything is okay. If the EMT suggested you go to the ER, seeing your doctor is important. You may feel things tomorrow you aren't feeling right now with the adrenaline still coursing through you."

He nodded in response, knowing that was most likely true and already feeling the aches and pain he'd be feeling more of the next day. He'd have to call Syed and... Fuck. He walked to his car as quickly as his aching body would allow and excused himself as he walked by all the emergency personnel. "Sorry, everyone. Need to get the phone out of my car and let my friend know I'm okay."

He grabbed his phone, his keys, his iPad, and his registration, handing the paper over to the cop he'd been speaking to, remembering Asher's keys at the last minute. "What about the young man's keys and personal things?"

The cop raised his brows. "I can grab the keys and check for anything he might need and take them to the hospital. They'll make sure to get everything to him."

Thornton nodded. "Thanks for your help, officer." He stepped away, making the call he'd nearly forgotten about.

"Jesus, Thorn, we've been worried sick." Damon's strained voice made him feel like shit.

"I'm sorry. I was helping the guy I ran into until the EMTs and cops arrived. The poor kid I T-boned is a mess. Fuck, guys, he's probably no more than twenty years old."

"Are *you* all right, though?" The worry in Sy's voice made him realize he should have led with that.

"Yeah. I'm all right. I'm feeling achy, but I'll be okay."

"Thorn, I don't want this to wait."

He sighed, knowing he wasn't going to get out of it, when Syed said, "How about you come over here now? I can check you over to reassure my worrywart of a husband that you're fine."

Damon, his voice full of sarcasm, replied, "Yeah, because I'm the only one worried about him."

"Watch yourself, D." Thornton smiled at Syed's warning.

To which Damon replied, "Sorry, Sir."

He interjected. "No. I need to go to the hospital and check on Asher."

Syed wasn't going to let it drop that easily. "Thornton." Syed's voice held a warning. "We're coming to pick you up. We'll stop back by our place so I can check you out, and then we'll take you to the hospital."

He sighed. Well, it would save him a Lyft ride. "Okay. Yeah, that'll work. Christ, you guys. His blood was everywhere. He'd hit his head on the driver's side window. He was in and out of consciousness, and right as the ambulance arrived, he managed to tell me he has an arrhythmia. Showed me his bracelet listing atrial fibrillation and coumadin. He was unconscious by the time the medics got to him. For all I know, he could have been having a heart attack."

Syed muttered, "Fuck," over the line, and Thornton's heart flipped in his chest.

"Tell me what to expect when I get there. Don't church it up, Sy. Tell me the worst case so I'm prepared."

He heard his friend sigh through the line. "There are several things that could be happening."

His friend paused, so he pushed. "Just say it. Rip it off like a Band-Aid. I need to finish here so I can call you and get to the hospital."

He wanted to hear it. Needed to, actually, but the words made him feel sick to his stomach when Syed finally gave him the details. "The impact and adrenaline from the accident could have put him into AFib. He's taking coumadin, the medication on his bracelet, to help him with that. It's a blood thinner. He'll be given an EKG, a CT scan of his head, and bloodwork. If he's in AFib at the time of arrival, they'll give him medication to try and stop it."

"Will that even work?"

Syed made a noise that was neither a yes nor a no. "It could. Hopefully, it does. If it doesn't or if his heart rate is too high, they'll do a cardioversion in the

ER. Because he takes coumadin, they'll have to check his levels to see if he's at risk to throw a clot during the procedure."

He sucked in a breath, scared to death for the boy. "Jesus, Syed, I don't even know what any of that shit means! I didn't see anything else, but fuck, who knows what was going on internally."

"Let's not borrow more trouble. It all depends on what medication he uses to control his AFib. If he's taking another drug for the arrhythmia, he may not be in quite as much danger of internal bleeding."

"And what the fuck is a cardioversion?"

"It's where they'll try to convert his AFib to sinus rhythm by shocking his heart with paddles."

"Jesus, Sy. You're not making me feel any better."

"Thorn, he'll be sedated. If his head CT is clear, with no internal bleeding, he could be released tomorrow if he's got a concussion, which he most likely does. Hell, you most likely do as well."

He ignored that part and asked, "And if that doesn't happen?"

"Depending on where the bleeding is, they'll give him something to thicken up his blood."

"Where could he be bleeding?"

"Internally, but we're not going to go there right now. You have enough information to help you understand what could be going on with him. Hopefully, he's just got a concussion, and he'll be fine."

He growled, "Sy, tell me."

Damon spoke up instead of his husband. "Thorn, you don't need to know every possibility. It's not going to help you, and we know you want to get there as soon as possible. Finish up with the cops and your insurance and give us a call when you're ready for us to come get you."

Jesus, he had to call his insurance too. He sighed, knowing they were both right. "Yeah. Okay. I'll call you soon."

***

Two hours later, cursing the insurance company and emergency personnel for the delay—all while knowing it wasn't their fault—Syed picked him up, took him to their house, and checked him over. Besides the bruising that would get worse and the achiness he'd feel in his neck and his body for some time, Syed thought he would be fine but warned Thornton to call him if he started to feel a lot worse. He gave Thornton a travel bottle of over-the-counter pain meds and had him wash the blood off his hands and borrow a shirt so he wasn't walking around with blood on his clothes.

They dropped him off at the hospital. When he approached the front desk, he saw the woman's gaze on him. "Where—" He cleared his throat, suddenly even more nervous about Asher. "Where is Asher Simmons? He was brought in a couple of hours ago, head injury, arrhythmia. I need... please."

Seeing the woman's expression soften, he knew he must be more of a wreck than he thought. She got onto the computer in front of her and typed what he assumed was Asher's name. While still typing and not sparing him a glance, she asked, "Sir, are you family?"

He couldn't go through not knowing how Asher was. He just couldn't do it. Fuck. Clearing his throat, he answered in what he realized was a whisper, "Y-yes."

She gazed up at him expectantly, so in a bit of a panic, he told her the only thing that came to mind. "I'm his husband."

She raised her brows at that, but he didn't know if it was because she didn't believe him or because he was gay. But the only way her feelings mattered at that moment was if she didn't believe him and he couldn't get to Asher. She tapped a few more keys and nodded. "It looks like he's been admitted and is on the fourth floor, room 418. Take the elevator around the corner to my left to the fourth floor, turn right, and you'll see nurses' station there. They will show you where his room is."

He swallowed and nodded. "Thank you."

She smiled at him in sympathy as he walked away to follow her directions. When he reached the fourth floor, he found the nurses' station and waited to speak with the nurse behind the desk.

He gave a halfhearted smile when the nurse acknowledged him. "Hi, my name is Thornton Hayes. I'm here to see my husband, Asher Simmons."

She nodded and turned, tipping her head towards the door. "Come with me. He's resting, but I'm sure he'll be very happy to see you."

As they walked into the room, her words faded into the background when he laid eyes on Asher. Jesus, he was tiny in that big bed, tubes hooked to monitors, surgical tape, and gauze wrapped around his head protecting the injury on his temple.

His straight blond hair still had remnants of blood. His eyes were closed, but Thornton would never forget the startling blue-green brilliance of them. He was pale as a ghost. Even his lips, which had been pink and full when he was in the car, now looked faded. Overall, he looked awful and yet still beautiful.

Tuning back into his surroundings, he watched as a different nurse checked Asher's vitals. She began to fill him in about Asher's injuries, and he was overwhelmed with just how much had happened since he'd last seen Asher. The young woman smiled at him. "Your husband is a survivor. He came through the procedure and is doing well."

She headed towards the door, and he managed a wobbly, "Thank you," as she left.

CHAPTER THREE

Asher

There was a pounding in his head unlike anything he'd ever felt in his life. He could feel his heartbeat in his temple, a steady bass drum making itself known with every thump. That alone was enough to wake him up. But it was the distinct smell filling his nostrils and the tug on the top of his hand cluing him into the fact that he had an IV drip going that pushed him towards opening his eyes.

He fucking hated hospitals.

Cracking his eyes open just brought more pain to his head, but he forced the issue. It was dim in his room as the beeping of the machines droned in the background. He turned and realized what it must have been that woke him up—or rather who—and jumped a bit in his bed.

"Hi, Asher. I'm Jess, your shift nurse. You were in a car accident. Do you remember that?"

God, did he ever. If he never drove again, he'd be happy as hell. But he didn't think she'd care about that, so all he did was nod, which fuck, that hurt.

She must have seen the pain he was feeling written all over his face as she smiled sympathetically and asked, "How are you feeling?"

"M—" He cleared his throat and tried again. "My head is killing me."

"Not surprising. You hit your head pretty badly and have a concussion."

"What else? My ribs hurt too."

"Yeah, three of your ribs are cracked. You also went into AFib so they had to do a cardioversion, the paddles on the chest. We're gonna keep you for observation for twenty-four to forty-eight hours."

With how he was feeling, none of that surprised him. He didn't have the energy to try nodding again, so he murmured, "Okay."

"I'm going to give you some meds to help with the pain, all right? You should feel better soon."

He managed to whisper an affirmative as she gave him a dose of pain meds through his IV, and the pain overtook him again. He slowly glanced around the room, his gaze coming to rest on a gorgeous sleeping man that had his mind buzzing. God, the man was perfection. He loved a nice, short beard and thick, wavy, dark hair. He was sprawled out in a chair, his legs impossibly long. Asher glanced back up at his face and noticed the longest eyelashes he'd ever seen. He couldn't help but sigh.

But, why was he in Asher's room? And come to think of it, why was he reacting so strongly to a man he didn't know? He'd never reacted to someone like he was to this stranger. Somehow this man was different, which he couldn't begin to understand. And while he'd normally panic at having someone he didn't know in his room; panic wasn't what he was feeling. And wasn't that just a mind fuck?

He turned back to the nurse, confusion in his eyes. Her smile was warm when she filled him in. "He's been so worried about you. You're one lucky man."

"I'm... what?" Did his concussion come with a side order of hallucination? Because something wasn't adding up. And why did the man look so familiar?

"You're lucky to have such a sweet, attentive husband. He hasn't left your side since he arrived."

Husband? On what planet... Pain lanced through his head, making him wince and let out a low moan.

Wincing with him, she patted his shoulder. "You'll feel better soon. In the meantime, I'm going to get you some water. I'm sure you're parched. I'll be back in a bit."

Nodding and then regretting it immediately after, he simply closed his eyes to ward off the pain as much as possible until the meds kicked in. But no sooner did he close his eyes than they popped right back open. Thornton. Asher hadn't been dreaming him. Hadn't conjured him up at the accident site. He turned to face the beautiful, sleeping man in the chair and didn't dare look away until the pain meds had him drifting off to sleep.

When he woke sometime later, his head finally feeling somewhat better, he immediately turned to see if somehow, he'd dreamed that Thornton not only existed but was sitting in the chair next to him. The beautiful amber eyes, gorgeous masculine features, and dark, sculpted facial hair was a jolt to his system, even though he'd half expected to see him there. He couldn't help but feel some level of tension; the man *was* a stranger, after all. But somehow, when he thought the panic would bloom, it just... didn't.

But, what was he doing here?

"Hey, you're awake."

"Thor—" His mouth had gone dry, but he had a feeling it was because of the sexy-as-sin man before him, rather than anything else. He cleared his throat and tried again as the near stranger leaned forward, placing his elbows on his knees and watching him intently. "Thornton?"

The sweet smile that graced the guy's lips did fluttery things to his stomach. Concern suddenly hit Asher. "Are you hurt? I'm so sorry."

Thornton frowned, and somehow even that was sexy. "Why on earth would you be sorry? *I'm* the one that hit *you*."

He shrugged, not knowing why he felt like he needed to apologize. Technically, he knew his light had been green, but he always felt so out of sorts when he was driving. So keyed up and stressed out, he couldn't imagine he wasn't partially responsible in some way.

Thornton shook his head, tilting it to the side, and giving him a disbelieving look. "You were doing everything right. I was glancing behind me as I was trying to change lanes and obviously not going slow enough when visibility was so bad. By the time I turned back around, I saw you in the intersection and realized the light had turned red. This was my fault."

Asher still felt bad, whether it made sense or not. "But are you okay?"

"Asher..." It wasn't censure in Thornton's voice so much as confused exasperation. "I'm a little sore, but I'm just fine. You're the one in the hospital bed."

He didn't have anything to say to that, so he stayed quiet as he kept eye contact with Thornton until the man smiled and said, "I'm surprised you remembered my name. I wasn't sure you would. You were pretty dazed."

Hell, he was *still* dazed and would remain so, as long as he was under such close scrutiny of a man so utterly gorgeous, out of his league, and most likely straight. He... Wait. The nurse had called him Asher's husband. Surely, she didn't just come up with that on her own. "Do I have amnesia? I don't think I have amnesia."

The confused look on Thornton's face nearly made him smile. Asher couldn't imagine any scenario where the man wouldn't appeal to him. On every possible level. Thornton shook his head. "I doubt you do if you remember who I am. What makes you ask?"

He bit his lip, for some reason embarrassed to even say the words out loud. "The nurse said I was a lucky man because I had such an attentive husband and that you were so worried about me that you hadn't left my side."

He thought the man might blush—hell, he knew *he* would have, if the situation were reversed—but he didn't look chagrined in the least. A sweet smirk was all he got. Well, that and an unrepentant shrug. "I *have* been worried, and I haven't left your side. I had to be able to see for myself you were going to be okay, and that seemed to be the only way they'd let me back here. That and it was the only thing I could think of at the time. We don't exactly look alike, so..."

Asher blushed and looked away. But surprisingly, besides being a bit embarrassed by the husband bit, he felt fairly comfortable with Thornton, and he *never* felt comfortable with strangers. He'd have to think on what that meant later. Asher gazed towards the windows, noticing for the first time how dark it was already. "What time is it? Are visiting hours over soon?"

He didn't want them to be. He had no idea why, but he didn't like the idea of Thornton leaving. He watched as Thornton checked his watch. "It's three-thirty."

"AM?" As soon as he said it, he felt like an idiot. Of course AM. It was pitch black outside.

"Yeah."

"But... it's no longer visiting hours."

Again, that smirk. "Husbands don't have to go home when visiting hours are over." His face flamed even brighter, and he couldn't help but look away. Thornton obviously didn't feel awkward about the situation at all as he continued. "I feel awful about what happened. I hate that you were hurt so badly. Is there anyone I can call for you? Anyone you want to be here with you?"

He glanced up quickly, and his brow creased in confusion, pain exploding in his head at the movement, radiating out from his temple. "Ow, fuck." Asher's voice was barely there, and no sooner had he whispered it than his hand was captured on its way up to touch himself where the pain originated. The much larger hand gently squeezed his and pulled it back down to the bed, holding it there. Yeah, okay, probably a good idea not to touch. That thought kept him from using his other hand to rub at his painful ribs.

"Shit. You should be resting, and here I am chatting with you as if everything is fine. Let me call the nurse."

No. He didn't want that. Not yet, anyway. He just wanted to... be. Just for a little while longer. He didn't even mind the direct and very intense gaze he kept being subjected to. "No. I'm okay."

Pain meds always put him out, and even with the pain nearly making him whimper, he was afraid if he woke up again, the gorgeous apparition before him would disappear. He'd learned his lesson, though. He knew well enough now not to shake his head or make any more facial expressions that might cause pain to lance through him.

The soft caress of Thornton's thumb on the back of Asher's hand nearly made him sigh. It was rare that he was touched, and when he was, it was never a caress. "Asher, there's no reason you should be in pain if they can make you more comfortable."

The man's authoritative tone brooked no argument, but... "Are you going to leave?"

Asher hadn't meant to sound so needy—or pathetic, for that matter. Thornton's raised eyebrows had Asher's heart pounding. Feeling embarrassed, he gazed down at his lap until he got another squeeze of his hand. He looked up just as Thornton asked, "Do you want me to?"

He nearly shook his head again before he caught himself. "No. Please don't leave." The echo of the words he'd said to Thornton earlier at the accident site lay hanging between them.

The barely there lines around Thornton's eyes crinkled when he gave Asher a soft smile. "I'm not going anywhere."

He'd never been an assertive person. All he could chalk his bravery up to was the situation: his pain, his vulnerability, and the fact that he had nothing to lose. If Thornton left, he'd never see him again. If he didn't, then being honest and asking him to stay would be well worth the embarrassment. Even if he didn't understand what he was feeling around this enigmatic man, he knew he wanted more of it.

"Is there anyone I can call for you? Family or friends?"

"No. Well, a coworker friend of mine drives me to work most days, so I'll need to call her in the morning to let her know she doesn't need to pick me up. She can tell my boss."

He waited for a pitying look from the man. Admitting he basically had no one in his life was a tough pill to swallow. But all he saw there was understanding. "All right. Well, I'll call the nurse, so you can get some relief. And then later this morning, if you need to you can use my phone to call your friend."

He closed his eyes, grateful the decision about the pain meds was being taken out of his hands. "Thank you."

He winced when the tinny voice of the nurse came through the speakers in the room. "Nurses' station. How can I help you?"

He looked at Thornton, but before Asher could answer the nurse, the little smirk was back, and Thornton took care of it for him. "Yes, ma'am. My husband is in a lot of pain. Can he have some more pain medication, please?"

"Yes, sir. I'll send his nurse in after she's finished with her current patient."

"Thank you."

The speaker clicked off. The wink and cheeky smile from Thornton set his heart racing. He didn't think his face would ever return to normal if he continued to spend time with the older man. He could feel the heat of his blush all the way down his neck. There had to be something illegal about what he'd done. He couldn't keep the scandalized tone from his voice when he whispered, "We could get in trouble."

The full-fledged grin zapped all the energy from Asher's body and left him reeling. Now *that* was illegal. One man wasn't allowed to go around being that gorgeous. It was some sort of crime. Had to be. Not to mention insulting to all the normal-looking people in the world. Goddamned blush.

Thornton leaned forward, his voice a soft, throaty purr. "God, you're adorable. Are you planning to tattletale on me, Asher?"

Struck speechless and not wanting to move his head, his default expression seemed to be wide-eyed shock, mouth gaping open, unable to form words. Words came to his mind, though. Words like *never, nuh-uh, nope, not gonna happen,* and even *no, Sir* fluttered around in there like butterflies, trying to flit their way out of their confinement.

Nothing was coming out, however, and he was saved from having to say anything at all when Jess breezed in, bright-eyed and energetic like it was nine in the morning instead of the middle of the night when normal people slept. "Hi there."

Her gaze drifted down, reminding him Thornton was still holding his hand. "You guys are so sweet together. How are you feeling, Asher?"

He cleared his throat and glanced once more towards Thornton, which was a mistake because, if he wasn't mistaken, there was a note of mischief in the man's eyes, and his raised brow and teasing smirk seemed to be some sort of challenge he knew he wasn't ready for. He looked back at Jess and realized she was waiting for an answer. "Pretty rough."

She nodded and took his vitals, making a few notes on the little pull-out computer next to his bed. "Ready for some more pain meds?"

"Yes, please."

She administered the meds and told him the doctor would be in later that morning and was off to help her other patients. Sometime while he'd been occupied with Jess, Thornton had moved his chair even closer. He leaned forward, resting his crossed forearms alongside Asher's thighs on the bed, the warmth of his presence seeping into Asher and making him feel somehow protected and safe, which made no sense.

Thornton's gaze was intense but his smile was sweet when he said, "Thanks for not turning me in."

The man was dangerous—that's what he was. Because even when Asher should have huffed and rolled his eyes, all he could do was say, "You're welcome."

CHAPTER FOUR

Thornton

"You're still here."

Asher's sweet voice drew Thornton's gaze away from his iPad where he'd been keeping himself busy trying to get some work done. Thornton smiled, noticing the pink in Asher's cheeks, happy he had more color, even if it was because he was shy. His gaze was captured by the most beautiful blue and green eyes he'd ever seen.

When Thornton and Asher had talked the night before, Asher remembered he had to call his friend to let her know he wouldn't be at work the following day and to tell their boss. That morning, with Asher's phone out of battery on the table next to his hospital bed, he'd asked to borrow Thornton's.

When Asher made the call, Thornton stepped out of the room for several minutes so he could give Asher privacy. He stretched his body to loosen his sore and achy muscles. He wasn't badly injured, but he was pretty damn banged up and didn't want Asher to feel guilty. When he came back in, Asher's face was aflame as he held the phone out to him. "I'm sorry. She wants to talk to you and won't let me hang up until she does."

Thornton smiled, liking the woman already, and brought the phone to his ear. "Hello?"

"Who are you?"

He knew Asher would have already gone over who he was, but he humored her. "My name is Thornton Hayes."

"And you're the one that ran over my friend and lied about being his husband?"

He couldn't help but grin at her brazenness. "Well, I didn't exactly run over *him. But I did run* into *him…"*

At hearing Thornton's answer to his friend's question, Asher had covered his eyes and whispered, "Oh my god, Madi."

He'd chuckled quietly, and when Asher glanced up at him, he'd winked at the boy, so he knew Thornton wasn't upset. He tuned back into what Madi was saying. "But basically, you're the reason he's in the hospital."

His shoulders sagged, feeling the weight of her words. "Yes. I'm responsible for the accident."

"He said you're being really nice to him, but you lied and told the hospital you're his husband. Are you a lying liar who lies and is going to try to manipulate him into admitting fault?"

Wow.

Okay, he hadn't seen that one coming. "No. I've already admitted fault with my insurance company. It was after visiting hours when I was finally able get away from the accident scene and deal with the insurance claim and could make it to the hospital to check on him."

"So, what, you were concerned about him?"

He took a seat in the chair he'd vacated earlier. "Yes, of course. I needed to make sure he was going to be okay."

"Are you going to stay with him or leave him all alone?"

"Stay, unless he wants me to go."

He watched as Asher's eyes widened at his comment.

"I think he wants you there. But he'll feel guilty you're staying."

"He shouldn't. It's where I want to be."

"Promise you won't leave?"

He'd chuckled at that. "I thought you'd want me gone." He couldn't help but ask, "You sure you trust me with him?"

"He seems to think you're good people, and from what you've said, he might be right."

"Well, thanks."

There was a significant pause. "Treat him well. He's fragile and too innocent for his own good."

Not knowing what she meant by that, he could only say, "I will."

"Okay. I'll stop by after my shift to take over."

"I'm sure he'd love to see you. But I won't be leaving unless he asks me to go."

Another significant pause. "You'd be good for him."

A thrill raced through his body at the thought. Surprised by her easy acceptance of him and not knowing how much Asher had shared about their interactions, he finally answered, "We'll have to see."

She hummed in his ear and said goodbye, leaving him thinking long and hard about her comment about Asher being fragile and innocent and about him being good for Asher.

"I promised your friend I wouldn't leave your side. And I'm responsible for putting you here in the first place. I'm not about to leave you alone without anyone to be with you."

It was entirely too early to tell, but something about the boy was burrowing deep inside him already, which he knew was insane. But he always trusted his instincts, so he'd just have to take it a day at a time.

He had to admit the vulnerability and sweetness of Asher was doing a number on him, and he knew how those two combined always made him yearn to take care. But he also knew it was ridiculous to even entertain the thought when the way they'd met wasn't exactly a meet-cute. More like a meet-disaster. And he wasn't quite sure he wasn't manufacturing the way he was feeling as a direct result of the way they'd met and the responsibility he felt.

That conversation continued to play over and over in his head ever since, but he shook it off, refocused, and watched as a frown marred Asher's face as the boy concentrated on his hands in his lap. "She shouldn't have made you promise that."

"She didn't make me do anything. I'm here because I want to be." More blushing on the boy's face. "Would you rather I leave?"

Asher slowly raised his head to meet Thornton's eyes. "No. I mean, you can if you want. I just... I don't want you feeling like you can't go if you need to. I don't know of anyone who would stay with a stranger in the hospital because of a car accident."

He gave Asher a gentle smile and said, "But I'm not a stranger. I'm your husband. And this is where a husband should be."

Thornton hoped that by joking about the strange circumstances of his being there with Asher in the hospital, he might bring a smile to the boy's face. It worked, and he grinned when he saw a tiny smile appear on Asher's sweet face. "Even if you hadn't asked me not to leave last night, I'd still be here because I want to be. Not to mention I put you in the hospital with my carelessness. Of course I'm going to make sure you're taken care of."

"It was just an accident. And it was raining really hard."

Thornton shook his head. "It still shouldn't have happened. Asher"—he waited until the boy met his gaze—"I don't want to leave unless you ask me to. I'd like to stay until I can take you home."

Thornton's heart squeezed when Asher bit his lip, hope in his eyes when blurted out, "You would?"

The boy looked away, obviously embarrassed to have reacted so strongly. He wanted to get up and hug him, give him comfort, but he wasn't sure it would be welcome. Figuring he could test the waters, he stood and sat on the side of Asher's hospital bed and clasped his hand. When their gazes met, he squeezed Asher's hand. "I would. So, what do you think, are you going to ask me to leave?"

Asher slowly shook his head, turning his gaze away. "No," he answered, as his eyes slid back to Thornton's. "Thank you for staying."

"You're welcome. I've already admitted fault with my insurance, so they should be paying out. Your car is totaled, so sadly, you'll need to get a replacement, but I'll help you with that. It's my fault you no longer have a car."

The color drained from Asher's face so fast he grew concerned, and the boy shook his head a little too quickly and gasped in pain, his other hand reaching towards the gauze, wincing. Thornton caught Asher's other hand in his before he could make contact. "I know you want to touch it, but that'll just make it worse. Okay?"

Asher's eyes closed at the pain, and he let out a slow breath. "Yeah. Okay."

Curious, he couldn't keep himself from asking, "What made you so upset? I'm the one that ruined your car, so I'm going to be the one to replace it."

"I don't want it."

He kept his voice as gentle as possible, "Asher—"

"No. I don't think I'll get another car. I get rides from my friend most days, and for the days I don't, I'll call for a Lyft, or… something. I just can't… I don't want to…"

He could hear Asher's breathing begin to get choppy, and he could feel the boy's whole body stiffen. Thornton's brother suffered from depression and anxiety, so he knew a panic attack when he saw one. Drawing Asher's hands to his chest, he spoke quietly, calmly, "Asher, look at me. There you go. You're having a panic attack. I want you to feel my chest moving and take slow, deep breaths when I do. Focus on our hands, all right?"

Guilt slammed into him like a battering ram. Goddammit. If the accident had caused Asher's panic at just the thought of driving again, he didn't know what he'd do. Asher struggled for another couple of minutes before he could slow his breathing. "That's it. That's better. Did the accident…?"

Asher closed his eyes, and his throat moved as he swallowed. "No. I hate driving." Asher pulled his hand free and lifted it to press against his ribs where they must have been throbbing. His fingers were trembling, and Thornton ached to help him. When Asher finally continued, his voice was a whisper. "Fucking hate it. I don't want to do it anymore."

"Hey." He squeezed Asher's other hand gently in his. "Deep breaths, okay? No one's going to force you to drive. I just thought since I totaled your car, I'd replace it. But if you don't want to drive anymore, you don't have to drive anymore."

"I just…" Thornton watched as Asher drew in a deep breath and was saddened when it caught several times with the boy's pent-up emotions. "I know it's stupid. But I don't want to."

"It's absolutely not stupid. I'm not sure why you hate it so much, but it's enough that you do. We'll figure something else out. Okay?"

"You don't have to do anything. It's my problem, and I'll deal with it. After this, I don't even want to think about driving."

"Jesus, Asher, I'm so sorry."

"No. It's not… It's not your fault. I've been afraid of driving for years. I… My parents died in a car crash, but even before that I hated doing it but forced myself to, just in case of an emergency."

Not knowing what that meant, Thornton decided to let it go. "Then it sounds like driving isn't worth the stress it causes you. Don't do it if it fills you with anxiety. It's not worth it."

Asher nodded, and his grateful smile warmed Thornton's heart. "Yeah. You're right. It's not worth it."

Thornton let a few moments of comfortable silence pass them by before continuing. "You mentioned your parents. Do you have any siblings?"

Asher shook his head. "No. I was an only child."

Thornton waited a few beats, hoping Asher would continue, but he didn't, obviously not feeling talkative. He wondered if Asher was extremely private or if he just wasn't a talker in general. Seemed he'd have to pull information rather than him offering it. But as he saw it, they had nothing but time, so he didn't mind. He wanted to get to know the boy, so he had no problem putting the effort into doing just that. Asher was worth it. Thornton had no doubt.

"What do you do for a living? I know you called to talk to your boss about being unable to come in for the rest of the week."

The first truly heartfelt smile, one that not only brightened up the boy's already beautiful face but reached his eyes, would have knocked Thornton flat on his ass if he hadn't already been sitting down. "I guess I'd call myself an uneducated horticulturist."

Thornton couldn't help but chuckle at the unabashedly self-deprecating grin on Asher's face. "Okay, I'm hooked, and I need to know more."

Asher blushed and let out a small chuckle, catching himself and raising a hand to his side. He grimaced a bit, and Thornton couldn't help but join him. "I shouldn't have teased you. Laughing isn't exactly good for you right now."

"It's okay."

"So, an uneducated horticulturist…"

Asher's little smirk had Thornton's heart beating just a little bit faster. "Yeah… So, my mom worked at a local flower shop where I grew up. She always used to bring me along with her when I was old enough because the owner, an older woman named Beth Channing, didn't mind it. I'd always sit in the back and sometimes read or do homework, but most of the time I'd do whatever I could to help with orders and eventually learned how to do some planting as well. Beth had a tiny attached greenhouse where she used to grow some of the flowers she'd sell and other plants she liked."

"Did you enjoy that?" He knew by the excitement Asher was showing, he did, but he wanted to keep him talking.

"Oh yeah. I think it was more of a hobby of hers because she mostly had flowers delivered to make her arrangements, but she loved growing and tending to her plants, and they sold well. So, I'm not sure why that wasn't a bigger part of her business. Maybe because it was so time consuming. Anyway, that's how I got interested in it. So, when I was old enough to stay home alone, I'd still go in with my mom when she could still work and sometimes even when she couldn't."

Thornton figured there was a story there when Asher got a sad, faraway look in his eyes, but he didn't want to take them down a path that would take away the boy's smile, so he asked, "What did you like about it?"

Asher shrugged. "There's just something about plants that calms me like nothing else. I never feel anxiety or stress when I'm growing and tending my plants. I guess I liked the quiet of it too, and the progress there always seemed to be each time I'd go in to check on the plants and flowers. Beth would let me stop in any time after school and tend to the plants I'd started and the ones she'd planted herself. I guess it kind of became my home away from home. I was there a lot, and eventually, when I was old enough, she started paying me."

"So, is she still your boss today?"

Asher gazed down at his lap and shook his head. "No. I work at The Glasshouse now."

"Wait, the huge greenhouse on the outskirts of town?"

Asher's grin was back full force. "You know it?"

"I think everybody knows it. It's huge. And you grow pot there."

Asher snorted out a laugh and then sucked in a gasp, clutching his ribs.

Fuck.

He rested his hand on the boy's thigh. "Jesus, Asher. It was an offhand comment, and I wasn't thinking. Are you okay?"

Asher nodded, breathing in and out shallowly. "I'm all right."

Thornton clasped Asher's hand when he rested it next to his on Asher's thigh. "I'll be more careful."

A small smile flitted its way across Asher's lips. "Yes, please don't amuse me."

"I know you're kidding, but I really will try not to make you laugh."

That smirk returned, and Asher nodded. "Yeah, maybe that's a good idea."

"So, you work at The Glasshouse as a horticulturist."

"Don't forget the *uneducated* part. I had to find a job when I dropped out of college, and I applied there at the right time. I was lucky because Beth knew the owner through a state chapter of a national association for florists and nurseries. When she learned where I was moving, she told me about Jennifer Cook, the owner of The Glasshouse."

Asher grinned, remembering how it had all just fallen into place. "It just so happened Jenn was hiring. It was kismet, because of the timing and the fact the job didn't involve working with a lot of customers, mostly just the plants. And since the women had known each other for years, Jenn gave me a chance. It probably helped I was the only person with experience who applied."

He watched as Asher used the remote to lay the bed back a bit more, obviously feeling worn out and uncomfortable. "Tired?"

"Yeah."

"Go ahead and rest. There's plenty of time to tell me more about the job I can see you love so much."

Asher's eyes brightened with a smile, and he nodded. "Okay. What about you. What do you do?"

"I own some local businesses."

"Wow, some?"

He shrugged, not wanting to go into just how many pies he had his fingers in. "Ever eaten at Mama's Chimichangas?"

Asher's eyes rolled back in his head, and he smiled an intoxicated-looking smile. "Oh my god, her steak fajita burritos are the stuff of dreams."

"Her steak soft tacos are my personal favorite."

"You own that?"

He shook his head. "No. Not really. I co-own it. For now, at least. Eventually, she'll buy me out, and then I'll have no excuse to stalk her on Taco Tuesdays."

Light dawned on Asher's face. "Ahh, so you're an investor."

Smart boy. "I am. But sometimes businesses need more than just funds. I also help them come up with solid business plans that include marketing and growth so they can eventually become self-sufficient and buy me out when my... services, for lack of a better word, are no longer needed."

Asher's grin was brilliant when he interjected. "So, you're helping people achieve their dreams."

It wasn't often that he blushed, but damned if that comment didn't hit to the heart of him. Because he might never have verbalized it, but that's exactly how he felt when one of his business partners was finally able to buy their way out of business with him. It's why he did it. Seeing the smiles on the faces of the people he helped become even more successful was the best feeling out there. "I guess I like to think I have a small part in helping some people do that, yeah."

The admiration in Asher's gaze kept his blush going and made him think he'd like the boy's admiring gaze for other reasons as well, which had him scrubbing his face and trying to change the subject before he got himself in trouble with a boner he couldn't explain. "So, I guess we both do something we love."

Asher smiled and nodded. "I guess we do."

After that, Asher asked about his own family, and he chatted about them for a while until he could tell Asher was drifting off. He sat and stared at the boy as he slept, taking in every detail of the boy's face he could and cataloguing it in his mind to remember for later.

The boy was stunning. Even all banged up. His blond hair was straight, thick, and looked as soft as spun silk. The boy's lashes were dark and long, in contrast to his light hair. His flawless skin and rosy lips were tempting his lips to explore. He knew—he just *knew*—he'd never have a hard time remembering the sleeping boy before him.

***

A little while later, there was a soft knock on the door, and Damon and Syed walked in carrying a "get well soon" balloon tied to a gorgeous vase of flowers. He'd told them he'd meet them downstairs, so they didn't bother Asher, but apparently, they'd ignored him. When he turned to glance at Asher, the shallow fast breaths he was taking, coupled with the stricken, confused look on his face, had Thornton's protective instincts coming forward.

He moved to sit on the side of Asher's bed, clasped his hand, and hastened to explain. "Asher, these are my closest friends, Damon and Syed Antoun. I just asked them to stop by to bring me a change of clothes, but I *told* them to wait for me downstairs."

He gave both men a pointed look, ignored by Damon, who strode forward, placed the flowers on the side table by the bed, and extended his hand towards Asher, who, though he seemed intimidated and somewhat nervous, took it, trying to smile through his unease. Though Thornton didn't miss the slight trembling of his hand.

Fuck.

Something made him want to shove his friend away from Asher, to protect him, even though he knew Damon wouldn't hurt a fly. He stood to at least pull his friend back when Syed did it for him. "Damon, you're scaring the poor boy. Stop looming over him like a hulking brute."

Damon, his enormous best friend who often forgot his size—which topped out at six-foot-five and 255 pounds of muscle—could scare mere mortals, straightened and let loose Asher's hand, chastened by his husband and Dom's stern voice. He stepped back immediately, a frown marring his perfectly chiseled features which turned into a teasing smile when he looked at Thornton. "I just wanted to meet the man who could so easily convince our Thornton here to give up his creature comforts to sleep in a hospital recliner."

Though his friend's smile was sweet—charming, even—and he'd genuinely been teasing without any malice whatsoever, the worried frown on Asher's face made Thornton's heart skip a beat. When the boy turned his gaze on him, Thornton moved closer, wanting to softly rub the wrinkles between the boy's brows until the worry lines smoothed out. Asher's beautiful eyes captured him, as they always seemed to do, and he nearly missed it when Asher whispered, "You must have been so uncomfortable."

The guilt he saw on Asher's face made his heart sink. He stepped forward and clasped Asher's hand, sitting beside him on the bed again and casting a pleading look at Syed, who tugged on his husband's arm at the same time he apologized for barging in unannounced. Damon followed it up with, "I fucked that up, didn't I?" Damon looked from him to Asher, genuine concern in his gaze. "I'm sorry. I was teasing Thornton, not you."

Syed smiled and reached up to grip his sub's neck, reassuring Damon he wasn't angry as he addressed Asher. "We'll just be going. It was nice to meet you, Asher. We're sorry we invaded your space."

He put the bag of Thornton's clothes and toiletries he'd been holding by the foot of the bed and turned to go. Syed gave an apologetic look to Thornton as he turned towards the door. Loving both of his friends equally for realizing Asher was overwhelmed and working to put him at ease, Thornton turned back to Asher, who was watching them retreat.

"You don't—" Asher's voice was gruff, so he cleared his throat and tried again. "You don't have to leave. It's okay."

Thornton could see the words had cost Asher. That he was still anxious. Thornton didn't know what was wrong or why Asher was worried, but it was enough that he was. Thornton turned towards Syed and Damon, knowing as a Dom, Syed would see the same thing he did and realize what needed to be done. He watched as Damon gave Syed a pleading smile, but Syed only shook his head. "We weren't planning on staying, and we both have to get back to work. Asher, it was great meeting you. I hope we'll meet again sometime soon."

Asher, looking surprised, said softly, "Oh, that's… Thank you. You too."

Damon gave Asher a genuine smile. "I'm sorry if I made you uncomfortable. It wasn't my intention. I often forget I'm like a bull in a china shop."

Asher's shoulders relaxed a bit, and his smile was sweet. "It's okay. I get nervous at silly things."

Damon's expression was kind when he answered, "They're not silly to you. We don't always have control over what makes us nervous." Damon leaned closer to the bed and whispered, "I'm afraid of heights and needles."

Asher's grin widened, finally putting Thornton at ease, and his heart swelled when Asher whispered back, "I'm afraid of rats and snakes."

Damon smiled. "See? Not silly at all."

Asher blushed and looked down at his hands in his lap. Syed cleared his throat. "Come, Damon."

"Yes, Sir." Damon smiled and waved at them, walking through the door Syed held open for him.

The confused look on Asher's face didn't go unnoticed. When people that weren't in the lifestyle heard one man calling another Sir, it tended to put that look on their faces. But he had a feeling Asher wouldn't ask, and he knew it wasn't the time. "I'm sorry about that."

Before he'd even finished talking, Asher was shaking his head. "It's okay. I acted so weird. I…" He wrung his fingers together and gazed back up at Thornton. "I have a lot of stupid fears. From driving to busy public spaces to strangers approaching me, it's… a lot."

"Like Damon said, they're not silly or stupid—they just are. Fears don't always make a lot of sense, and rarely do people have control over their own." Asher nodded but otherwise kept quiet. Thornton's heart hurt for the young man, and as much as he wanted to know what Asher had gone through that made him constantly battle his fears, he didn't want to pry. At least not yet. But if he had anything to say about it, he'd be prying into Asher's life in many ways. Only time would tell.

***

Later on that evening, when there was a knock on Asher's door, Thornton saw the tension in Asher's frame, so he reached over and placed his palm over Asher's fisted hand. But when two beautiful women walked in carrying flowers and balloons, concerned looks on their faces, he felt Asher's body relax.

"Oh, Asher! Honey, I've been so worried. How are you feeling?" This from the tall woman with silver hair in some sort of curly updo that made her appear both regal and approachable. She bustled in, no nonsense, and placed the huge vase of flowers on the countertop along the back of the room.

"I'm okay, Jenn. Just a little banged up."

The other woman—tiny, with naturally red hair shorn in a pixie style—had her arms crossed over her chest and was giving Thornton a thorough onceover. As the older woman fussed over Asher, the younger one, who he assumed was Madi, approached him. "So, you're Thornton.'

He smirked. "And you must be Madi, the protective best friend."

He squeezed Asher's hand—an act Madi watched with interest—before he stood up to shake her hand in greeting. "It's nice to meet you, Madi."

She met his gaze head-on, and he decided he already liked her when she narrowed her eyes and finally grabbed his hand in a surprisingly strong grip. "You too. Are you taking good care of him?"

He smiled, liking her boldness. "As long as he'll let me."

She smirked at that and finally released his hand. She moved to Asher's bed and gently sat down, clasping Asher's hand in hers as she leaned forward to kiss his cheek. "You look like shit, kid."

Asher chuckled, sucked in a startled breath, and clutched his side. "Dammit, Madi, you can't make me laugh."

"Well, I'm sorry. But you need to stop getting run over by cars, okay?" But Thornton could tell the fact she'd been the cause of Asher's fresh pain was making her feel awful. She rubbed up and down his arm. He watched as Asher turned his arm over and held his hand open for her. She clasped it again and brought it up to her cheek, leaning in closer to whisper, "I love you. I don't want you hurting. I've been a wreck all day."

"I'm okay. Really. Where's Gigi?"

"She's with the sitter still. Molly said she could stay and make dinner for her while I came to see you. My girl is gonna be beside herself when I tell her what happened. When can you leave?"

Asher sighed and spoke to both ladies when he said, "Tomorrow."

"I'll be working. How are you going to get home?"

He saw Asher tense up and had to step in. "I'll take you home, if you're okay with that?"

He thought he saw the tension in Asher's shoulders ease as he nodded. "Yeah. That would be great. Thank you." Asher turned back to Madi. "But I don't think I'll be able to work right away."

Jenn, sitting in a chair on the other side of his bed, replied, "Of course not. I've already worked the schedule to pull extra staff in for a while, and people that were on part time, hoping for more hours, are very happy right now."

"I'll come back to work as soon as I can. I don't want to be gone too long. I know you were supposed to tell us something today, and I messed that up."

Madi rolled her eyes. "Oh, don't get me started. She won't even tell *me* what it was about. Said she wanted us both to be together when she told us."

Both employees turned to their employer, and Jenn flushed under the scrutiny. "I don't think now is the time. It can wait until you're back with us. I want you to focus on getting well. I'll email you the paperwork for short-term disability. I want you to be covered if you have to be out for several weeks."

Asher shook his head, and Thornton could tell he was getting agitated. "I shouldn't be out that long. Maybe just a week or two."

Jenn gave a sad shake of her head. "Asher, fractured ribs take a while to heal. That and your concussion? I think you'll be out for several weeks. Three to four at least."

Asher's horrified expression, coupled with the way his free hand gripped the blanket on his lap in a tight, shaking fist, let him know the boy wasn't coping well with that info. "No, it shouldn't be that long. I'll figure it out."

Jenn merely gave him a noncommittal shrug. "Whatever happens, we'll make sure we handle it so that you have enough time to get well before you come back to join us. There's no rush."

"Can you please tell us what you wanted to talk to us about?"

Jenn shook her head. "It's not a big deal. I don't want it to worry you. We'll talk about it when—"

"Jenn, you know him. You know this will eat him up, and he'll worry himself into a panic attack if you don't tell us. You might as well get it over with."

When Jenn gave him a look, Thornton stood. "I can step outside if you all need me to." He reached across the bed to shake her hand. "And sorry, I'm Thornton, the guy who…" He cleared his throat and gave Madi a droll glance. "Ran Asher over with my car."

He felt a bit better when Asher let go of his fisted blanket to cover his face and shake his head. "Oh my god. Madi, you're awful." Asher gazed up at him imploringly. "I'm sorry. She didn't mean that."

Thornton smiled. "Yes, she did."

At the same time Madi replied, "Yes, I did."

An exasperated noise passed through Asher's throat as he rolled his eyes to the ceiling. "You're both ridiculous."

Thornton stepped around Madi and in closer to Asher. "It sounds like maybe Jenn has something she wants to talk to you about. Why don't I give you all some privacy?"

"No! I'm sure she can…" Asher's gaze turned to Jenn's. "Is it okay if he stays while you tell us?"

Jenn's brows rose, but she shrugged. "I suppose it doesn't matter if he hears."

Thornton gazed back down to Asher, trying to decipher what was going on in the boy's head. "I'm happy to step out…" At the quick shake of Asher's head that both women probably missed, his mind was made up, but just to be sure, he had to ask. "Asher, would you like me to stay?"

The relieved look on the boy's face went a long way towards settling down his protective instincts at the thought of having to leave Asher, even for just a few minutes. "Yes. Please, stay."

He ran his hand up and down Asher's upper arm and would have touched his cheek if he didn't feel like both women were hyper-aware of every move he was making. He sat back down in the lounge chair and gave them as much privacy as he could by picking up his iPad and pretending to get some work done.

Jenn sighed. "This isn't exactly how I saw this discussion happening, but I guess this is as good a time as any. You both are my best employees, and the passion you have for your jobs is something that makes me grateful to have both of you working at The Glasshouse. You've both been a huge part of making my business the success it is, and for that, I'm so thankful."

Thornton glanced up to check on Asher and saw his face had lost color. He gave it another moment before standing to lend his support when Madi cried, "Oh my god. Are you dying? Why the speech? Just spit it out—you're killing us!"

Thornton smiled when Asher rolled his eyes at her. "Madi, you're being ridiculous. I doubt she'd tell us she's dying by starting with telling us how great we are. Let her talk."

Jenn merely raised her brows at both of them, obviously knowing them well enough to wait them out. "Don't be shoving me in a grave too soon, Madi. What I'm actually doing is planning to retire."

Both Asher and Madi gasped, so Jenn plowed on, doing what Thornton was assuming was trying to allay their fears. "It's not going to be an immediate thing. My goal is six months, but that can change if it needs to. Anthony and I would like to start traveling."

Asher, obviously confused, asked, "Do you need to hire that manager you've always wished you've had, so you can take time to do what you want?"

Jenn smiled at him, shaking her head. "No. Actually, I wanted to approach you both to see if you wanted to buy the business, become the owners."

Well, *that* was quite the offer. Thornton's business mind kicked in and started whirling with the possibilities. So many ideas popped in his head for how that could work out when he realized both Asher and Madi were struck speechless.

"Wait, what?" Unsurprisingly, Madi was the one that came out of her stupor first. But it looked like Asher was just as confused. Shaking her head, Madi continued, "You want *us* to buy The Glasshouse?"

That had been more like a mini-shriek, and Thornton had to cough to cover up a laugh and look down at his iPad when Madi turned to glare at him. He heard Jenn sigh and glanced up. She had a smile on her face, though, and turned it on both of them. "I do, but only if you're interested in doing so. I don't want to saddle you with the responsibility if it isn't something you'd feel impassioned about doing."

When neither of her employees had anything to say, their utter shock obvious, Jenn continued, "I know you both love your jobs. You've expressed as much to me many times over the years. I trust you both implicitly, and I know if you decided it was something you wanted, you'd be wonderful, responsible, passionate business co-owners. *But* it is an enormous amount of work and responsibility, and you may not want that so early on in your careers. I understand that. Regardless, I'll be looking for a buyer. I just wanted to check with you both first, before I looked elsewhere."

Madi spoke up again. "But why don't you just hire a manager or something, like Asher said, and then you can travel whenever?"

Jenn smiled, reaching over and patting Madi's hand. "I don't want to have any ties keeping me tethered to a business that takes up so much mental time and energy. I want to truly retire and enjoy my travels with my husband."

Both Asher's and Madi's shoulders slumped, but Jenn's positive energy didn't flag. "Listen, this is a huge decision, and I don't expect you to make it quickly or without a million more questions. Why don't you take this time while Asher is out and healing to maybe talk together about it and just figure out if it's even something you'd be remotely interested in doing? We can work out the particulars later. Just take time to sort out your feelings about it. Maybe only one of you would be interested. I'm not against that. I just wanted to propose you both do it together because you both have such passion for your work and have the most interest in seeing to the success of The Glasshouse."

After that, Asher and Madi asked a few more questions, and things wound down. Both Jenn and Madi could see Asher was exhausted. Thornton could see the fatigue weighing the boy down, and it wasn't long after that when dinner was brought in for him. Not even an hour after he ate, Asher was asleep, and Thornton spent more time than he'd ever admit watching the boy rest, his mind a whirlwind of emotions.

CHAPTER FIVE

Asher

I t was bright and early on his third day in the hospital—the day he was going to be released—and he found himself even more nervous at that prospect. But for reasons other than his injuries, which was unexpected. Asher wasn't entirely sure how to handle the situation he found himself in. He'd never had a man's attention so focused on him before.

But there he was with a sexy-as-sin, older man who hadn't left his side since the accident, told the hospital staff he was Asher's husband, and was very obviously interested in him. He'd even alluded to that the night before. Hell, Thornton's, "I'm very interested in getting to know you, Asher. I hope you'll allow me to do so," was more blatant than alluding, but thinking about that made him nervous as hell.

He'd never dated, never had sex or even fooled around with anyone. He couldn't deny he was interested in Thornton as well, making the enigmatic man the *only* one he'd ever been interested in. He might have lacked any experience in the dating scene, but he wasn't oblivious to flirting and interest aimed at him. He'd just never wanted attention like that from people. It stressed him out because what the fuck else was new. Everything stressed him out. And he never understood why anyone would bother with him in the first place.

He didn't think he was ugly. He'd consider himself average, but he'd also consider himself an antisocial, neurotic mess. And he didn't understand why Thornton was showing such an interest in him. But he was, so Asher had a decision to make, which had never been a problem before because his decision had always been to say no. But he admitted to himself he didn't *want* to say no. Not this time.

The larger-than-life man, who was still asleep in the godforsaken hospital recliner, was just... *more* than he'd ever experienced. More virile, more confident, more gorgeous, more masculine, more intense, kinder, gentler, more straightforward, and more determined. It left him feeling untethered, adrift in a sea of questions he didn't have the answers to. And he *hated* not having the answers. But he couldn't think about it anymore. His brain hurt, and his ribs hurt, and suddenly he was exhausted again.

He woke with a jolt, unsure of what roused him. When he looked at the clock, he realized he'd slept several more hours. He was still foggy, but he took stock of his injuries, grateful some of the pain had dissipated. He looked towards Thornton's chair, and when he met those beautiful eyes, all thoughts left his head. The man's deep voice made goosebumps slide up his arms. "Good morning."

Asher cleared his throat. "Morning."

His eyes skirted away from Thornton, scared to feel that pull towards the man every time their gazes clashed. Asher watched as he stood up from the recliner with a grimace, stretched his limbs and his back, which popped, and then his neck. God, Asher felt awful. Guilt weighed him down again for making Thornton feel as if he had to stay with him. He couldn't help but apologize. Again. "I hate that you had to sleep in the recliner for the second night in a row. You must be sore. I should have told you to go home. That was selfish of me."

His gaze snapped towards Thornton as he sat down beside Asher on the bed, his skin tingling even under the blankets when Thornton's thigh brushed against his own. Shivers raced over his skin when Thornton clasped his hand between his much larger ones. "It's okay to be a little selfish every once in a while. I get the feeling it's a rare occurrence for you, isn't it?"

When Asher only shrugged, Thornton continued, "I *wanted* to stay with you. And before you tell me not to feel guilty, it's not guilt that is keeping me by your side. I *am* responsible for putting you here, but if you were anyone else, I can honestly say I wouldn't be here. There's a pull I feel towards you. I think you feel it too."

Still unable to come up with words, Asher merely nodded, unable to lie, even silently. "If you'd have told me you wanted me to go home yesterday, I'd have done so. I'd have hated it, but I'd have done it."

"W—" Asher cleared his throat and tried again. "Why?"

"Why would I have done it, or why would I have hated it?"

Wanting the answers more than he wanted anything else in that moment, he met Thornton's gaze and admitted, "Both."

Thornton's smile, which Asher somehow felt held pride in him, was melting his insides like goo. He couldn't take his eyes away from those dark, full lips as they spoke. "I'd have done it because I will always respect your wishes, and I'd have hated it because I don't want to be away from you just yet."

Warmth flooded him, and he could feel his face reflecting that with a blush. God, why did he like the idea of this strong, self-assured man not wanting to leave him? *Him.* Of all people. He had to at least be honest with Thornton for showing Asher the same respect. "I don't want to be away from you yet either."

"Good bo—" Thornton seemed to catch himself before he continued what he'd been about to say and cleared his throat before trying again. "Good. I'm glad you feel that way."

Had he been about to call Asher *boy*? He had no idea what that meant, no idea why goosebumps traveled up his arms and neck, and no idea why his heart started beating faster at the thought. Unable to come up with any answers for his body's physical reaction to what amounted to a slip of the tongue, he decided to ignore it, like he did anything he didn't want to look too closely at.

Asher's stomach decided that was the moment it wanted to make itself known with a loud, hungry growl. Thornton squeezed his hand and said, "How about I call the nurses' station and get them to bring you some food?"

There went Asher's blush again when he nodded in response. Why did Thornton taking charge, taking *care*, feel so damn good? It wasn't like calling the nurses' station was some grand gesture. But Asher couldn't convince himself it was simple either.

There was something about the *way* Thornton took charge that appealed to him. The man wasn't pushy, bossy, or aggressive about it. He could tell Thornton did what he did to ensure Asher got what he needed. He'd never had that. Well, he supposed Madi sometimes did that for him—she *did* drive him to The Glasshouse every day she was working—but somehow it felt different when Thornton did it. Somehow it felt more meaningful, more deliberate.

The beep before the nurse answered pulled him out of his thoughts. "How can I help you?"

He didn't even try to answer. Didn't want to. He felt the need to allow Thornton to take charge of him in that way. His skin warmed again, and a small grin graced Asher's lips when Thornton replied, "Yes, my husband is hungry. Can someone bring him a late breakfast?"

"Yes, sir. We'll have to order him a fresh one, but it should be up shortly."

"Thank you."

Shortly was more like forty minutes, and his stomach nearly ate itself during the wait. When he dug into the mediocre food with gusto, Thornton chuckled. "I'm glad you have such a healthy appetite."

Oh, god, was he being a pig? He chewed quickly and swallowed. "Sorry."

Thornton chuckled. "Don't be sorry. I just said I was glad. It's a good thing."

Asher shrugged, not sure what to make of that. Thornton stood, and Asher felt the loss of the man's warmth as he did. "I'm gonna wash up quick and change."

Asher nodded and watched as Thornton leaned down to pick up the bag Syed had left him the day before and headed into the bathroom. He continued to eat his breakfast, lackluster as it was, and just as he finished and pushed the rolling cart away from him, his doctor, Dr. Flores, walked in.

She approached him, her bedside manner apparent in her friendly smile. "Asher, how are you feeling this morning?"

He took stock of his pain, and though he still had quite a bit, he wanted to go home more than he wanted to stay in the hospital, so Asher told the doctor what he thought she wanted to hear. "Much better."

Dr. Flores raised a brow at his quick answer, probably aware he just wanted to get the hell out of dodge. She logged into the computer on the monitor stand attached to the wall and looked at his chart. "Your tests and vitals are looking good. I think you'll be fine to be released today as long as you'll have some help at home. But since your husband hasn't left your side, I'm sure you've got that covered."

He blushed at that and nodded because he wasn't about to admit the truth. And he didn't need help; he'd be fine. "I'll have it if I need it."

"We'll be sending you home with a script for oxycodone that you can take until your follow up with your primary care doctor. You can't lift anything over ten pounds..." She continued to talk about his restrictions, but he knew he'd never remember everything, and it would all be in his discharge papers. So he did his best to zone out and not stress about it.

When he heard the bathroom door open, revealing a casual, sexy Thornton in ripped jeans and a fitted, long-sleeve white tee, with a pair of black Vans, he breathed a sigh of relief, which only lasted long enough for her next words to sink in. "... and you'll want to take at least a couple of weeks off no matter what you do for work, but if your job is physical, you'll probably need at least four weeks off."

He could feel the stress reach in to grab hold and could hear it as the heart monitor started beating a little faster. He concentrated on his breathing, ignoring the pain that it caused, willing his heart rate to stay steady. It must have worked well enough for Dr. Flores, as she smiled before saying, "You'll have everything we just spoke about in your discharge papers. Be sure to follow them closely. It's the fastest way for you to recover."

She shook both his hand and Thornton's, who thanked her for everything she'd done. He felt bad he didn't do the same but was still concentrating on keeping himself from losing control in front of her. When she walked out the door, he continued to try and keep himself from flying apart. He couldn't be off work for four weeks. There was no way. There was harvesting and planting to do; there always was. He couldn't do that to Jenn. She'd have to work double duty as she was the only one with enough experience to do what needed to be done.

Thornton was at his side, sitting down on the bed, and clasping his hands, which were fisted in his lap. The man's long fingers slowly pried his fingers out of his fists, flattening them out as he murmured. "You're okay, Asher. I'm here with you. As much as the pain will allow, take some deep breaths with me. I'm going to count, and you're going to breathe in and out slowly as I do."

Thornton had a way about him that just exuded calm and tranquility, as if nothing in the world bothered him, and he had everything under control. What a foreign concept. But that calm seemed to seep into Asher's bones with each new breath. Even when his ribs ached, even when his head continued to pound, he was calming down bit by bit.

"That's good. That's really good, Asher. How's your pain?"

He shook his head, not wanting to answer, but Thornton repeated, "Asher, I asked you a question. I need to know how much pain you're in. Is it manageable? Do we need some meds before you're discharged?"

He shook his head again, managing to say, "No."

Thornton's voice was stern when he said, "Look at me, Asher. I don't think you're telling me the truth. So, I'm asking you again—is your pain manageable, or should we ask for some painkillers before we leave?"

He took a deep breath and nodded, finally able to admit he was feeling pretty awful. His ribs hurt, obviously, but he ached pretty much from his head to his feet. He'd seen the bruises all across his chest from the seat belt. It wasn't pretty. And he found it nearly impossible to lie to Thornton with his voice so serious. "Yeah. I think I need some."

Asher glanced up and met his eyes. Thornton's expression was serious when he replied, "Thank you for telling me the truth."

Thornton took care of ordering his pain relievers, and as soon as they began to kick in, he helped Asher put on the clothes Madi had brought him for when he was released. His day shift nurse, Rebecca, finally brought in his discharge papers and a wheelchair. Asher stiffened when he saw the chair, knowing what was coming. He just had to get through the next hour, and then he'd be home.

"I'm gonna go down and get your prescription so we don't have to make that stop on the way out, all right?"

He cleared his throat. "Can I borrow your phone and your earbuds? I just thought I could listen to… but you probably need it. Never mind."

"I can make do without it. Here." He handed the earbud case and his phone over. He put the code in so Asher could use it while he was gone. "You sure you're okay? I can stay if you'd rather, and we can—"

He shook his head. He could use the time to calm the fuck down, as much as possible, anyway. "No, I'm fine. Go ahead."

Thornton excused himself to go down to the hospital pharmacy. Asher took several deep breaths. He'd been able to ignore the fact he was in the hospital because he'd woken up in his room and hadn't had to be around a lot of people.

He'd only had a few nurses in and out of his room, and the doctor too, so he'd been able to distract himself enough to handle the situation. But now they were headed home, and he'd have to sit in that wheelchair and be pushed through the fucking corridors, and the thought of all the people and everything going on around him made him start to shake.

He found YouTube and searched for the background noise he often listened to, turning it up high and shoving the earbuds in his ears, and tried to use his mantras and his relaxation techniques to calm himself down. By the time Thornton was back, he thought he might be able to pass as normal without setting off Thornton's alarm bells. Thornton helped him into the chair and began the long, arduous trip to the lobby.

His hands were in fists in his lap, his palms were sweating, and he was practicing his breathing exercises just to get downstairs. Then he had the drive home to contend with. But he'd be home free soon enough. He wasn't driving, and for that he was grateful, but even getting in the car seemed like an insurmountable task. He was going to hold it together, though. If it was the last thing he did, he was going to hold it the fuck together without making Thornton look at him with pity.

The man had been kinder than he thought possible. If he could make it home without causing any more fanfare, Thornton would finally be able to leave him at home and go back to his own life. Asher was positive the man had shit to do, a life to live, and from what it sounded like, a business to run.

A sleek, black SUV was brought to the curb by the valet driver. Thornton locked the wheels on the chair and stepped forward, slipping some cash in the valet's hand, slick as you please. It was a practiced move, so Asher had a feeling the life Thornton lived was *much* different than his own. That impression was proven when Thornton opened the passenger door of the car and the interior was revealed.

Shinier than a car had any right to be, he was greeted with soft, supple, tan leather seats and wood grain and chrome dash accents. Jesus. It was fancier than any car he'd ever laid eyes on. He was positive he'd do something to mess it up, but it was his best—and realistically the only—option he felt comfortable with to get him home.

Thornton was by his side, practically lifting him to his feet without him having to exert himself at all, but even with the help, pain lanced through his side, and he sucked in a breath. "Fuck, Asher. I thought I was being gentle. Do you think you can take the few steps to the car?"

He took a couple of shallow breaths, gearing himself up more for the ride home and the inevitable pain he would feel. "Yeah. I'll be fine. You were gentle. I think I just sucked in too deep a breath, and my ribs weren't happy with me."

Asher took several steps to the car and slowly slid himself into the passenger side with a lot of help from Thornton, narrowly avoiding crying out in pain. Thornton helped him with the seat belt but hesitated before clicking it into place. "This is going to put pressure on your ribs. How about I put the top half of the belt behind you so it's not so painful?"

Fear lanced through him. He couldn't do that. He had to have the belt on properly. He'd end up flying through the window and getting killed if they got in an accident. He couldn't. He just… no. Shaking his head, he squeezed his eyes shut, unable to even respond.

"Asher, hey, look at me. Come on, let me see those gorgeous eyes of yours. There you go. We don't have to do that. You can wear it properly, all right? I'm clicking it into place. Maybe hold it out in front of you a bit so there isn't so much pressure. It's going to be okay."

Oh my god, you're such a pathetic freak. He got himself under control by the skin of his teeth and finally answered, "Thanks. I'm all right."

"We're gonna get you home and comfortable."

He nodded, unable to do anything else. "Yeah, okay."

He was in pain, he was a hair's breadth away from losing his shit, and he was feeling sick to his stomach. But after Thornton put Asher's address in his GPS, the man kept idle chatter going on the way to his place. He was grateful he didn't have to respond because the longer he was in Thornton's posh car, the less control he had over his mental and physical reactions to everything going on with him.

His head got foggy, and he found himself breathing harder as his heart kicked into hyperdrive. Humiliating himself wasn't on his list of favorite things to do. And doing it in front of the only man he'd ever truly been attracted to was more than he could bear. He was positive he was going to have to ask Thornton to pull over so he could be sick when he heard the man say, "We're here. Let's get you—"

Asher fumbled with the seat belt and pushed the door open, ribs protesting and pain lancing through his chest as he leaned out of the passenger door and emptied the contents of his stomach onto the pavement below, thankfully avoiding desecrating Thornton's car.

Oh, god, oh, god, oh, god, oh, god, oh, god.

A sob escaped before he could hold it back, and he swiped at his mouth with the sleeve of his shirt. He was trapped in a nightmare. Had to be. But as a hand rubbed his back and gently pried his own away from the door handle he'd been gripping like a lifeline, he realized it was reality.

"Jesus, Asher. God, I'm so sorry. Were you in that much pain? Shit. I really don't feel comfortable leaving you here alone. You need help. You can't—"

"No!" Shaking his head, he squeezed his eyes shut, sending the last of his tears down his cheeks. "No. I'll be fine. I just want to be in my own place. I can't be in the car. I can't... Don't make me be in the car."

"Fuck, Ash—

"Please..." His breath was heaving now, and he was feeling lightheaded. Jesus, he couldn't remember feeling so ashamed and humiliated in his life.

"Shhh, shh. Okay. It's okay. Let's get you inside, all right? We'll get you settled, and you'll feel much better."

There was no helping it. Anything he did, every move he made hurt. But if he could put on the performance of his life and convince Thornton he was fine on his own, he'd be able to break down in peace once Thornton was on his way home. He could do it. He knew he could.

Mind over fucking matter. He made his way to his apartment with a lot of help from Thornton, grateful the police officer had dropped his keys off at the hospital. He eventually found himself propped up in bed with a mountain of pillows he didn't even remember having, a glass of water on the side table next to him, and his cell phone finally plugged into his charger.

He was grateful for the help, but he *needed* the man to leave, all the while not *wanting* him to. But he couldn't hold himself together any longer, and with every minute that went by, he felt like he might fly apart into a thousand pieces he knew he'd never be able to glue back together.

"I'm gonna let you rest. But if you need anything, I'll be out in the living room getting some work done."

"No. Thornton, I'm fine. You need to go home and get back to your own life.

I'm sure Madi will come be with me if I need her, but I just want to sleep for now."

"Asher—"

He met Thornton's concerned eyes with as steady a gaze as he could muster. "Please. I just want to be alone." Asher could see the battle waging in the older man's eyes, see he was about to protest again, but Asher had to stop it. He could only hold himself together for so long and he'd humiliated himself enough for several lifetimes. "Thornton, thank you for all your help. I am so grateful to you for everything you've done for me the last several days. You have your own life to get back to, and I just want to sleep and try to recuperate on my own. When I wake up, I'll call Madi."

Thornton sighed but nodded. "I'd like you to call me every couple of hours until you go to bed. I know I'm being overly cautious, but please humor an old man. I don't think you should be left alone, but I'll honor your wishes if you make those calls."

Finally, he gave in, unable to say no in the face of those worried eyes. "I'll call. I promise."

Thornton finally acquiesced, and he gave the older man his phone number so he could text Asher and he'd have his number for later. When he heard his front door close behind Thornton, he let the tears he'd held at bay slip down his cheeks. He felt helpless, and the pain he felt from head to toe was so much more than he thought he could handle. But his tears were short-lived, and his body decided they weren't what he needed as he drifted off before he even realized it was happening.

CHAPTER SIX

Thornton

Thornton glanced at his watch and cursed himself six ways from Sunday for leaving Asher home alone. It didn't matter that he didn't have a choice. He was asked to leave, so he did. That didn't mean he felt good about it. As soon as he'd closed the door, it had locked from the inside. He'd tried to open it again, knowing it a fruitless endeavor. And he wasn't about to knock until the poor boy had to come to the door to let him in.

He didn't think Asher's body could take much more, and that was all the more reason to be upset with himself for leaving. He'd been stuck between a rock and a hard place, which was why he'd been pacing the floor of his family room off and on for the last couple of hours, unable to focus on much of anything. He'd tried to work, he'd tried to watch TV, he'd even tried to pay bills, to no avail. As soon as he got into a rhythm, his mind would drift back to Asher's pain-filled expression.

The phone rang in his back pocket, and he nearly fumbled the thing trying to answer it. His body relaxed as soon as he saw it was Asher. Nearly two hours and twenty minutes had passed since he'd left, and with every minute that went past the two hours he'd demanded from Asher, his stress levels increased exponentially. He knew, in the far reaches of his mind, he needed to calm the fuck down and allow Asher to take care of himself, but there was no turning off his Daddy side when he was so invested in someone.

He didn't want the boy to know he'd been out of his mind with worry, so he forced a calm he didn't feel. "Hey, Asher. Are you all right?"

Asher's long pause ratcheted up his concern, but when he finally heard the boy's sweet voice, his nerves calmed down a bit. "I'm okay. Sorry I'm late calling you. I just woke up."

"I'm just glad you were able to sleep. Is there anything you need? I'd be happy to bring you a late lunch or early dinner. I know you won't be up for cooking, most likely."

"No. I'm fine. I'm not really hungry yet."

"All right. Well, let me know if you change your mind later. I'd be happy to stop by with anything you might be craving now that you're free from hospital food."

He heard a chuckle through the line, but it felt forced. And he couldn't help thinking Asher's voice sounded strained, like he was still in a lot of pain. "I have lots of freezer meals, so I'm set. Thank you."

He nearly launched into Daddy speak, lecturing about the nutritional value of that type of food, but realized it would most likely not be welcome. "Well, I'd be happy to come by and keep you company later, so just let me know if you'd like that."

"You're being really nice. I'll be fine, though. I don't want you to worry about me. I'm a big boy and can take care of myself."

Thornton sighed. He knew that was true of the beautiful young man on an average day, but this wasn't an average day. The injuries Asher had sustained as a result of Thornton's negligence didn't make him weak; they made him wounded and vulnerable. But he didn't feel like it was his place to tell Asher that. Yet. Hopefully, that would change in the future.

His shoulders sagged, unable to think of any other reason Asher might need or want him to come check on him. "I know you can. It's just a lot harder to do when you're in so much pain, so please don't feel bad about calling if you need my help. I want to be here for you."

"I will. I'm going to see what's on TV and maybe grab something to eat later. Do you still want me to call you every couple of hours?"

God, yes. "I do. I'll worry otherwise."

"Okay. Bye, Thornton."

"Bye, Asher."

***

The call he got from Asher around five-thirty that evening went much the same. He asked several times if he could drop by to see him, but Asher said no each time. He had to respect the boy for being able to put his foot down, but it pretty much sucked on Thornton's end.

Surprisingly, he'd been able to get quite a bit of work done during the last half of the day. By eight, however, Thornton was losing his mind. He'd eaten dinner, cleaned up, fed his lazy pups—Beauty and Beast, the adorably enormous English mastiff puppies he'd gotten from the dog rescue and training facility he was in business with—and worked out. It had been two and a half hours since he'd heard from Asher, and he was at war with himself.

On one hand, he knew he was probably overreacting. The pain was probably making Asher tired, and he'd probably taken some more pain meds, so he knew the logical assumption was that he was sleeping. On the other hand, what if he wasn't overreacting at all? What if Asher had hurt himself and needed help?

He waited another fifteen minutes and then he picked up his phone, opened his contacts, and dialed. The other line finally picked up, and he started talking before he heard any type of greeting. "How worried should I be that Asher hasn't called me? He's supposed to call me every couple of hours, but it's been two hours and forty-five minutes."

Syed, obviously having heard in his voice how worried he was, answered immediately. "How did he say he was doing the last time he called? He could be sleeping. If he's on strong pain meds, and I hope to god they gave him some, they probably knocked him out. He's a pretty small guy, so it wouldn't surprise me if that's what's going on."

"He said he was fine, but I could hear the strain in his voice. He keeps telling me he doesn't need me to come over, and I know I should respect that, but I think it's because he thinks he's bothering me. I don't think he's telling me the truth. He said he'd call his best friend, Madi, if he needed help, but—"

"He doesn't have anyone there to help him?"

"He told me he'd be fine, and he'd call Madi to come over if he needed her."

"Have you called *him*?"

Fuck. "No. I'm worried sick, but he doesn't seem to want to accept help from me, so I've been holding off, hoping he calls."

"You need to call him, Thorn. He shouldn't be alone right now. Hopefully, Madi is there with him, but call him just in case she's not. Call me back when you're done."

He said a quick goodbye, feeling angry with himself for waiting to call and for leaving the boy to begin with. He dialed Asher's number and listened to it ring. And ring. And ring. And ring, until it went to voicemail. He hung up and tried again. Same thing. One more time. Same thing.

Fuck.

Syed answered the phone before it was done ringing the first time. "He's not answering. I called three times. Jesus, Sy."

"Take a deep breath for a second. Keep your head in the game. Do you know Madi's last name or a way to reach her?"

"Jesus. Yes. I have her number. He had to call her from my phone because his was dead. I'll call you back."

He hung up, found Madi's number, and dialed. "Hello?"

"Madi, this is Thornton from the hospital—"

"Yeah, I remember. Is everything okay?"

"I don't know. I was calling to see if you're with Asher."

The long pause had his heart nearly beating out of his chest. "No. Should I be?"

"Dammit. He said he was going to call you if he needed your help."

"He won't call. He doesn't ask for help. I always have to force it on him. When did he get home?"

"I drove him home around lunchtime, and he said he was going to be fine and I should go home. That he'd call you if he needed to, but I made him promise to call me every couple of hours just to be sure he was okay. He called twice since then, but it's been nearly three hours, and I can't reach him."

"Shit, shit, shit. That boy—"

He heard a little voice say, "Mommy, you said shit!"

He would have chuckled if he wasn't so worked up. "I know, baby. I'm sorry. I'll put a dollar in the jar, okay? Thornton, let me try to call him and see if he answers. I'll call you right back."

They hung up, and he waited, but when she called less than a minute later, he knew it wasn't good news. "He's not answering."

"Do you have a key?"

"Yeah. Let me just… Gigi, can you run and get your shoes and coat on?"

"But, Mama, I'm in my PJs."

"I know, baby—"

"Madi, I can come to you and get the key. I don't want you to—"

"No. I have to make sure he's okay, too. Meet me there if you want, but I'm going regardless."

"Okay, I'm leaving now. See you in a bit."

He was out the door a minute later and turning on the rental car his insurance had arranged for him as he told his phone to call Syed. "Did you get ahold of him?"

"No. He never called Madi either. She called him, and he didn't answer. She's meeting me over there. Fuck, Sy, I'm worried sick."

"I know. Thorn, he shouldn't be left alone. And I'm sure he would have been told that in the hospital when he talked to his doctor before they released him. He's going to need help with simple, everyday things. Getting dressed, brushing his teeth, showering, getting up from a chair or his bed—it's all going to hurt."

"I wasn't there when the doctor talked to him, or I'd never have left him to begin with."

"I know. Maybe his phone is on vibrate, and he's sleeping through it. I know you're thinking worst-case scenario, but you won't know until you get there. Stay calm so you get there in one piece. You're no good to the boy if you hurt yourself."

"Yeah. Okay. I'm gonna let you go, but…"

"You call me if you need me."

He let out the breath he'd been holding. "Thank you, Syed."

"No need. Be safe."

They hung up, and if he ignored the speed limit as he drove to Asher's apartment, Syed didn't have to know about it. When he got there, he pulled into Asher's spot, the same one Asher told Thornton to park in earlier. He didn't see Madi anywhere, so he got out and walked towards the building, stopping when he heard a car pull in the lot. Relief flooded him when he saw it was her. She jumped out of her car and tossed a keyring his way. "Go on. I'll get my daughter out of the car and be right behind you."

He caught the ring and jogged inside, skipping the elevator and using the stairs to get to the fourth floor as quickly as possible. He knew his achy, bruised body would pay the price later, but checking on Asher as soon as possible was more important than his discomfort. When he got to Asher's door, he knocked first, calling out Asher's name. After waiting a couple of seconds, he used the key, calling out Asher's name again. It was dark in the boy's apartment, the only light coming from down the hallway in Asher's room.

Panicked he didn't hear anything, he jogged to Asher's room. The bed was rumpled but empty. The door to his bathroom was slightly ajar. Thornton walked towards it, trepidation making his heart hammer like a bass drum as he pushed the door open a bit and knocked lightly, not wanting to scare him. "Asher?"

He heard a whimper and then a sob and shoved the door open the rest of the way. "Oh, Jesus. Oh, god. Asher."

What greeted him was worse than even he'd imagined, and he'd imagined some awful shit over the last hour. The bathroom was cold, so he knew the water pelting down on Asher's crumpled form had to be freezing. He was mostly covered with the shower curtain, which he was using to shield himself from the worst of the shower's spray.

Thornton was there by his side, turning the water off immediately. He reached back towards the door to grab Asher's towel. "Baby."

When the boy raised his eyes to Thornton's, they were filled with tears, and his lips were trembling and tinged blue. With chattering teeth, he whispered, "Hurts."

"Fuck. Ash, will you let me help you? I'll close my eyes if you want. I just…"

"Please. I'm sorry." His breath hitched. "I shouldn't have told you to leave. You don't have to close your eyes."

"Shh. Don't apologize, sweetheart."

He was a hair's breadth away from crying himself as he took in Asher's small, shivering frame. He tugged off the shower curtain, replacing it with Asher's towel. The bruises covering Asher's body were worse than his, and he'd thought *his* were bad. Asher was half his size. He couldn't imagine how much pain he must be in. When he tried to meet Asher's eyes, they were blurry. It was only then he realized he was tearing up. Blinking away his own tears, he wrapped the towel around Asher's tiny body.

Sliding one arm behind Asher's back and the other under his knees, Thornton whispered, "Brace yourself. It'll probably hurt like hell when I lift you, but I don't see a way around it. Keep your hands in your lap so you aren't straining to hold onto me. Trust that I have you, okay?"

"I do." Their gazes met, and Asher nodded, sending another tear down his cheek. "I trust you."

Thornton couldn't help but kiss the boy's forehead. "On three. One, two, three."

He clenched his teeth as he watched fresh tears fill and fall from Asher's eyes. When it seemed Asher couldn't handle it anymore, he cried out, eyes squeezed tight as Thornton carried him into his bedroom. He sat him down on the bed and wrapped the duvet around him.

He saw a large scar bisecting his pectorals and knew there was a story there but assumed it was related to his heart condition. He set it aside to think about later. He needed to deal with the pain Asher was feeling at that moment. Grabbing the pain pills beside the bed and the bottle of water next to it, he handed both to Asher and watched as he took the pills.

Thornton kneeled and began to softly rub Asher's feet and lower legs, then his hands and forearms with the towel. Standing, he did the same to Asher's hair, avoiding his injury and then gently patted his chest and back, satisfied he was dry enough.

Moving the blanket back around Asher's shoulders, he wrapped it around in front, so he was fully covered. Thornton squatted and clasped Asher's hands in his, squeezing gently. Thornton needed to convince him to come home with him, at least the first night or two. He knew he'd have to put up a fight, but he couldn't leave Asher again. He just couldn't.

Madi walked in, prompting a gasp of surprise from Asher. She held what smelled like hot chocolate, and Gigi followed with Asher's slippers. Emotions were riding high, and a shuddering sigh left Asher's body. "I'm sorry, Madi. It's so late for Gigi. I didn't mean to—"

"Hush. You should have called, Ash." She put the steaming travel mug down on Asher's bedside table. "I would have come. I think you should come stay with us tonight."

Thornton almost interrupted—wanting, almost *needing* Asher to come home with him—but he waited until Asher answered his friend. "I can't do that. You don't have the space, and I won't take Gigi's bed."

Gigi knelt beside Thornton and helped Asher slide his feet into his slippers. The sweet smiles they gave each other melted Thornton. "Thank you, for coming here to help me."

Gigi nodded. "I was sad. Belle was singing my favorite song. But then Mom told me we were coming to check on you, and I was happy."

Asher smiled and then looked up at Madi. "I won't interrupt your lives. I just need more pain meds, and I'll be able to sleep it off."

She began to protest, but Thornton raised his hand to interrupt. "I have more space than I need, and I'd really like to be the one to help you, Asher."

Asher shook his head, but Thornton squeezed his hand. "I wanted to take you home with me instead of leaving you here today, but I didn't want to force your hand. If you won't go home with Madi and Gigi, then, at least for tonight, come home with me. If you don't want to stay and recuperate there, then I'll find a dog sitter to take care of my puppies, and I'll come and stay with you here."

Gigi gasped and brought her tiny fists under her chin, vibrating with excitement. "Puppies! Mama, he has puppies!"

Madi smiled indulgently at her daughter and ran her hand over her daughter's soft curls. "I heard. That's exciting, isn't it?"

Gigi asked Madi, "Can we go see them?"

"No, baby. It's late."

"But…"

Thornton couldn't help but chime in. "How about if you're good tonight, and you go right to bed when you get home, your mom and I can figure out a way for you to meet Beauty and Beast?"

"Mama, Beauty and Beast! Like my favorite Disney movie! We gotta go home right now. I gotta go to bed."

As Gigi wandered out of the room on a mission—obviously ready to keep up her end of the bargain—the three of them laughed. Madi crossed her arms over her chest and spoke to Asher. "So, what's it going to be? His roomy house or my mini apartment?"

Asher sighed, obviously unhappy about having to agree to either, but Thornton wasn't giving in a second time. Just the thought of finding him in that freezing cold shower had him angry at himself all over again. Asher turned his exhausted gaze towards Thornton. "Are you sure I won't be putting you out?"

"I promise you won't be. I want you there so I can keep an eye on you. If you had someone else that could help you during the day over the next several weeks while you recover, I wouldn't be pushing so hard. Though, I must admit, I would have asked regardless. I want to help you."

Shoulders slumped, Asher nodded. "All right. But I'm not agreeing to anything more than the next couple of days."

Thornton would just have to work especially hard to get Asher to stay until he was able to go back to work. He was going to have nightmares of what happened to Asher when he was on his own.

Madi leaned over and kissed Asher's cheek. "Call me in the morning. Or else."

"Yes, ma'am."

Madi leaned down to Thornton, who was still kneeling on the floor in front of Asher, and kissed his cheek as well. "Thank you for caring enough to call me. I'm glad he's got someone like you to take care of him."

"I'm glad he's got such a wonderful friend in you, Madi. I'll text you my address later. You can stop by and see him anytime."

She smirked and tipped her head towards the front of the apartment. "You've gotten yourself into trouble with that one. She's gonna constantly be harassing me to see those dogs."

"The pups are great with kids. I don't mind at all."

They said their goodbyes, and Madi left the room. They could hear her talking to Gigi as they made their way out the front door. Asher made a move to get up. "I should get dressed and pack some things."

Thornton reached up and clasped Asher's chin, turning the boy to meet his gaze. "Asher, you can't keep overdoing things. I won't have you hurting yourself again. I need you to allow me to help you. God, I'm feeling so awful I left you alone today."

"Don't. Please. I made you go home. I'm too stubborn for my own good. I promise, I'll let you help me. I've never been in so much pain as when I fell tonight in that shower. I was so scared, Thornton. I couldn't get up. I thought I'd be there all night."

Thornton took in a shaky breath, whispering, "Jesus, Ash. You're killing me. No more protesting, all right? Promise me, sweetheart."

Asher's cheeks pinked, but he nodded. "I promise."

Thornton's shoulders sagged in relief, and he gently dropped his head on Asher's knee, still unable to get the image out of his head of a frozen, hurting Asher crying in the shower as he was being pelted by cold water. "I'm contemplating having Syed meet us at my place to check you over. I'll probably let it pass until tomorrow, if you think you'll be all right. But he'll be coming tomorrow, no question."

Waiting for a protest, Thornton met Asher's gaze with steely resolve, but when Asher only smiled a sad, tired smile and said, "Okay. Thank you," Thornton finally felt some of the tension leave his shoulders.

"Good. You're welcome. The pills should kick in pretty quick. From the way your eyes are blinking drowsily at me, maybe they already have."

Asher nodded but kept quiet. "I'm going to pack a bag for you with enough clothes to last a week. If we come back early and I stay with you instead, that's fine. But I'd rather be prepared. Stay sitting up, and I'll try to work as fast as I can. I'm afraid if I let you lie down, it will be too painful sitting you up again and getting you to the car. This way at least it's less strain for you."

Thornton made to stand up, but Asher reached out and clasped his hand in his much smaller, much colder ones. "Thank you. You're kind of amazing, you know that?"

"I'm not amazing. I left you here to fend for yourself and nearly put you back in the hospital."

The boy squeezed his hand. "Don't do that. I asked you to leave, and you were a gentleman and did what I asked. This was not your fault. If there's fault involved, it lays squarely on my shoulders."

Thornton stood, leaned over the boy, and kissed his temple. His voice was rough with emotion when he whispered, "Jesus, you scared me to death, Ash." He knew he was going too far. Hell, that was the second time he'd kissed Asher, and he'd let *baby* and *sweetheart* slip out more than once, but he had no fucks to give at that point. Sighing, he got his head back in the game, straightened up, and glanced around the room. "Where should I start? Do you have a duffel?"

He hurried to pack everything Asher asked for, his mind racing triple time when he saw the boy's socks with cute little designs on them and then boxer briefs that were similar. Trying not to read too much into it, he continued to pack the rest of the boy's clothes and a few extras, including any electronics he saw and toiletries he might need.

Taking the bag with him, he walked towards the front of Asher's apartment to see if there was anything he should include and stopped dead in his tracks when he saw what was stacked on the coffee table in front of the couch in the family room.

His legs carried him the rest of the way but gave out on him. He nearly collapsed on the sofa, his heart rate kicking up. He had to swallow down his emotions as he gazed at what was in front of him. A stack of adult coloring books of all different kinds was there: animals, mandalas, flowers, rainforests, one with quotes in calligraphy, underwater scenes, geometric patterns, even one with fantasy-type creatures.

He picked up the ones that looked the most used and tucked them in the bag, adding a few of those that weren't as well for variety. Next, he packed the large zippered pen, marker, and colored pencil case and the big box of crayons as well.

Knowing Asher was sitting waiting for him, he headed back that way, speaking before he got to the room. "I packed several of your coloring books and markers and stuff. Is there anything else you'd like me to pack?"

He saw Asher doing his best to quickly tuck something colorful under his pillow. Having moved too fast, the boy sucked in a breath and brought a hand to his ribs. Thornton got down on his knees in front of him. "Are you all right?"

"Mmm, I'll be okay. I just twisted wrong."

Knowing he was pushing too much too fast but wanting to make sure Asher knew he had nothing to be ashamed of, Thornton kept his gaze on Asher's and reached to pull out whatever it was he had tucked under his pillow. Asher turned away and closed his eyes, embarrassment coloring his cheeks, but Thornton reached up and cupped his face, turning it back his way.

Thornton could tell the threadbare, crocheted, stuffed train in red, white, and blue was a beloved, old friend. "There's no need for you to hide this away. There's nothing to be ashamed of or embarrassed about. Not with me. Is this from your childhood?"

Still avoiding his gaze, Asher merely looked down at his lap and nodded. "Asher?" Finally, those eyes met his. He placed the train in Asher's hands and watched as the boy's nimble fingers reached for the most threadbare spot on the stuffy and rubbed it between his fingers. "My grandmother made him for me."

"We'll bring him, okay?"

When all Asher could do was nod, Thornton stood, pulling the blanket back over the shoulder that had been bared. He went back to the drawers where Asher kept his soft clothes and pulled out a pair of socks and some sweats, knowing and hating that it was going to hurt Asher no matter how gently he maneuvered him into them. He cursed himself again, realizing just how impossible it would have been for Asher to take care of himself in the state he was in.

"I'm going to forgo boxers for now, so I don't have to jostle you twice to get them on before your pants." He put the socks on first and then managed to get the sweats under Asher's thighs without too much pain, finally lifting him just enough to tug them on the rest of the way, hating it when he heard Asher's pain-filled, indrawn breath. "Sorry, sweetheart."

Asher murmured that it was okay, keeping on his brave face, and Thornton looked back at the drawers full of shirts that he had no intention of making the boy put on. Pulling off his own sweatshirt that was at least three sizes too big for Asher left Thornton only with his long-sleeved tee. But he knew from earlier at the hospital that nothing Asher's size would easily slip over the boy's head and arms without entirely too much jostling.

Gingerly helping Asher put the sweatshirt on, he couldn't help the jolt of satisfaction he got seeing the boy in his clothes, not to mention the pleasure he felt when he saw Asher hold the neck of the sweatshirt up to his nose and breathe it in, eyes closed, as if Thornton's smell was an aphrodisiac to him.

Jesus. Get your head in the game, Thorn.

He put the slippers back over Asher's socked feet and squatted down to meet the boy's gaze. "Okay, this is going to hurt, but I want you to keep your hands in your lap like you did in the bathroom. Hold your train for comfort, all right?"

When Asher nodded and braced himself, Thornton picked him up, ignoring his own pain, and they headed down to his car. Relief filled Thornton when all was said and done and they were on the road, an exhausted Asher beside him where he couldn't help but feel the boy belonged.

CHAPTER SEVEN

Asher

He felt a hand on his thigh and startled awake, unable to keep himself from gasping when his ribs protested. "Shit. I didn't mean to startle you. We're home. I'm coming around to get you, all right?"

He nodded and hummed his assent, concentrating on taking shallower breaths to ward off the pain. He couldn't believe Thornton was real. Who did things like this? He'd packed for Asher; he'd even found his coloring books and his train stuffy, but instead of mocking him, he'd somehow made it all feel normal, which he knew it wasn't. It was so very far from normal.

Then he'd carried him down to his car, which Asher knew had to be painful for Thornton as he'd been hurt in the accident, too. He'd gotten Asher inside it with very little pain and without tipping them both over as he opened the door with him still in his arms, which was a miracle in itself, and then gone up to grab the bag and lock up after them.

The car door beside him opened, and as much as he wanted to twist his body and step out, there was no way in hell he could do that. He'd completely overestimated his ability to take care of himself. He was an idiot, but he also abhorred taking advantage of people. He'd had enough of his parents doing that when he was younger to last him a lifetime. He didn't want to be that kind of person.

As Thornton lifted him out of the car, he finally took in his surroundings. They were in the biggest garage he'd ever seen. It had four bays, making him wonder why Thornton was driving a rental to begin with, but he figured he'd have to find out why later on. The pain pills were making him woozy and sick to his stomach.

Oh fuck. No. Not now, not now, not now.

"I... I think I'm gonna be sick."

God, if he vomited on the man after everything he'd done for Asher, he was going to die. He sucked in as deep a breath as he could, closed his eyes, and willed the nausea to pass. Thornton sped up his pace, and the next thing he knew, he was sitting on top of a counter in some kind of gigantic laundry-mud room combination and handed a small trash can which, embarrassingly enough, he used immediately. And then again. And again.

Crying out from the pain in his chest when his ribs protested the violent use of the muscles surrounding them, he was unable to control his sobs and could only do his best to keep them as quiet as possible. It was only by sheer force of will that he got control of them before he couldn't stop and was a pathetic puddle of agony in Thornton's arms.

Jesus. Could things get any worse?

Thornton calmly rubbed his back, murmuring words Asher's fuzzy mind couldn't make sense of. When he was finally done and had nothing left in his stomach, he was able to tune back in. "I've got you. You're okay. It's probably the pain meds making you sick."

He shook his head, miserable, in pain, and weak as a kitten. "Oh my god. I'm so sorry."

"Don't apologize. Have you had any dinner? Pain meds sometimes don't settle right without food."

The thought of that nearly had him heaving again, but he swallowed convulsively to keep it down as he shook his head. "Hmm mm."

He was momentarily distracted at the clicking of puppy feet on the floors leading to the laundry room. Suddenly, two ridiculously cute, extra-large "puppies" were running around the corner together as if they were connected at the hip. It wasn't until they got closer that he was able to see one of the puppy's eyes were both gone. Shock had his own eyes popping wide, but he got distracted from asking about the blind pup when Thornton's voice went deep and authoritative. "Settle."

Something about that voice made him shudder, and he couldn't blame the puppies when they sat on their haunches, faces turned up towards their master in what seemed a lot like adoration, tails thumping on the floor, excitement held in check by sheer force of will to obey. Hell, he wanted to obey Thornton in that moment, and he couldn't understand why he was so affected by the man.

"Have you eaten anything at all since I took you home?" When he finally recovered enough to force himself to meet Thornton's eyes, the concern in them nearly did him in. Caught out, all he could do was look down at his lap as he shook his head again.

He heard Thornton suck in a breath, probably in exasperation, and he couldn't help but look up to apologize again, but the sadness and guilt marring Thornton's face caught him by surprise, even though it shouldn't have. And then he was apologizing for an entirely different reason. Disappointing this kind, generous, beautiful man broke his heart. "I'm sorry. I don't want you upset. I—"

Thornton gently rubbed his hands up and down Asher's arms. "I'm not upset with you. I'm upset with me. I should have listened to my instincts and stayed no matter what you said. Because of course you can't just get up and cook yourself food. Jesus."

His ribs protested when he reached up to touch Thornton's tortured face. "Don't do that. Because if you feel guilty, I'm gonna feel guilty, and then we're *both* miserable."

That got a tiny, rueful smile, which Asher returned. "You couldn't have known how bad it was or that I was supposed to make sure I had someone at home to take care of me. You couldn't have known that I'm stupid stubborn, even when I know it's to my own detriment. I promise I'll do better. I'll ask for help even when I don't want to. It's just... Thornton, you're practically a stranger, and the thought of you putting yourself out, putting your life on hold... doesn't sit well with me."

"Do I feel like a stranger to you, Asher? Hey, look at me. Don't tell me what your mind says is the right answer. Don't think about the fact we've only known each other for a handful of days. Tell me how you feel. Am I a stranger?"

His shoulders slumped, knowing the answer. Because no. He absolutely did *not* feel like a stranger. They'd spent countless hours over the last two and a half days getting to know quite a bit about each other. They'd been in such close proximity, and neither of them had wanted to pass the time watching TV or sharing idle chit chat. He'd felt a connection with Thornton, and for once in his life he hadn't wanted to ignore his feelings in fear of what might happen. Because maybe, what might happen could turn out to be amazing.

Back at the hospital they'd talked about his job, how much he loved it, and how grateful he was to Jenn for giving him a chance. Thornton knew how much he loved Madi and Gigi. Asher had shared the fact that he'd dropped out of college when things were too tight financially and how he eventually wanted to go back and finish. And Thornton had shared stories about his wonderful family and Damon and Syed. He'd shocked Asher when he told him about being owner and co-owner of a lot of local businesses and how he'd fallen into it and never looked back

His voice was rough when he finally whispered, "No. You're not a stranger."

Thornton sighed and leaned down to rest his forehead on Asher's, and he couldn't have stopped his heart rate from kicking up to high gear if he wanted to. That gesture—that intimate, gentle, sweet gesture—nearly did him in. He sighed and leaned into Thornton's strength. He didn't deserve a man as wonderful as Thornton, but he was unwilling to reject the man's care and comfort. He couldn't remember the last time anyone had taken his wellbeing so seriously.

It wouldn't last forever, so Asher vowed to himself then and there he'd soak it up while he had the chance. Thornton's expression was imploring when he asked, "Will you stay with me while you're on leave?"

Asher couldn't think of a reason not to—didn't *want* to think of one—but he knew he couldn't commit to that. He had to have an out in case he started to sense Thornton had changed his mind. He shook his head, trying not to feel enormous guilt at Thornton's defeated frown. "It's just... this is all so overwhelming. For now, all I feel comfortable with is staying my first week. Can we see how things go after that?"

Thornton let out a soft breath, a smile slowly lighting up his face. "I'll take it, for now. So, do you feel well enough for me to move you? I'm going to take you right up to the guest room across from my bedroom so I can be there when you need me, and I'll bring you some dinner." He was about to protest when

Thornton continued, "It won't be anything heavy, but you need to eat to keep up your strength."

Something deep inside of him, that he'd have to unpack and look at later, settled with a deep desire to do as this forceful yet kind man demanded of him. "All right."

"Ready?"

He nodded, warmed again by Thornton's kindness. "Yeah. But I can probably walk. I don't want you throwing your back out."

"You're light as a feather. Just let me take care of you tonight, okay? It will go a long way to easing my mind of the guilt I'm still feeling for leaving you today."

He sighed, knowing there was nothing he could say or do to rid Thornton of his unnecessary guilt except help him relieve a bit of it by taking care of him. "It's not your fault, but I'll let you take care of me. You're going to have to be careful, though. A boy could get used to this."

Something sparked in Thornton's eyes at Asher's admission. He didn't know what it was about, but Thornton's gruff voice sent shivers down his spine when he said, "And I'd be happy if you did."

Heat flooded his face, and goosebumps slid up his arms at the liquid sexiness of Thornton's voice. All he could do was sigh when Thornton picked him up as if he was made of spun glass and carried him through the most beautiful house he'd ever seen, the clickity-clack of the puppies' nails trailing behind them. Thornton continued up a grand staircase and down a long hall into a ridiculously large guest room with what he assumed was a walk-in closet and an attached bath.

His own apartment was beautiful, and he was very proud of the fact he'd worked hard enough to afford to live in a place like it, but this place was far beyond what he could have even imagined. He couldn't wait to see the outside of it, if the inside was anything to go by. He didn't think it was a mansion. It felt like a big, beautiful, yet comfortably lived-in home. From what he'd seen, there wasn't anything he'd be afraid to touch and no furniture he'd be afraid to sit on, and the fact that Thornton let his puppies run amok while he was gone was testament to that fact.

He felt comfortable immediately despite the residual pain that ached in his head and chest. Thornton set him down on a bed he'd swear was made of clouds and moondust, it was so comfortable. He watched, charmed, as Thornton bustled about grabbing extra pillows and blankets and propping them up against the headboard. He lifted Asher and pulled back the covers, setting him down so he could rest against the fluffy pillows.

A soft smile found its way to his lips as Thornton took off his slippers and rubbed his feet to warm them. "I'm gonna go heat up some of the beef stew I made earlier. Does that sound good?"

Shocked when his stomach gave a growl in answer, he couldn't help but blush and then melt into a puddle of sappy goo when Thornton squatted and brushed the hair back off his forehead, a sweet smile on his face. "Sounds like your stomach is on board with that idea. Rest a bit while I'm gone, or..." he stood and looked around, reaching for Asher's phone and handing it over, "entertain yourself while I get it heated up for you. If you fall asleep, I'll wake you long enough to eat some and then let you get back to sleep, okay?"

That sounded very okay to Asher, and he nodded, murmuring, "Yeah."

When Thornton stood, Asher couldn't stop himself from reaching out and capturing the man's bigger hand in his, stopping him short. He squatted again and waited quietly while Asher came up with words to express how he felt. "Thank you for your help. I know you don't think it's a big deal, and you want to do it, but, Thornton, you've shown me more compassion in the last seventy-two hours than I think I've ever had in my whole life."

His face grew warm at that admission, and warmer still when sadness slid over Thornton's features. But it was gone a second later when the man leaned forward, brushed his hair back again, and kissed his forehead. "You're welcome. I hope we can get to a point where you come to expect that compassion from me. Settle back and rest. I'll be back soon."

Thornton stood and made a couple of kissy noises, prompting Beauty and Beast to trot into the room as if they'd just been chomping at the bit to come in and visit. "They really want to say hello. Are you afraid of dogs?"

Eyes big and excitement thrumming through him at the thought, he couldn't keep a grin off his face. "No, I don't think so. I've never been around dogs before. I always wanted pets, but my parents never allowed it."

Surprise flitted across Thornton's face, but he recovered quickly and smiled wide. "Well, what they really want to do is jump up on the bed and fawn all over you, but I don't want them to bother you or hurt you. I'm going to order them to sit beside you, and they'll probably plonk their heads on the bed and stare at you sadly so you'll pet them. But don't feel you have to."

Oh, how he wanted them on the bed with him. "Can you... If you order them to settle, will they be calm on the bed?"

A soft smile slipped over Thornton's lips as he nodded. "They're good pups. They won't bother you. I just didn't want you to be overwhelmed."

Asher nodded and patted the bed beside himself. "I want them by me."

Thornton rolled his eyes and groaned. "God, they're going to have you wrapped around their big, clumsy paws in about five seconds flat. You've been warned."

Asher grinned. "You sound like you're speaking from experience."

"Pfft. I don't know what you're talking about."

Seeing that for the lie it was, he couldn't keep a giggle from escaping and then a sigh to follow when Thornton's dazzling smile brought the man's face alive with happiness. "Okay, so, I can order them to settle near you once they're up there, but there's no way they'd be gentle clambering up beside you."

Thornton picked each of the puppies up—which was no small feat—and placed them on the bed next to him as gently as possible. "Beauty, Beast, this is Asher. Be gentle."

He watched in awe as the huge pups slowly inched their way across the bed like soldiers on a training course, staying low and not shaking him at all. Curiosity won out and he had to ask, "What happened...?"

The sadness on Thornton's face made his heart wrench. "That's Beauty. She and her brother, Beast, were rescued from a puppy mill. She was born with some congenital defects which included glaucoma, so they surgically removed her eyes. One of my business partners, Dax, wouldn't separate them because Beast acts as her—well, I guess her seeing-eye dog, for lack of a better name.

"They go everywhere together, and he takes care of her. So, it was hard to find anyone to adopt them both, especially considering her health issues. I got to know them when I went into business with Dax and fell in love. Haven't regretted adopting them for a second. They're a handful, but so worth it."

Asher gazed down at both puppies, newfound admiration and love for them. He smiled as they rested their heads on his upper thigh, right beside his stuffy—which he'd have to panic about later—and he giggled again when they both sighed contented puppy sighs as they turned towards him. They turned their heads towards Thornton when he asked, "Does that hurt?"

Asher shook his head and reached out to pet them. "Not at all."

"Good pups." Both Beauty and Beast gently lifted their heads to wait for their next command. "Settle."

They did as their master ordered and lowered their big ol' adorable heads to his lap again, settling right down to keep him company while the three of them waited for Thornton to return. As soon as Thornton was out of sight, Asher picked up his phone and took a couple of photos of the puppies, texting them to Madi.

Asher: Show Gigi when she wakes up in the morning.

Madi: OMFG. Those are puppies?

Asher: LOL Right? They're enormous!

He grinned as the bubbles appeared and then chuckled when the emoji of the frustrated woman with a hand over her face popped up.

Madi: You know she's going to hound me until I drive her over there to the swanky neighborhood he's taken you to.

Asher: *snort* You said hound…

Madi: Asher… OMG you're ridiculous… Go to sleep.

Asher: I can't. He's making me dinner.

His phone rang, and he had to pull the phone from his ear when her excited voice got a bit too loud. "Dammit, Asher! How is it that you've never put any effort into finding yourself a man, and then one runs over you with his car and instantly becomes everything you've never been looking for and yet have always needed?"

Shocked, he shook his head. "That's not… that isn't—"

"Asher, he's gorgeous, he's sweet, and he was an absolute *wreck* when he called me. So worried about you and ready to do anything to get to you in case you were hurt. He doesn't want you out of his sight in case you get hurt again, and he's hell-bent on taking care of you. Oh. My. Fucking. God!"

Jesus. "What?!"

"Asher! You landed yourself a Daddy."

That threw him off. "What? I'm pretty sure he doesn't have any kids. I mean… We talked a lot, and he didn't mention—"

She sighed. "My sweet summer child. I love you."

Even more confused, he answered, "I love you, too."

"Go eat your dinner and then get some sleep. I'll talk to you tomorrow."

"Okay, night, Madi."

"Night, boo."

He hung up. The bewilderment he was feeling must have been showing on his face because once Thornton returned, concern colored his voice when he asked, "Everything okay?"

He shrugged and figured he'd better ask, in case he missed something huge and was the last to know. "Do you have kids?"

Thornton nearly bobbled the tray of food he held but got it settled on the table beside the bed. Confusion marred Thornton's brows. Good. That made both of them. "No. No kids. What made you ask?"

He scratched his head and gazed up at Thornton "Nothing, I... It's silly."

But Thornton just waited patiently, a gentle smile on his face, obviously encouraging him to continue. "It's just—Madi just said I found a Daddy, and I didn't remember you ever saying you had kids, so—"

Thornton's choked cough stopped him mid-sentence. "Are you okay?"

The man's eyes were watering, and he continued to cough into his fist, but he nodded. "Yeah." He cleared his throat. "I'm just fine, Asher. And no, I don't have children."

Asher smiled, glad he hadn't completely missed something so important. "Okay good. I would have felt bad if you'd said something and I'd completely missed it."

"Nah, you're good." The smile Thornton gave him made him blush. "You hungry?"

He breathed in, and the smell of the stew had him sighing. "Mmm, that smells so good."

Thornton glanced at the pups and spoke to them with that sexy voice again. "Away, you two. Gentle."

Both dogs moved gently away to the opposite side of the bed and settled as Thornton placed the lap tray over his legs, making it easy for him to feed himself. "How have you trained them so well already? And how can they move so gently? What are they, a hundred pounds?"

Thornton chuckled. "110. And I didn't train them—Dax did. We own a large dog rescue and training facility together. They stayed with him until they were fully trained, and I just had to learn the commands."

"Wow. That's awesome. Was Beauty able to be trained just like Beast?"

"Dax made some adjustments for her, but for the most part, yeah. Whatever she's unable to do, Beast leads her through so she can follow well enough."

Asher took a bite of stew and hummed around the spoon as he pulled it from his lips. "Mmm. Oh my god. That's so good."

Thornton pulled an upholstered, armless chair next to the bed and sat as he grabbed the bowl he'd set on the side table for himself and settled down, crossing an ankle over his knee. "Glad you like it. It's my mom's recipe."

"It's yummy. Thank you." He put the spoon down in the bowl and met Thornton's eyes. "You're doing so much for me. I don't really understand why, but, I'm grateful."

"Because I want to. Because you deserve it. And because I care about you." Thornton uncrossed his legs and leaned forward, placed the bowl on the table, and reached to take his hand. "I know it's early, and I have no idea what, if anything, will happen between us. But I'm drawn to you, Asher, and I'm not going to hide that or play games."

He took another bite of stew with his other hand and sat for a moment, chewing while he tried to figure out how in the hell to respond to a man who wore sex appeal and confidence like a second skin. "I wouldn't know how to play those games anyway, so I guess that's good." He cleared his throat and decided he had to be honest. "I'm drawn to you, too. But you don't know me. You know only bits and pieces. I'm messed up in a lot of ways, Thornton, and the me you've seen over the last several days is different from the me of reality. I'm afraid you'll be disappointed."

"I promise you, I won't be disappointed, but you won't believe that until you see it in my actions, not just my words. I'm never going to pressure you to do anything you don't want to do or to be anything you're not. I didn't bring you to my house to seduce you and manipulate you. I want to take care of you while you get better and get to know who you *really* are."

Asher drew in as deep a breath as he dared and nodded. "Okay. Just, please, if you decide you don't like the real me or that I'm not worth the effort, don't pretend you do because you feel sorry for me. I couldn't take that."

Thornton squeezed his hand again, concern and, if Asher wasn't mistaken, sorrow furrowing his brows. "Who have you had in your life that made you feel less than?"

He pulled his hand away from Thornton and felt the loss immediately, but the vulnerability coursing through him demanded a bit of distance. "Most everyone that really mattered."

CHAPTER EIGHT

Thornton

*M*ost everyone that really mattered...

The words hit Thornton like a sledgehammer to the gut, and he sat back hard into his chair, staring at the beautiful man before him. God. How could *anyone* treat Asher in such a way? It broke his heart. He must have been taking too long to respond because the boy's shoulders fell, and he whispered, "Don't feel sorry for me."

Fuck.

"Asher, the last thing I'm feeling right now is sorry for you. I'm feeling a lot of things, but not that." Thornton leaned forward to clasp his hand again. "I'm having a hard time wrapping my mind around the fact that you've been made to feel like you're not worth someone's time. If you were mine, you'd never question how much you meant to me. You'd have no doubt that you were the most important person in my life."

He watched as Asher blushed and played with the napkin on his tray. And when he finally whispered, "That would be really nice," it was almost too quiet for Thornton to hear.

But he wasn't going to pretend like he didn't. "I think so, too."

After a few long moments of charged silence, they both tucked back into their meals. When they were finished, he asked if Asher wanted to get some sleep. "Can we watch something on TV? I sleep better if it's on. It makes me feel..."

For some reason, Thornton had a feeling what Asher had been about to say was important, so he pressed. "Makes you feel what?"

Asher shook his head, but when Thornton just waited him out, he shrugged. "I guess like I'm less alone."

God, this precious boy was going to shatter his heart into thousands of pieces. "I'm happy to turn it on if you truly want to watch something. But if you just don't want to be alone, I'm happy to stay here with you until you fall asleep."

The shy gaze he got in return melted him. "You don't mind?"

"I don't mind at all, Asher. I'd prefer it, actually. I don't like the idea of leaving you alone when you're feeling vulnerable."

Thornton stood and gathered their dishes, taking them out of the room and placing them on the hall table to deal with later. When he went back into the room, Asher was struggling to get off the bed. "I need to use the bathroom and brush my teeth."

He approached and helped Asher from the bed. "Here, let me help."

Thornton helped him up and led him to the en suite. "Your toiletries are there on the counter. I'll be just outside if you need anything."

Asher blushed but nodded. "Thanks."

When Asher came back out of the bathroom, he was moving more slowly, and Thornton could see the pain in his eyes. Helping him into the bed, he turned out the lights. They chatted for a few minutes until Asher's eyelids drooped. "Close your eyes. I'll stay until you're asleep, and I'll leave both bedroom doors open so if you need me in the night, you can call me, okay?"

Asher hummed his assent and snuggled down into the pillows at his back. Thornton stayed long after Asher had fallen asleep, thinking he might just start to believe a bit more in fate than he had in the past. He couldn't attribute the way they met to anything else. Obviously, he hated that he was responsible for hurting Asher in the first place, and if he could go back in time and do something different, he would, without a doubt. But he couldn't, and all he could feel was grateful Asher was here with him in his home, trusting Thornton to take care of him.

***

He'd checked on Asher several times during the night, going so far as waking him up when he'd been moaning a bit in his sleep. He'd settled right back down after taking some more pain meds, and the grateful look in the boy's eyes had him leaning down, brushing Asher's hair from his brow, and kissing his forehead. He sat in the chair beside Asher's bed again until he was sure he'd gone back to sleep.

The dogs wouldn't leave the boy's side, and if he and Asher did end up getting involved, he knew Beauty and Beast would treat him like a member of their pack, one they'd protect and be careful of. He couldn't blame them. Thornton was already in protective mode, and they weren't even in a relationship. He'd left Asher to sleep in as he'd prepared them breakfast. He couldn't help but want to see the boy well fed, so he'd pulled out all the stops and made his mom's stuffed French toast.

He was just about to load breakfast on the tray to take it upstairs when he heard the dogs whining from upstairs. He left the food where it was and walked quickly to the stairs, knowing Beauty and Beast would be doing more than whining if Asher was in any real trouble. What he saw when he got to the bottom of the stairs had him smiling.

Asher was leaning against the wall at the top of the stairs, an exasperated look on his face. "They won't let me go downstairs."

Thornton chuckled and headed up the stairs. "They're feeling protective of you. And I'm glad. I don't want you to hurt yourself getting up and down the stairs."

When he reached Asher, he couldn't help but grin when the boy scowled at him and then the dogs and then back up at him again. "I can't just be a lazy bed blob for days on end."

"Oh, I don't know. I kind of think you're an adorable bed blob. But I have breakfast for you, if you want to come downstairs to eat. Did you take some meds for your pain?"

"Yeah."

"Good. How about I help you downstairs?"

He shooed the dogs down the stairs and held out his arm, which Asher took. They started down, their pace slow. "What are we having for breakfast?"

"My mom's stuffed French toast."

Asher's eyes went wide as saucers, and that grin Thornton was getting used to seeing slid over his features. "That sounds yum."

Thornton chuckled. "It *is* yum."

When he had them both settled with their meals and fresh coffee, he watched as Asher took the first bite. The blissful sigh and little moan Asher let slip as he closed his eyes and chewed had Thornton's pants tightening as his dick plumped up. God, if he had anything to say about it, he'd make it his life's mission to get that reaction from Asher as often as possible. And not just with food.

"God, Thornton, that might be the best thing I've ever had in my mouth."

Thornton couldn't have stopped the chuckle that comment elicited, but the embarrassed blush his laughter brought on had him leaning forward and trailing a finger down the boy's cheek. "So sweet, that blush. I'm glad you like the food. I like feeding you."

"You're quite the chef."

"Nah. My mom's the chef. I learned from the best. My whole cooking repertoire is just a result of watching her in the kitchen. If you ever meet her, she'll most likely end up cooking for you, and *then* you'll know my skills are sorely lacking by comparison."

"What's your favorite meal of hers?"

"Oh man, that's a hard one. But her crab-stuffed filet mignon is pretty phenomenal."

"Mmm, that does sound good."

"I'll have her cook it for you someday."

Asher looked down at his lap and when he looked back up, his eyes were sad, making Thornton's heart twist. "I don't think we should talk about a future that might never happen."

Everything in him wanted to push back against that statement, but he couldn't blame Asher for wanting to protect himself, especially if he had no confidence in them even remaining friends after he'd recuperated.

Thornton would just have to prove to him that there could be a future between them. "I'll try to keep your wishes in mind, but I think no matter what, we'll be friends, so the possibility of you meeting my mom in the future is pretty realistic. All right?"

Asher shrugged as if he wasn't convinced, moving the food around on his plate.

"Asher?"

The boy's gaze flicked to his and held. "Yeah?"

"I want you in my life. Whether we can make a relationship between us work remains to be seen, but I know enough about you to know, no matter what, I want you in my life as a friend. Can you trust that much at least?"

When Asher didn't answer, merely sat in his seat gazing at his food as if it held the answers, Thornton thought he wasn't going to answer him at all. But when he finally nodded and lifted his gaze, decision made, his small smile went a long way towards easing Thornton's mind. "Yeah, I can trust that much, at least."

He hadn't realized he'd been holding his breath, until he finally released it. Thornton watched as Asher finally continued to eat his meal and he did the same. They sat in comfortable silence for a few minutes as they finished eating. He sat back and watched in amusement as Asher surreptitiously took the last two forkfuls of his food and gave one to each of the puppies. And then busied himself with wiping his hands and drinking the last of his coffee, as if nothing was amiss.

And as his heart did a little flip in his chest, cementing his decision to pursue this boy with single-minded determination, he tried to figure out what obstacles he had to remove in order to be able to do that. Because suddenly, it wasn't something he wanted to think about working towards in the future. It was something he wanted to work towards immediately. And he knew he had to address a situation he hadn't even had time to deal with yet. "There is something that I need to be honest with you about, but I don't want you to take it the wrong way and think it's more important than it is."

He saw the deep breath Asher tried to draw in, the pained look in his eyes as a result, and the straightening of his spine as he geared himself up for what was to come. "Okay."

He leaned forward, elbows on his knees, and reached for Asher's hand. "I've been dating a man off and on for several weeks. We've both agreed it's run its course. I just don't want you thinking I'm trying to hide anything from you. We had plans to get together one last time…"

His voice drifted off when he saw Asher's shoulders sag, but before he could reassure him, Asher asked, "When?"

He was happy Asher wanted to know when it would officially be over. He hoped that meant he was interested in Thornton enough he didn't want him seeing anyone else. "Tomorrow. I'm going to call and cancel today. I just wanted to be honest wi—"

The doorbell rang unexpectedly, prompting him to get up. "Let me get that, and we can finish talking, all right?"

He squeezed Asher's shoulder as he passed by to answer the door. When he pulled it open, expecting to have to sign for a delivery of some sort, he found his arms full of an exuberant Jimmy.

"Hi, Daddy! I know we don't have play time until tomorrow, and it's kind of our last playdate really, but I got out of class early, and you're so close to campus. I thought I'd stop by because I know you work from home on Fridays so I thought maybe today would be better for you, or we could have two or something. I don't know. Look, I brought treats!"

Jimmy held a white paper bag aloft and shook it a little. He couldn't help but smile at the boy's enthusiasm, regardless of the fact this was going to be quite the conversation later with Asher. He wasn't upset Jimmy had stopped by and would treat him as he normally would because the boy was already in little mode, and taking him out of that headspace too quickly wasn't something he'd ever do. He didn't want to make him feel vulnerable and like he'd done something wrong. He ushered Jimmy inside and closed the door as he continued to talk a mile a minute.

"I got a good grade on the paper you helped me with, and I just got so excited. I know I'm not supposed to have a lot of treats, but when I walked by the candy shop I could smell the fresh fudge, and I just couldn't help myself. Can you take a chocolate break? Everyone should take a chocolate break once in a while, right? I mean, it's chocolate. I… Oh…"

Thornton sighed, bracing himself for the inevitable, and turned towards the hallway that led to the kitchen, a sheepish smile on his face. The shock in Asher's eyes reminded Thornton just how sheltered the boy really was. Thornton had known that when Asher had asked if Thornton had kids the night before. He knew his particular kink wasn't exactly mainstream, so he was doubly sure Asher's mind was reeling.

"I was going to call you this afternoon to cancel our playdate tomorrow. I have a—"

"—new boy?" Jimmy's eyes were alight, and he smiled at Thornton, making his heart twist that the lovely, sweet boy before him hadn't been the one. Jimmy fairly skipped across the room and held his hand out to Asher, who did the same more out of reflex than anything. "Hi! You must be Daddy's—oops, sorry. You must be Thornton's new boy. I'm Jimmy. Oh, ouch! Your head looks like it hurts. Are you okay? I bet Daddy's taking good care of you. He's the best, isn't he?"

"Jimmy, this is my *houseguest* Asher."

Jimmy's eyes popped comically wide, and Thornton could see him slipping out of little space into his adult headspace as he tried to backpedal. "Oh, um." He turned his body fully towards Thornton, a horrified expression on his face, and mouthed, *I'm so sorry!*

Thornton chuckled and ran a hand up and down Jimmy's arm to reassure him. "It's all right. We were just talking about you. I mentioned tomorrow was our last date and that I was going to call today and cancel. Asher and I are getting to know each other, and I wanted to be sure—"

"—nothing stood in your way." Jimmy smiled in understanding and nodded, turning back towards Asher. "I'm sorry to burst in on you like this. It was spur of the moment. I'll get out of your hair. It was nice to meet you, Asher. Thornton's a great guy. He'll be really good to you."

Thornton smiled and wrapped his hand around the back of Jimmy's head, pulling him into his chest. He kissed Jimmy on the head and hugged him tight, hoping his actions were enough to relieve the boy of any guilt for coming over unannounced. "I'm sorry to cancel."

Jimmy reached up and touched his face, just a gentle caress. "Don't be sorry. I hope things work out. Be happy, Thorn."

Charmed by the sweetness of him, he rubbed Jimmy's shoulders. "You too, Jimmy."

He wrapped an arm around the boy and led him to the front door. Jimmy pulled away for a second and rushed towards Asher, who jumped at Jimmy's quick movement. "Here." He handed over his bag of fudge, and Thornton was about to protest, but Jimmy continued, "I always want sweets when I'm in pain. I hope they help."

He turned and patted Thornton on the chest, reaching up on his tippy-toes to kiss his cheek and whisper, "Good luck. You got this, Daddy Thorn."

And then the boy was flitting across the room and out the front door before Thornton could say or do anything further, the door closing behind Jimmy with a soft click of finality. He turned his gaze back to Asher and grew concerned when Asher cast his gaze about as if looking for something. When his gaze latched onto the seating area in the living room, Thornton wanted to steer him towards the family room where the couch was much more comfortable.

Thornton held his hand out, and Asher took it, leading them to the family room. When he settled Asher on the sofa and flicked on the fire, Asher gazed down at the bag of fudge in his lap, the paper crinkling in his hand. He opened his mouth as if he was about to speak but shut it quickly, obviously unsure of himself.

Thornton was about to say something, but Asher finally found his voice, flushing with embarrassment "Jesus. That's... that's what Madi meant?" Asher's face turned an even brighter red. "Oh my god, and I asked you if you had kids. Oh, for Pete's sake."

He couldn't help but chuckle at that. "You didn't know. You couldn't have known. That's not something most people would assume, Asher."

Asher covered his face with his hands and shook his head at himself but finally met his gaze, confusion etching lines between his brows. "I don't know what that... Is that what...? I don't understand, Thornton."

Thornton approached the skittish boy, pulled the large coffee table away from the sofa a bit, and then sat on it in front of him, but not so close he'd crowd him. "It's a lot to take in. I know that. I wanted to talk with you about it after we'd gotten to know each other a bit better."

"But... Was he, I don't even know, he seemed... Was he playacting? Is it some kind of game, or...?"

"No. It's not a game, and it's not acting. Not... well, not like you think. It's age regression, what some call age play, but sometimes the word play makes it sound trivial when it's not. Not for people in the lifestyle, anyway."

"The lifestyle." Those words, whispered, didn't sound disgusted, so Thornton had to take heart in that. But Asher's grip tightened on the bag, and it crinkled even more.

Thornton winced at the state of the fudge and gently pulled it from the boy's hands, setting it on the table beside him. "It's… wow, this is hard to explain when you've been blindsided like you just were. Your friend Madi was right when she called me a Daddy. Although I have a feeling she didn't mean it quite that literally."

Asher's snort had Thornton smiling. "I'm part of the BDSM and kink lifestyle, Asher. So are Syed and Damon."

A lightbulb went on for Asher at that. "Sir."

Thornton nodded. "Yes. Syed is Damon's Dom, and Damon is Syed's sub. It's not the same as being a Daddy, but the power exchange is similar in a lot of ways. Damon cedes control to Syed, and Syed ensures Damon's needs are met. In that way, it's similar."

"So, you control Jimmy?"

"No. I'm not technically a Dom, not in the strictest sense of the word anyway, but I am dominant. I didn't control Jimmy, I cared for him. When we spent time together, Jimmy gave me the gift of his submission more in the form of being a caretaker or Daddy to his little self. Does that make sense?"

Asher's bewildered gaze let him see he wasn't quite there yet. "I don't know. Why would he want to do that?"

"There are many reasons people like to regress. Jimmy is a pretty carefree guy, and he doesn't stress over much, but he has the need to let go occasionally. To sink into the role of a much younger boy. He liked to forget about what he calls 'adulting' for a while and play in his little headspace. To let the mantle of his adult self fall away."

"It just seems strange, I guess. Why do it?"

"For Jimmy, it allowed him to step out of his world and let anything that had bothered him since we last played float away so I could take care of him and his needs without the burdens of having to make decisions or be in charge of anything."

"But if he's carefree, why would he need that?"

"Jimmy is a happy boy. His life is good, and he loves it. He's a pre-med student, and he's brilliant. He spends his life learning, head in a book or taking classes to prepare him to become a trauma surgeon. As you can imagine, that's a lot of responsibility. When he was with me, he was safe to let all of that go and fall back into the child he used to be."

"And that helped?"

"It did. He would always leave here refreshed and ready to dive back into his everyday life. For some people, age regression takes them out of the 'real' world and allows them to be free in a way they don't feel they can be in their own lives."

"So why did you end it with him if he likes what you do for him?"

Thornton shrugged. "He didn't need me for more than an occasional session a couple of times a week or so. I'm the type of Daddy who needs to take care of someone who needs more from me. I want to be someone's safe space at the end of every day. The one they rush home to because they know as soon as they walk in that door," he pointed behind him to the foyer and the front door beyond that, "I've got them. I'll keep them safe, happy, and whole."

Asher's shoulder slumped. "That sounds... nice, I guess. But I don't think... I mean, I don't know if I can..." The boy sighed, obviously unable to voice what he was feeling or too confused to do so.

He clasped one of Asher's hands in one of his own, scooting forward. "Asher, last night when I found the coloring books at your place..."

"That's not—" Asher shook his head, his embarrassment showing in the pinking of his ears.

He held his hand up. "Let me just try to explain this in a way that might make the most sense to you, all right?"

Asher's nod was jerky, but he sat and waited patiently for Thornton to continue.

"When you color in those coloring books, does it give you a sense of peace?" He watched Asher closely for a reaction, but the boy's face still only showed confusion as he nodded.

"But I'm not a little boy when I do it."

"I know you're not. You don't know anything about the lifestyle, so that wouldn't be where your mind would automatically go."

When Asher only shrugged, Thornton continued, "Okay, so maybe you had a stressful day at work, or something was making you feel really worried and unfocused. If you were to sit down when you were feeling that way and color in your coloring books, would all of that tension sort of slip away?"

Asher's nod that time was more emphatic. "Yeah. That's why I do it. I was over at Madi's place playing with Gigi one time. I'd had a bad day, and I sat down, and Gigi asked me to color with her, so I did. And it made me happy, playing with her, but it was the coloring that made me feel better."

Thornton squeezed Asher's hand, nodding. "It kind of lets you stop worrying so much about whatever is stressing you out, I bet. Did you go find some for yourself after that?"

"No. Madi ordered a couple of adult ones for me online and a set of colored pencils. It felt silly, but I tried it when I got home one night, and now I do it a lot. I have stacks of finished ones at home. It's silly, really, but I have a lot of anxiety, and sometimes it fills my head and makes it feel fuzzy, gives me migraines and stuff. So that's one of the ways I can calm myself down."

"What's another way you calm yourself down?"

Asher shrugged. The hand Thornton held in his nearly pulled out of Thornton's grip as a result, but a warmth filled his chest when Asher ensured it didn't. "I do, like, meditation and I have a mantra. It's stupid and doesn't really work at all, but it lets me function enough…"

He clammed up at that, probably feeling as if he'd shared too much, but Thornton couldn't let it go. "Function enough to what?"

Asher did pull his hand away that time and folded them in his lap where his gaze went. "Just function enough to get through things that are hard."

He reached forward and placed his hand on Asher's thigh, drawing the boy's gaze to his. "What's the hardest thing you go through on a daily basis?"

"Driving. Or even being driven places." Asher couldn't help but sigh, admitting, "But that's only because I've found workarounds for most everything else."

"Can you tell me about that?"

CHAPTER NINE

Asher

That was a good question. *Could* he tell Thornton about his fears? He hoped he could. He thought he could. But that didn't make it easy. It didn't make him want to flay himself open and spill his guts, but it did scare him just thinking about it, and wasn't that just pathetic? He had fears about his fears.

Jesus, he was a basket case.

But was he a basket case in need of a Daddy? Now *that* he was having a hard time wrapping his mind around, because… What?! It all seemed very strange to him. A foreign concept he'd never thought of or even known existed. Sure, he'd heard things about BDSM and kinky stuff, but watching a few porn vids with a little slap and tickle was one thing. Talking to someone about it in real life was a whole 'nother ball game.

Seeing it face to face in the form of a gorgeous, apparently brilliant, and ridiculously sweet pre-med student calling the man Asher had just had breakfast with Daddy was a punch to the solar plexus he didn't think his ribs could handle. When Jimmy had been faced with Thornton possibly having a new boy, he'd smiled an utterly charming and absolutely genuine smile and wished them luck. Who did that?

Confident, brilliant pre-med students did apparently. And he was none of that.

So it begged the question, if Jimmy wasn't good enough for Thornton, how in the hell would Asher ever stand a chance? What on earth could a man as sophisticated, driven, mature, and so mouthwateringly sexy want with a twenty-four-year-old uneducated college dropout who could barely force himself to leave his apartment and go to work every day?

So many fucking questions he didn't have the answers to, and he just didn't have the energy for—

"Asher?"

Shit.

"Sorry, I... What?"

The patient smile he got from Thornton told him he'd missed the man's question several times. "I asked if it would be all right if I sat on the sofa next to you while we talked."

"Oh, yeah, sure." He glanced to one side and was met with Beauty and Beast's upturned faces. Beauty on the sofa beside him, her pretty face lifted for what he got the feeling was approval, so he couldn't make her wait for it and reached out to pet her and scratch behind her ears. Beast was on the floor, standing sentry. Asher wasn't sure if he was doing so for Beauty's benefit or his own. If he had to guess he'd probably say both.

Petting them, he'd forgotten Thornton was going to move beside him until the sofa dipped on his other side. The man was more imposing than he'd thought. They hadn't really sat so closely before, and everything about him was bigger. His legs were longer, his thighs thicker, his torso larger. It was overwhelming in a way, but in another, not so much.

Asher thought he might feel eclipsed by him. Hell, he was tiny compared to Thornton, but when the man lifted his arm and laid it on the back of the sofa behind him, surrounding him without even touching him at all, he felt a sense of calm settle over him he'd only ever felt in Thornton's presence.

He didn't know what that meant. Hell, he was afraid he was imagining it or wishing that feeling into being. He couldn't say which was true or if they were both false. Doubts plagued him, which was par for the course. When weren't doubts plaguing him? It was a wonder he got any sleep at night, but he supposed the drugs he took every night helped him with that.

He felt the sofa dip again and turned to see Thornton bring his knee up onto the cushion to face him, his arm still behind Asher along the back. Thornton's other hand reached to clasp his, a gentle squeeze reminding him they were supposed to be talking.

"Asher, I'm not going to force anything out of you. If you don't want to talk about it, we don't have to."

"It's just... There isn't much I don't struggle with or fear. I've been known to jump at my own shadow."

He was trying to make light of what was essentially his reality, but it fell flat, as jokes often did when they're based on sad truths. He turned a little towards Thornton. The man's earnest expression drew him in and somehow, against all odds, made him want to share his secrets. The ones that no one else knew. The ones he was often afraid to admit to himself.

"Start with something small. Something you struggle with that you've overcome."

He scrunched his face up in frustration. "I don't think I've overcome much of anything."

"I doubt that's true."

Thornton couldn't know because it was true. But all he did was shrug. "I fear crowds. I struggle being around a lot of strangers. It's too much for me. I start to panic and shut down."

"Where do you think that comes from?"

He pulled his hand from Thornton's and rubbed both of his suddenly sweating palms along his pant legs. "My parents were..." He gazed across the room, then closed his eyes, trying to come up with the right word for them. One that wouldn't give too much away. "Negligent. They were forgetful, easily distractible. They would take me places and forget I was there with them and leave me."

He felt Thornton tense beside him and couldn't stand the thought of his horror-stricken face, so he plowed on, wanting to get some of it out so Thornton would understand just how fucked up Asher was and they could stop talking about it. "So, once, when I was about four, maybe five, they took me to the mall around Christmastime—"

"Jesus, Asher—"

Just get it out. Get it out and get it over with. "So... Um, it was pretty busy on a Saturday afternoon, and I remember seeing Santa at the center of the mall and asking if I could meet him. I should have known better—"

"You were a child."

Asher shook his head. "It wasn't the first time, just one of the really bad ones."

"Fuck." Thornton brought the hand that was behind him on the couch to the back of his neck and squeezed, gently, just letting him know he was there. It was nice. It grounded him.

"They ignored me, so I turned to take another look, and when I turned back, they were gone. Maybe I thought Santa could help because I walked closer and got swallowed up by the crowd, I think. I don't know. Some bits are fuzzy. Some are crystal clear. I'm pretty sure I drifted around for hours trying to find them. But I was short, and everyone else seemed so tall, and everything was moving really fast. I remember getting knocked into by shopping bags, women's purses, other kids. It was pretty scary."

"Sweetheart."

He shook his head, not even sure why, and continued, "The mall was so big. It was two floors. I tried to remember where they said they were going to go, but I couldn't. I knew my mom liked those warm, freshly baked cookies they had in the food court because I loved them too, and sometimes she'd get us each one." He laughed a nervous, self-deprecating laugh. "I hate them, now."

Thornton's fingers carded through the hair at the nape of his neck. "So when I saw the cookie place, I thought for sure I'd find them. But I didn't. I sat down close to it, though, and waited, almost positive they'd eventually come because they'd know I'd go there. They didn't. People kept approaching me, asking if I was okay. I probably looked scared to death. But they were strangers, and I wasn't allowed to talk to them." Asher met Thornton's eyes, earnestly. "Kids aren't supposed to talk to strangers."

"Shh, Asher. Shh. You're shaking, sweetheart." He was? He felt strangely empty. "Come here."

He felt himself being lifted and ignored the little stab of pain in his ribs because then he felt protected, surrounded by warmth. Realizing he was on Thornton's lap made his body go lax, and he rested his head against Thornton's chest as he continued, unable to stop now he'd started. "Hours passed. I know because when we'd gotten there it was daylight, and when I passed by one of the exits, I could see out the windows that it was completely dark outside."

Thornton rubbed his hands up and down Asher's back. "I was hungry and scared, and I had to go to the bathroom. So I wandered down one of those long hallways that has the restroom signs outside of it. I used the bathroom, and then when I came out, I just remember being exhausted. So tired I didn't want to move. There was a little alcove just behind the bathrooms, and I huddled into it and sat down and eventually fell asleep."

"Goddammit, baby."

"A woman found me as she was coming out of the family restroom with her own kids. I think her little girl pointed me out. Anyway, she took me to mall security, who called the cops. I could remember my parents' names and my last name, but I guess I was too young to remember their phone numbers or our address."

He sighed, tired suddenly. "They took me to the police station. And when my parents finally remembered me and went to the mall looking for me, mall security must have sent them there because they came to pick me up with stories of me running off and them looking all over the mall for me."

"Jesus, and the cops believed them?"

He shrugged, his movement hindered by pain, and he felt Thornton's arms wrap around him. "They were charismatic, larger than life. They could spin a tale, and people would be hooked. By the time the cops released me into their care, they were laughing and joking with my mom and dad."

"That's fucking awful, Asher. I hate that you had to go through that. You should be able to trust your parents."

He shrugged again because really, what else could he do? "So, all that's to say I hate crowds and don't like being around strangers."

"That's understandable. And you've overcome—"

He gave a quick jerk of his head, denying that. "I haven't overcome anything, Thornton. Don't you see? I don't go to malls, or theme parks, or regular parks... You don't know how hard it was, being in that hospital."

Thornton made a dismayed sound in his throat. "Did they... Were there more...?"

"Times they left me? Sure. They left me at our local park several times. But I knew my way home from there, so I'd just walk home, and they'd show up eventually."

He felt a kiss on the top of his head. "I think the worst one was when my dad's job gave their workers free tickets to a water park."

"No. Oh, Asher."

"Somehow, we got separated on one of those kid water structures with all the different slides. Or maybe they just walked away thinking I'd be entertained. I dunno. When I realized they weren't there, I started looking around for them, but god, that place was huge. It was hours before I finally stopped a worker and told them what happened. They'd put my shoes and shirt in a locker, so by that time my feet were raw and bleeding, and I had the worst sunburn. They had to have the medics come take care of me because I was dehydrated, and then the cops came. I was six at the time, so I knew my address and phone number. But it was still hours before my parents finally picked me up."

"Jesus. I don't even know what to say, Asher. I can understand why you might not like being in huge crowds of people."

He pulled away and met Thornton's gaze, pleading with his eyes. He had to explain it wasn't that simple. "It's not just huge crowds. Look, you said you wanted to date me, but you don't know—you can't possibly understand who I really am."

"I *want* to know who you really are. Dating you will help us get to know each other, Asher."

Frustrated, he huffed out an incredulous laugh. "There is no *dating* me, Thornton. The real me avoids leaving his house unless it's to go to work. The real me can't go out on dates like a normal person. A crowded restaurant? A packed movie theater? Jesus, I can't go shopping in the supermarket or on a walk in the park. I had to close my eyes and turn the volume on your phone to blast while you steered me through the hospital to get to your car. And then the drive home —Jesus, I can't... I can't..."

"Shh, shh, baby. You're okay."

He hadn't realized he'd been crying until Thornton was brushing away his tears and leaning down ever so slowly to kiss them away. His breath caught in his chest. He wanted more of those lips, but he couldn't let Thornton misunderstand. Pushing Thornton back was both harder and easier than he'd thought it would be. Harder because he didn't want to do it in the first place. And easier because the slightest pressure on the man's chest, and he was releasing Asher completely and leaning far enough away to show Asher his hands, palm up, as if Asher was afraid Thornton would hurt him or force more contact.

His shoulders slumped at that. He didn't want to make Thornton wary to touch him; he just wanted him to understand what he'd come to realize over the last twenty-four hours. There was no way they'd be able to work out. He'd thought—hoped—maybe they'd find a way. He'd convinced himself he'd somehow make it work if he just wanted it enough, but after talking about his bullshit craziness, that hope went out the window.

He took a deep breath and shook his head. "But that's just it. I'm not okay, Thornton. Let's not pretend I am. This... This can't possibly work between us. You have a life, a busy, full life outside these walls, and I'm one marble shy of losing it completely and becoming a total recluse."

"That's not true. You're so strong, Asher. You have a career you love and friends—"

He snorted a laugh. "*A* friend. One."

"You have Madi and Gigi. Hell, from the way you were talking about your boss, it sounds like you can probably consider her a friend as well. And now you've got me, Syed, and Damon."

"I just met the three of you. That doesn't count."

"I count, Asher. I count as a friend to you. Hopefully, you'll eventually feel the same." The crease of Thornton's brow when he frowned made him feel guilty.

Fuck.

His shoulders slumped, sad that he'd hurt this beautiful man. "You do count. I didn't mean... I'm just... I'm not normal, Thornton."

A soft, sad smile appeared on the man's lips. "Fuck normal, Asher. Just give me a chance. Give *us* a chance. You've trusted me with so much today, and I'm still here wanting to get to know you, to help you, to see where this can go between us. Don't shut the door on what could be before you know for sure if it will or won't work."

Asher looked away, unable to hold Thornton's hopeful gaze. Could he do it? Could he give Thornton a chance? Could he risk putting his heart on the line and then having it destroyed when it didn't work? Because he was positive it wouldn't work. The man before him was larger than life, and he knew sitting around at home day in and day out wouldn't keep Thornton by his side.

But what if he gave himself this chance? He knew it wouldn't work, but he'd have so much to look back on. Surely, he'd have fond memories of his time with Thornton. He already did, and it had only been a handful of days. If he gave it a real chance, even if he didn't believe anything would come of it, maybe he'd be able to take another chance with someone else in the future. Maybe it would help him move past some of his fears.

There was only one way to find out. He'd open himself up to it, to giving whatever Thornton had in mind a try. He met Thornton's gaze and nodded. "Okay. I'll give everything a chance."

CHAPTER TEN

Thornton

E*verything?*

God, could the boy really mean that? He didn't think so, not with the shocked reaction from Asher when Jimmy had stopped by. But he didn't want speculation on either of their parts. "I'm so happy to hear that. But you said you'll give everything a chance. I'd like to understand what you mean by that so there are no misunderstandings between us."

He watched Asher's face turn a pretty shade of pink, and he couldn't help but think the boy's other cheeks would look beautiful in that color, warm and rosy from a spanking. God, did he want this boy over his lap. He couldn't ever remember wanting someone on such a visceral level that he could feel it under his skin, a bone-deep ache of longing for the sweet boy in front of him.

Jesus. Get your head in the game, Thorn!

"I mean, I don't know. Are you still interested in, well, um, other things besides friendship? Did I misunderstand?" Asher's hands were up, covering his face, cheeks not just pink but red in humiliation. "Oh my god, I'm so stupid. I thought—"

He pulled Asher's hands away from his face, captured those warm, red cheeks in his own palms, and drew the boy in for a kiss. And as first kisses went, he couldn't have asked for more. The boy went pliant against him, melting into him so much Thornton had to wrap his arms around him. He kept their kiss chaste. He didn't lick or delve into Asher's mouth like he wanted to. He didn't want the boy to feel overwhelmed. He knew actions spoke louder than words, so hopefully this kiss would make things clear. Clear that he *did* want more than friendship, so much more.

As his lips moved over Asher's, taking the boy's upper, then lower lips between his own in a gentle, teasing caress, he hoped he was letting the boy feel how much he was wanted, how much he was desired, without fear clouding his mind. The sweet whimpers coming from Asher reassured him and made his dick so hard he thought he might burst.

What was it about this boy? This boy that broke his heart and made him ache, made him feel so protective and made him yearn for so much more than even he could understand. He should have been scared. He wasn't in love with the boy. He didn't know if that was in the cards for them, but god, he could see it happening.

He could see Asher, all his sweetness, all his innocence, and all his fears laid out before him. He could see the boy was already becoming someone he wanted to praise, someone he longed to cherish, and someone he needed to spend time reassuring until he felt the same confidence in himself as Thornton did.

Thornton had a sinking feeling the things Asher had shared with him about his childhood were only the tip of the iceberg. He couldn't help but fear how much more Asher had to tell him, how much more the boy had had to endure. But a man with that much fear, that much anguish eating him up inside, needed someone strong and steady and sure in their life. Thornton wanted to see if he could be that person for Asher. Wanted it so desperately he wasn't sure how to deal with the feelings coursing through him.

When he finally pulled away and watched as Asher's eyes slowly opened, their fathomless beauty causing an ache in Thornton's heart, he couldn't have stopped himself from leaning in again for another gentle kiss—and again, and again. They were soft, barely there kisses that filled the empty places inside of him, and Thornton feared he'd never ever get enough. "Does that make things clear, sweetheart?"

When he only blinked up at Thornton, a dazed look in his eyes, he smiled and leaned in yet again, the boy's eyes fluttering closed. One kiss on each eyelid, one on the tip of that sweet, upturned nose, and one last kiss on those sweet cherry lips. "I don't want to hear you say you're stupid ever again. And if those kisses didn't clear everything up, let me tell you in words so you have no doubts. Yes, I absolutely want more than friendship with you."

Asher's small, shy smile melted him to his core. "Okay."

He let out a chuckle, feeling happiness in every cell of his body. "Okay. Are you feeling overwhelmed?"

The nod Thornton received didn't surprise him. "Yeah, a little. I just... I think you're going to have to be really patient with me. I don't have much to give. My life consists of nothing more than me being at home and being at work. It's not much to offer, really."

"I'm a very patient man, Asher. And I think your life consists of much more than that, even if those things are your reality when broken down to the basics. I'm going to make sure that you understand how very much you have to offer not just me, but yourself as well. Because I get the feeling you're hard on yourself, and I want you to understand how wonderful you are."

Asher shook his head, but before he could speak, Thornton covered Asher's lips with a finger. "Let me be the judge of how I feel about you and what I think of you. And maybe, just maybe, after you come to believe what I feel is true, you'll see some of those wonderful things for yourself."

Asher nodded and then looked away, shifting uncomfortably. "You're tired and in pain. What do you think about a bath and then a nap?"

The light was back in Asher's eyes, and he couldn't have been happier. "A bath sounds really good. My failed shower last night was disappointing to say the least."

Thornton chuckled. "I don't doubt it. I bet you're feeling like you just want to get clean."

"I really do. I feel so gross. I think I still have dried blood in my hair."

"Will you allow me to help you bathe?" He hurried on to make sure Asher knew he could say no. "If that makes you uncomfortable, I'll leave you alone once I've helped you into the tub. It's deep, and I don't want you to hurt yourself climbing in. But if you allow it, I'd like to help you."

When Asher bit his lip and nodded, Thornton's stomach did a flip. This boy was going to destroy his ability to keep any type of objectivity where he was concerned. "I'd like your help. I didn't want to admit how much I might need it yesterday when you dropped me off. I didn't want to be a burden."

"You could never be a burden. I think you're going to come to understand that I'm a caretaker at heart. I *want* to take care of the people in my life. Drives my friends and family crazy at times, but I can't help it. I'd love to be able to take care of you, Asher. It would be my pleasure."

"I think I'd like that."

"Good. But before we go upstairs for your bath, I want you to know you can always say no to me. If I'm overstepping, or you feel overwhelmed, if you need me to back off or just need time to think about things, I will always listen to you. Your feelings are valid, and I never want to diminish them."

"Even with that thing you mentioned before?"

"What thing was that?"

"The control thing? Power change?"

"Power exchange. Yes, even with that. *Especially* with that. In an exchange of power, the submissive partner offers up control to the dominant partner. The submissive makes the choice of what power to give to his dominant and how much he's willing to give."

"Okay."

"Asher, we aren't going to rush headlong into a Daddy/boy relationship. I don't expect that from you, and I won't push you for more than you're willing to give. We're going to get to know each other and maybe see how you feel about trying some things out. I think you're well-suited to the lifestyle, but in the end, it doesn't matter what I think. It matters what *you* feel."

"Okay."

Thornton smiled. "Okay?"

When Asher only nodded, Thornton had to ask, "Do you feel like you can tell me no? If I asked you to do something and you didn't want to, would you feel comfortable enough to say no to me? Without any equivocations, just straight up no?"

Asher rubbed his hands on his thighs. "I think so."

"Until you can say a definitive yes to that question, we won't be entering into any type of power exchange. You don't have to worry about any of that. We have to establish trust between us first. And while I feel like you do trust me in a lot of ways—you wouldn't be here with me otherwise—I think there's a long way for us to go."

"Yeah, I guess that's true."

"So, in that vein, would you be willing to stay here while you recuperate fully? That way we'll have more time with each other so we can figure out if this thing between us will work."

Asher took a deep breath and let it out, his gaze serious. "Yeah, okay."

Careful not to show too much of a reaction to that, he only smiled and said, "Good. That makes me happy. So, going forward, if you want something, I'm going to make sure I ask specific questions and that you give specific answers. Yes and no isn't enough right now. I'll need you to verbalize what you want. Do you think you'll feel comfortable enough to do that? That way, if you don't feel like you can say no, you're at least able to tell me what you *do* want. Do you think that will help?"

Asher nodded. "Yes. I can do that."

"Good." Thornton ran his fingers lightly over the boy's knee. "Today kind of went sideways on us, didn't it?"

Asher shrugged, and Thornton clasped one of the boy's hands in his, prompting Asher to meet his gaze. "All I was going to tell you today was that I was cancelling my final date with the man I was dating. And that I hoped you'd give me a chance to get to know you while you're here to recuperate. But Jimmy showed up and tossed my plans out the window."

"I'm sorry."

Oh, this sweet boy was going to kill him. "Asher, you have absolutely no reason to be sorry. Honestly, *I'm* not even sorry he came by. I wasn't going to bring up a discussion about being a Daddy yet. I thought it was too early, and I didn't want to scare you off. But now you know the type of relationship I'm looking for, and that's a good thing, I think. It gives us both time to learn each other and figure out if that's something we'd like to explore together."

"Yeah. I hadn't thought of it like that."

"I don't ever want you to be worried about trying to change who you are to try to be what I want you to be. I will only ever want you to be you. And I will only ever be me. And we'll just have to see—with you being you and me being me—if we can become an us. And if not, we've each made a new friend. How does that sound to you?"

He watched as the boy's whole body relaxed, and he let out what Thornton thought was probably a relieved breath. "That sounds good. But, will you help me understand what it means to be in that type of relationship? I've never even heard of it. It sounds strange to me, but that's probably only because it's new, and I don't know anything about it. Hell, I don't even know what normal relationships are like, so I'm starting from scratch either way. And I won't know if it's something I want unless I understand what it entails."

He thought he knew what Asher was getting at but wanted to be sure. "Asher, are you a virgin?"

The boy's blush was becoming something he didn't want to live without. "Yes. I don't know anything about anything, especially the Daddy stuff."

So sweet and innocent. Thorton loved that Asher had never belonged to anyone else. He was already feeling overly protective and wanted to make sure he took very good care of Asher.

"We'll only ever do what you're comfortable with. There's no rush. I'll tell you anything you want to know, and you can ask me as many questions as you want. I can even give you some blogs to read if you're curious to learn more on your own. You might find answers to questions there that you're uncomfortable asking me at first. And that's okay."

"Yeah. I think I'd like to read about it too. Thanks."

"We'll get you set up on my iPad later. Why don't we get you upstairs for a bath now, and then you can rest for a bit?"

Asher agreed, and they slowly made their way upstairs. He showed Asher into his bedroom and had him sit down on the chaise lounge he had in his little reading nook in one corner of his room. He went about running a hot bath for the boy with eucalyptus Epsom salts and some bubble bath. There was a mesh bath toy organizer suction cupped to the tiled wall beside the tub. He didn't think Asher would use them, but he also didn't want to hide them.

He was going to be as open and honest as he could be about his preferences so Asher could see he was comfortable with what he desired in a relationship and unashamed of it. If that led to Asher being comfortable and unashamed by it, all the better. But if it turned out the trappings of his lifestyle weren't for Asher, and if they were going to be friends, he'd need to understand it was a part of Thornton's life.

When the tub was ready, he went to get Asher and found him asleep on his chaise. He didn't want to wake the boy and would have let him sleep, but when he crouched down and lightly caressed a finger down the boy's cheek, he woke slowly, blinking up at him, vulnerability showing in his gaze. "Hey. Would you rather just sleep for a bit? This is a comfortable chair to rest on. I can put the blanket over you and let you sleep if that's what you need."

Asher hummed. "I do want a nap, but that bath sounded really good. I don't want to waste the hot water."

"There's plenty more where that came from. If you need a nap right now, you can still have a bath later."

Asher shook his head and tried to push himself up, wincing with the movement. Thornton helped him up and led him to the bathroom where the boy looked around in wonder. Thornton had to admit it was one of his favorite rooms. He'd spared no expense making it just right for himself, keeping the possibility of a future partner in his mind as well.

"This is beautiful."

"Thanks. I was happy with how it turned out. Are you comfortable with me helping you undress?"

Asher turned a sweet smile his way. "Well, considering you found me completely naked, in a heap on the floor of my shower, covered only in a plastic shower curtain, and then proceeded to help me out and get me dressed and just generally take care of me while I was basically at my worst, I think I'm good with it."

Thornton grinned, chuckling at Asher's slightly nervous rambling. "All right, but, Asher," his gaze turned serious, and Asher's did the same, "remember what I said about saying no. I *want* you to say no if you're feeling uncomfortable. I'd feel awful if you said yes but you really meant no."

Asher met his gaze head on. "I understand. But I really am comfortable with you helping me take a bath. I'm in a lot of pain, and I don't know how much I'll be able to manage on my own. And," the boy blushed and averted his gaze, "I like it when you take care of me. I haven't had a lot of that, so it's new and it feels... I don't know. Special?"

Thornton couldn't have stopped himself from stepping closer to Asher if he'd tried. That sweet admission had his heart racing and feeling like a million bucks. He cupped Asher's cheeks and tilted his head up so their gazes clashed again. If he wasn't mistaken, there was heat in the boy's eyes, though it was tempered by nerves and what he guessed was pain. He leaned down and kissed Asher's nose and grinned when that nose wrinkled as the boy's face scrunched up in confusion.

"Come on then. Let's get you undressed and washed, and then you can just lay in the bath and relax for a bit."

He slowly undressed the boy and realized that normally, just the act of doing so would have made him hard, but Asher's body was covered with bruises. Bruises *he'd* put there with his carelessness. There was nothing sexual in his touch, only care and gentleness. He couldn't help but hope for a day when he'd be able to undress Asher just like this when his skin was flawless and without the vestiges of pain.

Thornton wanted nothing more than to be able to show Asher pleasure in every way he could possibly imagine. He wanted to send the boy flying and ensure he was there to catch him when he landed. When it finally came to removing his own sweatshirt from the boy's body, he hated the pain it brought and the instant loss he felt when Asher no longer wore his clothing.

The scar in the middle of his chest caught his eye again. He traced it with his finger. "When did you get this scar?"

Asher's eyes got distant, and his voice was stilted when he said, "When I was a baby. I had to have open heart surgery."

Asher ran his finger down the scar, and Thornton couldn't help but ask, "And the arrhythmia is from the same issue?"

"Yeah. I'll always have it. I have to take blood thinners for the rest of my life. But other than that, it doesn't really affect my day-to-day life."

Thornton nodded. He wanted to ask more but dropped the subject, not wanting to bring the boy any more pain, physically *or* mentally.

There were a couple of steps up to the platform surrounding the tub and then a deep step down into the tub itself, all of which was relatively painless for Asher, thankfully. He slid his hand into his new soft cotton bath mitt and dunked his hand in the hot water, only realizing belatedly he should have asked about that. "I forgot to ask if it was too hot."

Asher, head leaning against the back edge of the tub, slowly shook his head. "Hmm mm. S'perfect."

He soaped up the mitt and was ready to start taking care of the boy's needs, but with the boy's eyes closed, he wanted to make sure he asked permission before touching him. "Is it all right if I wash you?"

Asher's eyes blinked open and met his. A blush bloomed on his face, but he nodded, his expression warm, his smile soft. "Yes, please."

"Good boy."

Oh, fuck.

He let out a deep sigh. That had just slipped out so easily he hadn't even thought of holding it back, even though he should have. "Damn. That was... inappropriate."

He met Asher's gaze, not wanting to try to avoid it when he knew he'd misstepped. Asher's blush deepened, and they stared at each other for several, drawn-out moments until at last, Asher's sweet voice interrupted the silence. "It didn't feel inappropriate. Is that wrong? Is it bad that hearing you say that felt good?"

Jesus, it was a good thing he had no intention of guarding his heart where Asher was concerned because there was absolutely no way that would be possible. He was so blessedly innocent; Thornton could hardly believe it. But he was so brave to be so clear with his thoughts and feelings. He knew a lot of men who wouldn't have been able to be so free with their truths. "No, sweetheart. It's not bad. Your feelings are always valid, and I always welcome hearing them. I'm happy those words felt good to you."

"That feels good, too."

Thornton gave the boy a questioning look, and he admitted, "When you call me sweetheart. It feels nice."

God, this boy was destroying him with his softly spoken words. "I'm glad."

He kept his eyes on the boy and saw indecision when he bit his lower lip and started nervously sifting his fingers in the water, avoiding his eyes. "What is it?"

"You said... You called me baby, before."

"I shouldn't have. It just came out. I don't want to make you uncomfortable."

"You didn't. I don't mind it. I—" Asher took a deep breath, as if gathering courage. "I've never had anyone call me by anything other than my name. It feels like it means something. Is that stupid? I mean, I know we just met, but... but when you say those things, I like the way it makes me feel inside."

"No, it's not stupid at all. I honestly don't know that I'll be able to keep myself from saying them. They fall from my lips so naturally with you. But I also don't want to blur the lines and make you feel pressure with the familiarity of them if you're not ready. Does that make sense?"

"Yeah, but if I want you to say them?"

The day he'd be able to deny Asher would be a cold day in hell. "If you want me to say them, if they make you feel good, then I would love to keep doing it."

Asher's tentative smile melted him. It was a habit Thornton was growing to like. "Thank you."

"You don't have to thank me. Saying those words to you makes me feel good, too. It's kind of like a happy warmth in my chest. Is that how it feels for you?"

The shyly whispered, "Yes," had him nodding in response. Not wanting to push too hard or take their conversation somewhere neither of them were ready for, he decided moving onto the job at hand was probably best for them both.

As he began to wash Asher, lifting one leg at a time out of the water to wash every last inch of skin, Asher giggled and wiggled his toes when Thornton's ministrations must have tickled him. He chuckled and admitted, "I'm going to have a hard time not filing that tidbit in the back of my mind for a later date."

Asher giggled again when he washed the arch of his foot, and he grinned. "Another secret tickle spot?"

"No." The boy's denial rang false, and he couldn't have kept the smile off his face if he'd tried, without further comment. He just continued washing the boy's foot and then his beautiful leg. When he moved onto the other foot, he got the same reaction but didn't draw too much attention to it. When he was done with both legs, he moved up to his stomach, torso, chest, shoulders, and arms. He sat the boy forward and washed his back and then took the spray attachment and washed the boy's hair, doing his best to keep his head injury dry while cleaning off the surrounding dried blood.

When he was finally done with almost everything, Thornton gazed up at the boy and found him watching everything he did with single-minded focus.

"Would you like to wash your own private parts?"

"I can try, if you'd rather not. I'm not sure if I can reach my… my bottom. But…"

"Asher, I am more than happy to wash every single square inch of your sweet body. And I know I asked if I could bathe you already, but I don't want to push you past your comfort zone."

"I'd like for you to do it, please."

Thornton nodded and gave the boy a smile of reassurance. He could tell Asher was nervous but that he wanted Thornton to take care of him. He washed Asher's half-hard cock without much fanfare. He didn't want to push the boy too far. He only had one more thing to finish. "Raise your knees and place your feet flat on the floor of the tub. There you go. Spread your legs for me, sweetheart, so I can wash your bottom."

When Asher followed directions beautifully, without a hint of hesitation, Thornton lathered up the mitt again and took special care to be gentle as he washed Asher's most private place.

CHAPTER ELEVEN

Asher

Asher couldn't help but lift his bottom up off the floor of the tub to make sure Thornton had all the access he could possibly need to clean him thoroughly. Every swipe and press of the soft fabric of the mitt against his desperate flesh was heating his body and revving him up. He lifted up just a little bit more, Thornton thoroughly cleaning his crease and rubbing soft circles around his anal pucker. Asher gasped and let out a moan before he could stop himself, which seemed to break the spell Thornton was under, causing him to pull away. He felt his face flame. But god, he felt bereft when the man's hand left his most intimate place.

Thornton's gaze was intense, but instead of making him feel ashamed for enjoying the brand-new sensations, Thornton waited calmly, his hand caressing the outside of his thigh. "Are you okay? Does exertion affect your arrhythmia?"

He swallowed and nodded. "I... yeah. That," he took a deep breath, "that felt good. And no, my heart is fine with exertion. It's just... I wasn't expecting it."

The sweet smile Thornton gave him made his heart flip in his chest. "I'm glad it felt good. Don't ever be ashamed of what makes your body and your mind feel good."

"Okay."

"You ready for me to continue?"

He nodded, spreading his legs again. He half expected a teasing glint to show up on Thornton's face, but it didn't. His curious gaze met Asher's. "Tell me what you want, baby. Use your words."

"I liked... can you do that again?"

"I can. I want to make you feel good. But we can't do too much. I don't think orgasming is a good idea for you with your fractured ribs. There are too many muscles involved, and I think you'll regret it. If you still want me to give you special touches, I'm happy to continue."

Special touches. Why did it sound so erotic when Thornton said it like that?
"I just like how it felt. I never knew it would feel like that."

"You've never fingered your little hole to make yourself come?"

Oh, god. His little hole. So much blushing. "No. I was always too scared it would hurt."

"When something or someone first breaches your special place, it probably will hurt a bit, but it can still feel really good."

"Can we do that sometime?"

"Perhaps, if we discuss it and it's what you truly want."

He couldn't think of a reason it wouldn't be what he wanted. Losing his virginity to the man who was softly caressing his skin in a bath full of bubbles he'd drawn just for Asher didn't feel like such a daunting thing. And even if they never worked out in a relationship, he didn't think he'd regret giving himself to Thornton. He knew he'd be taken care of properly. But he supposed it would have to wait and they could work up towards that, if the man was even interested.

Spreading his legs again, he whispered, "Please?"

"Be a good boy and don't strain. Try to stay still while I make you feel good."

"Okay."

"But, Asher, keep in mind being edged can be very frustrating."

"What does that mean?"

"It means if I continue to give you special touches and you aren't able to orgasm, you'll grow increasingly frustrated because I'm edging you to near completion and yet you can't come."

"I just want a little more. I won't come, I promise."

"Okay, baby boy. I'm going to use some lube and touch you with my fingers instead of the mitt."

He swallowed and nodded. "Yes, please."

"You're such a good boy, Asher."

"Thank you."

Sweetheart, baby, good boy.

He felt silly loving the sound of each of those endearments, but he couldn't help himself. He'd never been called by any term of endearment, even by his parents. They'd been selfish and neglectful. They'd kept a roof over his head and clothes on his body, food in his belly, and had taken his physical health seriously. He knew they'd cared for him as much as they possibly could, but there were no soft words, no emotional connection, no holiday celebrations, and no true sense of security.

He'd been given the bare minimum, but he supposed the minimum was better than others had grown up with, so complaining about it and moping around about it wasn't going to do him any good. Thinking about it, however, made it so starkly clear that just the simple care Thornton had given him since the accident was such a drastically different feeling. He was in real danger of becoming addicted, and they'd just met, for fuck's sake.

But from the moment Thornton had arrived by his side at the accident site, the man had shown more care and compassion than Asher had ever had aimed his way. Hell, he'd practically begged the man not to leave him when he was scared and hurting in his car, and the very fact Thornton had only left him long enough to handle the details of the accident before he'd gotten back to him said so much about the type of man Thornton was.

The man had told hospital staff they were married. If that wasn't shocking enough, Thornton had stayed with him every second of every day since then, until Asher himself had forced him to leave. And what a mistake that had been. He didn't know if he'd have the strength to walk away from such a kind, generous man. He didn't know if he'd want to.

"I want you to relax, slide a bit further down so your chest is covered and you don't get cold. All I'm going to do is make you feel good. I only want to give you pleasure."

Oh Jesus, Thornton's deep, gruff voice was making him quiver inside, and he wasn't even touching Asher yet. He did as he was told, sliding down deeper and loving the warmth that surrounded him. "That's a good boy. Spread your pretty legs open. You're so lovely, Asher."

And then the man's fingers were at his entrance, rubbing ever so softly up and down his crease over and over. Glancing over his pucker. God, it was bliss. Why had he waited? He'd never felt something so good. The slick heat of Thornton's fingers was almost more than he could take. He wanted more. He wanted those fingers inside of him. But he knew that was too much, too fast.

He'd watched porn—what gay man didn't? But he hadn't ever felt the confidence to see if touching himself there would feel good. Or maybe it was just that he wanted to save that for a time he might be with someone. Make it more special or something. He didn't know. He let his fears get in the way of a lot, so it was most likely a combination of both.

When Thornton finally zeroed in and put all his focus on teasing Asher's pucker, the mewling sounds he let slip out of his mouth had the red hue of humiliation slip over his skin. But he couldn't seem to stop them. He was just so much more sensitive there than he'd ever realized. He started moving his hips in time with Thornton's ministrations, ignoring the twinge in his ribs at the movement.

Thornton put pressure on his hole, swirling his finger over that sensitive spot three times and then putting pressure on it. Not enough to pop inside, but close. Three times more and then pressure. He was going out of his mind and cried out when it was almost too much. He clamped his mouth and eyes shut, taking deep breaths, trying to calm down. But when he did so, Thornton pulled his fingers away.

He whimpered and opened his eyes. Panting, he met Thornton's gaze. "Why did you stop?"

"Because you seemed to be getting overwhelmed, and I was worried you might lose control. Your cock is hard as a rock, and I don't know just how easily you can come. Were you close, baby?"

The whimper that escaped him as he nodded must have been something Thornton enjoyed because his eyes sparked with heat, and he leaned over and kissed Asher. God, those lips were like heaven. "I think we should stop. As much as I want to keep exploring what makes you feel good, I don't want to push you over the edge and cause you to be in more pain. You've got enough of that without making matters worse."

Asher sighed and nodded. He knew Thornton was right. He just hadn't wanted it to stop, and he knew he wasn't going to stop wanting more from

Thornton. He didn't think he could say no to the man, but not because he didn't feel strong enough to turn him down when he didn't want something, because he didn't *want* to say no. Suddenly, he wanted too much—he wanted everything—and he had no idea what that even meant with a man like Thornton. The thought scared him and thrilled him in equal measure.

***

After his bath, he hadn't been as tired as he'd been before it, so he'd put off taking a nap, and they'd watched a movie together and eaten lunch. He took some pain meds with the food, so by the time the movie ended and the food was all gone, his eyes were drooping. But instead of going upstairs to rest, he'd fallen asleep with his head on Thornton's lap, the man's fingers playing with his hair but ever careful of his head wound.

When they first started the movie, Asher was sitting farther away from Thornton than he'd really wanted to, prompting Thornton to ask, "Do you want to sit so far away from me?"

The man was too observant by far and seemed to know exactly what he was thinking and feeling because it *had* felt way too far away, but he hadn't had the guts to move closer. "No."

"Good. I don't want you that far away either. Come cuddle with me."

Besides earlier in the day when he'd been pulled into Thornton's lap, he'd never cuddled with anyone. He was going through so many firsts, his head was spinning. He couldn't remember ever being so content in someone else's presence. They'd had ice cream for dessert after lunch—Thornton had coffee ice cream, and he'd chosen double chocolate brownie. They'd traded bites back and forth using each other's spoons. Another first.

He must have slept for several hours because when he woke, it was dark when he looked out the window, and he could smell something yummy coming from the kitchen. Somewhere along the way, Thornton had replaced his leg with a pillow under Asher's head. Who knew how long the man sat, carding his fingers through his hair. If he had to guess, it was a while. Thornton had seemed content to sit there earlier while he did something on his iPad and Asher rested.

He slowly sat up, the ever-present pain making him suck in a breath. He straightened the huge sweatshirt he was wearing—another one of Thornton's—which had gotten rucked up, exposing his stomach as he slept. He secretly loved wearing the man's clothes and thought about hiding one in his bag that he could take home with him when he was done recuperating. But in the end, he'd probably just ask Thornton for one straight out because the thought of stealing anything from the man, even if it was something Thornton apparently had tons of, didn't sit right with him.

He grabbed the glass of water from earlier and took a few sips, standing and walking towards the kitchen. When he rounded the corner, he froze, shock making his heart burst out of his chest and his stomach plummet. He backed out of the room before he was noticed and made his way as quickly as he could upstairs and to his room.

He went straight to the bathroom and started stuffing his toiletries in his dopp kit, his hands unsteady and his breaths coming in short bursts. He was going to keep it together if it was the last thing he did. Done packing his toiletries, he picked up the kit and turned to head back into the bedroom when he knocked his water glass from the counter where he'd stupidly placed it on the edge. It hit the tile floor and shattered.

"No, no, no, no, no, no, no. Oh, god."

He couldn't leave a mess behind like this. It wasn't right, and the dogs might get hurt. He stepped forward to start cleaning it up and gasped as pain shot through his foot. Collapsing onto the little bathroom rug, pain lancing through his chest at the jarring movements, he gasped. "Fuck. Oh, fuck, fuck, fuck."

He looked at his foot and pulled out the large piece of glass, getting blood all over the rug. It was all just too much. He ignored his foot for the time being and began to pick up each piece of glass he could find, slicing his finger in the process. He turned and grabbed the trash can beside the toilet and yanked a bunch of toilet paper off the roll.

"Asher? Oh Jesus, baby. What happened?"

"I broke it. I'm so sorry."

"It doesn't matter. Sweetheart, let me help you. You're bleeding."

"I'm okay. I'm okay. I'll be just fine. I just need to…" He wiped ineffectually at his foot, realizing he hadn't gotten all the glass out when it hurt like a motherfucker. "Shit."

He rubbed the sweatshirt sleeve across his eyes and realized it had blood all over it. "Oh, no. Your sweatshirt. I'm… I'm…" Suddenly, he couldn't breathe.

"Asher, hey, baby, look at me. Come on. Take some deep breaths."

But he couldn't. He couldn't take any breaths at all. He clutched at his chest.

Why couldn't he breathe? Dizzy, he reached out to try to grab something solid. Something to tether him, to make the world settle under him again. What he gripped in his hand was Thornton's arm, saddened at the strength in it, knowing he'd never be able to count on that strength again.

He couldn't slow the gasping breaths he was trying so desperately to take. He heard a snap of fingers. "Beauty, Beast, stay back."

He gasped out, "The glass."

"They're fine. They won't step on the glass. Sweetheart, I'm going to pick you u—"

He shook his head. His chest was wracked with pain at the quickly drawn breaths and shaking body. He couldn't calm down. Why couldn't he calm down? He hadn't had a panic attack this bad in years.

"Boy!" He jumped, jerking his head back to meet Thornton's worried gaze. "Keep your eyes on me. Feel my chest moving in and out. Feel it expand and contract with my breaths. In and out, sweetheart. In and out. Do it with me, please."

He shook his head, unable to focus enough to do what he was being asked to do.

"Asher, you'll do as I say. Focus on your senses. What color are my eyes?"

What? Why would he...? He blinked rapidly to bring his eyes into focus. God, those eyes. Specks of brown surrounded by golden hues. But that sounded too romantic, so he settled on... "Amber."

Thornton smiled. "And here I thought they were brown."

He shook his head, trying to breathe but only able to pull in short, shallow breaths. "And my hair? What color is my hair?"

"Br—brown."

"That's right." Thornton. "Listen. What do you hear?"

He closed his eyes and heard the puppies crying. "Beauty. Beast."

"That's right. They're worried about you. You don't want them worried about you, do you?"

He shook his head. He didn't want to worry the pups. Thornton pulled one of his hands up to his cheek. "What do you feel?"

He moved his fingers under Thornton's, and his breath caught before he was able to draw in more air. "Your beard."

"That's right. You're doing really well, Asher."

He didn't understand why Thornton's words were getting to him, but he found himself focusing on the man's muscular chest as it breathed in and out, and slowly, his vision started to clear when he began to draw in regular breaths. In and out. In and out, like Thornton said. He hurt all over. His head, his chest and ribs, his foot, and his stupid finger. Everything hurt.

His silent tears fell unchecked down his cheeks. "You're all right. You're breathing just fine. Everything is okay. Keep breathing with me. That's it."

They sat there together, dogs whining from outside the bathroom, both him and Thornton on the floor breathing in time with each other. When he finally felt steadier, he pulled his hand away, unable to touch and receive comfort from Thornton. He couldn't count on him. He'd never be able to count on him again. He closed his eyes at the heartbreak of that. Of what he was losing before it was even his to claim.

Gathering himself together, he glanced down at his foot and realized it was still bleeding. Grabbing the toilet paper he'd dropped on the floor, he held it to the cuts on his foot, pressing down hard, ignoring the pain it caused and the knowledge he must still have some little pieces in there. He'd deal with them later. He just had to go home. Once he was home, he'd be okay. Everything would be okay.

Once he got the bleeding under control, he realized Thornton had been talking to him, and he hadn't heard a word. "... me what's wrong? I don't understand what happened. You were sleeping on the sofa, and then I heard the crash of glass on the floor and rushed up here."

"I have to go home."

The silence was deafening, and then finally, "What? Asher, you can't go home. You're in no state to take care of yourself. You need help while you're getting better. You said you'd stay and recuperate here. What changed?"

He shook his head as he got up on his knees and gripped the counter to help pull himself to stand. His foot hurt like a bitch, but so did his chest, and what the fuck else was new? Once he was steady enough to move, he watched as Thornton scrambled to his feet, towering over him, his expression confused and, if he wasn't mistaken, sad. He couldn't let that deter him. It was how his parents would look at him when he wasn't doing what they wanted or needed from him.

Firming his resolve, he used the wall to hobble a few steps over the rug and then was about to take a big step over the glass and onto the carpet of the bedroom when he was scooped up in strong arms, making his chest ache with what he could no longer have. "I need to pack my things. I have to go home. Please, put me down."

He was placed gently on the bed, where he tried to get right back up. But hands were on his cheeks, wiping them free of tears and turning his gaze up to meet Thornton's. "Talk to me, baby. Please. I know you're hurting physically and emotionally right now, but I don't know why."

The tear at the corner of Thornton's eye had his own eyes filling with them again. He shook his head to dispel the urgency to do as Thornton asked and pulled away. "I can't. I just... Thornton, I want to go home."

After several beats of silence, he heard Thornton breathe out a shaky breath. "Okay. All right. Let me pack your things for you, and then I'll take you home."

"No! No, Thornton. I'll call a Lyft or a cab."

"I'm not sending you home in a Lyft car with a stranger, Asher. I'll take you there myself."

He shook his head, panic hitting him full force at the thought of being forced into a car with him. "I won't go with you. I won't. You're not fit to drive."

"What the hell? Where did that come from?"

"You're drunk!" Asher practically spat the words at him.

"Drunk? Asher, what are you talking about? I haven't had anything to drink."

How could he say that to his face? "Don't lie to me."

"Sweetheart, I'm not lying. I haven't had anything to drink. I got out a—"

Asher covered his ears and rocked back and forth on the bed, unable to hear anymore. "Don't. Please don't. That's what they used to say. All the time they'd lie and tell me they hadn't had anything to drink. It was always a lie. Don't do that to me. Don't lie to me, Thornton."

He didn't know how to handle lies coming from Thornton. He was supposed to be different. Realizing that he was just the same as his parents shattered his heart into millions of pieces. He'd started to care. Too much, too fast. And he hadn't controlled his feelings like he should have.

They'd never have what he had imagined. They'd never be the friends Thornton had promised him they would be. He sat there, curled up as tight as his ribs would allow, hands still over his ears, eyes closed tight against the pain, and he cried.

CHAPTER TWELVE

Thornton

Oh, god, the sight of Asher protecting himself from Thornton's words and what he believed to be true broke Thornton in a way he couldn't even specify. His feelings were all over the place. Pain, sorrow, frustration, determination, horror, anguish, and *pride*. God, he felt proud of Asher for standing up to him, for pushing back, for refusing to back down. He had a very brave boy on his hands, and he was going to reward that behavior.

But first things first. The boy had to see for himself he wasn't lying. Asher wasn't in a place that would allow him to see reason any other way. He slid his arm under the boy's legs and wrapped his other around the boy's back, lifting him as gently as he could. The moan and whimper, most likely a result of pain, nearly did him in. "I'm sorry, baby. I'm taking you downstairs. I need to show you something."

Asher just sighed and went limp in his arms, the fight suddenly slipping away, leaving only a husk of what he'd been before. Thornton would move heaven and earth to bring back the boy he'd been with earlier that day. The boy who had told him secrets of his past, the boy who had enjoyed the first sexual stimulation he'd ever received from someone else, the boy who had cuddled up to him, admitting that he felt protected when Thornton surrounded him with his warmth, and the boy who said he loved being called sweetheart, baby, and good boy.

He walked downstairs and into the kitchen with Asher still held snug in his grip, murmuring words to him as he went. "You're all right, sweet boy. I'm here. We'll get you home if you need to go. I promise I'll take care of you. Don't be scared. I'll never hurt you, Asher."

He sat Asher down on the counter beside the crockpot where their dinner sat warming. On their way downstairs, Asher had placed his hands in his lap, and they stayed there as Thornton clasped the boy's cheeks in his hands. When Asher's heartbroken eyes met his—lashes still shimmering with the tears that had fallen—it was all he could do to draw in a breath and forge on with his plan. Not sure it was the best thing to do but not knowing what else would convince him.

"I didn't lie to you, Ash." Thornton shored up his determination, heart aching. "Open those beautiful eyes, baby. I won't ever lie to you. That's a promise. I think you must have seen my beer sitting here on the bar."

Instead of looking at the bottle, Asher turned his head away, almost like it was just too much for him to bear. "Asher, be my brave boy for a second, please. Give me your trust once more. I promise I won't squander it. Let me prove to you it's not misplaced."

There was a spark in the boy's eyes, but his emotions were all over the place, so Thornton couldn't tell if it was anger, disbelief, or a challenge. Probably a combination of all three. "Look at the bottle. All I did was take the lid off. It's completely full. I thought it sounded good when I started making the chili, and then I forgot it was even there."

Asher's eyes blinked up at him, and then, almost against his will, they seemed to turn towards the bottle and then back to him, as if he wasn't sure he could handle seeing it, especially if Thornton was lying. But he wasn't, and he hoped like hell Asher would see it for the truth. Jesus, his boy had suffered enough. When Asher finally found the strength to glance over at the bottle, he just stared at it in disbelief.

"I swear to you, I haven't had a drop. It's been sitting there for over an hour. No more condensation. It's warm." He turned and pulled out the drawer containing his recycling bin and his trash. "Look, there are no other bottles either. I'm one hundred percent sober."

He picked the bottle up and held it between them. Asher lurched back and sucked in a breath, as if he'd been burned. God, it was so much worse than he'd thought. He set it down again, gently picked Asher up, and set his feet on the floor. With his arm wrapped around Asher's slim waist, he walked them over to the sink and began pouring out the beer.

Asher turned in his arms as if he couldn't bear to watch it, burying his face in Thornton's armpit and wrapping his arms around Thornton's waist. That was something. No, that was more than something. That was everything. Having those arms wrapped around him when Asher had just been so distrustful meant the world to him.

He leaned down and kissed the top of Asher's head and then stretched the remaining distance to throw the empty bottle in the recycle bin. Capturing the boy's face between his gentle palms, he lowered his head until it touched Asher's. Wrapping his arms around Asher's shoulders, he whispered, "I won't ever lie to you, Asher. I promise you."

He pulled away enough to look into Asher's eyes and said it again to be sure. "I promise, baby."

Thornton drew him in, and they just stood there for a bit, Thornton swaying them both for comfort. Pulling back finally, Thornton asked, "Do you still want to go home?"

Asher hesitated but nodded, sending Thornton's heart plummeting. But this wasn't about him any longer; it was about Asher, so all he did was pull him in for another hug. "All right. I'll drive you then."

"Thank you. I'm sorry. I can't be around someone who drinks. I just can't. It's a trigger for me. I should have asked you before I came here. Alcohol isn't a part of my life anymore, and I have to keep it that way. It's not about you. It's about me and what I can and can't handle."

He nodded, feeling an enormous sense of loss when he stepped away from Asher and turned to head upstairs. "Let me go pack your things."

Searching his mind for some solution that didn't involve Asher leaving, the obvious finally occurred to him, and he stopped in his tracks. "Asher, if the alcohol wasn't here, would you want to leave?"

The boy closed his eyes and opened them again, taking several deep breaths while Thornton looked on, waiting for Asher's decision. When it finally came in the form of a shake of his head and a whispered, "No," Thornton couldn't believe the overwhelming sense of relief he felt.

"Oh, sweet boy. You're being so brave. I'm going to dump everything, all right? And I want you to watch so you know I'm not hiding anything from you."

"But I don't want you to have to do that. It's not fair to you."

"You've essentially given me a choice. Whether you meant to or not, that's the long and short of it. And I choose you, Asher. I choose you over having alcohol here. You mean more to me than any alcohol ever could. So much more."

That must have been the breaking point because Asher crumpled in front of him, as if releasing all the tension he'd been under. Thornton gently scooped him up again and walked them out of the kitchen and into the family room. Sitting down on the couch, he nestled Asher in his lap.

"Asher, I'm so proud of you right now."

The boy's exhausted eyes turned up to meet his. "Why?"

"You said before you thought you might not be able to say no to me. And you said no to me in a monumental way. No matter what I said, you told me no. I had to prove myself to you for you to change your mind. I love that you did that. You've shown me that you are strong enough to say no to me and mean it. And I think you proved that to yourself as well. That's a big deal."

Asher sat on his lap in silence but finally looked up again. "I guess it is."

"Will you stay with me if I remove every trace of alcohol from the house?"

"Yes. But I feel bad I know it's expen—"

"The expense doesn't matter to me. You matter to me. Will you let me take care of you properly now? I think your foot has stopped bleeding, but I'm worried about more glass being in there."

"Yes, please."

He slipped Asher from his lap and went to get the things he'd need to fix the boy's foot and finger. After tweezing three tiny slivers of glass out of his foot, he wrapped gauze around it and put a bandage on his finger. He pulled the sweatshirt gently off the boy and wrapped the soft fleece blanket around his shoulders to keep him warm while he was gone. He handed Asher the remote control. "Here, watch something for a few minutes while I make sure everything is cleaned up in the bathroom."

"There's blood on the rug. I'm—"

"Don't. Don't apologize. You were afraid. Give yourself a break, sweetheart. The blood will wash out; I've got a ton of glasses just like the one that broke. Okay?" When Asher nodded, he leaned down and kissed his head.

Upstairs, he grabbed a new sweatshirt. Once he had everything cleaned up and Asher's toiletries unpacked, he dug in the boy's bag for his coloring things, knowing the noise in Asher's brain needed to be smoothed out, softened. He had a feeling coloring was the one constant in Asher's life he could count on to take him out of what Thornton thought of as his "adult" headspace. He knew Asher would think of it as a simple stress reliever.

It broke his heart Asher hadn't had security in his life except that which he made for himself. He knew Asher would thrive in a setting where someone else was providing that security, and he just hoped age regression would be the way he could finally find that, with a proper Daddy to help him feel secure and strong even when he didn't feel as if he was. If anyone needed a Daddy, Asher did. He also had to admit to himself he was already thinking of Asher as *his* boy.

He didn't know if it would work out. But god, did he hope it would. He didn't worry if they were compatible. He felt a closeness with Asher he hadn't felt with his other boys. There was a deep-seated need in Asher to be loved and cared for, to be coddled and cherished. He wanted to be the one to show Asher how he should be treated, how he *deserved* to be treated.

"I brought you some coloring books. Do you want to sit on the floor at the coffee table, or do you want to sit here and I can bring you a lap board?"

The happiness in Asher's eyes when they met his finally settled the remaining doubts he'd had since he'd seen Asher bleeding on the floor of his bathroom. "I'll sit at the coffee table."

"Here, let me pull it out so you don't have to struggle to get under it, and I'll put a pillow on the floor and behind you." He helped Asher down on the pillows. "How's that?"

The boy glanced up at him and smiled. "Good."

He arranged all the coloring things in front of Asher. "I'm going to go get started dumping everything out, okay?" The solemn look on Asher's face tore at him. "I want you here with me. It's as simple as that. Most of the stuff I'm getting rid of I've had for years. I won't miss it."

When Asher's shoulders relaxed, he reached to clasp him under the chin and tilt his head up, kissing those sweet lips. He headed into the kitchen, and when he opened his liquor cabinet over the fridge, he realized he had a lot more than he'd thought he did. His house was a good party house, so he'd thrown parties often enough he'd wanted to be fully stocked. Shaking his head at the absurdity of the quantities he'd collected over the years, he dove into his task.

He started with the bottles that were less than halfway full. Pulling them down, he shut the cabinet after he was done, not wanting Asher to come in and see how much was there. He dumped those without thought and put the bottles in the recycle bin drawer. Next came the ones that were opened but not even halfway empty. He was in the middle of pouring out a large bottle of bourbon when Asher walked in, a small smile on his face. "Can I have someth—"

Asher's eyes popped wide at the three large bottles he had out, one of which he was holding above the sink, pouring. The boy's face got ashen, and then he was covering his nose and mouth and running.

Fuckfuckfuckfuckfuck.

He set the neck of the bottle into the sink drain and ran after the sounds of retching he heard coming from the bathroom down the hall. Jesus. He hadn't expected such a visceral reaction. He should have been dumping them in the laundry room sink, farther away from his boy.

"Baby, I'm so sorry." He leaned over Asher, rubbing his back, a slow up and down motion meant to soothe. "I didn't know you'd react that way to seeing it or smelling it."

Asher took deep breaths, and Thornton cringed, knowing those breaths and all that heaving had to be killing his ribs. His heart was breaking, and he felt like the biggest failure. Once the vomiting stopped, Asher just leaned his head on his forearm on the seat of the toilet, trying to slow his breathing. He knelt, Asher's small body between his knees.

Leaning forward, he flushed the toilet and pulled Asher back against his chest. "I know how awful it feels to be sick, but to be sick when your ribs are fractured…" He let out a sigh. "I can't even imagine."

"It's not your fault."

"I should have known."

Asher shook his head against Thornton's chest and turned his head sideways to look up at him. "I didn't even know, Thorn."

He loved hearing the shortened version of his name coming from Asher's lips. "I still feel awful I didn't think about it."

He stood and pulled Asher up with him. He grabbed Asher one of the little paper cups he kept in the dispenser by the sink and filled it with water. As Asher swished his mouth out, he reached into the cabinet above the toilet and pulled out a small bottle of—thank sweet fuck, alcohol-free—mouthwash, meeting Asher's eyes in the mirror. The boy handed the empty cup back to him, and he poured a generous amount inside, handing it back.

He stayed with Asher, his hands on the boy's sides, rubbing up and down in a gentle caress, lending his support the only way he knew how at that moment. When Asher was done, he crumpled the little cup in his hand and tossed it in the trash beside the toilet.

They walked back to the family room, and he sat down beside Asher, who was fidgeting with his fingers in his lap. "That was my mom's favorite. That drink, whatever it was. It's the same bottle, same color liquid, and smelled the same."

God, would he ever know the depths of shit this boy had needed to crawl his way out of? "What made you come in the kitchen?"

"I was going to ask for a snack and a drink."

"Do you want food right now?"

"Ugh, no."

He smiled at the sound of Asher's disgust. "How about some ginger ale?"

Asher nodded. "Yeah. That sounds good."

"Let me go grab it for you. Do you think you can settle down to color for a bit, or are you too upset?"

"I think I'm okay."

An idea brewing in his head, he stood to grab the boy some soda with a straw. He very nearly put it in a kid's cup with a lid and straw but caught himself just in time, knowing Asher wasn't quite ready for that. He'd had enough thrown at him for the day. "Here you go. I'm gonna finish up with this. If you need something, call me in here so you don't have to see any of it."

"Thank you."

He gave Asher a reassuring smile. "You're welcome, sweetheart. Do you want to watch a movie? I've got all the regular channels, movie channels, Netflix, Prime Video, Hulu, and Disney Plus."

Asher bit his lip as if thinking whether or not he should do what he really wanted to do. Those shy eyes met his, though, and he asked, "How do I watch Disney Plus?"

God, those pretty eyes, so earnest, would be the death of him. He was thrilled

Asher felt comfortable asking to watch Disney Plus. He dealt with switching the TV over to the Fire Stick and loaded Disney Plus. He thought maybe the shy look meant Asher was embarrassed by what he wanted to watch, but when he was nearly vibrating with energy, toggling to episode one of *The Mandalorian*, Thornton grinned and then chuckled when the boy clapped his hands in excitement.

God, he was the perfect little already. Not wanting to get ahead of himself, he crouched down. "I'm on episode three myself, so when you get there, we can start watching together. I'm going to make a phone call, okay?"

Asher nodded absently, and he headed into the kitchen, knowing a better way to handle the alcohol problem. It was going on seven o'clock, and he was getting hungry. He hoped Asher would be feeling well enough to eat in just a little bit, but in the meantime, he had to make a call.

"Thornton, you better not be calling to cancel tomorrow."

Shit. "Well, I wasn't, but yeah, I guess I'm doing that too."

"Aw, come on, man!"

"It'll make sense later, but listen, I need a favor. Are either one of you free right now?"

Damon had obviously heard the seriousness of his tone. "Uh, yeah. We both are because we're getting ready to come over. You wanted Syed to check your boy over, remember? We were gonna fix a quick dinner and then head over, but we can bring something to eat or eat when we get home if you need us to come right away."

"Jesus, I forgot about that. It's been... quite a day. Why don't you come over and eat chili with us? There's plenty here. And I'd like you to pick up a couple of boxes of booze."

The snort on the other line had Thornton rolling his eyes. "You think we need booze? Have you *been* to one of our parties?"

"Listen, brat, I'm being serious. For reasons I can't really go into right now, I can't have any alcohol in my house."

Several long moments tick by. "Uh, that's weird, Thorn. But—"

He heard muffled voices and knew Syed was probably asking what was going on. "Thorn, everything all right? We were gonna head over there soon, but do you need us to come right away?"

He sighed. "Hey, Syed. I told Damon you guys can come over and eat chili with us. Least I can do for you stopping by to check on Asher. And I think everything's gonna be fine, but I just learned Asher can't be around alcohol. I opened a beer earlier, never drank it, but he saw it, and it's some sort of trigger for him. He was packing his shit to go home when I went to look for him."

"Packing to leave because you had a beer out?"

"Yeah, it was bad. I gotta get it outta here. I can't dump it all in the drain because the smell..." Fuck, he shouldn't have been telling them this, but they were his closest friends, and he wanted them to understand the seriousness of the situation. "I don't think it's enough to put it in the trash in the garage. It might work, but he's feeling vulnerable right now, and I don't want to chance it not being enough to make him feel safe here. I just need it gone."

"We'll be there in ten minutes."

"Thank you."

He went to the garage and dragged out a couple of large plastic totes. Bringing them inside, he began filling them both with bottles of alcohol and the beer from the fridge. He made a mental note to grab the two cases of beer he had in the garage. The doorbell rang, and he walked into the family room, seeing Asher frantically trying to put away his coloring things, his expression panicked. "Hey, hey. It's only Syed and Damon. I'm a Daddy, remember? They've seen my boys playing with their toys, and they've been to my playroom. Coloring books aren't even going to register as anything but normal with them. I promise you."

Thornton paused the show as Asher gazed at everything on the table—the crayons, pencils, markers, pens. He must have come to the decision he was going to leave it because he stopped trying to put everything away. "Are they coming for dinner?"

"Yeah, I offered to share the chili I made. I forgot I'd asked Syed to come over to check on you since you took that fall last night. And they're going to take the alcohol. I didn't want it in the house or the trash in the garage. But I didn't want to dump it all out in the sink if it's going to make you sick. This way they can make use of it, so it won't go to waste, and it's all out of the house." He saw his boy get ready to apologize again and cut him off at the pass. "Don't apologize. I want to do this."

Asher nodded, picked up a purple pen, and then put it down, folding his hands in his lap. Thornton smiled as he walked towards the foyer. "Watch. Damon's going to want to stay and color with you."

Asher looked like he wanted to ask something but decided against it when Thornton moved to open the door. He waved his friends inside. "Hey, guys. Thanks for coming. I've got the totes in the kitchen."

He hugged them both, appreciating they'd drop everything to lend a hand. Damon walked through the foyer into the family room. "Hey, Asher. Oh man, coloring and *Mandalorian*? Best Friday night ever."

The grin on Asher's face went a long way towards reassuring Thornton things were going to be all right. As he watched, Damon pulled the nice, large, leather-bound sketchpad Thornton kept for him out from between a coffee table photo book and Thornton's iPad. He sat down on the sofa on Asher's left side, taking off his shoes and reaching for a few of Asher's colorful pens. "Can I use these?"

Asher, taking it all in with wide-eyed wonder, nodded. "Yeah. Sure."

Damon brought his legs up onto the cushion to sit criss cross, flipped the sketchpad open to the last page he'd been working on, and started drawing. "Do you wanna play the show?"

He had to hand it to Damon. He'd changed tactics with Asher, not giving him too much direct attention that might make him uncomfortable. He hadn't even looked up from his sketch when he'd asked about the show. Asher glanced at Thornton, smiled, and shrugged, pushing play on the remote. As he and Syed walked further into the room, he watched, bemused, while Syed gripped Damon's thick hair and yanked back his head.

Damon didn't make a sound, obviously used to being manhandled like that, and closed his eyes as Syed kissed him quite thoroughly, before whispering in Damon's ear, causing him to shiver, bite his lip, and say, "Thank you, Sir."

That got Asher's attention, and he turned to see Syed letting go of Damon's hair and smoothing it out, blushing when Syed kissed his boy again and then turned a wink on Asher. Thornton chuckled and waved Syed towards the kitchen. "I think your boy is fully ensconced on my sofa for a while. Thank you for coming by to help. I've got chili keeping warm in the crockpot."

"I'll never turn your mama's chili down."

They carried both heavy totes through the garage so Asher wouldn't be upset. They loaded them in Syed's SUV and then grabbed the cases of beer and did the same. Back inside, Thornton leaned into the family room. "You boys want some chili?"

They both turned towards him, smiles on their faces, and nodded. "You wanna keep watching and drawing while you eat?"

When they both gave him more smiles and nods, he chuckled and asked what they wanted to drink. Back in the kitchen, he got everything ready for the boys and took it in; coming back, he filled two bowls and brought the remaining cornbread muffins to the table. Sitting down with Syed, they ate and chatted while their boys enjoyed their show, drawing, and dinner.

After they ate, Syed grabbed his stethoscope from the car, and Asher sat on the barstool in the kitchen waiting, tension obvious in the set of his shoulders. Syed walked back in, a smile on his face. "Asher, I'm sure you have your own family doctor, so you can set up an appointment with them for your follow-up, but Thorn told me about your fall last night and would like me to check you over. Is that all right with you?"

Asher glanced at Thornton and then back to Syed. "Yes. It's fine."

"Okay, I'm going to listen to your lungs, check your breath sounds, and make sure there aren't any breathing issues. Then I'm going to palpate your ribs to make sure there are no further issues as a result of the fall."

"It's gonna hurt, though, right?"

Syed nodded, his smile sad. "I'm afraid it won't be comfortable. I'll be asking you to take deep breaths, which is going to hurt, and then I'll be putting pressure on your ribs to check them. I'll do my very best to do it all as quickly and as gently as possible."

"Okay." Asher nodded, his shoulders sagging, and Thornton's heart broke for him. He wished like hell they could avoid this altogether, but he needed to make sure Asher hadn't hurt himself even more.

Syed donned his stethoscope and asked Asher to take deep breaths as he listened. "Good job, Asher. I know it's uncomfortable. I'm going to have you lie down on the sofa, so I can palpate your ribs."

They headed to the family room. Damon moved over to the chair next to the sofa and ignored the goings-on as he continued to draw, which most likely helped Asher not feel like a bug under a microscope. Thornton sat on the coffee table and held Asher's hand during the exam, the boy's grip stronger than he thought possible for a boy his size. He made a few small noises of discomfort, but when his eyes squeezed tight at the obvious pain he was in, Thornton knew he'd been holding his reactions back.

Finally, it was over, and when Syed apologized for any discomfort he'd caused, Asher merely nodded and sat in the corner of the couch clutching his ribs. "I don't think you did any further damage, Asher. Your ribs will continue to ache for a while tonight. Take your next dose of pain meds as soon as you're able. Your lungs are clear, no punctures, and your breathing is fine. Did the hospital give you instructions about deep breathing several times a day to avoid getting an infection in your lungs?" When Asher answered that they had, Syed continued, "Good. Make sure to follow those instructions. We don't want you to catch pneumonia."

Asher nodded. "Thank you."

"You're welcome, Asher. We're going to get going. It was good to see you again."

"You too." Asher smiled, kindness radiating from the boy even as exhaustion weighed him down. Thornton watched, a warm feeling in his chest as Syed shook Asher's hand and rubbed the boy's shoulder as he said goodbye. Damon, always more exuberant and demonstrative, leaned down and gently hugged Asher.

"I'm gonna walk them out, sweetheart. I'll be right back."

Asher nodded and sat back on the sofa to wait for him, looking through Damon's drawings in the sketchbook after having shyly asked permission. He walked his friends out to their car and hugged them both. Damon hugged him longer than normal, and, when he pulled away, said, "He needs you, Thorn. He's a little, and he doesn't even know it. He'll be good for you."

He appreciated those words, especially coming from Damon, as he was often a bratty sub that didn't take too many things seriously. "I think we'll be good for each other, if we can work things out."

CHAPTER THIRTEEN

Asher

S tretched out, trying to get to sleep, his mind was moving a mile a minute. He'd had a good ending to a long, rough day. But the day hadn't all been bad. He'd cuddled with Thornton, shared some of his past with him, which felt like he'd unloaded a heavy burden, he'd learned about what type of relationship Thornton desired, and he'd had the best bath of his life.

He smiled to himself, remembering he'd had fun talking to Damon. The man was seriously talented with a pen and paper and not too shabby on the eyes. He was enormous and so muscular, but the most striking thing about him was his dark facial hair coupled with his dyed gray hair with light purple undertones, which was a moppy mess on the top of his head. His facial features were angular, his gray eyes piercing.

In contrast, Syed had dark tanned skin and wavy, thick, dark brown hair, his skin shaved smooth, and his eyes a deep, warm brown. He was probably at least six feet tall but had a runner's build. They were a striking couple, to be sure. Syed was definitely the more dominant of the two, while Damon seemed pretty laid back. He felt comfortable around both of them, which was so rare for him.

But the reason both Syed and Damon had been there in the first place was the worst part of his day. He'd been so humiliated by his own actions before

Thornton's friends had arrived. The way he'd treated Thornton was awful. Guilt was plaguing him.

But instead of being upset or resentful, Thornton calmly found a solution so Asher could stay with him. Thinking about it made his heart feel full, it humbled him, and it gave him so much hope. After everything that had happened, he realized how much he'd truly come to trust Thornton. He'd never been cared for like Thornton cared for him.

Part of him worried he was confusing feelings of gratitude with romantic feelings, but when he laid them all on the table, he realized he could clearly separate them. In his mind, he knew it was too soon to make any decisions about jumping into a relationship with Thornton, but there was a tender, aching, hopeful part of his heart that longed to do just that. And he knew if Thornton expressed his interest in taking those first steps, he wouldn't say no.

Thornton was beautiful, inside and out. He was funny, smart, successful, thoughtful, protective, and kind. And if the man was to be believed, he was interested in Asher, of all people. How could that even be? He was a mess. A complete and total wreck. And yet, every time he showed Thornton more of who he truly was, instead of moving further away, the man kept inching closer. And closer, and closer still.

The man was under his skin, inching his way into his mind, interrupting his thoughts, and squeezing his heart. He was ensnared by him. And instead of feeling suffocated by his strong, masculine presence, he wanted to curl up into a ball and be surrounded by him. By his kindness, his strength, and his warmth. Was that dangerous? It probably was, but he wanted it all the same.

He thought about the conversation they'd had before Thornton had essentially tucked him into bed. Once he'd brushed his teeth and Thornton had helped him into a pair of boxers and one of the larger man's long-sleeved tees, he'd helped Asher into bed and sat next to him, his own iPad in his hand.

"I made a list of different websites and blogs about the lifestyle that you can read through whenever you want. You'll be able to see some of the things that make both Daddies and boys want to live their lives like I do, from their own perspectives."

He'd only nodded and watched as Thornton opened a document with more links than he'd been expecting. Clicking on several of them, Thornton pointed out which were blogs written by Daddies and which were written by boys. There were several websites he opened that focused on age play/age regression dynamics and even one that had a list of different ages and traits Daddies might see in their littles and how to help guide and nurture them.

If he was being honest with himself, it was all rather strange. Not a bad strange, but strange all the same. When Thornton stood, made sure Asher was tucked in, had everything he needed, and then headed into his own room, Asher could admit he liked being taken care of, and perhaps the lifestyle had more to offer him than he could have imagined. And that alone gave him the courage to do as much research as he could, his mind open to possibilities he could never have imagined prior to meeting Thornton.

He'd stayed up for hours reading everything he could get his hands on. The more he read, the more he needed to know, and the more he learned, the closer he'd ever felt in understanding a part of himself he realized had always been elusive. His mind was working a mile a minute, cataloguing things about himself he'd never truly realized were behaviors already geared towards the lifestyle. Things started slotting into place.

How had he never known something like this existed? How had he gone his whole life completely unaware of a relationship dynamic he could literally see himself in if he closed his eyes? The images came to life in a myriad of ways, things he already did and, even more thrilling, things he *wanted* to do. Coloring, watching cartoons, eating off kids' plates, drinking from straw cups, and sleeping with a stuffy were all things he did on a daily basis. And being cuddled, caressed, cared for, and cherished by a Daddy? God, he realized with surprising clarity, he'd never desired something more. That in itself was a shock.

He found himself hard just thinking about things that weren't even sexual in nature. Why? What was it about the dynamic that made him feel more alive and filled with yearning than he ever had? Sure, he was a virgin, but he obviously wasn't new to masturbation and the concept of sex. He'd had fantasies like any other red-blooded person, but they'd been so cookie cutter, so run of the mill. He chuckled at himself when the new meaning of the word *vanilla* came to mind. Yeah. They'd been so vanilla. Was it wrong it thrilled him just a little that the fantasies he had in his head at that moment weren't vanilla at all?

His own searches led him down several rabbit holes which had also included Daddy kink porn because, well, porn. His dick had never been so hard or responsive. He'd been leaking precum with barely a touch, and when he finally did reach down and grip himself, the puddle of the shimmery liquid on his tummy grew quickly. But because he didn't have the energy or the strength but *did* have a lot of pain, he didn't do anything more then give himself a few soft tugs and caresses.

Frustrating himself more than anything else, he'd eventually stopped the touching and stopped the watching, not wanting to continue the torture. But the fact he'd been ridiculously turned on by reading some of the blogs and watching quite a bit of porn had him admitting he had more than just a passing interest in trying it out himself. He felt like he was seeing his deepest desires playing out before him.

It was nearly two in the morning when he'd finally stopped. His eyes had grown tired. The day had taken it out of him. His whole body hurt, but his ribs had been killing him. But it was too early to take another dose of pain meds so he did some deep breathing exercises.

Finally he closed his eyes and drifted off to sleep, feeling secure and optimistic. He might not have fully understood everything about Thornton's preferences, but from what he'd read, he was intrigued, and frankly aroused, much more than he thought he'd be.

***

He had his seat belt on. He couldn't stop himself from checking over and over again to make sure it worked, his hands shaking, palms sweating, and stomach churning. Lights were coming towards them, and they were passing by other cars so fast they were like a blur. He kept hearing car horns blast and counted in his head the amount of times it happened. He closed his eyes to block out the lights, but he couldn't block out the sounds, so he gripped the hand rest on the door and held on for dear life as he counted all the way up to thirteen.

But the fourteenth, that time was different. That time was followed by screeching car wheels, curses, screams—his own for sure, probably his parents—and a jarring impact that tested the strength of his seat belt. When he dared open his eyes, he wished he hadn't. The screaming argument that came from the front of the car ratcheted up his heart rate, and the tears from the fear, and the pain, and the adrenaline, made his vision blurry.

And then they were moving again, and he blinked the tears out of his eyes long enough for him to see the carnage they were leaving behind.

***

He sat up in bed, gasping, hands clutching at his chest where the seat belt caught him. The remembered pain of the car accident from so many years ago coincided in tandem with the pain from his most recent one. He was covered in sweat from head to toe, shaking, and feeling out of control. He was panting and trying to catch his breath, a sob creeped its way up his throat and, he swallowed it down before it could escape.

Beauty and Beast whined and scooted closer to him, and petting them both brought him some measure of comfort, but it wasn't enough. Both dogs hopped down from his bed, walking as if glued together, and waited in the doorway of his room. He stared at them, and Beast whined, Beauty joining in. They edged out the door and sat in front of Thornton's, and suddenly he didn't want to be alone anymore, the dogs understanding what he needed even before he did.

Crawling out of bed, he glanced at the clock and saw it was 3:45 in the morning. Guilt hit him, something he seemed to be feeling a lot over the last two days since he'd gotten out of the hospital. He stopped and sat back down, not wanting to wake Thornton for something so silly. He was no longer that helpless child. He'd be fine if he just took some more pain meds and went back to sleep.

He reached for the bottle of pills and roughly wrenched the cap off, and the pills went flying. His breath hitched, and suddenly he was exhausted. It was all too much, and he was just so tired. He slid down the side of the bed to pick up the pills and fell apart. He heard the dogs whining and moving around but didn't have the energy to make sure they were okay.

It was dark, and he couldn't see the pills amidst the light carpet, so he just sat there as the tears slid silently down his face. When the hall light flicked on, he turned towards Thornton, who was beside him in an instant, checking him for injuries, his voice frantic. God, Asher was a fucking mess.

"Baby, what is it? What happened? Did you fall out of bed?"

"I dropped them."

"Dropped what, sweetheart?"

"The pills. And I can't find them."

"Okay. It's all right. I'm just going to turn the bedside light on."

He nodded and wiped his nose with the sleeve of his nightshirt. "It hurts."

The light clicked on. "I know. I know it does. The pain woke you up?"

His breath hitched. "No."

Thornton slid his hand up and down Asher's back. "No? What did?"

Asher leaned into the touch. "A nightmare."

"Asher, you should have called out for me."

He wiped his nose again. "I was going to. I didn't want to be alone."

"Then why didn't you?"

He looked at the clock and shrugged. "It's the middle of the night. I didn't want to ruin your sleep."

"I need you to call me when you need me. Do you understand?"

"But..."

"No buts, Asher. I need to know you're feeling safe and secure, taken care of. This is important to me."

Asher nodded, knowing just from what he'd read earlier what Thornton said was true. He leaned into the man's touch. "Okay."

Thornton made quick work of picking up all the pills while Asher sat and sniffled pathetically. Holding out two of the rescued meds, he handed them over to Asher and grabbed the water glass by the bed, handing it to him. Asher took the pills, his equilibrium returning. He steadied his breathing and wiped his eyes, so sick and tired of humiliating himself in front of this man.

"Asher, do you want to sleep alone tonight?" That had his breath hitching again as he shook his head. "Look at me, sweet boy, and use your words."

"Can I sleep in your room? I can sleep on the chaise. I just don't want to be alone right now."

Thornton clasped his chin and lifted his face, so their eyes met. "Do you want to sleep on the chaise?"

Asher refused to be a coward and opened his eyes, shaking his head. "No."

Thornton's smile was a reward in itself, but his words were even better. "That's my good boy. I don't want you on the chaise either."

He helped lift Asher to his feet, turned off the bedside lamp, and then held his hand, leading them into the master bedroom and over to his massive bed that came up to Asher's hip. He made to crawl on the bed, but Thornton put a hand on his back to stop him. "Wait a second and let me help you."

Asher nodded and stood back as Thornton pulled back the covers and picked Asher up, laying him down. Thornton drew the covers up, leaned down, and kissed his lips, a soft caress of warm skin on skin. He watched as Thornton held up a finger and headed back into Asher's room. A few seconds later, he returned, Asher's stuffed train in his hands.

His face flamed as Thornton handed it over. But before he had a chance to feel too embarrassed about it, Thornton pulled the blankets up again, leaned over, and kissed him softly on the lips. Asher's heart thrummed a quick cadence as he watched Thornton round the bed and get in. Turning on his side, he reached for Asher's hand, holding it firm in his. "Is this what you wanted?"

Asher started to nod but caught himself. Forcing himself to be brave, he shook his head. "What do you want, Asher?"

"Will y—" He cleared his throat and tried again. "Will you hold me?"

"I would love to." Thornton slid closer, careful not to jostle the bed. "I'm really proud of you for telling me what you want. It's pretty scary sometimes, isn't it?"

He sucked in a deep breath, the hitching of it making him blush, which in turn made him grateful it was dark and wouldn't be seen. "I'm scared all the time."

Thornton hummed. "Lift your head."

Asher did and felt Thornton's large bicep slip under it, the perfect cushion in the cradle of his arm. The larger man curled himself around Asher, careful with his injuries. "Everyone gets scared. You're not alone in that."

"It never seems to end. If it's not one thing, it's another."

"It's hard to feel safe and secure when you've never been properly taken care of. It doesn't sound like your parents made you feel that way." Asher shook his head, shuffling a bit closer to the heat emanating from the man. Feeling surrounded by Thornton, protected and cherished, was perhaps one of the best feelings he'd ever had. "I want to make you feel safe and secure, sweetheart. I would love to be that person for you. Would you like that?"

"Mmhmm. I feel... I don't know. I doubt myself a lot. And when I'm with you, somehow, I feel less uncertain? Like maybe just having you verbalize that my feelings are valid, and my fears aren't stupid, makes me feel more confident? I know it sounds silly. We've only known each other for a short time."

"That's the best compliment you could give me, and it's not silly at all. I think some people just need to have someone in their lives who helps them see it's okay to be who they are and to feel safe in letting their guard down."

Asher nodded and rubbed his face against Thornton's soft T-shirt. "This feels nice."

Thornton wrapped an arm over Asher's stomach, careful of his ribs, kissed his temple, and murmured into his hair, "I agree. Do you think you can fall asleep now?"

No. He didn't. But he also didn't want to keep the man up all hours of the night dealing with his ridiculous thoughts and fears. So, he did his best not to lie when he said, "I'll try."

"That's not what I asked you."

God, how did he know? "No, I don't think so."

"Good boy. Do you want to tell me what your nightmare was about?"

He pulled in a shaky breath and squeezed his eyes shut. "A car accident."

Thornton squeezed him a bit tighter, careful as ever not to hurt him, his voice shaky when he said, "Fuck, baby. I'm just so angry at myself."

Shit. "No. Not... not ours. It was the night I got lost at the water park."

"You mean the night your parents left you to fend for yourself at the water park."

Right to the heart of it. And he couldn't even argue the fact. "Yeah."

"Do you want to tell me about it?"

"From the police station, my parents took me back to some guy's house. When we got there, everyone was partying and welcomed them back, so—"

"You're fucking kidding me." Asher hunched in on himself and shook his head. "Fuck. Baby, I'm sorry. I'm not upset with you. I'm so... Goddammit. I'm so fucking angry at them."

God, why did that feel so good? Why did he need that validation? Of course, he felt the same exact things, in hindsight. And hell, if he was honest with himself, even at six, he probably felt some of those same feelings. Just remembering it now made him feel so many things. Anger, sadness, and fear.

"It's okay. The guy's wife, or girlfriend, asked me if I was hungry. I was starving, so she microwaved a frozen mac and cheese dinner and left me in the kitchen to eat it. I stayed there because I didn't want to be in the middle of whatever was going on in the other room, which was full of people, alcohol, junk food, empty bottles and cans, trash. The TV was on, there were arguments, people yelling and laughing, and eventually a bunch of strange noises—what I know now was probably sex. In the kitchen at least I was alone and didn't have to see it."

Thornton buried his face in Asher's hair, snuggling closer to him, his stuffy between them. His breath was warm and soft as he murmured, "Jesus, baby."

Asher tried to shrug. "None of it was new. It was like any other time they brought me along with them when they didn't find a sitter. And they never found a sitter. I would have been better left at home, but for some reason they thought they weren't being neglectful if they brought me with them."

"Christ."

"Sometimes I was lucky, and they'd forget I was in the backseat, and I'd sit in the car and wait. It was always nighttime, so I'd started to bring blankets with me, hoping I'd be able to stay in the car, even when it was freezing out.

"Anyway, that time I was in the kitchen. It was hours later, and I had fallen asleep at the table. They came to wake me up, said we were leaving. I knew they shouldn't be driving. I knew. I was fucking six and I knew."

Asher took strength from the soft kisses Thornton placed on his head. "I told them we could just stay. I was comfortable, and they could just crash there. My dad wasn't having it. So, we got in the car."

"God, Asher." He could feel Thornton's body vibrating. Asher knew he was holding back his anger, his protective instincts urging him to fix what couldn't be fixed. It helped somehow. With Thornton's tension rising, Asher's began to fade.

"I put on my seat belt. My six-year-old brain thought I could insulate myself with the pillow I'd brought, so that went beside me against the door, and I bundled the blanket in my lap. I kept checking my seat belt, though, to make sure it worked."

His body relaxed into Thornton's as the man's body thrummed with pent-up energy. Curving his body to the larger man's, he continued, feeling as if he was giving his fears over to the man that surrounded him because he trusted Thornton could take it. Why he knew Thornton could carry the burden, Asher didn't know, but it didn't change the fact that he did.

He continued on, talking about the lights, the speed, the honking horns, culminating in the last one, and the impact, the screaming, and then his parents' escape. The blood and carnage they left behind. "I don't know why they didn't get caught. The park was an hour's drive away, so maybe that was part of it. I don't even know what happened to the people they hit. I don't know if they lived or died. And my parents never mentioned it again."

Thornton murmured in his ear, soft, reassuring words that helped him gain back control so he could continue, "Anyway, I started losing my shit every time they'd try to take me somewhere with a crowd or try to get me in the car when they'd been drinking. But they were always drinking. To this day, I can't get into a car without some spike of panic.

"By the time I was a teenager, there had been several more accidents. None of them were too bad, fortunately. I was fifteen, and god, I didn't want to get my license. Driving a car was the scariest thing I could think of besides being a passenger in my parents' car. But I thought maybe, if I had a license, they'd allow me to drive everywhere, and then they wouldn't get hurt or hurt anyone else. After I got it, I'd offer to drive them wherever they wanted to go. I hid their keys, anything I could do to keep them from getting behind the wheel."

The steady caress of Thornton's fingers, such soothing touches, lulled him into sharing more than he normally would. "They were remarkably adept at functioning in real life. For the most part they kept their jobs. I always had food, a roof over my head. But they always had booze as well, so maybe if we'd been starving, they'd have been sober."

"Jesus. I'm so fucking sorry. I don't know what to say. I can't fix this for you, and I want to so badly it's like a knife in my gut."

"Don't. I'm not telling you this to make you feel bad."

"God. I know that. I know, but I hate it all the same. I hate that I can't go back and be someone you could count on. But I swear to you, I'll be someone you can count on now. Please believe that."

"I do."

He could feel Thornton's body relax around him. "I'm glad. Do you want to…"

"Finish?"

A soft kiss on his head and a murmured, "Mmhmm," had him continuing. "They would sober up every so often. I'd get my hopes up. But it was always so random I never understood the timing. They'd last for a week, a month, six months, and then one would inevitably fail and drag the other down with them. It was one of those failures when it all ended."

Thornton's body tensed up again, and he rubbed his hand over the man's arm, laying on his stomach. "I was going to college. Online courses, which was normal for me. When I began panicking in crowds when I was younger, they'd had to take me out of school, and I'd started taking virtual classes where I could attend school with an actual teacher in live video classrooms. I guess I was lucky they didn't just leave me at home without seeing to my education."

"Jesus."

He squeezed Thornton's arm, reassuring him or perhaps reassuring them both. "Anyway, I was almost twenty and still living at home obviously because I'm nothing if not consistent in my fear of, well, anything remotely related to being a fully functioning adult."

"Stop it." The growl in which those words were issued sent shivers up his spine, but he said nothing. "I won't have you talking about yourself that way."

The tension left his body in a rush, and he felt almost defeated as he continued, "I was living with them to save money while in school. I worked at the flower shop as much as I could to pay for classes. Anyway, one night they were arguing about some party they were going to, and I went out to find their keys while they were distracted, but they saw me, and Dad waved the keys in his hand and told me he didn't need a ride from his kid to get where he needed to go. I tried arguing with him and even appealed to my mom, but she just hugged me and said they were fine."

"Asher…"

It was like Thornton knew this was the end, and it wasn't going to be good. But he couldn't stop the retelling. It wasn't exactly cathartic, or perhaps it was, but it didn't feel good, just necessary. "They weren't fine. I kept trying, but nothing worked. When they left, I called the police, and I think they put out some kind of alert, but they couldn't find them in time, I guess, and I had no idea where they were going. It didn't work, though."

Asher took a deep breath and continued. "They were driving home from whatever party they'd drunkenly driven to, their blood alcohol levels through the roof. They ended up on the wrong side of the highway and ran headfirst into a minivan. They died immediately, but the woman they hit? It took weeks for her body to give out. She left behind three kids under the age of eight and a grieving husband."

He heard Thornton suck in a breath, and he turned onto his side, ignoring the pain in his ribs so he could cuddle into the man who was feeling his pain. "I dealt with their funerals, sold the house, and left town to come here. It wasn't far, a few hours' drive, really, but it was far enough away I felt I could make a fresh start. I was stressed beyond what I thought I could handle. I don't know how I did it, honestly. Desperation, probably. And I think I was in a daze for the first six months."

"You did something for yourself that you needed to do. That takes strength."

Asher made a noise in disagreement. "I couldn't stay in the small town we lived. People knew whose kid I was. And yeah, I rarely left the house, but when I did, even if it was my own paranoia, it felt like I was being blamed by everyone there for what my parents had done, and really, I didn't even disagree. Not then anyway. I've come to realize it wasn't my fault, but it's not like it makes me feel any better about it."

"I'm so glad you understand there was nothing you could have done. They were adults, and mistakes parents make are never a child's fault. Jesus, you're so brave, Asher. So strong."

Asher shook his head, knowing what Thornton said was bullshit. He wasn't strong at all. He was weak in every way.

"Asher, listen to me. Hear me. You had a shit childhood, and even though you may not see it, you're living a good life. You have a beautiful apartment and a career you love. You have friends."

Thornton gently turned his face towards him so he couldn't avoid eye contact like he'd been doing. "You may hate crowds, and driving might give you panic attacks, but you go to work every day. That, in itself, is amazing with your anxiety. You spend time working out. I saw the equipment in your spare bedroom. So, I know you're taking care of yourself. You're healthy, and, in a lot of ways you may not be able to see, you're thriving."

"I feel like a failure, every single day."

The sad noise Thornton made had Asher's heart aching, and he closed his eyes as the man spoke, his voice a soft whisper. "I wish you'd give yourself more credit."

He didn't have anything to say to that. What could he say? Maybe some of that was true, but when he was ordering everything he needed online and having it delivered because he was too scared to leave his house for any other reason than needing to earn a living so he could afford the apartment he locked himself up in, he didn't feel like he was thriving at all.

How could he pat himself on the back when he broke out in cold sweats every time he knew he was going to have to drive somewhere? That wasn't brave; that was cowardly. That wasn't strength; that was weakness. He heard and felt Thornton taking a deep breath before he felt a kiss on his lips. Opening eyes that were gritty with fatigue, he took in the man's beautiful face. Even in the dark he could see his strong features and considered it a minor miracle he was lying in Thornton's bed, held in his arms, receiving kisses from him.

"I'm going to do my best to help you see how wonderful, strong, and brave you are. But right now, I think you're exhausted and need some rest. Are you comfortable like this?"

He didn't want to move, so he nodded. He didn't want Thornton to pull away. The pain meds were still working, and he was comfortable within the circle of Thornton's arms. Feeling just a tiny bit of that bravery Thornton kept insisting he had, he brought his hand to Thornton's chest and gently grabbed the man's shirt in his fist, needing to anchor himself, or maybe anchoring Thornton to him. As he watched, Thornton's eyes moved down to his fist, and then the arm wrapped softly around his waist gently tugged him closer.

"You don't have to hold onto me like I'm gonna go somewhere. I'm not going anywhere unless you want me to. Wrap your arm around me. There you go."

He still didn't think they were close enough. God, why was he suddenly feeling so needy? But Thornton either felt his need or was feeling the same thing he was because he reached down and lifted Asher's leg over his hip as gently as he could, sliding his thigh between Asher's. And suddenly all was right in his world.

He was being held in an embrace that felt like home, taken care of in every way, and made to feel safe and at ease. Two things that were so rare in his life he could probably count on one hand how often they'd happened... before Thornton. And that made him wonder. Would his life forever be segmented in his mind of memories *before* Thornton and memories *after* Thornton? Warmth settled in his chest, something in his brain he barely recognized as hope began to flourish, and he drifted off to sleep wondering how long it would last.

CHAPTER FOURTEEN

Thornton

T hornton woke slowly, a feeling like he was being watched bringing him out of his sleep. He knew not to make any sudden moves, wanting Asher to be able to look his fill without worrying or stressing about it, so he stayed quiet and feigned sleep. And he was happy he did because as he lay there, partially curled around the boy's small frame, Asher's tentative hands began to softly wander over his body.

He was shy with it. It felt more like Asher was learning something brand new, trying to figure out how it worked. It felt worshipful and yet so tentative. He imagined it was like a blind person trying to learn what someone looked like by touching them. It wasn't sexual, but it was hands-down the most sensual thing he'd ever felt, and his body was reacting to it.

He hummed a little, letting the boy know he was awake and slowly opened his eyes. Asher's exploration stopped, and just as he was about to pull away, Thornton moved to capture his hand, which had traveled to his stomach. He rested his palm against the back of it to hold it there. "Don't stop."

Asher let out a little distressed noise, and Thornton let go, feeling such loss when Asher pulled his hand away. "I'm sorry. You were asleep. I shouldn't have…"

"I want your hands on me. I thought you understood that. I would love it if you wanted to explore my body."

When Asher bit his lip, Thornton clasped his hand and placed it back where it had been. Asher gripped his shirt in his hand and gazed into Thornton's eyes. "I should have asked first."

"I'm telling you now: whenever you want to touch me, however you want to touch me, I want you to. If you want to hold my hand, if you want to sit on my lap, if you want my arm around you, you have my permission to touch me however you want. You never have to ask me. If my body can give you comfort, you take whatever comfort you need."

"But, aren't you in control of my body? I thought you wanted control of me. I… I read everything you showed me last night on your iPad, and some of it—"

"Everything?"

Thornton was shocked. He'd given the boy a lot of things to look up. Asher blushed and admitted, "Plus more I found on my own."

Thornton raised his brows. "Asher, did you watch porn last night?"

Jesus. The boy nodded. "A lot of the Daddies wanted a lot of control of their boys."

God, Thornton's dick turned to steel at hearing those words. "There is a measure of control I would want over you. I'm dominant in that way, but it's more about making sure I give you what you need, what you want, within reason, and ensure you and I are doing what is best for your mind and your body."

"So, you wouldn't order me not to touch you? I read that sometimes…" The boy cut himself off.

"Asher, these types of relationships aren't cookie cutter. They aren't one-size-fits-all. When I tell you what I want you to feel comfortable doing, it will probably be different than what another Daddy or Dominant would want. But it's not about them. It's about what works for us. The type of power exchange you are talking about is not the type I want."

"Okay?"

The questioning lilt to that word had Thornton continuing. "You can tell me if I'm wrong. But what I think you need most is someone to help you feel calm and confident, safe, and secure. Someone to help you when you are struggling and someone to take away some of the hard decisions and things you feel you have to do that bring you an enormous amount of stress. Would you like that kind of help and care from someone, or am I off base?"

"I don't know. It sounds... good. Too good to be true, really. I don't even know how that would work. I'm scared I'd do it wrong. I—"

Thornton leaned forward and kissed Asher's lips, effectively silencing him. He leaned their foreheads together. "That's the beauty of this type of relationship. You don't have to stress over doing things right. You don't have to make those decisions. I will make them for you if you are willing to give up that control to me and let go. But you can always tell me no, Asher, no matter what it's about. I will always respect your limits."

"Will I need a safeword? I thought..." Asher shook his head and closed his eyes. "I'll stop asking questions."

Thornton tipped Asher's head up and waited until he opened his eyes again. "You can ask me anything, anytime. I'm happy for you to pick a safeword if you're worried about telling me no. Whatever makes you feel safest."

"I wouldn't need one?"

"Well, safewords are used a lot in relationships where pain play is involved, and the submissive needs to be able to have a word they'd never normally say in a situation where they are receiving pain. The submissive may say *no* or *stop* but not want the pain play to end. The Dominant would know not to stop because they didn't use their safeword. Does that make sense?"

"I don't want that."

"No, and I don't either, Asher. That is not the type of Dominant I am. But if you feel more comfortable with a safeword, then you can choose one for yourself, and I will always listen when you use it. For instance, something I might do where you might need a safeword is wrestle with you and tickle you. If I found a particularly ticklish part of your body, and you screamed and laughed and said no, but you didn't really want me to stop because it was all in fun, you could say *chinchilla*, and everything would stop immediately."

That had its desired effect when Asher giggled. "Chinchilla?"

He chuckled and booped Asher on the nose. He loved seeing the lighthearted look in the boy's eyes. "Well, it's not something you'd normally say in everyday conversation, let alone when I'm tickle-torturing you. So, it would definitely let me know you were serious, if you said it."

"All right, chinchilla it is." Asher let out a snort and then giggled again, grabbing his side when the movement hurt his ribs. "Shit. How do I keep forgetting? It's a constant pain, but sometimes it dulls enough that I don't remember to be careful."

He ran the back of his hand over Asher's ribs in a feather-light caress. "How about some pain meds?" Asher nodded and began to move to get them. "Stay, sweetheart. I'll bring them."

He crawled out of bed and into Asher's room, grabbing a dose of the meds and bringing them back with the boy's water. "Here, take these. I'm going to use the bathroom, and you can do the same if you need to, and then we can continue to chat if you'd like."

"Okay."

He used the toilet and brushed his teeth, then helped Asher out of bed to do his own business and ran downstairs to feed Beauty and Beast. Whenever they wandered back inside the house through their dog door, they'd be hungry. Smiling to himself, he grabbed a few things for himself and Asher as well.

When he got back, Asher was just getting back on the bed and turned as he came in the door. His eyes popped wide, and then he was laughing, clutching his side. "Must you keep making me laugh?"

He chuckled. "I'm sorry. Truly. I wasn't trying to make you laugh. I was trying to bring you a balanced breakfast."

"Pop-Tarts and—what are those—breakfast cookies and juice boxes?"

"Breakfast of champions."

"You really are a Daddy, aren't you?"

He knew Asher was teasing, but he couldn't help but take the question seriously. His face must have shown it too because Asher's smile dropped, but his face remained open, as if waiting for his response. "I really am."

"And you like to spoil your boys?"

"On rare occasions when I'm feeling very generous and my boy has been *very* well behaved."

He rounded the bed and crawled back in next to Asher, dropping his spoils on the duvet. When he glanced at Asher, the boy was biting his lip. "And was I? Very well behaved?"

Jesus, that hit him right in the chest. Did Asher mean what he hoped he meant? He leaned over, clasped Asher's chin, and moved in for a kiss. After several chaste ones, he pulled back. "Yes, sweetheart, you've been very well behaved."

Asher blushed at that and broke eye contact, glancing down to the pile of sugar on the bed. When he didn't appear to want to make a move, Thornton grabbed one of the juice boxes, poked the straw in, and handed it over. The grin on Asher's face before he began to drink from it was one he'd probably remember for years to come. Thornton grabbed one of the silver Pop-Tart pouches and tore it open a little bit, looking in. Hmm, probably not...

He opened the other and showed Asher, who glanced inside. "What's wrong with the other one?"

"Oh, nothing. They're just the kind I like and no one else does."

"Unfrosted?"

Thornton smiled and nodded. "Yeah, they're the best."

"They are."

His smile grew wider. "Seriously?"

Asher grinned and nodded. "*Real* frosting isn't hard and crunchy. Frosting should only ever be soft and sweet. Their version of frosting is like biting through a rock to get to the good stuff."

Thornton laughed, finished opening the pouch containing the unfrosted brown sugar cinnamon Pop-Tarts and handed one over. "I have strawberry ones downstairs, too. We'll have to divest my cupboards of the rocky subpar Pop-Tarts so we can stock more of the good stuff."

Asher grinned, nodding, as he bit into one of the unfrosted treats. He closed his eyes in ecstasy—as one does when tasting unfrosted Pop-Tarts—and hummed as he chewed. "So good!"

Thornton bit into his, eyes closing much like Asher's had. "They really are."

Asher laughed and tossed another piece in his mouth, then followed it up with a sip from his juice box. The noise of the air sucked through the empty box made Thornton laugh. He poked the straw through the second box and handed it over. Asher smiled and drank Thornton's juice down. Once finished, Thornton took both empty boxes from him and put them on his nightstand.

When he turned back, Asher's face was serious when he whispered, "Thank you, Daddy."

Ahhhh, fuck, fuck, fuck. God those words had never sounded so good.

But he couldn't have Asher saying them if… "Don't say it if you don't mean it, sweetheart."

Asher met his gaze straight on. "I mean it."

"Asher…" His voice was a low growl.

Asher shuddered, and Thornton had to file that away for later, enjoying, probably too much, how his voice affected the boy. "I do. I promise. I'm not playing with you. I don't know what the hell I'm doing, and I'm scared to death, but when the hell am I not scared to death? You said you'd help me. You said you'd make the hard decisions. You said all I had to do was let go. You said—"

"Shhh, baby, shh." He moved closer, shoving the remaining food away, careful not to jostle the boy, and rubbed the pad of his thumb over Asher's lips, dislodging a crumb. "I meant what I said."

"So did I." The stubborn set to Asher's jaw made him smile. His gaze took in every inch of the boy's face, looking for doubts and indecision. He saw none. A bit of trepidation, yes, but the boy was resolute in his choice and that's all he needed.

Nodding, he leaned in. "Good boy."

He captured Asher's whimper with his lips as he kissed him with a hunger that was born of desperation. He slid his tongue over the boy's lips, receiving a soft gasp of surprise that allowed him to slowly lick his way into his boy's mouth. "Mmm, baby boy, you taste so sweet." Asher moaned and tried to push forward, to move closer. "Be careful. Let me do the work. I don't want you to hurt yourself."

Asher nodded, closed his eyes, lips parted, and waited. He'd never seen a more beautiful sight. His boy, waiting patiently for him, as he'd been told. He leaned in, but instead of kissing Asher's mouth, he started at the base of his throat and gently kissed his way up Asher's neck, lightly nipped on the boy's ear, and nibbled his way over to those luscious lips.

"You're gorgeous, baby. Just perfect."

Asher began to shake his head and opened his mouth to disagree, but Thornton was having none of it, placing his finger over Asher's lips. "Don't. No negativity towards yourself, Asher. Rule number one."

Asher's eyes popped wide at that. "Ru—" He cleared his throat and tried again. "Rules?"

Thornton gave the boy a soft smile. "What Daddy worth his salt doesn't have rules?"

Asher's bewildered expression wrenched at his heart, but he had to begin as he meant to go on. "We'll talk about all of that later. I don't want to overwhelm you right now."

"But what if I don't agree with the rules?"

He rubbed the back of his hand against Asher's soft cheek. "We'll settle on the rules together. We'll talk about them so we're *both* in agreement. But the one most important to me that I'd like to start with immediately is negative self-talk. You don't give yourself the credit, care, or compassion you deserve. So, I think it's a good idea if we work on that together. What do you think? Are you willing to do that with me?"

Asher nodded. "Yes."

"Yes, what?"

Confusion wrinkled the boy's brows before they smoothed out and he whispered, barely loud enough for Thornton to hear, "Yes, Daddy."

"That's my good boy."

Asher's breath hitched, and Thornton sipped at his lips, sliding his tongue in and groaning when Asher surprised him by sucking on it. Fuck if that didn't get his dick rock-hard. He glanced down at Asher's lap, then his own. "Naughty little boy. Look what you did to us both."

Asher glanced back and forth between them and shook his head. "I didn't…"

"Oh, but you did. You said, 'Yes, Daddy,' in that beautiful, soft whisper. It sounded so needy. I bet just saying it made you hard, didn't it? I know just hearing it made me hard as steel."

A soft whimper, followed by an even softer, "Oh, god," had Thornton nodding, his cheek brushing along Asher's. "I know. I know, baby. You're a natural at this. You're going to be my sweet, perfect boy. Would you like that?"

"God, yes."

"Me too, sweetheart. Me too."

Asher made a needy sound, and Thornton leaned closer, Asher resting his forehead against Thornton's shoulder. He brought his palm up to grip the back of Asher's neck to hold him in place and whispered in his ear, "Your mind is working faster than you can keep up with, isn't it? I want to help you slow it down, focus, so you aren't worrying yourself into a panic attack."

When Asher nodded against his neck and drew in a deep breath, he tightened his grip and began a massage of the boy's neck and shoulders. "I want you to clear your mind of the clutter. Take deep breaths. Close your eyes and think of ocean waves. Can you hear them? See them?"

Asher nodded, his hand making its way to Thornton's shirt at his waist and gripping the fabric tight. Thornton slowly rocked them to mimic the movement of the waves for several moments. "Better?"

The soft, "Mmhmm," helped Thornton relax a bit as well. He kept rocking slowly back and forth, barely moving, just enough for both of them to be aware of the movement. Asher's grip eventually loosened on his shirt, and then those soft, warm fingers found their way to the skin at the waistband of Thornton's pajama bottoms, with sweet little caresses Asher probably wasn't even aware of doing. The boy's tentative touch sent little jolts of electricity straight to his cock.

He ignored it as best he could. "I want you to think about the one thing you want most right now. Not something that is unattainable, but something realistic, something you can have right now if you could only ask for it. It can be anything; a real breakfast, a bath, seeing Beauty and Beast, coloring, or watching TV. Anything at all. Can you visualize it?"

Asher's hitched breath had Thornton kneading the boy's shoulder again and kissing his ear as he whispered, "Can you tell me what it is?"

"I want to touch you."

Fuuuuuuck.

Okay, Asher *was* aware of what he was doing. His sweet boy was going to slay him with his innocence. "You *are* touching me. Is that not enough?"

Asher's fingers stopped moving, and he made to pull his hand away. Thornton clasped Asher's hand and held it right where it was. "Don't pull away. That came out wrong, so let me rephrase. You're already touching me. But do you need more?"

"Mmhmm."

"I need to hear your words."

"Yes."

"More?"

The barest of whimpers escaped Asher's lips. "Yes, more, please."

"You've been so good, so brave staying calm, asking for what you want. You can have more, Asher. You can have everything. Do you want to just feel my skin against yours, or do you want to explore my body?" A shiver ran through Asher, the movement making Thornton's cock leak. "Tell me what that shiver was about, baby. Tell Daddy what you want."

"Oh, god. To explore. Please. Can I explore?"

"Yes. Do you want Daddy naked?" He felt the need to use Daddy as much as possible with Asher. Thornton wanted him to feel comfortable hearing it, so he'd feel more comfortable saying it. That, and it thrilled Thornton to be able to use it with Asher.

Asher lifted his head at that, and their gazes clashed. The boy's eyes were wide, his gaze heated and pupils blown. "Yes, D—Daddy."

"Good boy." Thornton reached behind his head, gripped his shirt in his fist, and dragged it over his head, wincing a bit when his battered body protested the movement. Next, he divested himself of his pajama pants and leaned back against the headboard, pillows behind his back, and watched as Asher took in Thornton's long, lean, muscular build. "Look your fill. Take your time."

But Asher's gaze turned sad as he reached out to touch the bruises on Thornton's torso. "I'm sorry you were hurt."

"Baby, I'm fine. I promise. I'm just a bit achy but it's absolutely nothing like the pain you're feeling. Please don't let this discourage your exploration. I think I need it just as much as you do."

That admission had Asher blushing, but it worked because the boy's gaze went from concerned to heated again. His cock, having already been hard, was pulsing with the beat of his heart. When a minute ticked by and Asher hadn't made his next move, he held his hand out, palm up. Asher finally pulled himself out of his daze and clasped it.

"You can touch me, anywhere. You won't hurt me. I *want* you to feel free to explore. I know this is new. I know it's probably scary your first time, but there's no right or wrong way to learn my body, Asher. I want your hands on me, but there's no rush."

It was like those words broke the spell that had been holding him immobile. Asher's hand, still clasped in his, tugged Thornton's closer, placing Thornton's hand in his lap. Asher traced each finger, one at a time, turned his hand over, and ran his fingers over Thornton's palm and up the inside of his forearm, feather-light touches up and down.

The boy made a noise in the back of his throat, a frustrated sound Thornton wasn't expecting. "What is it?"

Asher tried to remove his own shirt like Thornton had. He watched pain pass over the boy's features and sat forward immediately. "Hey, hey." He pulled Asher's arm down where he knew it wouldn't hurt him. "Do you want me to take it off for you?"

Asher nodded, so he slowly pulled the shirt off him. Sitting back again, he could only smile when Asher made another frustrated sound and pulled the string to his pajama pants loose. Thornton's mouth went dry, knowing what Asher wanted. Sitting back up, he helped the boy free himself from his pants.

What he wanted to do was pull his boy on top of him, flip them over, and kiss and lick every square inch of his boy's skin. But he knew that wasn't possible. Not yet. So he had to let Asher take what he wanted. He folded his hands behind his head so he wouldn't touch. He wanted Asher to take his time and move at his pace. But again, it seemed like the boy had lost his nerve.

"Are you all right? Do you need my hands to guide yours? If you're feeling overwhelmed, you don't have to do anything, sweetheart."

Asher's chest rose and fell as he seemed to come to a decision, and Thornton's heart rate shot through the roof as Asher slowly scooted closer to him on his knees. Then, before he knew what was happening, the boy sat astride his thighs, Thornton's cock lying flush against Asher's. He groaned, but he forced himself not to move.

"What a brave little boy you are."

The sweet blush blooming on Asher's cheeks was Thornton's very own brand of kryptonite. The urge to reach out, draw the boy flush against him, and ravish those sweet lips was almost impossible for him to deny.

Fuckfuckfuck.

The reward was worth it, though, as Asher squirmed on top of him and then leaned forward, their dicks pressing against each other, both of them groaning that time. But instead of touching their cocks, Asher's innocent touch on Thornton's face was a surprise, more a dusting of fingertips over his cheeks and trimmed beard. When Thornton didn't move, the boy's hands moved to his hair, carding through Thornton's thick, dark strands. His palms then ghosted down his arms and into his armpit hair, lightly tugging on it.

Thornton closed his eyes and leaned his head back against the headboard.

And then Asher's breath fanned over his underarm, and the boy was rubbing his face in his armpit. Thornton's eyes popped wide, and he glanced down, eyes glued to the top of Asher's head as his boy continued to breathe him in. Asher's gaze turned up towards his, and he licked his lips and then looked down at the thatch of hair he was rubbing against and rubbed his nose in it again, inhaling.

But it was when the boy's tongue flicked out and licked him there that Thornton nearly lost control and came. "Fuck, baby. What made you do that?"

When Asher pulled away, embarrassment reddening his cheeks again, Thornton lowered an arm and held him right where he was, not wanting him to move further away. "Look at me. Asher, that's the sexiest fucking thing. You surprised me, that's all. I just wondered what prompted that."

"I like your smell there. When you have shirts on and you put your arm around me, I've wanted to do that. It's weird, isn't it?"

He sat forward a bit, cupping Asher's warm cheeks and kissing him, quite thoroughly. There was no mistaking Thornton's arousal as his cock grew even harder against Asher's. The boy's wet, kiss-darkened lips let out little puffs of air, showing Thornton just how affected by him he was. "It's not weird. Nothing you find arousing, nothing you want to do with me, nothing you want to share with me is shameful, Asher. What turns you on is going to turn me on, even if it hasn't been something that has done so in the past, because it's you and because your arousal heightens mine."

"Really?" Christ, when the boy dipped his head, closed his eyes, and then opened them while peering up at him, Thornton's breath caught. That timid, sweet, hopeful look was going to be the one that tripped his damn heart into love sooner rather than later, he just knew it.

"Yes, really."

Asher nodded and then smiled a tiny, little devilish smile, the tease of it making Thornton's cock drip with his arousal. "Okay, then sit back so I can keep exploring."

Thornton smirked and raised a brow, Asher's blush and a stammered, "Please, Daddy," had him complying. "Good boy."

He sat back into the pillows, careful to stay upright so the boy didn't have to strain to touch him. He tucked his hands behind his head again, waiting. Asher's movements were more confident as he leaned in that tiny bit they were separated, sniffed, rubbed his face in the hair there, and then licked. His tongue lapped him there, over and over. Thornton's eyes nearly rolled into his head. He'd never experienced a feeling like it. How the fuck did he not know his own armpits were a damn erogenous zone?

His cock was dripping copiously at that point, and he thought if Asher kept going, he'd come without actually touching his own cock, which blew his fucking mind. But before he could start to worry he was going to go off before he was ready, Asher pulled back, the dilated eyes, pink cheeks, and wet lips almost enough to kill him. "God, you're so fucking beautiful."

CHAPTER FIFTEEN

Asher

Asher had a hard time trying to understand how Thornton could think of him as beautiful, but what he saw in Thornton's eyes couldn't be faked. There was reverence, lust, and so much tenderness in the man's gorgeous eyes, Asher could barely hold his gaze. So he believed it—he believed Thornton looked at him and found him beautiful. He felt his cheeks heat up, a common occurrence around this enigmatic man. Would he ever get used to being the target of Thornton's full attention?

He had never thought of himself in that way. Of course, he had looked at himself in the mirror his whole life, but when he thought about it, truly thought about it, he realized he had only seen the parts of himself individually. His eyes, his hair, his lips. He didn't know why that was. He didn't think of himself as someone with self-esteem issues. He didn't hate what he saw when he looked in the mirror; he was just indifferent to it.

He looked down at Thornton's chest, raised his hands, and ran his fingers through the hair between Thornton's pecs. He could feel Thornton's gaze, but he knew if he met the man's eyes, he might lose his nerve. The fact he was sitting on the man's lap, their hard cocks rubbing against one another, was just too much to be believed.

Thornton wasn't a very hairy man. He had chest hair and a beautiful treasure trail leading down to the thatch of hair above his cock. God, the man's cock was a thing of beauty. He was uncut, a bit longer than average length, but the thickness… holy fucking hell. The thickness was as mouthwateringly sexy as it was terrifying. Because how the hell was he supposed to fit that thing anywhere?

Thornton was so aroused his foreskin had pulled back, fully revealing his deep, dusky, red glans. God, how he wanted to lean down and taste the precum that was dripping down the length of his cock, along the raised line of a vein that he could imagine himself licking from tip to base and back again.

He had to wonder. If he wasn't injured, would he have the confidence to do it? He knew in the past that he wouldn't have had the guts. But something about Thornton and how the man made him feel had him believing that he might just be able to.

It hit him then, what a big deal this was. It was like he'd been given a gift, the most important gift he'd ever been given, and the enormity of that had him frozen in place. Then and there, touching Thornton's chest, the man's coarse hair between his fingers—the magnitude of what he'd said yes to hit him. And Thornton must have seen it or felt it in the shaking of his fingertips, the tension that seeped into his frame. Because suddenly he was wrapped in the man's warm embrace, being offered comfort he didn't even know he needed.

He sucked in a breath, and his whole body started to shake. "Shh, baby, you're all right. I'm here. Wrap your arms around me. Let's just breathe. Feel me take in a breath and let it out. Focus only on that, in and out like waves. Can you picture them?"

He could. He could picture the waves, and he began to calm. He sank into Thornton's embrace, resting his head on the man's shoulder. He felt the tension float away on the waves he could see in his mind's eye. It shocked him how well it worked. How could Thornton come along and not only give him so much but understand him so deeply in such a short time? He had no idea what he'd done to deserve to have garnered the interest of a man as good as Thornton, but he'd be forever grateful.

The fact was, he'd never been in a position to be close with anyone. Being what amounted to a hermit didn't exactly help with that, but being infernally shy when he actually *did* leave his house didn't help matters either. And how the hell could he ever expect anyone to understand his issues? He hated the constant fear and stress he felt, but having someone else be a part of that? It was never something he'd even entertained.

Frankly, he was shocked he was even giving this thing with Thornton a chance. But the man had a hold of him. From the moment he'd opened his eyes at the crash site, Thornton had made him feel less afraid. He thought it had just been a fluke, his scared brain telling him Thornton was some kind of savior, but when the man had refused to leave the hospital and remained with him every second of his stay, he knew those feelings of peacefulness, strength, and trust weren't all in his head.

It wasn't his imagination making him feel like Thornton was somehow going to be an important person in his life. Every moment they were together, Thornton had been proving himself. Every time he talked about his past and learned about Thornton's, he knew, no matter what happened, Thornton would be in his life as a friend, at the very least.

But to be offered so very much more than he thought he'd ever be given... it was like a dream come true. He wasn't about to squander such a dream. He knew it was a once-in-a-lifetime chance to feel normal, to feel a part of something, to be made to feel special to someone, someone who was already special to him. He was a fucking mess, but he wasn't stupid.

So he was going to grab onto that chance, hold on tight, and jump in with both feet. He never thought he'd find himself diving headfirst into a kinky relationship. He could barely even conceptualize a vanilla one, let alone this new world he'd been dropped down into. But something about it, something about the Daddy/boy dynamic, intrigued him.

He wanted to let go. He wanted to be carefree. He wanted to be able to hand over his worries and his constant fears and his ever-present stress. He couldn't think of anyone who wouldn't want to do that. And sure, it may have been offered in a strange, unique package, but that didn't make it any less desirable, any less wonderful, any less intriguing.

He was going to put his everything into figuring out if he could make a man like Thornton happy and maybe, just maybe, make himself happy in the process. Just the thought of it gave him a sense of peace, and he pulled back a bit from Thornton, smiling. "Thank you. I don't know how you do it, but you're like the calm in my storm."

"God, Asher, the things you say. I'm so glad that's how it feels. I want to be that for you. So much."

He nodded, leaned in, and kissed Thornton, tentatively at first, and then with more confidence built on the passion the man made him feel. When he ended it, he pulled back. "Can I keep going?"

"Of course."

Thornton settled back again and left himself open for whatever Asher wanted to do, and Asher wanted to do so very much. But since he was limited, he thought he might just be brave enough, and well enough, to make Thornton feel amazing. Feeling a bit of trepidation, but not enough to stop himself, he trailed his fingers down Thornton's chest, over his beautiful abs, and down into the treasure trail of hair, brushing his fingers in a feather-soft caress there.

When his fingers slipped lower, Thornton's cock was too big a prize to ignore. He trailed a finger from base to tip and down again, tracing a particularly dark, thick vein. But the glans held his attention, so he slid his finger back up and dipped his finger into the shimmery precum that dripped out of it. He slid the pad of his finger down the side of his glans and back up, gathering more of the slippery fluid on his skin and spreading it down the side of Thornton's flared head over and over, until every centimeter of the large helmet head of his cock was shiny with it.

He realized then that Thornton was the one that was full of tension, body shaking beneath him. He glanced up, into Thornton's eyes, and saw a storm brewing in their depths. But instead of scaring him, it gave Asher confidence. He licked his lips and then pulled his bottom one between his teeth and glanced back down.

He looked at his own leaking cock, circumcised and smaller in both width and length. Lighter in color, too. Ignoring his erection, knowing he didn't have the strength nor the pain tolerance to do anything about it, he trailed his finger through another fresh drop of precum at the slit of Thornton's dick. Suddenly, he needed to taste it. He'd tasted his own, of course, but he knew somehow Thornton's would taste different. And he was right.

The groan Thornton let out sent a thrill zinging through him. "Goddamn, baby boy, you're killing me."

Excited by just the thought of that, Asher couldn't hold in his grin, feeling more confidence than he'd thought possible. His voice was breathy when he asked, "Do you like it, Daddy?"

The growl he got in answer had his own drop of precum sliding down his shaft. "You know I do. You're going to be Daddy's naughty little boy, aren't you?"

He gasped at the thrill that shot through his body and straight to his dick at those words. "I think I am." He felt playful and daring when he looked into Thornton's eyes, a flirty smile on his lips, and asked, "Is that a good or a bad thing?"

"Aww, god, baby. It's a good thing. Such a good thing."

Thrilled by that, completely at the mercy of his own hormones, and high on more confidence than he'd ever felt in his life, he wrapped his hand around the girth of the base of Thornton's cock, just enough to move the foreskin up and down his steely shaft. The growled, "Fucking hell," ratcheted up his own arousal even more.

He tightened his grip, loving the helpless noises Thornton was making, and feeling a sense of empowerment at bringing so much pleasure to a man like Thornton. Jacking his hand, agonizingly slow, up and down the large shaft, was almost as pleasurable as it would feel to have Thornton's fist wrapped around his own cock and doing the same.

He tugged on the man's turgid length at a pace he knew would drive Thornton crazy. He'd done it to himself enough times to know that while going fast and hard had its own rewards, going slow and steady, just shy of it being painful, made the inevitable orgasm that much sweeter, that much more powerful.

He paused for several long, drawn-out seconds, met Thornton's eyes, and then started again as he held his gaze. Wanting—no, needing to see Thornton's reaction to the pleasure he was giving him, he refused to look away. Thornton was the first to break when he closed his eyes, tilted his head back, and growled. A sound that made Asher's dick leak so much precum, he was worried he'd be unable to stop himself from coming.

But he didn't want that. He didn't want his own pleasure. He just wanted to give it all to Thornton. And with that single-minded intensity, he began again. He didn't quicken his pace, he didn't tighten his grip, he just. Kept. Going.

Until he stopped. A long-suffering groan escaped Thornton's lips, and he raised his hands and scrubbed his face in obvious frustration. "You're edging me.

Jesus, baby. Who'd have thought you'd be the consummate tease? When I said you could do anything to me, I should have realized you'd be the one man in my life that could bring me to my knees at the first touch."

God, he couldn't mean that, could he? And if he did? Did Asher truly have that power? Did he want that power? It seemed like a heavy weight to bear, and yet, something about it bolstered his confidence and had his heart beating even faster.

He resumed his ministrations: the slow pump, the soft grip, up and down, the foreskin gliding along with him, engulfing the glans on the way up, revealing it on the way down. Up and down, up and down. He lifted his other hand from Thornton's abs and trailed his finger through the precum at Thornton's slit, and he continued using his other hand to jack Thornton's fat cock.

"Fuck, yeah, that's it. So good, Asher."

He could feel Thornton's muscles contract beneath him. Both of Thornton's hands lightly gripped Asher's hips. He knew from the tiny movements of Thornton's hips, his tightly coiled body was doing its best to keep from pumping up into Asher's hand. He could see it was a battle of wills for Thornton, and the thought spurred him to continue the agonizingly slow pace of his movements.

Their eyes clashed again, and he had no words that could describe the animalistic glint he saw in Thornton's. His chest was heaving, and Asher's own breathing was labored, fast little pants he had no hope of slowing when Thornton's piercing gaze wouldn't allow him to look away.

His heartbeat was a fast staccato in his chest, and when Thornton closed his eyes on a groan, he tightened his grip an infinitesimal amount, and that was what tipped Thornton over. The man's eyes opened a fraction, and he lifted one of his hands and brought it to the side of Asher's neck, where he gripped Asher just enough for Asher to feel his domination, even as Asher controlled his orgasm. He felt the first spurts of cum escape Thornton's cock and dribble over his fist: hot, thick, and creamy.

Thornton hadn't moved his gaze away for a second once he began to come. The muscles in Thornton's jaw tightened with every volley of his release, and his eyes narrowed to slits as he growled out between clenched teeth. As Thornton's orgasm wound down, it felt like their connection intensified. Nothing was said between them as they both recovered from what they'd just gone through.

It was the single most intense moment of Asher's life, and his whole body felt more alive than it ever had before. The smell of Thornton's seed was so potent in the air around them; he had the burning desire to taste it. He kept his eyes riveted on Thornton's as he slowly lifted his hand to his mouth and licked Thornton's cum from the backs of his fingers to taste. Thornton's tortured groan as he watched Asher taste his release had Asher's cock leaking more precum.

Thornton sat up, wincing with the effort, carefully wrapped his arms around Asher, and took his mouth in a bone-melting kiss, Thornton's cum still in his mouth. Their kiss was passionate, and Asher whimpered at the taste of Thornton's seed, the combination salty and sweet, their tongues circling around each other, making the kiss all the more potent. He knew he'd never get enough of it and couldn't wait until he could make the man come with his mouth.

"God, baby, that was the most intense orgasm I've ever had. You made Daddy feel so good. I can't wait until I'm able to do the same for you."

Asher blushed and tucked his head into Thornton's neck. "I'm glad you liked it. Thank you for letting me explore."

"I will always be happy to have your hands on me, learning my body, learning what I like. I can't wait to learn yours."

Thornton cleaned them both up and got them dressed. A long-sleeved, button-up flannel pajama shirt made things easier on his ribs, which he figured would help when he had to go back to work. They headed downstairs, Thornton mentioning he was going to fix them something more substantial for breakfast.

"I need to fill out the paperwork for short-term medical for Jenn to submit. Can I use your computer?"

"Yes, of course. Here, I'll show you where the office is and get it booted up. You can work on the paperwork while I make us some real food."

Asher chuckled and followed him downstairs. At the foot of the stairs, Thornton turned left, out of the foyer and down a hall. Asher peeked into each room as they went by them: a couple of spare bedrooms, a bathroom, a...

Holy shit.

He let out a quiet gasp and pushed the door open to what could only be the playroom Thornton had mentioned the day before. The walls were a stunning clash of color and design Asher knew after looking at Damon's sketchbook the night before were all his doing. There was a cityscape featuring a highway leading out of the city with cars, trucks, motorcycles, and semi-trucks. Running parallel to the highway was a train track with trains on it, houses dotted along the hills in the background.

As the highway turned into streets, the streets led to a neighborhood, which led to woods with wildlife of all kinds, which led to a river and then the ocean full of sea creatures, which led to the shore and back to the city. He'd walked into the middle of the room and just taken it all in. All four walls had been painted with such intricate detail he could hardly believe his eyes.

He felt Thornton's presence behind him before he felt the warmth at his back. He didn't know what to say to a man that committed himself so wholeheartedly to making someone else happy. And this room was happiness personified. He'd never been so charmed and delighted, and yet felt so calm and peaceful, as he did in this room. And he'd never wanted to explore a space so much in his life.

CHAPTER SIXTEEN

Thornton

Thornton headed down the hallway leading to his office. Walking to his desk, he woke his iMac, the monitor lighting up with the spreadsheet full of numbers he'd been looking at for one of his businesses. "I'm assuming you have a Google accou—"

When he looked up and found the office empty, he retraced his steps into the hallway and realized Asher must have peeked into the playroom on their way past it. The door had been left partially open, as it always was, but he hadn't thought about it. He could understand why it would have drawn Asher's interest, though, because Damon's artistic talents covered the walls in the room.

Thornton still loved the mural he'd done for his little space. He hoped Asher did too. If not, he'd have to work with Damon to do something more to Asher's liking. He realized that thought was getting way ahead of himself, but he looked at Asher and saw permanence, so he'd be thinking and acting accordingly, with himself *and* Asher, until the time came that he didn't. He sincerely hoped that time never came.

When he stood behind Asher, Thornton gripped his hips and stood flush to the boy's back, resting his chin on Asher's head. "You found the playroom."

Asher fairly vibrated in his grip. "When you said playroom, I didn't... This isn't what I envisioned."

Concerned, he pulled back and turned Asher around, taking in his pink cheeks and vulnerable expression. "Asher, talk to me. What's wrong?"

Asher shook his head, bewilderment obvious. "It's like... It's the perfect room for a little. A wonderland. It's so big—why is it so big?"

Thornton shrugged. "I think it was meant to be a media or movie theater room, not sure. But it's perfect for a playroom, isn't it?"

Asher nodded. "It is. There's even a bed. Is it also a bedroom?"

"No, that's for naptime."

Asher's eyes got big. "Naptime?"

Thornton nodded. "Sometimes little boys need naps when they've had a long day or are feeling overwhelmed."

Asher nodded slowly and turned to look at everything again, still appearing a bit shocked when he said, "I didn't... I don't know what I expected, but..."

"This is a room I put together with my future little in mind." Thornton hoped he put enough inflection in that for Asher to understand it had significance, but he couldn't say more than that. Not yet. Asher was so new to everything; he didn't want to add pressure or stress to the situation.

"Your future little." Asher whispered that, and his eyes grew big.

He turned back around before Thornton could say anything. Thornton watched, heart in his throat, as Asher walked around, hands gripped together in front of him as if scared to touch anything. When he got to the bookshelf with its assortment of children's books, he watched Asher's hand—shaking with some kind of emotion Thornton couldn't decipher—reach out as if to touch the spine of a book.

Turning back to Thornton, Asher's gaze was almost pleading. "Go ahead. You can look at, play with, and touch anything in this room. Nothing is off-limits to you in here." That didn't feel like enough. "That goes for everything, actually. Absolutely nothing of mine is off-limits to you, baby."

Approaching, he watched as Asher touched the spine of one of the books. *The Polar Express*, with its gorgeous illustrations and inspiring message to believe, had always been one of his favorites. The boy's finger traced down the spine, and finally, he found the courage to pull it from the shelf.

Asher held the book in one hand and opened it with the other, turning page after page, his fingers sometimes tracing reverently down the beautifully illustrated drawings that had been done by the author using oil pastels. He couldn't help but ask, "Is that a favorite?"

Asher turned his gaze towards Thornton, and his heartbeat sped up when a tear trailed down Asher's cheek. Stepping forward, he caught the tear on the back of his finger as he traced the track of the tear up Asher's face until his finger brushed Asher's eyelashes. "What is it, Ash?"

Asher closed the book and held it close to his chest, hugging it as he turned and looked around the playroom again. "Why does it feel like home?"

Oh, Jesus. This boy, this beautiful boy was taking him apart piece by piece.

He gathered Asher into him, the boy's arms still holding onto the book, and rubbed his hands up and down Asher's back, soothing him. Not sure he understood, he asked, "It feels like the home you used to have?"

Asher let out a huff. "No. God. My home never felt…" He pulled back a bit and glanced around the room. Thornton sensed he wanted to touch and explore, so he let his inquisitive boy go. "It never felt anything like this."

Asher placed the book back where he'd gotten it and walked slowly around the room, touching the animals in the toy chest of plushies, tapping on the keys of a piano keyboard, and finally trailing his finger up the side of the crane lamp. Its cab was lit, and the hanging wrecking ball was a lightbulb. He turned towards Thornton again, a look of wonder in his eyes.

"Thornton, this is… Wow. I don't think I truly understood what you *meant* by age regression until I saw this room. Reading everything online helped me understand the concept of it, in a big-picture sort of way. It helped me see what it's like for the littles I read about. But it was nothing compared to this. Seeing it firsthand, finally understanding what it could be like for *me*? It's completely different. This is *tangible*. This is *amazing*. And if I'm being honest, a little overwhelming."

Thornton's heart sank at that admission. "I'm sorry you're so overwhelmed."

Asher's head shook, and he made his way back to Thornton, placing a hand on his chest. "God, no. Don't be sorry. It's a *lot*, Thorn." He chuckled and looked around. "I mean, it's *a lot*… but it's… I don't know how to describe it except to say I walked in the door, and my cares, my worries, the stress I feel as a low-level hum in the background of my every day—it slipped away. I felt carefree and excited to discover everything that made up this space. I said it before, but it truly was like coming home, a home I've never had before, but, maybe, the home I'd always dreamed of having."

Thornton felt *so many things*, the biggest of which was mesmerized, truly entranced by this special boy he'd somehow been lucky enough to find, albeit in a rather unorthodox way. Regardless, by some stroke of luck Asher had come into his life, and he couldn't imagine ever wanting to let him go. His voice was rough with emotion when he said, "I'm so glad you feel at home here. That means more to me than you'll ever know, baby."

He gathered Asher into his embrace and held him in his arms, loving the feeling of it and needing the simple comfort. When Asher gazed up at him and touched his cheek, Thornton's heart melted. "Daddy, you've given me a gift. A gift I didn't even know I should have asked for. One I wouldn't have ever known I could have. Thank you."

Thornton leaned down to kiss his beautiful boy, his lips were soft and warm. He couldn't have spoken if he'd wanted to, didn't know what else he could possibly say to make this moment better, so he didn't say anything at all.

They smiled at each other, and he watched as Asher moved around the room, continuing to explore. Fingers grabbed a rubber sensory ball and touched the points of a castle's turrets. And then he bent down and pulled a bin halfway out of one of the cube shelving units and peered inside.

Thornton knew the bin contained wooden trains and train tracks, and Asher looked back at him again, as if seeking approval. Thornton smiled and nodded, wondering what Asher would do. "Do you like trains?"

Asher nodded and pulled out a couple of wooden trains and just looked at them, turning them over in his palm. "I used to play with trains when I was little. I had a small set that looked like one my dad had. I used it until it fell apart. When it finally broke, they wouldn't get me a new one because they said I was too old to play with trains anymore. I always wanted to play with my dad's, but it was a really nice, old, Lionel train set, and he always said I'd break it."

Thornton's heart went out to Asher. "What ever happened to it?"

Asher shrugged, not meeting his eyes. "I have it. It's in a box in my storage closet."

Thornton's shoulders slumped, knowing Asher hadn't ever felt comfortable playing with it on his own. Whether because he still didn't feel like he was "allowed" to or whether he just felt like he shouldn't be playing with toys,

Thornton didn't know. Either way, he'd be doing his best to change both of those feelings. "Maybe you should play with it sometime. It's yours now."

Asher looked around the room as if still taking it all in. "I just…" He shrugged. "I felt silly."

"Why?"

"I guess because trains are toys, and toys are for kids, and… I'm no longer a kid."

"But you can be, if you want to. I can feel the yearning in you to let go and be that carefree child again. Your childhood was stolen from you, in a way. You may have gone through it, but you never felt safe to live it. I don't even know how early it all started for you."

Thornton pulled Asher into him again, felt the boy stiffen in his arms. "Birth."

Horrified, he leaned back to look in Asher's eyes. "What do you mean?"

Asher brought his hand between them and touched his heart and the scar that bisected his pecs. "My arrhythmia is from fetal alcohol syndrome. I had open heart surgery when I was a baby."

Thornton closed his eyes and drew Asher back into his chest. "Goddammit, Asher. I'm… Fuck."

He felt Asher shrug in his arms, as if having a heart condition as a result of his mother's negligence was commonplace. Leading Asher over to the soft, leather, upholstered chair, he moved the ottoman aside and sat, pulling Asher into his lap.

The boy laid his head against Thornton's shoulder and sighed. "I think it scared the shit out of them both, because I had to have surgery so quickly after I was born. They must have realized what they'd done to me. Nothing like the possibility of your baby dying to sober you right up. They went to rehab, and for the first four years of my life, off and on, they were sober. My grandmother was still alive then. She watched me while they were getting their shit together, but then she got too old to take care of me a few years before she passed. She died when I turned eight but was a fairly steady presence in my life until then."

"It sounds like she was there when you needed someone to rely on most."

Asher's voice was quiet in the stillness of the room. "She was. I loved her."

"I'm so glad you had her."

They sat there, Asher snuggled in his lap, and his world felt right. He rubbed

Asher's back, and they were quiet for a while. But when Asher's stomach started protesting, Thornton helped Asher stand. "Your stomach sounds angry at me."

Asher's giggle went a long way towards settling them both. "I think it is. You're obviously not feeding your boy enough."

Your boy.

He'd never ever get tired of hearing Asher call himself that. "Obviously. Why don't you explore the room? There's lots of train track. Some trains are wooden, but there are other trains that are battery-operated. Not to mention a ton of other things you may love."

Asher bit his lip and gazed at the room around him. "I should fill out my paperwork for medical leave."

He rubbed Asher's arms up and down, clasping his hands in his. "There's plenty of time for that. I'll make sure you have time to do it. The last twenty-four hours have been a lot for you, physically and emotionally. I think you could use a little playtime."

Asher glanced over at the train bin and then back up at him. "Are you sure?"

"That's what they're here for, baby boy. Have some little time. I'll make us a quick breakfast, and then when we're done with that, I'll come in here with you, and you can show me what you've been working on."

Asher brought his hands up under his chin as if he was trying to contain himself, and a grin spread over his face. A grin so wide Thornton was sure his cheeks were hurting. He couldn't help but grin back when faced with all that happiness. "Okay, Daddy."

"That's my good boy. I'll come and get you in a bit."

He watched as Asher made his way over to the train bin and chuckled when Asher got down on his knees and gasped as he pulled out another bin that was also full of train paraphernalia. He made a mental note to start looking up the best train sets for kids. He had a feeling he might need to have Damon back to add some more trains to the mural.

He glanced at the tracks painted there already and frowned. "Asher?"

Asher turned, a smile on his face and a bunch of wooden track in his hands. "Mmhmm?"

"Would you like me to have Damon remove the highway and the cars and trucks?" He turned to look again at that part of the mural. "I don't want it to—"

Asher was in front of him then, tugging his head down for a series of kisses on his lips before pulling back. "Don't you dare change a thing. It doesn't scare me or stress me out. This room, the toys, the books, the mural—it's all perfect. I feel like the luckiest boy alive."

"God, baby, the things you say."

Asher's stomach growled again, and he patted it, looking up at Thornton. "It's angry, Daddy."

Chuckling, he leaned down to peck Asher on his nose and then walked out as he said, "Breakfast for my boy, coming right up."

***

When he was done fixing breakfast, he made his way back to the playroom and found Asher asleep against the life-sized bear sitting in the corner by the cube shelving unit. He glanced at the two bins of train track and saw some track built and other pieces scattered about, with a few trains coupled together on them as if his boy had started to play with them and then given up.

He realized then and there it was way too early for his boy to be playing with toys on the floor. He'd probably started hurting and had realized the most comfortable spot close by was the enormous panda bear. He knelt beside Asher and ran his hand down the boy's cheek until his eyes opened. "Hey, sweetheart. It was too much, too fast, wasn't it?"

Asher nodded, blinking sleepily up at him. "It started to hurt."

"I shouldn't have left you alone in here."

Asher smiled. "It's okay. I'm glad I got to see the room. I'm excited to be able to play when I'm feeling better."

"I'm going to pick you up off the floor. I think if I tried to help you stand, it would hurt even more. Keep your hands in your lap, okay?"

Asher nodded, and then he had the boy in his arms and headed to the kitchen. "I can walk if you put me down."

"I know you can, but I've got you. I'm feeling a bit guilty. I should have realized how quickly you'd tire out."

"I knew you were coming back soon. That's why I didn't call out for you. If I'd have been really hurting, I'd have called for you, I promise."

"Thank you. That makes me feel better. I don't want you suffering when I could be helping you."

He set the boy down at the kitchen table in the spot he was coming to think of as Asher's. They both dug into their food, the silence between them comfortable.

When they were done, Thornton cleaned up and led Asher to the office, waking his iMac and letting him do what he needed to do in order to get paid while he was out of work with his injury.

"Do you want me to leave you alone?"

Asher shook his head. "Please stay. I'll try to hurry."

"Baby, there's no need to rush. I'll get some of my own work done while you're doing that."

Asher stood. "If you need the computer, I can probably figure out how to deal with all this on my phone or your iPad."

Thornton walked around the desk until he was standing only inches away from Asher. "I'm used to getting work done while I'm mobile. I'm perfectly capable of doing what I need to do on my iPad while you use the computer."

Asher nodded and got to work, and Thornton did the same, sending an email to one of his assistants to cancel his face-to-face appointments the following week to allow him to be at home with his boy. He'd either have to make them up when Asher was better able to care for himself and could be left alone or take care of them over the phone.

That done, he went through several contracts he'd been mulling over, signed them, and sent them back to his lawyer to deal with. By the time he was wrapping up, so was Asher, and the boy looked exhausted. "Why don't we go watch a movie or some TV, and you can rest?"

Asher sighed and rubbed his eyes. "I'm tired of being tired."

"I know. I'm sure it's frustrating when you're not used to being so inactive. You can color if you'd prefer, or we can talk if you want. Maybe this afternoon, after you've rested a bit, we can take a short walk outside if you're up to it."

"I'd like that."

"Good."

Asher got up, rounded the desk, and held out his hand for Thornton to hold, a vulnerable look clouding his expressive eyes, as if doubting Thornton would take it. Thornton clasped it immediately but turned to face him.

"Don't ever be shy or feel worried to reach out to me. Touching and affection isn't something I'll ever reject from you. It doesn't matter when or where we are —I will always welcome it."

His sweet boy was starved for human contact, and he craved giving it to Asher so badly he was worried the boy would eventually feel drowned by it.

They'd have to see. He settled Asher on the couch, his soft, fleece throw blanket tucked around him. Handing him the remotes, Thornton said, "Find something you want to watch. I'm gonna grab us some drinks. Do you want milk, water, or juice?"

Asher's cheeks pinked. "Juice, please, Daddy."

"Okay, be right back." He mentally chastised his dick for being so reactive to that word coming from Asher, and headed into the kitchen. He wasn't going to second-guess himself this time and opened up his drawer full of his little supplies, grabbing a cup with a lid and straw. Grabbing himself some water and filling Asher's cup with apple juice, he headed back into the family room. He sat in the corner of the couch, where Asher curled into him without any prompting, warming his heart.

Still flicking through channels, Asher hadn't paid attention to what he'd brought with him until Thornton handed it over. The TV forgotten, Asher stared at the clear cup with the swirly blue straw that spiraled along the edges of the inside of the cup. They sat in silence for several moments, the TV a low hum in the background, some Shopping Network show Asher had stopped on when Thornton had handed him his drink.

He waited with bated breath, wondering how Asher would react. His boy turned his gaze to Thornton's and then back down again and up once more, a small smile morphing into a much bigger one. Thornton smiled back and chuckled when Asher shimmied a bit in his seat and took a sip of his juice, settling back into the crook of Thornton's arm.

That sweet bit of enthusiasm for something so simple made Thornton excited to share other things with him as well. He realized he should have served Asher breakfast on one of his fun plastic plates and given him the matching silverware as well. He'd just have to do that at lunch.

After a bit more flipping, Asher settled on some kind of baking contest. Asher fiddled and looked at the cup more than he did the TV. Thornton knew he had something on his mind and was trying to come up with the words to express it.

He felt rather than heard Asher's deep breath and winced when the boy realized it was too deep and rubbed gently at his ribs. "I have plastic and metal insulated cups at home with lids and straws. They aren't kid's ones—they're the adult ones people use for ice water and coffee, you know? But I put stickers on them. I have regular glasses too, but I always end up using the insulated ones with the lids and the straws. I tell myself it's to keep myself from spilling, but… maybe that's not the reason?"

He turned his gaze towards Thornton, confusion marring his brows. Thornton reached to smooth out the wrinkles between his brows. "Maybe it's not." Shrugging, he continued. "What other things can you think of that you do or use that might also be used by a little?"

Asher looked down at his cup again and took a long sip of his juice. "When I'm eating things like yogurt, pudding, or ice cream, I always use these tiny little spoons. I bought some of those plates where kids can paint on them and then you bake them, so you can eat off them. I got them for Gigi, but she gave me one of the ones in her box, and I made one with her."

"Do you use it?"

Asher nodded, still not meeting his eyes. "I got myself a box, and now I have five. I don't eat off anything else."

God, his boy had been a little aching to be let free for probably longer than even Asher would ever know. "What else?"

Asher shrugged and took another sip. "You've seen my train stuffy. I like wearing socks with little pictures on them, and some of my underwear has designs on them too."

"I noticed that when I packed for you."

More blushing. "Maybe it's not really a little thing, but I play a lot of kids' games on my phone, like Bejeweled, Candy Crush, Mario Run, and Bubble Coco. Oh, and I have a nightlight in my room."

"And when you use these things, do you feel guilty or silly?"

"Sometimes, yeah. If I have Madi and Gigi over, I'll give the plate that I drew with Gigi to her to use, and I'll use regular stuff for Madi and me. And I always bought adult coloring books only because I didn't want to think of it as being for little kids. If it was for adults, it was okay, you know?"

"I do know, but now you don't have to worry about that anymore. With me, you can get into your little headspace without worry or fear of being caught or judged. You needing to regress isn't something to be ashamed of. It's okay to play with trains and stuffies. It's okay to color with crayons. It's okay to use whatever dinnerware makes you happy. This isn't about what you think you *should* do; this is about what your heart knows you *want* to do. I hope it's something you'll come to embrace in time. Something that feels natural for you."

The smile on Asher's face was tentative. "Yeah, I hope so too. I really can't wait to use the playroom and—I don't know—maybe I can get myself some of the coloring books I've wanted to buy but wouldn't allow myself to."

"That's my job now, Asher. You let go, and I take care of you and your needs, whether they are physical, emotional, or material. That's my job as your Daddy. Your job is to allow yourself the freedom of being your little self. You are always safe to do that with me. Your desire to play and color and let go of your adult self to allow yourself to be little—it's not something to be embarrassed about. I don't ever want you feeling ashamed to be who you truly are."

"Just... can you be patient with me? It's going to feel strange at first. I think a good strange, but it may not come easy for me."

"I'm a very patient man, Asher. I won't be rushing you into anything you feel uncomfortable with. That's a promise. But I don't think it's going to be such a hard transition for you. I think there's been a little inside of you since you were young. A little boy craving and needing approval, supervision, guidance, and love. I will give you all of those, sweetheart."

"Yeah, I think I've needed those things too. I don't think I'd have ever seen it on my own, though. I don't think I'd have understood what I really craved until I read about it and saw for myself what it would feel like. I think I've needed it for a long time but didn't know what it all meant or why I felt the way I did."

"I think all you're going to have to do is allow the instincts you've buried under perceived socially acceptable behavior to be free. It's okay to get excited and to show that excitement about toys and games and such. I can't wait to see you take to it with enthusiasm. If it comes slower than I think it will, like you're worried about, that's okay. But if it comes quickly because you lean into it and yearn for it, that's okay too."

Asher nodded and took another gulp of his juice, and then the sound of the straw drawing in air let Thornton know he was all done. He took the cup from Asher and set it down beside his water glass. Knowing it was a lot to process, he said no more and just enjoyed the feeling of Asher snuggled up next to him. They finally settled into the show, and eventually, Asher took a short nap.

His business brain took over at that point. He often couldn't help himself, but this time around it wasn't for his own business—it was for the potential of

Asher's and Madi's joint purchase of The Glasshouse. When Jenn had spoken about it at the hospital, he could see the nervous looks on Madi and Asher's faces, but he also hadn't missed the spark of interest they'd both felt.

It had been obvious to him and, he assumed, Jenn as well. She was clearly a savvy businesswoman. He remembered the controversy years ago when she'd decided to grow cannabis. The local newspapers were all aflutter in both outrage and support. It was a business that could grow even more, if given the chance. He wondered how much land Jenn actually owned and if growth was physically possible in that single location. He'd need to look into the legalities of it all as well, if he was going to help Asher navigate the purchase.

He wouldn't be pressuring his boy in any way, but he'd definitely be sharing his opinions on the subject before too long. He didn't want Asher to put off thinking about it while he was recuperating. It was an enormous decision, and he'd need the time away from the daily grind to really work through how he felt about it and to understand all the angles before he could figure out if it was what he truly wanted.

As Asher's Daddy, he wanted to jump in feet-first and navigate all the business decisions with him, but throwing his weight around so early on in their budding relationship wasn't the best idea. So he'd have to put together some of his thoughts and ideas and see what Asher thought about it. With that in mind, he started making a list of questions, research needed, and possible ideas for his boy. It was just the type of thing that got his creative juices flowing.

CHAPTER SEVENTEEN

Asher

It was Sunday, five days after the accident. In a lot of ways, he was feeling so much better. Physically, he had a long way to go, but taking deep breaths was getting a bit easier, and he could go longer without needing to sleep the day away. They'd taken a walk the day before and planned on another one before dinner. But it was nearly two in the afternoon, and Madi and Gigi were on their way over to visit them so Gigi could meet Beauty and Beast.

Asher was nervous for their visit, and he didn't understand why. Or, rather, he was trying to deny understanding the reason why. He recognized the changes in himself, even just over the last couple of days. There had been a fundamental transformation in the way he saw himself, in the things he thought he knew about himself. That seismic shift couldn't happen without ripple effects.

He'd somehow gained and lost confidence, which was quite a mindfuck. Gained in that he'd admitted the truth about his needs and wants now that he had a name for them. Lost in the way that change always left him reeling and feeling unbalanced. Madi would see the changes in him and call him out on them, or at the very least inquire about them, and he wasn't sure he was ready to verbalize the swirling thoughts and emotions in his head yet.

At the same time, he knew he could trust Madi completely, so he knew he'd cave if she poked and prodded enough. And she would. It was one of her superpowers: seeing things people didn't want to be seen and delving right into them with a strong desire to help. Asher loved her for it. He also hated her for it. Okay, perhaps hate was a strong word, but she had a way about her that made it nearly impossible *not* to tell her your innermost thoughts and feelings.

It was how she'd ended up driving him to work four out of the five days he worked each week and how she managed to know just when he'd been alone one too many days and would show up—sometimes with Gigi, sometimes without—at his place, forcing him to be sociable, if only with her.

She'd bring him his favorite takeout or bake him a lasagna; she'd stop by during the times he usually spent working out and use his home gym with him or tell him they were going to watch a movie she somehow knew he wanted to watch but would deny it until halfway through the movie when she'd poke him in the side and make him admit she'd been right.

The fact those movies were often animated, or kid-rated, maybe should have clued him into what he needed, but again, how could it have done so when he never even knew what he desired even existed? Jesus, it was all a jumbled mess in his mind. A jumbled mess she'd see when she looked in his eyes. She had an uncanny instinct about when he needed to unload his emotions. She was a true friend that way.

The doorbell rang, and his nerves must have been showing because Thornton leaned down and clasped his face, kissed his lips, and rubbed their noses together. "It'll be all right. You guys have lots to talk about."

"I know. I'm just… So much has changed."

"Ash, who you are at your core hasn't changed one bit. You are still the same caring, loveable, sweet, smart, beautiful boy you've always been. The only thing that's different is that now you know yourself better than you did a week ago. I hope you can take comfort in that."

Thornton was right. He *was* the same person; he'd just discovered some new things about himself that had opened his eyes to a whole new world. That wasn't a bad thing, especially since he hoped the things he'd learned would lead to him being a happier version of himself. There *was* a certain amount of comfort in that, but also a certain amount of uncertainty as to the shift in his status quo. But he knew it was only a matter of time until those changes became his every day, his normal, and, he hoped, eventually brought him a level of happiness he'd never felt before.

They walked hand in hand to get the door, and when they opened it, Gigi was bouncing on her toes. "Where are the puppies? I want to—" She let out a gasp and a squeak as she started towards them. Madi caught her arm before she could launch herself at the dogs.

"Gigi, where are your manners?"

Gigi, looking a smidge chagrined, waved and smiled. "Um, hi, Asher and Mr. Hayes."

Thornton chuckled. "Hi there, Gigi. Just call me Thornton."

Madi ran her hand down her daughter's intricate braids. "And you can't just go running at a pair of huge dogs like that. You could get hurt if you're not sure they're safe."

"But, Mama, they wouldn't have invited us over to see them if they weren't safe."

Thornton crouched down to Gigi's level. "They're super safe," he gazed up at Madi and added, "and fully trained. And I told them you'd be coming, so they're excited to spend time with you. Beauty is the pretty girl in the purple collar, and Beast is the one in the blue collar. Beauty is blind, and Beast is basically her seeing eye dog. But she can pretty much do anything he can do, including play fetch, which I know they'd love to do with you."

Gigi's eyes continued to get bigger and bigger with every word Thornton said. When he was done, she was bouncing on her feet and clapping. "Fetch, Mama. Can I play with them now?"

Madi chuckled. "Yeah. Go for it."

Gigi squealed and ran towards the dogs, falling to her knees in front of them and hugging them both. She giggled when both puppies licked her face, and then she proceeded to ask for dog toys so they could play. Thornton glanced at them and smiled. "That is a girl after my own heart. I think we'll go outside and see how many times we can get the dogs to fetch. How's that sound, Mom?"

Madi's smile was huge as she nodded. The way to Madi's heart was to treat her daughter well. Warmth filled Asher's chest when he realized Thornton would be good for Madi and Gigi too. As Thornton headed with Gigi towards his mudroom to grab some toys from the dog bin there, Madi turned her shrewd gaze on him, and his face flamed under her scrutiny.

"Wow, do you have a lot to tell me."

Asher's mouth dropped open. That was fast, even for her. "How do you *do* that?"

She crossed her arms over her chest and smirked. "Your face is very expressive, and I know you. Come on, let's dish."

She put her arm through Asher's, and he led them through the foyer and down the hall towards the family room, where they both sat on the sofa, facing one another. He winced when he turned his upper body a bit too much, and she placed a hand on his shoulder. "Shit, I didn't even ask. How are you feeling?"

Asher wiggled his palm back and forth. "Eh. So-so. I get tired easily, and I can't do much of anything on my own, really. So that sucks."

She raised her brows at him, a smile playing at her lips. "But does it? Does it *really*?"

Catching her meaning, he blushed and covered his face with his hands. "Oh my god, Madi. Yes, it sucks! Okay, not *all* of it, but it's not fun having to ask for help for the simplest things or forgetting you can't do them and the pain nearly taking you to your knees when you do things without thinking."

She pouted and rubbed his thigh. "I'm sorry, boo. I know it's painful, and it really does suck. I was just giving you shit. I know some of the attention and help he's giving you is probably amazing, but some of it is probably embarrassing and frustrating."

That pretty much summed it up, so he nodded. "Yeah, that's it exactly."

She leaned in then and brought her hand up as if to cover her mouth so no one else could hear—regardless of the fact no one else was in the room—and whispered, "I bet he's really thorough when he's giving you a sponge bath or a shower."

Asher blushed from the top of his head to his waistline, the heat of it burning him up. He closed his eyes and shook his head. "I am *not* talking about this with you."

She let out an indelicate snort. "Yeah you are. You won't be able to help yourself. That man is the first one you've ever let near you long enough to get to know you, and you're practically shacked up with him as he takes care of you while you're convalescing. You've been *dying* to tell me every sordid detail."

Covering his face again, he whispered, "Not *every* detail, but I will admit he's very, very thorough."

She let out a squeak, much like her daughter's, and wiggling a bit on the sofa. "I *knew* it!" She rubbed her hands together, a maniacal gleam in her eyes. "Spill."

So he did, sharing a lot of what had physically happened since they'd last seen each other. When he was done, she narrowed her eyes. "There's a lot you're not telling me. What secrets are you keeping?"

Asher groaned and squeezed his eyes shut. When he opened them, the look in his eye must have let her know this was something he wasn't going to treat as a joke. She reached forward and clasped his hand. "What's wrong? Isn't he treating you well? The look on your face is making me nervous, Ash."

Not wanting her to get a bad impression of Thornton, he reassured her immediately. "God, Madi, I don't have anything to compare it to, but I've never been treated with more care, more affection, or more thoughtfulness. There isn't a thing I need that he hasn't thought of or tried to take care of before it even becomes bothersome. Thornton's so attentive, and god knows I don't understand it, but he's interested in me. Like seriously interested."

"That's amazing! I'm so happy for you, Ash." She paused and searched his face, her brow furrowing. "All of that sounds like great news. What are you worrying over?"

Asher sighed and shook his head. "You know me too well." She waited calmly, not responding, just watching him too closely for comfort. "It's complicated."

She didn't even need to roll her eyes at him; her exasperated expression said it all. "Then uncomplicate it for me."

He knew she'd eventually get it out of him, and he didn't know how long they had before the dogs got tired out. "Do you remember when we talked on the phone the first night I came here?"

"When you were waiting for that gorgeous male specimen to bring you dinner in bed, you mean?"

Asher's cheeks heated, and he looked down at his lap, picking nonexistent lint from his sweats. "Yeah. Do you remember what you said about him?"

"What, that he wanted to take care of you and didn't want you to get hurt again?"

His gaze slid away as he shook his head. "Um, no. The other thing."

She got a far-off look in her eyes as she tried to remember before she shook her head.

He leaned in closer and whispered, "You said I'd landed myself—"

She gasped and clapped her hands over her mouth, eyes big as saucers. Pulling her hands away, she exclaimed, "No way!"

Asher's eyes, feeling as wide as hers were, stayed on her face as he nodded without saying another word. She covered up her mouth again, her words a bit muffled when she spoke. "Oh. My. God! He's a Daddy?" He nodded again. "Holy shit, Asher, he's a Daddy!"

"He is." It was a whisper, and he didn't quite know what else to say about it.

"I mean, obviously I said it for a reason. He acted like one, but sometimes guys are just that type. But like, a real *lifestyle* Daddy?" He apparently couldn't stop nodding. "Wow. That's…" Her tone gentled. "… kind of perfect for you."

That surprised him. He hadn't known what to expect, but the fact she saw it right away baffled him. "Why do you say that? Am I *that* broken?"

"Ash, we're all a little broken. You've been through more than most, but that's not what this is about. You need someone in your life that will make you his top priority. Someone who will care for you like no one ever has. Someone who will give you attention and affection, both of which are things you've been starving for, even if you didn't know it. I don't know why I didn't think of it before now."

"I didn't even know it was a thing."

She snorted and rolled her eyes, laughing. "You said you didn't think he had any kids."

Asher covered his face. "Oh my god. How can I be that clueless?"

They both dissolved into laughter, and though his ribs hurt like hell, it was the best feeling. When they stopped, her eyes popped wide again. "Wait. What kind of Daddy is he? He's into age play, isn't he?"

"Thornton doesn't like to call it age play because he said it makes it seem like it's all a game. He calls it age regression."

Her smile was full of emotion, and her eyes got a little misty when she said, "You're a little. It makes so much sense, Asher. I never would have thought of it as a possibility, but now that it's right in front of me, I'm like… duh."

"At least you knew it was a thing that existed. I had no clue. But he's helped me see the things I already have and do in my life that are part of my regression —the coloring, straw cups—"

"With the stickers," she interrupted.

He nodded. "The easy little kids games I have on my phone, the plates I decorated…"

"The one you made at my place with Gigi?"

"Yeah, but I got my own set of four and decorated those for myself. And I have a stuffy I sleep with, and I still have my dad's train set."

"Wow. I didn't know all that. But it all makes a lot of sense. I think it's pretty remarkable he found you."

Asher smiled. "Ran over me, you mean?"

She snickered. "It was serendipity."

Asher thought about that for a few moments. "Yeah. Maybe it was."

"I'm so happy for you."

"Thanks. It's kind of scary and fast, but it feels good. I haven't had a lot of that in my life."

"You haven't. But you deserve it more than anyone I know."

"Thanks." Asher looked down at his hands and then realized he needed to talk to her about the elephant in the hospital room. "Speaking of scary." He looked at her, and she must have sensed his change of mood because she sat up straight and met his gaze head on, a serious expression on her face.

Understanding hit her, and at the same time, they both said, "The Glasshouse."

She sighed and deflated, and he could feel her overwhelm because it mirrored his own. But they needed to talk about it, no matter what, and Thornton was right —they needed to make use of the time they had while he was on leave. It was a huge decision and not one that should be made without thinking it through and understanding all the ins and outs.

Asher reached out and touched her hand. "So, what was your initial reaction when she asked us?"

"You mean besides the heart attack she nearly gave me?"

He smirked. "Yeah, besides that."

Madi huffed and shook her head. "I don't know. Fear?"

"What scares you most?"

"Everything."

"You sound like me, my whole damn life."

She turned her hand over and clasped his. "It sucks."

"It does. But can you maybe narrow it down to the biggest fears you have about it?"

Madi lifted her other arm and rested it on the back of the couch, leaning her head into her palm. "I guess I'm scared if we don't do it, another buyer will come in, change everything, fuck it all up, and make it something we don't want it to be. And…" She heaved a sigh so big he felt his heart constrict. "I'm also worried if we do this together, it will come between us. I can't lose you because of some business. I don't want to do it if it's going to break us. And, like, what if it's too much for us to handle alone? We don't know what the fuck we're doing when it comes to owning our own business. I mean, jeez, Ash, this business makes millions of dollars, and… and… we're still practically kids!"

Asher had felt every single one of those fears since Jenn had talked to them about it. He couldn't blame her for any of those thoughts, but… "You know me. You know how I am. My anxiety hits me hard sometimes. I don't want to be the partner that doesn't pull their weight or causes issues."

Madi scowled. "Asher, you know more about every single plant in the greenhouse than anyone else, including Jenn. You rarely ever need to help customers, that's *my* job. I think we're perfectly suited to run it together if we can get past the other stuff."

He looked down at his lap and sighed. "I know. It's really the only thing in my life where I'm one hundred percent confident. But still, I've gotten overwhelmed with customers before. I just worry I'll fail you in some way."

"That won't happen. You care too much. I've seen you in the past when you've been out of your depth and feeling stressed—you always make sure to get the customer the help they need with one of our associates before you excuse yourself. But that rarely happens. You usually handle customers just fine when it's one on one and they are talking about the plants you love."

He let out a relieved breath, knowing what she said is true. "Are you sure you trust me that much?"

Madi made a disgruntled noise. "I'd trust you with anything, Asher. You're my person. Not to mention, we wouldn't sell half of the things we sell if it wasn't for you growing everything, learning about new plants to add to our ponds, and basically making everything flourish around there. The place wouldn't be as successful as it is without you. I wouldn't go into business with anyone else."

His shoulders relaxed and he nodded. "You're my person too. I wouldn't want to do this with anyone else. Thank you for trusting me." She leaned in for a gentle hug, and when she leaned back again, he grinned. "So, what about it excites you? You're obviously interested enough to really be thinking about it. What are the things that make you the most enthusiastic about it?"

She leaned a bit forward, a spark alight in her eyes. "This is a solid, longstanding, very successful business. And we know it, inside and out, when it comes to making it run. We don't know the money or paperwork side, but we know everything out front, the stuff that actually makes the money, right?"

He nodded, her enthusiasm catching. "Right."

She squeezed Asher's fingers in hers. "And I already said it—The Glasshouse makes millions every year, and I honestly don't think we know the half of it. She pays us well, and we have great benefits. I can't complain. But I still wonder how I'm going to put Gigi through college. And before that, I'd like to own a home where she can have a backyard to play in and a puppy of her own."

"Those are all good reasons to get excited about it for sure."

Her gaze grew serious. "And if I am going to own a business with anyone, I'd want it to be with you. I don't trust anyone else in this world as much as I trust you."

Asher sucked in a breath and made the leap. "First, regarding your fears, the only way we can ensure there isn't another buyer that could possibly fuck it all up is if we say yes. Second, you could never lose me. Nothing business-related would ever mean more to me than you. If we do this, we won't let it come between us. Third, we're not kids. Not really. We have careers. Sure, we fell into them because the jobs interested us, but we're both managers there and have been for a couple of years because we love what we do, and we do it better than anyone else. Jenn doesn't make stupid business decisions, so you know we're the right people for the jobs she's given us *and* for the one she's offering us now, or she wouldn't be offering."

Madi's eyes grew wide. "You want this."

His shoulder slumped. "A big part of me does. Another part is scared to death. But I can't figure out if that's the fear that always seizes me when things are new or about to change, or if it's really the thought of owning this business and possibly failing at it that's doing it."

"Who the hell is going to approve us for a loan of the size required to buy it?

I mean really. I don't have bad credit, but we're in our early twenties, and I don't know any bank that would be willing to take that risk."

He nodded. "Yeah. I get that. But she is motivated to sell it to us, and I'm sure it helps that we have worked there for years. She's probably got all her ducks in a row, all the I's dotted and the T's crossed, just waiting for us to give her the nod. You know her. She wouldn't be asking us if she wasn't A, totally confident in us, and B, ready to help us do what we need to do to move forward with her plans."

Madi snorted, nodding. "She's diabolical like that."

Asher chuckled, agreeing. "She really, really is." He sobered up then. "So, I'd been avoiding thinking about it, and Thornton brought it up. He's the one that kind of pushed me to stop ignoring it and to make use of the time we have while I'm out on medical leave. He's offered help in any way we can use it."

"Really? Does he own a business?"

"Yeah, actually. This is basically his job. He runs a business that is all about buying other businesses. He's a very successful business investor, from what I can tell. From the size of this house for one, but I've also..." He felt his face turning red, covered his face with his hand, and cleared his throat. "Googled him."

Her guffaws embarrassed him further. "You googled your Daddy."

"Oh my god, stop."

She continued to giggle. "I can't. It sounds so dirty, and it's just so... you."

Asher rolled his eyes at her. "Yeah, yeah. Anyway, so he will know everything there is to know about buying a business, getting loan approvals, working up a business plan and prospectus, and all those little details we would know nothing about. I think we have a real chance, if we're both fully on board and ready to commit. But I know we need time to think about it and start to figure out how to deal with everything."

"Okay, so are you, like, one hundred percent sure you want to do this?"

He sighed and admitted, "No. But, I'm leaning towards it. That place is my life and I love it too much to see it get taken over by some greedy corporate types looking to make bank on a business they know nothing about and have put zero work into making a success."

Madi nodded. "I know. I'd be miserable if that happened."

"Exactly. So, are you sold on the idea of us doing this?"

"I want to. I'm just not completely ready to commit to it yet."

"Yeah, it's a lot to think about. Do you wanna mull it over, and we can talk again tomorrow?"

"That sounds good." And just as she finished speaking, they heard the back door open, Thornton chuckling, Gigi giggling, and the mad dash of Beauty and Beast's nails on the hardwoods. They grinned at each other, and both said, "Perfect timing."

"Mama, oh my gosh, the puppies are amazing! They can fetch. Even Beauty, and she's blind! It's like she just knows. She runs like she's connected to Beast and when he slows down, she starts sniffing around for the toy and finds it before he does sometimes. And other times they both wrestle for it and see who wins, and then sometimes they both run back with the same toy in both of their mouths. They're so fun! I want a puppy, Mama!"

Gigi jumped in Madi's lap in her excitement, but the jarring movement of the sofa bouncing under Asher shot pain through his ribcage, causing him to gasp and clutch his side. Gigi stopped moving when she realized what she'd done. "I'm sorry, Asher. I didn't mean to."

Her sniffles made him feel horrible, so he reached out and clasped her hand in his. "It's okay, Gigi. It was an accident."

Tears spilled down her face, and her chin wobbled. "But I should have known better. I should have been more careful. Mama always says I need to be more careful."

"It's all right, little one. I'll be okay. I promise. It's just sore, but it will get better."

She hid her face in Madi's neck as her mom soothed her, rubbing a hand up and down her back. She mouthed, *I'm so sorry*, to Asher as she comforted Gigi.

Asher shook his head, mouthing his own, *It's okay.*

Thornton came and sat on the coffee table and clasped his hand. Asher gripped it like a lifeline, trying to breathe through the pain. Asher would never blame a child for being happy and exuberant. It was an accident. It hurt like a motherfucker, but that wasn't for Gigi or Madi to worry about.

When Gigi finally settled down a bit, she was rubbing her eyes. Madi kissed her cheek. "I think you're tired, huh? How about we take you home so you can have a nap?"

Gigi nodded, slid off her mom's lap, and gently hugged Asher. "I hope you'll be okay."

"I'm already feeling better. Thank you for coming. Beauty and Beast had fun with you."

Gigi turned towards the pups and got down on her knees to hug them both. She giggled when they gave her licks. Madi gave him a gentle hug. "Get well. Call me tomorrow, and we can talk more about it."

She knew Asher was hurting, so she got Gigi ready to go. Thornton led them to the front door, thanked them for coming, and then made his way quickly back to Asher's side. "Fuck, Ash. Are you all right?"

Asher nodded. "Yeah, I'll be okay," though he wasn't altogether sure he believed it himself.

"You lost all color, and your hands are shaking right now. I know you're hurting."

Picking the pill bottle off the side table, Thornton shook out a couple of Asher's pain pills and handed him a cup of water. Asher drank them down and just sat, trying not to move. "Why don't you take a rest, sweetheart?"

"Yeah, I think I need it."

"Do you want to sleep down here on the sofa or upstairs in the bed?"

Asher wondered if Thornton meant the guest bedroom or the master suite. Either way, a bed sounded better than the sofa at that point, so he told Thornton he'd prefer the bed. Thornton helped him to his feet, and they made their way slowly upstairs, where Thornton led him to the master suite, making Asher's heart melt even more. When he got Asher comfortable, he lay down beside him.

"I'm going to stay with you until you're asleep, and then I'll go get some work done and start dinner. Text me when you wake up if I'm not up here with you, okay? I think you could use some little time for the rest of the night once you're awake."

God, that shouldn't have sounded as wonderful to him as it did, but just the thought of letting go of the stress he was feeling about The Glasshouse felt like a reprieve he desperately needed. He met Thornton's eyes and nodded. "Thank you for knowing what I need."

"You're welcome, baby boy. Get some rest."

CHAPTER EIGHTEEN

Thornton

Later, when they sat down at the dinner table, he watched as his boy realized his food was on a kid-sized plastic plate and in a bowl, both with robots on them. His silverware and straw cup matched the plate. And there was a plastic placemat with geometric patterns in primary colors underneath it all, and the paper napkin beside him was colorful too.

He hadn't wanted to shock Asher, but he thought the boy was ready, and tiptoeing around being a little wasn't how he wanted to start things between them. Sure, he knew it was all new to Asher, but he believed his boy was a natural little and would settle into things just fine. But he started to second-guess himself when Asher sat there without moving a muscle as he stared down at the place setting before him.

He seemed to be taking it in. It felt strange. Thornton had hoped it would all be reassuring somehow. Familiar, even though it was something new. But it seemed the boy's nerves were getting the better of him, and the last thing he wanted to do was cause a panic attack over something simple, even if he did understand it wasn't necessarily simple for Asher.

He crouched down beside Asher and placed a hand on his thigh. "If this is too much, just tell me. I don't want to rush you or pressure you into doing something you're not ready for."

Asher took a deep breath and shook his head. "No. I'm ready. It's just… a lot to take in. I eat on my special plates at home, but I guess doing it in front of you, with you, feels important somehow. But it's still scary."

He rubbed Asher's thigh. "I understand that. It's a big step to take. Do you need to take a timeout?"

The sadness that slipped over Asher's features had his stomach doing a flipflop. He reached up to caress the boy's furrowed brows until they were clear of any visible worry lines. "Did I do something bad?"

That sent a jolt through Thornton's system. "No, baby, why would you think that?"

"You said I needed to take a timeout. Did I make you upset?"

The very real fear he saw on Asher's face made his heart plummet. God, his sweet boy. He collapsed on his knees from his crouched position and captured Asher's cheeks in his palms. "Sweetheart, you haven't done anything. I didn't mean timeout in any behavioral way—I just meant it as a break. I wanted to make sure, if you needed a minute or you want to talk about this, that we could do that before we moved forward."

Asher's face cleared, and he gave Thornton a hesitant smile. "Oh. Okay. But I don't think I need one. Besides, the food's getting cold, and lasagna is one of my favorites."

"You're such a good boy." Thornton sat down at the place setting kitty-corner to Asher's. "Dig in, sweetheart. There's extra cheese just for you."

Asher clapped his hands and nearly bounced in his chair at that bit of news. Thornton chuckled at his excitement. He watched as Asher picked up the fork and dug in. It was like watching a kid at Christmas. Thornton knew it wasn't about the lasagna—or at least it wasn't all about the lasagna. His boy was feeling a new kind of freedom. Thornton knew this was only the beginning for his boy. He was going to thrive in this new lifestyle.

He continued to watch as nearly half of the piece of lasagna was devoured, red sauce on Asher's lips and even on his chin. He had a feeling if Asher was alone at home, he would have been much more contained. He probably wouldn't have let himself get so carried away. But something about it made Thornton's heart rate speed up as he grabbed the boy's napkin and wiped his face, receiving the biggest grin in response.

"Don't forget to eat your salad, boy." He picked up his own fork and watched as Asher scowled at the mixed greens in front of him.

"But, Daddy, I don't like limp lettuce."

Thornton had to cover his chuckle with a cough, utterly charmed by the little boy transforming before his eyes. He put on his most serious Daddy expression, using his own fork to point at Asher's salad bowl. "Asher, good boys eat their vegetables to grow up big and strong."

Asher lifted his arms and flexed his muscles. "But I'm already big and strong, Daddy."

Thornton had a hard time keeping his face devoid of expression. He felt his lips twitch, wanting so badly to smile. "You are very strong. But you need to be healthy, too." He pointed at the array of different salad dressings on the table. "Tell me which dressing you prefer, and I will add some."

He wanted to kiss that damn pout off his boy's face. "Fine, Caesar. But I want shaky cheese on top. And croutons, Daddy."

Oh, he had a little bit of a brat on his hands. Why did that please him so much? He'd never in his life wanted a bratty boy. But he realized he would take any version of Asher he could get. And the more his boy bloomed into the little he was meant to be, the better Thornton would feel. The fact his boy felt comfortable enough with him to let his naughty side out to play was more than he could have hoped for.

Nevertheless, he used his deep Daddy voice when he chastised him. "Asher, good boys don't talk to their Daddies like that. If you would like cheese and croutons, ask nicely."

The pout and the sad eyes nearly had him backing down, but he knew he needed to stay firm so his boy learned his lesson. But the whisper—oh man, the whisper nearly killed him. "I'm sorry, Daddy. I'll do better. Can I please have some shaky cheese on my salad and some croutons?"

He leaned forward and kissed his boy's forehead. Pulling back just enough to meet Asher's eyes, he gave him a proud smile. "That's Daddy's good boy. Let me get some shaky cheese and check and see if we've got croutons."

Finding both, Thornton brought them back to the table and doctored up his boy's salad. He sat back in his chair and began to eat his own dinner, happiness spreading through him when Asher started to hum as he ate. When they were finished, Thornton asked his boy to bring his dishes to the sink. He did so without causing much of a fuss.

"Why don't you go watch some cartoons and color in your coloring books? I'm going to get all the food put away and the dishes done."

The wide-eyed hopeful look on Asher's face was followed by the boy's hands raised together as if in prayer. "Can I have dessert? Do we have ice cream? I want ice cream! Please, Daddy, I'll be good."

He booped the boy on the nose and raised a brow. "You'll be good regardless, won't you?"

His tone made it clear he wasn't going to take any answer but yes. And when he got it, he softly pinched the boy's chin between finger and thumb and kissed the nose he'd just booped. "Good boy. Let me see what we have when I'm done cleaning up the kitchen. All right?"

Asher grinned and clapped his hands. He could tell Asher wanted to bounce on the balls of his feet when he raised himself up on them and then slowly lowered himself down when he realized it would most likely hurt like hell. Thornton drew his boy in for a kiss. "Go on then."

When Asher turned, Thornton gave him a soft swat on his pert little ass and got a gasp and a giggle in response. "Daddy!"

He chuckled as he worked to clean up and put everything away. Starting some water in his electric kettle for coffee, he grabbed a couple of cinnamon and almond biscotti from a clear sealed jar on the marble countertop by the coffee beans. He opened the freezer door and pulled out the three ice cream flavors he had. "Ash? Cookies n' cream, triple chocolate fudge, or coffee ice cream?"

He heard a whine from the family room. Worried Asher hated them all and he'd have to buy vanilla of all things, he wandered into the family room, hands on his hips. The cute pout coupled with furrowed brows had him laughing. "What is it, sweetheart?"

"I want all three. Can I have a scoop of each?"

He chuckled and shook his head. "No. You can have two small scoops of whatever combination you want."

Asher's eyes grew wide, and he bit his lower lip. "Chocolate and coffee, please! Do you have ice cream cones?"

He shook his head in exasperation. "You are a greedy little boy."

Asher rubbed his tummy. "It's my belly. He's very demanding."

Thornton snorted. "He is, is he?"

The serious nod had him raising a brow. "He is. I promise, Daddy."

"Mmhmm. I'll see what I can find."

But he already knew he'd find three different kinds of cones, so he'd just have to surprise his boy with a new one every night. Scooping both flavors into the waffle cone, he brought a small bowl, a spoon, and a damp paper towel out with him.

Asher was on the floor at the coffee table, purple crayon in hand as he colored in his mandala book and watched *How to Train Your Dragon*. Setting down the bowl with a little spoon, he handed over the cone to his excited little. "Thank you, Daddy!"

"You're welcome. The bowl is if you think you'll make a mess and don't want to hold it anymore. You can just tip it upside down in the bowl and eat it that way."

He nodded enthusiastically as he licked the ice cream, humming in happiness at his treat. The boy had a serious love of good food, if his humming was anything to go by. Thornton went into the kitchen, made himself some coffee, and brought it out with the biscotti. He lifted his leg as he sat on the couch so he could straddle his boy from behind him.

He drank his coffee and ate his biscotti as Asher colored, ate his ice cream, and watched a strange-looking black dragon swoop through the air on the big-screen TV he had mounted above the fireplace. When he was done with his coffee, he sat and waited for his boy to finish his ice cream. When he did, he leaned forward, grabbed the damp paper towel, and used it to wipe the boy's hands and mouth. He tossed it in the bowl and sat back again, carding his fingers through Asher's thick, straight, blond hair. It was soft, and as soon as his fingers went through it, the strands slid right back into place.

Touching his boy was an addiction he never wanted to quit. He knew he'd never, ever get enough and couldn't wait for Asher to heal so he could get his hands all over his beautiful, sweet, little body. He heard a low hum, different from what Thornton thought of as Asher's food hum, where it was more like he was humming a tune. This hum was low, sultry, pleased.

"Do you like when Daddy plays with your hair?"

"Yes, Daddy. It feels really good."

Asher tipped his head back between Thornton's legs until their eyes met. He couldn't help but lean forward and kiss his boy's sweet, chocolatey lips. As kisses went, it was a bit awkward being upside down, but when he drew away, he wrapped his palm around Asher's exposed throat. He didn't squeeze; he just kept it there, caressing his thumb just under Asher's jaw as they gazed at each other.

It was definitely a possessive, claiming sort of touch, and when Asher's head tipped back a fraction more, allowing a better grip, the boy's eyes closed when Thornton spread his fingers wide to touch as much of it as he could. His cock was rock-hard, and he leaned down to kiss Asher again.

"What does that feel like to you, baby boy?"

Asher opened his mouth and let out a long, slow breath. "Submission. Possession."

"Mmm, and how does that feel?"

"Intoxicating."

Christ, this boy was going to bring him to his knees. He'd never felt like he wanted to own a boy. Be their Daddy, care for them, and nurture their little side, yes, but possession hadn't been something he'd desired. He wanted to own Asher, consume him, make him his in every possible way. He wanted to take him over entirely.

It wasn't about bending Asher to his will. But he did want more of a hand in Asher's everyday life. He wanted to make decisions for Asher. Perhaps not all of them. They'd have to discuss how much his boy was willing to give. It was in Asher's hands; the decision would be his and his alone. But if he gave up that control to Thornton, he'd make sure his boy was taken care of and wanted for nothing.

Unable to stop touching him, Thornton leaned farther forward, trailed his other palm down Asher's chest, and leaned in for one more kiss before he pulled back, allowing Asher to resume his coloring and dragon watching. It was still too early to go to bed, but Thornton wanted to give his boy a bath. Wanted to make him feel good. Wanted to touch his sweet body, even if he couldn't bring him to climax. He'd never tire of exploring every bit of Asher's skin, inch by tantalizing inch.

***

While Asher slept in, Thornton was downstairs with the pups, making Belgian waffles for his boy and thinking about the night before. Asher had taken to regression like he'd been made for it or like it had been made for him. Watching Asher regress had been a near-visceral thing, Asher's little self finally being allowed out to play, being set free. His shoulders—hell, his whole body—had relaxed. Thornton could see the tension he always held drain from him as he let go and embraced that side of himself. His boy's smile had remained a constant throughout the night.

The dogs ran towards the front of the house, and seconds later, the front door slammed shut. Thornton's heart raced when he remembered what day it was and who he had a breakfast meeting with. Well, fuck. He was quite possibly about to have two stressed-out young men on his hands.

"Hello, Beauty, my gorgeous girl. Have you been taking good care of Beast since I saw you last? Hmm? Gotta keep your brother in line, don't you, princess? It's a tough job, but somebody's gotta do it."

Thornton's brother, Trenton, walked into the kitchen holding a bag Thornton knew would contain pupcakes, which were cupcakes made for dogs from a local gourmet pet bakery called Pawsitively Edible. Trent brought them for all three dogs to enjoy at least once a week. Trent's own puppy, a chocolate lab named Guinness, loped into the kitchen to greet Thornton.

Thornton bent to pet him, Trent's voice coming closer. "Waffles? Wow, if I'd known you were gonna be making me waffles this morning, I'd have tried harder to be here on ti—what's wrong?"

The look on Thornton's face must have caught Trent off guard because he stepped back, wariness obvious in the set of his shoulders. He smiled and walked towards Trent, not wanting to set off his brother's anxiety. "Nothing's wrong, I just forgot you were coming by this morning."

Trent shrugged and set the bag down on the counter. Thornton was about to explain about Asher when he smelled a waffle burning. "Fuck."

Turning back around, he lifted the lid from the waffle iron, forked out the charred waffle, pulled out the trash drawer, and tossed it in.

"Daddy?"

He looked up at Asher, dressed in his own pajama bottoms and Thornton's button-up pajama shirt. His boy was rubbing his eyes and looking ridiculously adorable and, from what Thornton could see and hear, might still have been in his little headspace. He glanced at his brother, whose eyes were wide. He looked at Thornton and raised his brows, a smile on his face.

"I thought I heard the—" Asher's words cut off when he realized someone else was in the kitchen. Thornton's heart took a jolt when Asher's face drained of color, his hand raised to his chest, and he took a step back, not necessarily in fear, but in surprise.

"Asher, baby, look at me." He approached his boy and gave him a reassuring smile. "You're all right. This is—"

Asher's voice was a choked whisper when he interrupted, hurt obviously clogging his throat. "Another boy?"

Asher's sad eyes nearly killed him. "God, baby, no. There's no one but you. Hey," Thornton cupped Asher's cheeks in his hands until their gazes locked, "this is my brother, Trent. I forgot I had a breakfast meeting with him today, or I would have warned you he was coming."

Asher wouldn't have seen any resemblance because his brother had been adopted when Thornton was six. His mom had been unable to have more children on her own, but his parents had wanted another child, so they'd adopted Trent when he was just a baby.

"Trent, this is Asher Simmons."

Trent's smile was gentle when he asked, "Your husband?"

Thornton couldn't help but laugh. However, he sobered when he saw Asher's bewildered expression as he looked at Trent. "That's just what I told the hospital staff so I could be with him. But…" Asher met his gaze again. "Who knows what the future may bring?"

Thornton pulled Asher into a gentle embrace when he saw the shock and maybe even a little hope in Asher's eyes. He leaned his head on the top of Asher's as they embraced and turned his gaze to his brother. "He's very special to me."

Trent's smile was beatific as he stood, slowly approaching them. Thornton could tell Trent understood Asher was trepidatious around him. If anyone understood anxiety, it was his brother. Trent held out his hand to Asher as they pulled apart. "Then I'm really glad to meet you, Asher. I shouldn't have teased you about the husband thing. When my brother told me that's how he'd gotten past the hospital's rules, I thought he was crazy, but I guess it worked out perfectly, didn't it?"

Asher's shy smile peeked out as they shook hands. "Hi, Trent. I guess it did."

Thornton let out a breath he didn't even know he'd been holding and returned to start another waffle. He turned back at Asher's gasp, his excitement evident when he asked, "May I pet him?"

Trent smiled, nodding. "He'll be sad if you don't."

Asher kneeled to pet the beautiful dog. Asher's giggle was that of his little side. That and the fact he'd already called Thornton Daddy had Thornton making the decision to treat Asher as such until Asher made it clear he didn't want that.

He guessed Asher was feeling a bit vulnerable around a stranger and might be more comfortable as his little self and letting Thornton take the lead. "That's Guinness, Trent's therapy pup. He takes him wherever he goes. Beauty and Beast love him."

All three puppies gathered around Asher and waited patiently for pets and scratches. He walked over and helped him up and then eased him onto the stool at the bar. He poured Asher some orange juice in a straw cup and handed it over as he flipped the waffle iron. "Trent always likes my chocolate chip waffles, but I can make a cinnamon one, a blueberry one, or a plain one for strawberries and whipped cream. Which kind would you like, boy?"

He hoped calling Asher *boy* would help him understand he didn't keep things a secret from his family, and he was safe to stay in his little headspace. Asher's shy gaze slid to Trent, whose smile was reassuring as he said, "His chocolate chip ones are the best. And you can put whipped cream on it and even some chocolate sauce."

Asher's face lit up. "Chocolate, please, Daddy."

"Good boy. Coming right up."

He fed them both, settled Asher in for some morning cartoons, and brought out some of the wooden train track for him to use on the big coffee table, hoping he'd enjoy that and be able to play without the pain of bending over. Asher's eyes lit up, and he dug into the bins as Thornton went back to the kitchen to work with Trent. The day he'd hired Trent as his CFO was the day he'd stopped worrying about his investments, portfolio, and the financial health of his company.

Trent was a brilliant man who needed a boss that understood his limitations. His brother had battled with his anxiety disorder as far back as Thornton could remember. It was one of the reasons he understood and could help Asher with his own anxiety and panic attacks. Once Trent felt secure in his position with

Thornton as his boss, he'd thrived, and business had doubled when Thornton had been able to focus on things besides finances.

They met weekly to go through the prior week's numbers, so it was pretty standard fare. By the time they were done and Trent was on his way out with Guinness—saying his goodbyes to Asher and promising to see him again soon—his boy was hungry for a snack.

As he brought in some apple slices and cheese cubes and a straw cup with milk, Asher was just putting all the train track and trains back in the bins. The concerned look on his boy's face had him helping his boy into his lap, snack forgotten. "What is it?"

"Did I embarrass you?"

He pulled back in shock. "Jesus. No, baby. Why would you think that?"

"I called you Daddy in front of your brother."

His sweet boy. "First, Trent is fully aware I'm a Daddy. Hell, my parents are too for that matter. Years ago, before my parents moved to San Diego, my mom and my brother used to like to walk in my house unannounced. Trent walked in on me and a boy I was seeing, and then my mom did the same a month later. That cured them of that habit, but the beans were spilled. I'm lucky my family is supportive. My parents may not understand, but they love me and will love whoever I choose. Okay?"

Asher shrugged, still not fully convinced, so Thornton continued, "Second, I'm pretty sure my brother is a little. I think he's in denial. He won't ever use the kids' place settings when I've offered, but I've seen the longing in his eyes when he's been around other boys I've dated. He's straight, though, and I think he's worried he'll never find a Mommy, someone who wants to nurture him rather than needing to be nurtured."

Asher nodded and picked at the sleeves of his shirt and murmured, "That would be hard."

"I think it is."

Asher lifted his gaze. "Why does he have a therapy dog?"

Thornton raised a hand to Asher's cheek, rubbing his soft skin with the pad of his thumb. "Trent has an anxiety disorder."

The soft gasp and sorrow his boy had on his face made Thornton inch a little closer to the precipice of never wanting to let go of this precious boy in his arms. "Is he okay?"

Thornton nodded. "He is. He's found ways to cope, one of which is medication, another of which is therapy, and the last of which is Guinness. Since I hired him as my CFO, he's really come into himself, and his confidence has grown. I'd love to see him settled down eventually. He'd make an amazing husband to a lucky woman someday."

Asher nodded, resting his head against Thornton's chest, where they sat in silence for a few minutes. "Have you ever gotten therapy for your anxiety?"

Asher shook his head. "No. My parents took care of my medical needs but not my mental health ones. And after they died, I was just trying to survive and get through every day."

His boy wasn't alone anymore, though, and he wouldn't have to handle his burdens on his own. "That's understandable. I think it could be really helpful, but we can talk about that down the road when we're through this rough patch. Would you be open to that?"

"I guess. Maybe?"

"That's my good boy. So, how about we talk about The Glasshouse?"

"Okay." His nod was much more enthusiastic that time, probably happy to change the subject from his own personal battle with anxiety.

"What are your thoughts about it? Are you leaning one way or another?"

Asher shrugged. "I'm leaning towards wanting to do it. I think Madi is too. It's just such a huge commitment, and I'm completely out of my element. It wasn't something I ever would have considered, and I'm not even sure I'd do a good job of it."

"I don't think you realize just how capable you are. You're one of the strongest people I've ever met, Ash. And from what I've seen, Madi is pretty amazing herself. Jenn, from what I gather listening to local news, politics, and the comings and goings in the business community, is a very shrewd businesswoman. And she wants you and Madi. That's the decision she's making for her business's future. That says a lot."

Asher regarded him, his gaze assessing before he finally nodded. "Yeah. I guess that's true. I mean, I don't pay attention to those things. Not really. But I trust that you do, and I know for a fact The Glasshouse is hugely successful, so I don't know why I'm still hesitating."

"Because this is a life-altering decision, you haven't done it before, and fear is a powerful thing."

Asher chuckled. "That pretty much sums it up."

"I'm not going to pressure you about it. You have to make this decision on your own, for yourself and your own future. What I will say is that I have every confidence in you, every confidence in Madi, and every confidence Jenn is making the right decision. She wouldn't make a choice like this just because she likes her employees."

"That's true." Asher smiled, more confidence reflecting in his eyes than Thornton had seen earlier. If that was all Asher would be allowing him to help with, it was enough. That confidence was worth everything.

Thornton added, "I will offer my help in any and every possible way to you both, whether it be simple business advice, aid in forming a proper business plan for a bank loan, or financial backing and support for you both, whether I'm involved from a business perspective or not. I want you to succeed, and if I have the tools to help you in any way, I will gladly do everything in my power to see that you get what you need."

"You'd help us that way? Financially?"

He nodded, gripped Asher's chin, and drew him in for a kiss. "I would."

Asher's brows furrowed. "I don't want to take advantage of you like that."

One more kiss and Thornton pulled back. "It's not taking advantage if I offer. But if you decide to go elsewhere for financial help, I'll ensure you get the backing you need. It would be an honor to be able to do that for you."

Asher's eyes were wide, awe written all over his face. "You're the best man I know, Thornton. I'm so lucky to have you in my life."

Thornton grinned. "I'm the lucky one. So, what do you say? Are you going to go for it?"

Asher's matching grin was all Thornton needed to know his answer. But the, "I think I am," sealed the deal. His boy was going to be a business owner, and he couldn't be prouder.

"You might want to call your business partner."

Asher bit his lip, eyes wide, grin spreading. "I think that's a good idea. Wow. Hearing it like that is crazy."

Thornton chuckled and leaned forward to grab Asher's phone from the coffee table. Handing it over, he watched as Asher put the phone on speaker and dialed his best friend. When Madi answered, his boy's voice was excited and confident. "Yeah, I was hoping I could speak to my new business partner."

Excited screaming filled the air, followed by a gasp, and "I'm so sorry, ma'am. I didn't mean to startle you. When you check out at the register, tell Lena to give you twenty percent off your order today."

The woman's, "Oh, thank you dear! A bit of enthusiasm is nothing to apologize for," had them both laughing.

CHAPTER NINETEEN

Asher

I t had been four unbelievable weeks since the day his life had irrevocably changed. He'd endured some of the worst physical pain he'd ever known, and the pain wasn't all gone. His ribs still gave him trouble and, while most of his bruises were gone, a few were being particularly stubborn and taking too long to fully heal. But his mental and emotional wellbeing had never been so stable and in sync. He'd enjoyed a full month nearly anxiety-free, something he couldn't ever remember feeling. And prior to the accident, happiness had seemed fairly elusive.

He also realized, as happy as he was becoming, he still had work to do. A lot of fucking work to do. They'd talked a lot over the last several weeks about him going to see a therapist. He'd never felt comfortable about the thought of spilling his guts to a perfect stranger, but when Trent was over one morning for another breakfast meeting, Thornton had asked for the name of his therapist.

When he'd asked why, Asher had plucked up the courage to explain, and that was when he'd begun to make a new friend. They'd bonded over stories of the worst location they'd ever had a panic attack in, stories about their worst ones and what started them, and about how they'd both learned to deal with them. As new friendships went, it was a fairly unorthodox thing to bond over, but he'd take all the friends he could get. They'd been few and far between in his life.

He wasn't exactly ready to take on the world and felt sick at the thought of even getting in a car to *ride* to the therapist's office, but he'd made the fucking appointment. It helped that the therapist had a phone intake consultation with him about his biggest fears and triggers and what he wanted to get out of therapy. He'd said, if worse came to worst, Asher could call him if he was unable to get himself to the office. And when it came down to it, the thought of leaving the house the following morning to go back to work had him needing to do his deep breathing exercises, so that wasn't exactly out of the realm of possibility.

It wasn't like they hadn't left the house in a month. They'd gone on walks, which had gotten longer the better he felt. And he'd eventually caved when Thornton had continued to ask him to get in his new car and go for a ride with him, as Thornton said, "Even if the first one was just around the block." He'd had a panic attack when he'd stepped into the garage. Though he hadn't even gotten in the fucking car yet, he'd bent at the waist, hands on his knees as the breath sawed in and out of his lungs.

Fucking humiliating.

But he'd moved past it with Thornton's help. Always, everything, with Thornton's help. And somehow, he felt no shame about that. He'd leaned into every new thing he could experience with Thornton, and it had been a lot. So much, in fact, it had often felt overwhelming, but only in the best possible ways.

So many new things brought him joy. Everything from new clothing, jammies, and underwear for his little self from Daddy, to story time, and set bedtimes and bath times. He'd come to love bath time so much. He got to play with toys and Daddy washed him from head to toe, which was always special for them both.

He'd also been surprised when Daddy started singing him to sleep some nights. His voice was so deep and beautiful, Asher could never stay awake long enough to hear the whole song no matter how much he wanted to hear it. The nights he went to sleep as his little self often ended up being the nights he slept the best. So even if they had adult time beforehand, Daddy had often brought him back into little headspace before sleeping when he saw what a difference it made for Asher the next day.

Some things had been awkward and embarrassing at first. Like the shorts, all of which were soft, short, small, and tight, and the T-shirts, which were either half shirts or shirts that were fitted with cute little cartoon characters on them. He'd loved them immediately, but the thought of actually getting dressed in them felt scary.

He'd blushed all over when Daddy had first started helping him get dressed in his little clothes, but when he understood Daddy didn't think it was silly at all, he realized how quickly they helped sink him into his little headspace. Asher especially loved the intense, desirous gazes Daddy gave him. That, coupled with his blown pupils and hard cock, made it clear how much Daddy loved seeing him in his little clothes.

Little things he never thought he'd enjoy became some of his favorites. When Thornton removed the napping bed in his playroom he never ended up using and replaced it with a beautiful, swivel-glider recliner, Daddy rocked him while he read him stories and then held him close as Asher napped in his lap. Every step of the way, with every new thing he was introduced to, Thornton had been there to guide him and nurture him, and Asher had thrived. Really, truly thrived.

He'd continued to recover, and almost before he knew it, he was getting ready to go back to work. A month had never gone by so quickly, but by the same token, he felt like he'd been there with Thornton forever. Syed had approved his return to work, but only part-time for the first two weeks before he was allowed to return to a full schedule.

Asher both hated and loved the idea of returning. He was ready. Or at least he was *getting* ready to get back to his real life. It felt like he'd been in a fantasy world for the last several weeks. And in a lot of ways he had. But for the last week, he'd been thinking about returning home and what that would mean for them. He didn't know, and if he was honest with himself, it scared him to death.

Would he lose everything he'd so quickly come to hold dear?

God, he seriously hoped not. Asher wasn't sure what he'd do if he did. But real life was beckoning, so while Thornton was on a conference call, Asher was upstairs packing his things to go home. He hadn't spoken to Thornton about leaving; they'd only talked about him returning to work. He'd waited for Thornton to bring it up, and he never had.

Asher feared perhaps Thornton wanted him to go but felt guilty asking. So, he'd made the decision to get everything ready and let Thornton know when he was done with work for the day. He couldn't pretend living with Thornton was a permanent thing. He had no idea where Thornton's head was at regarding where their relationship would go once he was back at work, but he wasn't going to make assumptions.

Besides, what if Thornton, when he finally understood the extent of Asher's anxiety, decided Asher was more trouble than he was worth? Thornton didn't truly know how bad his anxiety could be. Asher had told him, but seeing Asher in real life was very different than seeing Asher in the privacy of Thornton's home. They'd been in a fucking bubble. A gorgeous, well-kept, beautifully decorated bubble, but a bubble nonetheless.

He was a lot of trouble, too much for even himself at times. He couldn't expect Thornton to want to take that on permanently. He couldn't go to the movies, he couldn't go to restaurants, he couldn't go to grocery stores, he couldn't go to malls or busy parks. What *could* he do, really? Nothing. He couldn't go anywhere with Thornton in public, and who would want that?

What, were they going to sit around in Thornton's house for the rest of their lives? Four weeks in, and Thornton was already changing his life for him: staying home, taking as many conference calls as he could instead of meeting people face-to-face. If things kept going as they were going, Thornton was going to end up a hermit as well.

He couldn't do that to him. He couldn't... he just... His knees gave out on him in the middle of Thornton's bedroom, a couple of folded shirts in his hands suddenly a crumpled heap on the floor. Heart racing, dizzy, shaking with chills wracking his body, he tried to slow his racing heart. He heard Beauty whine and felt her snout on his cheek. He closed his eyes, trying to breathe, trying to concentrate on the puppy's wet nose touching his skin.

In the distance, he heard a bark, but that couldn't be right because Beauty was kissing him, and Beast never left her. He shook his head, the edges of his vision blurring. This was what Thornton had to look forward to. This was what he'd saddle the man with. He couldn't do that to him. He couldn't...

He blinked his eyes, tried to focus when he heard Thornton's voice. "Come on, baby. I've got you." He felt Thornton's strong arms wrap around him, rocking him on the floor of his room. "I'm here."

They sat there for several minutes as he got himself back under control. Thornton rocked him, and he concentrated on breathing. Finally, he shook his head and tried to pull away. "What are we doing?"

The confusion on Thornton's face was reflected in his furrowed brows. "What do you mean?"

He sighed. "My time with you here. It's been... Thornton, it's meant more to me than I can even express. But what am I even bringing to the table? You've been stuck in this house with me for weeks now. This can't be your life."

Thornton narrowed his eyes. "First, it's my call what I want for my life, and if I haven't made it abundantly clear, *you* are what I want. I haven't once considered myself stuck. I've left the house when I've needed to—"

Asher shook his head. "But you—"

"Boy, do not interrupt me when I'm speaking."

He held his breath at Thornton's admonishment, but nodded. Thornton was in Daddy mode, that was clear, and Asher was frozen to the spot as the authoritative deep voice held him in thrall. He'd never spoken to Asher that way, and as a shiver wracked Asher's body, he couldn't say he hated it. "Yes, Daddy."

Thornton took a deep breath at his response, perhaps to center himself; Asher wasn't sure. "I've taken meetings at home when I could because I wanted to. My focus has been getting you well because it is imperative to me that you are made whole after what happened. Not only that, but I also want you happy and thriving."

Asher nodded, knowing that was true. "I know."

"I cannot operate my business from home all the time. A lot of what I do needs to be face to face with my clients. But as I am an investor, I don't work at the businesses I invest in because they are not my home base. *This* is my home base. It was my home base before you came into my life."

Some of the tension he'd been holding in released. He breathed in deep and closed his eyes, laying his head on Thornton's chest, his body relaxing into the strong solid man holding him so securely. Thornton kissed the top of his head and continued. "My being home with you hasn't felt like some kind of sacrifice I'm willing to make. I'm here anyway because I have chosen to make my home my workplace."

Asher sighed, annoyed at himself. "I thought maybe you were only here because I was forcing you to be here."

"Hmm mm. Come on. Let's get off the floor." He helped Asher stand and then got up and led him to the chaise lounge in the corner. He sat and pulled Asher right back onto his lap, wrapping his arms around him and settling them in. "This isn't something I've chosen lightly for myself or my employees. Trent and my assistants, Jason and Laura, have all made it clear they want the flexibility of working remotely. That works just fine for me. I prefer it, actually."

He pulled back to look up at Thornton. "I wouldn't have guessed that."

With a smile and a kiss to Asher's nose, Thornton nodded. "It's true. I'm what you'd call a social introvert."

Asher chuckled. "That's an oxymoron."

Thornton shrugged. "You'd think. But somehow it works for me. I like people. I want to help them achieve their goals and, in turn, reach my own by helping them. That takes a lot of people skills and interaction with my clients. I love that. But most of that comfort is derived from interactions one-on-one or in small groups. I'm not one for big parties and tons of people I don't know."

"Really?" That surprised him because he thought of Thornton as larger than life.

"Really. So the guilt you've been feeling for keeping me here is absolutely unfounded. Sure, I've cancelled a few face-to-face meetings, but the work was done easily over the phone. I just prefer to meet my clients face-to-face to check on them and see firsthand how things are going with them. They like seeing that I'm involved and willing to jump in if needed, and I like seeing their hard work and passion in person."

Thornton shrugged that off like it was no big deal, and Asher's heart tripped with so much affection for him. "You're kind of amazing, you know that?"

Thornton shook his head. "Not really. But, Asher, I need you to understand even if it *was* a sacrifice, that is *my* choice to make, and I'd make it again and again for your well-being because your health—mental, physical, and emotional —means everything to me."

God... "How did I get so lucky?"

"I think we're both really fortunate to have found each other. I also think your anxiety about going back to work and what that means, from the physical act of leaving this safe space to the aspect of becoming part owner of The Glasshouse, has you feeling really out of your depth."

Asher huffed. "I think that's the understatement of the year."

Thornton chuckled, hugged him a bit tighter, and kissed the top of his head. "Come on. I think you need some playtime to get you out of your own head. Why don't we go downstairs, and you can play for a bit in your playroom while I make you lunch?"

His playroom.

That hit home, hard. Thornton always knew what Asher needed, and with that came a sense of confidence in them and in himself he'd been lacking just moments ago. How he could do that with such ease, Asher had no idea, but Thornton was coming to mean everything to him, and Asher was about a breath away from falling head over heels for the man. And while that did scare him a bit, it didn't petrify him as it would have in the past.

That was something, right?

For the second time in so many minutes, Thornton helped him to his feet and followed after. As he led them towards the door, Thornton stopped them, his gaze serious when he stood to face Asher. "And, boy?" That deep, commanding tone had a thrill racing through his body but also had him on high alert. It was no-nonsense and stern, and somehow that both thrilled and terrified him.

But he met Thornton's gaze head on. "Yes, Daddy?"

"Don't think I didn't notice you were packing your things in preparation for leaving. We'll be talking about that later, after playtime, because if you think for one minute I'm going to let you leave without a fight, you've got another think coming."

He gulped, eyes wide, and nodded. "Yes, Daddy."

Once downstairs, he settled quickly into his little headspace and dragged all three of his train bins out at once. Daddy had surprised him with new pieces and some super cool additions that helped him create a really big track, and every single time he made one it was unique. When he was allowed to regress, he lost himself in his own little world.

Unbeknownst to him, he began to hum as he strategically linked piece after piece of wooden track that looped around, over, and through itself until it was a maze of interconnected pieces making a whole. It zigged and it zagged, went under trestle bridges, through a covered bridge, and over a drawbridge, and included curved hills and valleys. He continued until the very last piece of track slid into place, his heart racing in excitement as he realized it was the first time he'd been able to use every single piece and still have all the pieces connected.

He stood to take it all in, bouncing on his feet as he clapped, a huge grin on his face. Then he got to work again, adding little houses, stores, a coffee shop, a fire station and police station, and a farm with a barn, farm animals, and fencing to keep the animals from going on the track. He added cars stopped at the railroad crossing and trees on the outskirts of town. And finally, he added the people.

When it was all done, he surveyed everything and giggled when he realized there was hardly any free space on the floor. And it was a really big room. He made a couple of adjustments and then gasped when he realized he'd forgotten to add the trains.

"Oh my gosh!" He crawled over to the mega train pile he'd created as he'd gone through the three bins for train track. Sorting them into separate groups, he began adding trains to various sections of track.

"Sorry it took so long, baby. Daddy got a phone—" Thornton cut himself off and just stood in the doorway, awestruck. So involved in what he was doing, he hadn't heard Daddy approaching, and he startled, letting out a squeak and bringing a hand to his racing heart. "Ash, this is amazing!"

He pouted. "Daddy, you scared me!"

Thornton chuckled and approached, crouching down beside him and ruffling his hair. Daddy's hand continued down and rubbed his back. "I didn't mean to, baby. I fixed our lunch, and then I had a work call I had to take. When I peeked in almost thirty minutes ago on my way to my office, you were so busy I didn't want to interrupt you."

"It's okay. But look! I used every single piece. The bins are even empty. And —and..." He was so excited he crawled over to a looped section that smoothed out into a straight stretch leading into town. "Oh no, there's a fire at the diner!"

He leaned over and pushed the siren on the fire engine, drove it towards town to the railroad crossing, and pushed the button when he got there. The bells rang as he lifted the gates so the engine could pass through on its way to the fire.

He moved the people around, outside of the diner. "Help! There's a fire! Help!"

Once he made sure the fire was out and everyone was okay, he crawled over to a different section of track and pulled the long line of train cars over a drawbridge, under the highway overpass, and around to the old covered bridge by the farm. A tree got knocked over by his knee. "Oh no, there's a tree on the track! We have to stop the train!"

He made screeching noises as the train's brakes finally stopped the train, just in time. But it was such an abrupt stop, two of the boxcars in the back tipped over, straight into the fence and halfway through the field, narrowly missing the sheep.

"Oh my goodness! Daddy, did you see? The train almost hit the tree and then the box cars knocked over the fence! The farmer is gonna be so upset! And look, now the sheep might get loose." He turned, mouth agape at the tragic accident.

He cocked his head when he saw the camera on Daddy's phone aimed his way. He scrunched his nose and then giggled. "Are you capturing real-time footage of the crash for the six o'clock news?"

Turning his gaze Daddy's way, Asher was surprised by his expression. It was serious, and yet a tender smile played around his lips. He looked poleaxed and mesmerized, but with what, Asher didn't know. Asher waved his hands in front of his face. "Daddy, did you see? The crash?"

Daddy blinked himself out of his daze, and a brilliant smile lit his face. "I did. And I think I caught it all on tape for the news team."

Asher beamed and clapped. "Oh good! Maybe Farmer Bob will use the fallen tree to cut into pieces for the new fence he has to build."

Thornton chuckled. "That's a good idea, little man. I'm so proud of you for building such an amazing track. It's the best one yet. But I see a spot that might need a little something extra."

Asher turned and surveyed the whole room, unable to see what was needed that he hadn't already added. "I dunno. I'm pretty sure I used everything, Daddy."

"Not everything. I might have a little something that could go perfectly over there." Daddy pointed to a section behind him and to the left, where there was a big loop of track.

He turned back, a grin growing. His whole body vibrated with excitement, and he squeezed his fists together, shaking them in excitement. "Did you get me a prezzie?"

Thornton chuckled, nodding. "I did. Don't move. Daddy's gonna be right back."

He wiggled back and forth on his butt, so excited. He loved prezzies! When Daddy returned, he had a box in hand that had been wrapped in blue paper with trains all over it. "Trains!"

"I thought you might like that. This is a good-luck-tomorrow gift I thought you might like. I was going to give it to you later, but the track you built is perfect for it."

He wanted to snatch the box out of Daddy's hands, but he waited patiently. Daddy smirked, like the meanie he was, but finally handed it over. He set it on the floor and went to town on the wrapping, unable to slow down in his enthusiasm. When the manufacturer's box showed a picture of what was inside, he gasped. "Oh my gosh! Oh my gosh! Daddy! It's the roundhouse and turntable I saw last week on your iPad! Look, it'll fit perfectly over there."

He pulled the huge, semicircle train garage and attached spinning turntable out of the box, ran over to the other end of the track, and slotted the roundhouse into place. He crawled to the closest train and coupled coal car and rolled them towards the roundhouse. "Chugga chugga, chugga chugga, choo choo!"

He rolled the train through the turntable and into one of the many garages in the roundhouse. "Look, it fits!"

"It does. That's exciting, isn't it?"

Asher wanted to show Daddy just how excited he was, so he scrambled over to him on his hands and knees and launched himself on him, knocking Daddy back off his heels and flat on his back. "Whoa, careful, little man."

Chuckling, Daddy caught him and kept them from crashing too hard into each other as he wrapped his arms around Asher, tugging him in close against his body protectively. Asher peppered his face with kisses. "Thank you, thank you, thank you, thank you!"

The adoring smile on Daddy's face made Asher's tummy do flipflops. "You're welcome. Is it the one you liked?"

"Yes, yes, yes. It's perfect."

"Good. I'm glad."

Asher groaned as his ribs protested, suddenly realizing launching himself at anything still wasn't a good idea. They were nearly healed, and he felt great compared to where he'd started after the crash, but sometimes he forgot he was still healing and went a little too far.

Thornton's hands ran up and down his back as Asher tucked his head under Thornton's chin. "You gotta be careful, sweetheart."

He sucked in a breath and nodded. "I know, Daddy. I forget sometimes."

"I know you do, baby."

Asher's tummy decided that was a good time to start talking. "Uh-oh. My tummy is mad."

Thornton chuckled. "Well then, let's go to the kitchen and eat lunch. I might have a tiny surprise on your favorite plate as well. Why don't you go see?"

At the thought of another surprise, he was up like a shot, ignoring his protesting ribs and running out of the room. "Ash, slow down. Don't hurt yourself."

Grumbling, he slowed to a power walk and made it to his place setting at the table, where his new train place setting was, and... "Oh my gosh! Daddy! It's train-shaped sammiches!"

"It is! How fun is that?"

"So fun, Daddy!" He clambered onto his seat, knocking the table in the process, which in turn knocked over his milk cup. He gasped as it fell over and tried to catch it as it rolled towards the edge of the table but couldn't catch it in time. It hit the floor on its side with a clatter, the lid popped off, and chocolate milk went everywhere.

He gasped. "I'm sorry!"

Thornton clasped his shoulder and squeezed. "It's okay. Accidents happen."

Asher started to get up to grab some paper towel, but Daddy stopped him. "You don't have shoes on, little man. Stay in your seat while I clean it up."

He watched as Thornton cleaned up his mess. He knew it wasn't a huge deal, but he felt awful. He'd just been given two super-fun gifts, and this was the thanks he gave his Daddy? He whispered, "I'm really sorry."

Thornton looked up from his final swipe of the floor with the paper towel, his smile turning into a look of concern as he dropped the paper towel on the floor and turned more fully to kneel in front of Asher. "Hey, hey. What's this?"

Asher drew in a ragged breath. "You got me prezzies and I wasn't careful and now I ruined lunch, and..."

Thornton pulled Asher down on his lap so he was straddling him and kissed Asher so sweetly. "You haven't ruined anything, Ash. It was an accident. I promise. I'm just gonna make you some more chocolate milk, and then things will be right as rain."

He sniffled. "Yeah?"

A kiss on his forehead made Asher feel better. "Yeah, sweetheart."

"I can help?"

"With your milk?"

"Yeah. I can be really careful. I promise. I just got so excited because of the train sammiches."

Thornton chuckled, nodding. "I know you did. Okay, hang on a minute. Let me finish this and get the milk and chocolate syrup."

Thornton came back with a new cup, milk, and the syrup, and Asher helped make himself some fresh chocolate milk. When he was done, he'd only dribbled a bit of chocolate on the table. He swiped it up and licked his finger, making Daddy chuckle at him. "All better?"

Asher nodded. "All better. Thank you, Daddy."

"You're welcome. I think your emotions are running pretty close to the surface today, so everything seems bigger, more overwhelming."

He bit into his peanut butter and jelly train and shrugged. His mouth was full when he mumbled, "Maybe."

"Asher, what have I said about speaking while your mouth is full?"

He swallowed and ducked his head, feeling sheepish. "Sorry, Daddy."

"It's okay, but don't do it again."

"Yes, Daddy."

"Good boy."

CHAPTER TWENTY

Thornton

T hornton set the table for dinner, which was chicken enchiladas and Spanish rice, a meal Asher had said was one of his favorites. Asher had been in little space most of the day. After lunch, they'd gone on a walk, and then he'd wanted to color and watch a movie. Thornton had wanted to make his boy's last day at home as stress-free as possible. The more time Asher had to regress before his first day back, the better.

His boy was healthier than Thornton had ever seen him, happier too. His posture was more confident, his smile ever present, he laughed easily and seemed to feel more comfortable and able to sink deeper into his little headspace. As Thornton watched Asher settle into the little boy he'd always kept hidden away, he'd felt as if his own growth as a Daddy had happened simultaneously. They were both learning from each other and growing stronger together.

"Hey, Ash. It's time for dinner. Can you turn the TV off and clean up your coloring stuff, please?"

"Yes, Daddy."

"Good boy. Wash your hands afterwards, all right?"

"Okay."

The sweet timbre of Asher's little voice was music to his ears. It was higher than his normal voice and had all the earmarks of full regression into little headspace. His boy had taken to the lifestyle like a duck to water, and Thornton was happier than he could ever remember being.

When Beast had barked outside his office during a conference call earlier, he'd barely excused himself from the call before hanging up and running upstairs, scared to death what he'd find. Seeing Asher on the ground struggling to breathe had his heart racing a mile a minute. He hated when his boy suffered with his anxiety.

After he'd gotten Asher settled, he'd notice the bag on their bed, half full of Asher's things. His heart nearly stopped, seeing that. He'd failed his boy, obviously. He hadn't even entertained the thought of Asher leaving. In his mind, Asher was still recovering and only working part-time, and after that they'd chat about him moving in, but the fact that Asher had doubted for a second Thornton wanted his boy there for always broke his heart.

He'd put off that discussion for the remainder of the day because the most important thing was for Asher to get the time he needed to let go of himself and let the stress of what was to come drift away while he played with trains and colored pictures in his new train coloring books.

He knew his boy was worried about the impending business buyout, and he couldn't blame Asher one bit for it. Over the last couple of weeks, he'd been working with Asher and Madi to understand the ins and outs of running The Glasshouse.

While he did not know the details of the financials, he knew enough about them from his conversations with his boy to have a rough idea of what was to come for Asher and his soon-to-be new business partner. Madi had a good head on her shoulders and, if he wasn't mistaken, would thrive in the role Jenn would be vacating when she sold the successful business to her two most trusted employees.

He had helped them see different ways of looking at their jobs from an ownership perspective. He knew it wasn't easy making that mental shift, but they were both willing, and eager, to learn. Jenn had stopped by a week prior, to check with them about their interest in the business. When Asher and Madi had finally told her they were interested, the excitement in the room was palpable.

Jenn hadn't stayed long. In her words, she had just stopped by to check on Asher and see if they had any questions for her in order to help them make a decision. When they'd explained their decision had been made, she'd been just as excited as Asher and Madi about it. And she hadn't pressed for anything more. Had made it clear Asher was not to be worrying about work while he was recovering, and when he came back, they'd talk about it and start nailing down the details.

All Thornton had done was talk to them about running a business, any business, and the many different things owners ran into. They'd both been pretty stressed after that conversation, and he'd done his best to assuage their worries. They weren't building a company from the ground up; The Glasshouse was a successfully run business that they were essentially taking over.

Once they understood that they had a leg up because of how much they already knew about the business, they both had relaxed and been able to talk to him and hear some of his advice. Other than that, he had done his best to only step in when he was asked to do so. But over the last couple of weeks, Asher had been picking his brain, and the questions he'd asked, the advice he'd wanted, was that of a man taking things very seriously. Someone who would do well in charge.

His biggest worry was getting Asher back to work the following day in a good headspace. The car ride was going to be an issue. That was why he'd pushed the boy into driving with him several times over the course of the last few weeks.

He knew the next day for Asher was going to be a tough one. Not only was he going to be getting a ride to and from work, but he was also going to be around more people than he had been around since he'd last been at work. He knew that Madi and Asher would be having a business meeting with Jenn in the morning, and he assumed that was when she would go over financials and other things they needed to know in order to put a good business plan together for their business loans.

He still hoped that he would be able to help them in some way to financially reach their goals. He wanted his boy and his boy's best friend to thrive. He could see the excitement growing in Asher's eyes when he talked about possible changes he would make in the future. Thornton had liked Asher's ideas and tried to help build upon them and had even introduced some of his own ideas he had to grow their cannabis business.

All in all, he felt like Asher was ready to return to work—he was feeling much better physically and, from what Thornton could tell, emotionally and mentally as well. He hoped he had had some small part in helping Asher along the way.

When Asher walked in the room, Thornton could tell, somewhere between walking to the bathroom, washing his hands, and walking to the kitchen, Asher had pulled himself out of regression. There was trepidation in his steps, and Thornton knew Asher assumed they would be having the conversation they had put off since earlier that day. And he wasn't wrong.

"It smells good, Daddy."

Thornton approached Asher and pulled him slowly into a hug, rubbing his hands up and down his boy's back. He pulled away, hands on Asher's shoulders, and gazed into his eyes. "I made one of your favorites."

Asher smiled, shyly. "I can tell. Thank you."

"You're welcome, boy. Have a seat, and I'll bring in your food."

As Asher sat at the table, Thornton filled their plates and brought them to the table. Perhaps Asher had noticed Thornton had used regular dinnerware rather than the plastic place settings he used when Asher was regressing. At least they were on the same page.

They started eating, and he decided to wait until they were finished for the heavy conversation, so they kept their conversation light. When they were done, Asher helped him carry their dishes to the sink, and they both set the kitchen to rights, somehow both understanding the sooner they got done, the sooner they could talk about the elephant in the room. Once everything was cleaned and put away, he led Asher to the family room couch, the place they spent most nights, and sat them down on the sofa.

He didn't know what to do to make Asher feel more secure about their conversation, so he figured he wouldn't put it off any longer. "I'd like to apologize."

Before he could continue, Asher's shocked gaze met his, and he asked, "What do you have to apologize for?"

"I left you floundering when I should have been very clear in my intentions. The fact that you are packing your clothes to leave and go home means I did not take care of your needs. I caused you undue stress."

Asher shook his head, but before his boy could speak, he raised his hand to hold him off. "The reason I did not mention how I was feeling about you leaving was because it wasn't even a thought in my mind. I still consider you recuperating since you are only going back to work part-time. And I figured we still had a couple of weeks to discuss our future. But obviously, it has been on your mind enough for you to have doubts about your place here."

"I didn't want to presume…"

"Sweet boy, I *want* you to presume. But again, I didn't make that clear, and for that, I'm sorry. But let me clear up any confusion you may have. I want you here with me. There are no ifs, ands, or buts and no prevarications. When you are one hundred percent recovered from the car accident, I will still want you here."

Asher's mouth had dropped open, and his shock had Thornton smiling and reaching out to clasp his hand. "Asher, if I have not made it clear, you make me very happy. In fact, I can't ever remember being as happy as I am with you."

"I feel the same way, Daddy."

God, hearing his boy call him Daddy never got old. The more he said it, the more comfortable he seemed to feel saying it. And that warmed Thornton's heart. "I'm so glad, baby boy."

Asher looked down at his lap, hands fidgeting there with nerves. Asher's voice wavered, uncertainty clear. "Are you… I mean… Just so I understand, are you asking me to move in with you?"

"Yes."

Asher's brows furrowed. Thornton couldn't help himself. He reached out and caressed his thumb over them, smoothing them out. "But… It's only been four weeks. I just… Isn't it too soon? I feel like we just met, but…"

"But?"

Asher shook his head. "In other ways, I feel like we've known each other forever. I don't understand how that's even possible, but it's how I feel."

He couldn't hold back any longer. He picked Asher up, sat him on his lap, and leaned back into the cushions so they could be more comfortable. "I feel the same. I think it's in large part due to the lifestyle. It takes a lot to trust someone as much as you have learned to trust me when you are regressing. You took a leap of faith in me, and for that I will be forever grateful."

Asher smiled shyly up at him. "You're very persuasive."

Thornton chuckled, knowing there was some truth to that. "There's also the fact that I basically haven't left your side since the day I became your husband."

That surprised a giggle out of Asher, and he smiled, loving the sound of his boy's sweet laugh. When Asher finally sobered, he nodded in agreement. "Yeah, I guess that's true."

"We've essentially squeezed in—at least by my estimation—a six-month relationship into four weeks. Add in the fact we're living as Daddy and boy, which might add another six months of trust and relationship growth to the mix. Hell, and the fact I became your husband the day we met adds in at least six more months."

Asher snorted. A disbelieving look coupled with exasperated amusement was written all over his boy's face. "So, eighteen months… by your estimation."

He grinned and nodded emphatically, glad Asher understood. "Exactly."

Asher huffed and rolled his eyes. "You're ridiculous."

"Be that as it may, there's some truth to everything I just said. We've basically lived a condensed version of a lengthier relationship within the last month."

Asher thought about that for a couple of beats. "So, you feel like we're ready for cohabitation as a result of this condensed relationship timeline you've created in your head?"

He shrugged. "In a nutshell."

Asher shook his head. "Thornton."

Thornton gave him the sexiest, most persuasive smile he could muster. "Asher, who am I to you?"

"Daddy." When Asher sighed, and doubt creeped into his eyes, Thornton sat up, knowing he needed to be serious, or he'd feed into Asher's fears that they weren't real or they were moving too fast. He lifted his sweet boy and lay him on the sofa, stretching out on top of him, careful not to put too much weight on him. He lifted Asher's thigh along his, hooking Asher's foot behind his own calf. "Wrap yourself around me, baby."

Asher followed orders and wrapped his arms around Thornton. His boy had been starved for touch for so long, the simplest of caresses seemed to ignite him, but in a position like they were in now, Asher's eyes dilated, and his breathing got heavier. He clasped Asher's cheek in his hand and met his gaze. "I know I was teasing you, but that doesn't take away from the fact that what I was saying is true. Do you understand that?"

Asher nodded, but that wasn't enough, so he waited on a proper response. "Yes, Daddy."

"Asher, I want you in my life, but not just that—I want you in my home. I want this to be *our* home. I don't want our relationship to backslide. I want it to move forward. The only way I see for that to happen is for you to stay with me, be mine. I can't fully take care of my boy if I barely see you."

"But it doesn't mean we can't see each other."

"I don't think you'll be happy going back to your apartment. Are you going to want to sleep alone after this? Are you going to be satisfied eating dinner alone and being unable to regress fully because Daddy isn't there to take care of you?"

"I don't know," Asher replied. "Can I think about it, Daddy?"

"Yeah. Of course you can."

Asher nodded. "So, I'll move home—"

He closed his eyes, and that, along with his expression, must have given away his displeasure because Asher rushed to explain. "I just... I feel so overwhelmed by you and by this and by us. It's like I'm in this happiness fog, and I can't tell what's real and what's imagined because I don't have a dose of reality to bring me back down to earth. I have to step away to see if I feel the same... when I'm not..."

"Under my influence?"

Asher gave him a sad smile but nodded. "Yeah."

God, that was the last thing he wanted for them, but he had to give Asher the space to figure out what he needed, even if he wanted to take over and run every single bit of Asher's life until he had nothing to worry about and no anxiety plaguing him.

He knew that was too much—he knew his urges with Asher were borderline controlling and overprotective—but he couldn't help what he wanted. His boy brought out every single protective instinct he had. He knew he'd have to come clean about what he wanted. He hadn't shown half of the possessiveness he felt towards Asher because, frankly, he hadn't wanted to scare him away.

Asher bit his lip, worrying it between his teeth. Thornton nudged that plump lip with his thumb, pulling it out, running his thumb along its soft surface. When Asher's tongue slid out and gave it a tentative lick, Thornton groaned and buried his head in the crook of Asher's neck. "Daddy?"

His boy's sweet whisper tipped him over the edge into full on arousal. His cock strained the confines of his jeans. He kept his face where it was while he answered. "Yeah, baby boy?"

"Remember your promise?"

That brought his head up because, for a second, he actually didn't. And then… he did. A week prior, he'd finally acquiesced and given Asher the orgasm he'd been waiting for. He'd pleasured his boy for as long as he could stand it and then finally sucked his beautiful, hard cock until he spilled deep down Thornton's throat. And his poor boy had loved and hated it with equal measure when his clenched muscles had hurt his ribs like hell at the same time he was coming.

Thornton figured it had been quite a mindfuck, and he'd sworn he wouldn't try again for a week. And it had been *exactly* a week. "I don't know if you're ready, sweetheart. It killed me when I hurt you last week."

"I'm ready. Please. I need you. You've been prepping me. I promise I can take it. I need to feel you inside of me. Please."

"Baby boy."

"Daddy, it's our last night."

God, he hated the sound of Asher calling this their last night. "Don't say that, baby. It's too final."

Asher acquiesced with a nod of his head, but still, so much desire burned in his eyes. "Daddy, I need to feel you filling me up. I want to feel you come deep inside of me. Please."

Jesus god, such sweet begging. He'd gotten tested during their wait. Asher hadn't wanted a condom between them, and honestly, neither had he, so it hadn't been a hard sell. And he *had* been prepping him. While he hadn't allowed his boy to orgasm before or after that single time a week back, he'd begun prepping Asher for his cock. It had started almost from the very beginning.

Every night when he gave his boy a hot bubble bath, he'd started with one finger, then two, finally three. From there, he'd used a few dildos similar in size to his own cock, and those had taken a while for Asher to get used to. They were much longer than his fingers. He needed to use the dildos to stretch his boy's greedy hole, but he always started with his fingers because he had to have a piece of him inside of his boy.

Asher's lip was between his teeth again, waiting for his response. And the blown pupils, flushed cheeks, and earnest expression were more than he could handle. He licked up Asher's throat and nipped across his jaw until he could kiss Asher's sweet lips. He gripped Asher's chin in his hand, turning his head to the side, and nibbled his way over to his ear before biting the lobe. "Does my boy want to give his sweet hole to Daddy?"

The whimpers were like music to his ears. "Yes. Please, Daddy."

Suddenly, he wanted it just as badly. Four fucking weeks was a long goddamned time to wait for such a delectable little morsel. It had been painful—so painful—holding off. And he'd allowed his boy to explore him and get him off whenever the mood struck, and for Asher, the mood struck. A lot.

He lived for the days his boy was playing in his playroom and then wandered into his office, sometimes walking, sometimes crawling, to make him come with his nimble hands or his talented mouth. He'd needed a lot of direction at first, but to be the one to teach his boy exactly how to lick, suck, bite, nip, caress, rub, and massage him to perfection was a gift that kept on giving.

Asher was a sponge, soaking up praise, attention, and direction, relishing being touched and thrilling in doing the touching. He stood and helped Asher up and then walked ahead of his boy, his hand outstretched behind him, fingers splayed for Asher's smaller ones to slip between his own. He led, Asher followed, it was their way and they both thrived in that space.

Asher's hand was still in Thornton's as they quietly made their way upstairs, he was aware of Asher's soft skin against his own. The boy's hand was just a bit bigger than half the size of his. Everything of Asher's was dainty and small. Asher seemed to think it could be attributed to his Fetal Alcohol Syndrome, but there was absolutely nothing wrong with his boy. He was perfection, through and through.

Once he had Asher in their bedroom, he slowly tugged his boy flush against him. He clasped his boy's face in his hands and murmured, "Are you sure about this?"

Asher nodded, eyes wide. "Yes. I can't wait any longer. I need you. Make me yours."

Thornton pulled Asher in for a soft kiss, but when Asher gripped his shirt and tugged him closer, he let out a growl and plundered Asher's mouth. His lips, tongue, and teeth took possession of Asher with every kiss, lick, and bite. When they were both breathing heavily, utterly consumed with each other, Thornton pulled back and smiled at the way Asher leaned forward, chasing his lips for more.

Thornton couldn't help but give his boy what he wanted, but in the form of several chaste kisses, chuckling when Asher pouted. "I'll take care of you. Let me unwrap my gift."

The blush that bloomed over Asher's skin warmed Thornton's heart. He'd never tire of the fact he could affect Asher with just a few sweet words. He knew it was an addiction he'd be adding to his list. His ever-growing, Asher addiction list of things that drove him absolutely crazy about the sweet boy in his arms.

He made slow, sensual work of taking Asher's clothes off. For every bit he revealed, he trailed kisses, licks, and nips along Asher's skin, branding him inch by tantalizing inch. But his boy wasn't idle, waiting on him for permission to touch. Asher's hands were in his hair, his nails scratching over his scalp, down his neck, along his shoulders, up his arms. Always touching.

The sensation of Asher's roving fingers mapping out his own body was something he'd always treasure. When his lovely boy was naked, cock proudly jutting up from his body, Thornton stood and walked a circle around him, trailing his fingertips up his arm, down his back, along his lower back, up his side, and over his belly, making Asher shiver.

Loving the fresh goosebumps all over Asher's skin, he leaned in and could feel the warmth of Asher's cheek nearly touching his own. "You're so beautiful, baby boy."

And he was; just perfect in every possible way. Lust shot through Thornton as Asher shuddered from his words alone. He started to yank his shirt over his head, but Asher stopped him with his hands on the bottom hem of his tee. "Daddy, can I undress you?"

He nodded and had to take a deep breath to calm himself down. Asher inched his shirt up, his fingers caressing over Thornton's skin, grazing his nipples, sending shock waves of pleasure zinging down to Thornton's dick. But when his shirt was gone and he'd assumed Asher would divest him quickly of his pants and the rest, all he did was slip a single finger into the band of his jeans and brush the back of it against Thornton's lower abdomen, back and forth.

How that exact spot had become some new erogenous zone, Thornton had *no* idea. But by the time Asher had finally stopped his torture, it took everything in Thornton not to toss Asher on the bed and fuck him senseless. He couldn't keep a growl from escaping his throat, though, and he watched as Asher's skin pinked with another blush, and the boy met his eyes as he bit his lip.

"Take the rest of Daddy's clothes off, now. I can't wait any longer for you to be stretched out on our bed underneath me."

Asher nodded. "Yes, Daddy."

Fucking fuck.

He knew Asher wasn't trying to manipulate him with his sweet, innocent, soft voice, but it really fucking did it for him. Finally, his pants and boxer briefs were down around his ankles, and he stepped out of them. But when he thought Asher would stand, his sweet boy gazed up at him as he gripped Thornton's steely length. "Daddy?"

His voice grated out when he replied, "Yeah, baby?"

"I want to worship your cock someday."

His brow furrowed. "You've already sucked Daddy's cock. But I'm always willing to have my boy on his knees for me."

"Hmm mm." Asher shook his head and leaned in to breathe in the smell of Thornton's manhood, rubbing Thornton's cock along his smooth cheek, eyes closing in near ecstasy like Thornton's dick was something he'd dreamt about but never been allowed to touch. Thornton cupped the back of his boy's head, holding him close. When Asher finally opened his eyes, his pupils blown, lips open as he puffed out little aroused breaths, Thornton nearly lost it then and there.

Thornton cleared his throat, swallowed. "No?"

Asher slowly shook his head but kept Thornton's dick against his cheek, and somehow the movement of his dick against Asher's soft skin was enough to have him dripping precum. But then Asher said, "No, Daddy. I want to be your cock warmer all day. I want to be on my knees worshiping it. I want to touch it and take care of it and make it happy over and over again."

Fucking hell. His voice was a guttural whisper when he replied, "How is it that this dirty boy at my feet is the same shy man I met only weeks ago? You wanna be my little cock warmer? Hmm? My pretty, naughty, little cockslut?"

Asher nodded without saying a word, Thornton's dick still pressed up against his cheek until Asher turned to the side, licked up his shaft, and took it into his mouth. Moved his sweet, hot mouth up and down Thornton's cock, eyes never leaving Thornton's. He finally let it go with a pop. "Yes, Daddy. I want to be your pretty, naughty, little cockslut more than anything. Does that make me a bad boy?"

He squeezed his eyes shut and tilted his head back, unable to believe his sweet innocent boy had all these hot little fantasies he'd never shared. Fuck, but they were going to have fun together. Finally, after getting hold of himself, he lowered his gaze back to Asher. "Do you want to be my bad little boy?"

"Yes, Daddy."

"Yeah? You want Daddy to use your body for his own pleasure? Take you rough, use you hard? You want to be under Daddy's control, ordered to get on your knees and present your ass whenever I want? Is that what my sweet boy wants from his Daddy?"

"Yes, please."

"But you also want to remain my sweet, shy, innocent boy too, don't you?"

"Yes, Daddy."

"My little angel boy and my little devil boy, all wrapped up in such a pretty package. You continue to surprise me, baby, and that makes Daddy very happy."

Thornton leaned down and helped Asher up, sitting him gently on the edge of the bed. He longed to toss Asher back onto it and fuck into him fast and hard after his dirty request, but not for his first time and not while his ribs weren't ready for it. But to know Asher craved rougher handling and more control, when they'd never even talked about it? Oh fuck, did he want to give it to him.

He liked the rougher side of sex, but if his boy had never wanted to explore that, he would have been fine without it. Asher was worth more than the loss of that part of himself. But knowing he didn't have to cheat himself of those urges more than thrilled him. He liked a good hard fuck, and he liked taking a boy over until he was well-used and wrung dry.

His cock was about to explode, and he knew he had to get himself under control for Asher's sake. He leaned over Asher. "Wrap your arms around me."

Scooping his hand under Asher's ass, the boy's legs on either side of his hips, he maneuvered Asher further up on the bed. When his boy's head lay against the pillows, he moved back a bit and kneeled between his legs. Asher's eyes met his, and his knees, which were bent, slowly lowered out to his sides, opening himself to his Daddy's hungry gaze.

Unable and unwilling to deprive himself of such a gift, he lay down on the bed, gently palmed the back of Asher's thighs, and pushed them back to split the boy even wider open for his mouth. God, the first taste of his boy's most intimate place, the sweet musk revving him up even more, was unlike anything he'd ever tasted. Asher's body was made for him and him alone.

The moans and whimpers he got when he licked from the boy's hole up to his taint and back down again were music to his ears. Asher, unable to curl enough to grip Thornton's hair, reached as far as he could, hand cupping his cock and moaning. But when his tongue breached Asher's sweet hole, the boy cried out and began to undulate as much as he could, pushing back against Thornton's face.

"Daddy… please." His boy's breathless, desperate whisper had him gazing up, but Asher's eyes were squeezed shut, head thrown back into the pillows.

"Please what, baby?"

"I don't want to wait. Don't make me wait."

"You want Daddy inside of you, little boy?"

"God, please! Yes, yes, yes."

Kneeling on the bed again, he reached over Asher to grab the lube from the nightstand drawer, loving Asher's hands roaming over every part of Thornton's body he could touch. Thornton squeezed some lube onto his fingers and slowly, methodically readied Asher for his cock. It wouldn't take long—they'd been prepping him for weeks—but he wasn't going to shove in without every precaution to make sure his boy was ready for him.

He met Asher's gaze, pouring more lube in his palm. "Nothing between us?"

CHAPTER TWENTY-ONE

Asher

A sher shook his head. "Nothing between us, please, Daddy."
Thornton nodded, expression serious. "I'll give you what you need, baby boy."

God, yes, he knew Thornton would. Knew it deep down in his bones. He didn't want anything between them. Never, ever, anything between them. He wanted his first time to be perfect, and perfect was feeling Thornton slide into him, knowing it was him only, no latex separating them, and Daddy's cum deep inside of him when he finally came. He needed Daddy to fill him up, to leave part of himself behind, to make him whole. Needed it like he needed oxygen to breathe.

He watched as Thornton wrapped his huge palm around his long, hard cock and slowly jacked himself with his lube-slicked hand. God, Thornton was a beautiful man. When Thornton raised his eyes to meet Asher's, they were burning with intensity. He leaned over Asher, weight on one hand beside Asher on the bed, and slowly guided his huge cockhead to Asher's entrance, nudging it against Asher's tight pucker, eliciting a gasp. He was ready—he knew he was—but he couldn't keep himself from tensing up.

Thornton lifted his gaze to Asher's face, confidence oozing from him, a gentle smile of reassurance relaxing Asher before he even spoke. "I'm gonna take care of you. Trust me. Open yourself up for Daddy. Let me in, baby boy."

He let his body relax and pushed out at the cock that was—even though he'd been prepped—a bit larger than the biggest dildo they'd been prepping him with. It was a stretch, and the pull of his taut skin as it surrounded Thornton's crown hurt, but in the best way. Because it *should* hurt, shouldn't it? The pain etched itself indelibly into his brain, never to forget, always to remember this first time with the man he loved.

Oh, god. He loved Thornton. He fucking loved this man with everything he was, everything he had.

Asher met Thornton's eyes, and the passion between them ratcheted up several notches as what he realized sunk in, just as Daddy's cockhead slipped past his second ring. Asher took the pain and reveled in it, opened himself wider, drew Daddy inside of him, his eyes stinging from the physical and emotional intensity of it all. Thornton's gaze heated. "You're my good boy, Asher. Take it for me, for us." Asher closed his eyes and forced himself to relax even more. "That's it. Ahh, Asher, baby."

Thornton slid in, bottoming out, and he slowly lowered to his elbows, hovering over Asher but otherwise holding still, waiting. Thornton's face was so calm, so serene, breathing confidence into Asher as the seconds ticked by. But god, he could feel what it was taking for Thornton to remain still, to keep himself from pulling out and thrusting back in. Daddy's body was shaking with it.

He reached up, clasped Thornton's face, and pulled him down for a mind-numbing kiss. "Make me feel good, Daddy."

Thornton groaned and nuzzled into the crook of Asher's neck as he slowly pulled nearly all the way out and slid back in. Asher whimpered. He'd never felt anything so good. His body was humming like a live wire, and he gasped as Thornton pushed back in a third time. And then Thornton was moving faster but with so much gentleness Asher could hardly believe it. He was expecting his ribs to hurt, and while he felt them twinge at the repeated movements, the pleasure far outweighed the pain.

Thornton pulled back a bit to raise himself up on his knees, spreading them wide and, in turn, spreading Asher's leg's even wider, before settling back down on his elbows. Just that change in angle had Asher's nerve endings singing. As Thornton slowly pistoned in and out, Asher's prostate was being pegged over and over and over.

Thornton growled in his ear. "Fuck, baby, you feel so good."

He whimpered. "Daddy."

"Yeah, sweetheart. You're taking Daddy's cock so well."

They lost themselves to the rhythm of it, Thornton's grunts, moans, and groans clashed against Asher's mewling, whimpers, and sighs. And suddenly he couldn't take anymore without touching himself. "Daddy, please, I need…"

"I know what you need."

And he did. He shifted his weight to one arm and reached between them, gripping Asher's cock in a tight fist, the same fist he'd used earlier on his own cock, the small trace of the lube remaining was enough to smooth the way. Asher gripped onto the back of Thornton's head, pulling him in for a deep kiss. Nearly out of his mind with the need to come, he tipped his head back, and Thornton took advantage of his movement to suck and nip on Asher's neck and then bit down on the juncture between neck and shoulder, causing him to cry out.

"Daddy, please, please, please."

"Almost, baby. Almost."

Asher whimpered, no longer in control of his body, giving it up to Thornton and floating in the whirlwind of feelings. Thornton's hips lost their smooth movement, choppy half thrusts punctuated by Thornton's groans, nearly tipped him over the edge, but he wouldn't, not until…

"Come for Daddy, baby boy."

He let go, blissfully releasing everything he'd been holding back, cum splatting his stomach. Thornton jerked with a groan, stilling inside him for several seconds before he continued his uneven pace. "Fuck, fuck, fuck, fuck. Asher, god, baby."

Several long moments slipped by them as they both caught their breath, aftershocks seeming to rip through Thornton several times. He ran his hand up and down Thornton's sweaty back, loving that his man had worked hard enough to pleasure them both that he'd worked up a good sweat.

He felt when Thornton's body had no more energy to hold him up and braced for their bodies to make contact, but ever careful of him, Thornton gently pulled out, leaving him feeling somewhat bereft, until he lay down beside Asher and tugged him close, into the crook of his arm. Resting his head on Thornton's chest, Asher couldn't ever remember feeling so relaxed, so happy, and so sated.

***

Everywhere he turned, there were more people. It felt like they were crawling out of the fucking woodwork. There was a sale going on at The Glasshouse, and the portion of the greenhouse that was open to customers seemed to be twice as busy as it normally was.

He'd been fine at first. He'd done his deep breathing exercises, and he'd kept to the area that was for employees only, but he hadn't counted on the sale bringing in so many customers, and he'd saved his data collection from the open part of the greenhouse until last minute for some fucking reason, working his way from the back to the front.

He'd always done it the opposite way, so he rarely had to deal with customers. But his mind was such a mess and he wasn't coping well. And on a good day, he could have handled it better, but this… this wasn't a good day.

He was struggling. And for as far back as Asher could remember, it hadn't been this bad. He knew—deep down he knew—he'd created the current state he was in. But that didn't make it easier to breathe; that didn't make it easier to function. Nothing seemed to do that. All the normal things he used to do to keep the anxiety under control weren't working anymore. It was like his security blanket was yanked out from under him.

There was pounding in his head and pounding…

"Asher, open the door."

"I—" He cleared his throat and tried again. "I'll be right out."

"Asher…"

"I'm fine, Madi. I—"

"You're not fine. Do I need to call Thornton, or are you going to open the door?"

His stomach plummeted. She wouldn't, would she? "Madi, don't…"

"Then open the door because right now you're scaring me, and if you won't let me help you, you need to call Thornton, or I'll do it for you."

He sighed, knowing she'd do it if he pushed her. He got up from the floor of the supply room, where he'd been leaning against the door so no one—namely

Madi—could come in. The irony that he was opening the door for the very person he'd been trying to keep out wasn't lost on him. He took a couple of breaths—they weren't deep; he didn't have it in him—but they were fortifying, so that was as good as he could do.

Opening the door, he made to walk out into the stockroom, but her hand on his shoulder kept him right where he was as she passed him on her way into the small room and closed the door behind her. "Come on, I told you I'm fine. Let's go."

"You're not fine. What's going on with you, Ash?"

"Nothing. I just got overwhelmed. I'm fine now. I just needed a few minutes, that's all."

She frowned. "You were white as a ghost when you walked out of the greenhouse. I haven't seen you like that in a while. I think you should call Thornton to pick you up early."

He shook his head. The truth was he'd felt a panic attack looming, and he'd escaped before it hit and humiliated him in front of paying customers. He wasn't about to let Thornton see him like this. There was no way. "He's in meetings all day. I'm sure he's catching up on stuff he put off while I was staying with him."

"You know he'd drop everything to come get you, right? That's what Daddies do."

"Yeah, but I don't want him to have to rescue me, Madi. I'm an adult, and I should be able to take care of myself."

She looked disappointed in him, which made everything worse. "Everybody needs help sometimes, Asher. Maybe it's time for you to ask for it."

He resented her as much as he was grateful for her in that moment, and he wasn't about to take his panic and piss-poor mood out on her. "If I'm feeling rough this evening when he's done with his meetings, I'll give him a call. Please, just let me handle this myself, all right? It's important to me."

She looked as if she might push back, might try to convince him otherwise, but with a slump of her shoulders, she relented. "Okay, but you should think about trusting him to take care of you."

"I do trust him, Madi. I just... I want to be able to take care of myself."

She hugged him, and when she pulled back, she whispered, "You've proven you could do that your whole damn life, Ash. But now that you have Thornton, you don't have to anymore."

She opened the door and walked out, leaving him there. The truth of her words hit him hard as he finally made his way back out to the floor, but that didn't change the fact he couldn't count on Thornton every second of every day. It wasn't realistic, and it wasn't fair to Thornton. His anxiety was an albatross around his own neck; he wasn't going to bring Thornton down with him. He just had to sort his own shit out, get himself under control, and then things would even out.

But as things often went, things never evened out, and his week had continually gotten worse as he went along, carried by the currents of whatever anxiety attack hit him next. It was like a perpetual game of whack-a-mole. As soon as he took care of one thing causing him to panic, something else cropped up.

Thornton had been driving him each day. And so far, he'd been able to keep his shit together around him. Except for Monday, when he'd had a meltdown before Thornton had even pulled out of the driveway. But he'd half expected that, and by *that* time, he'd panicked around Thornton enough that he was *embarrassed* but not completely humiliated.

When he'd finally gotten himself under control and Thornton had dropped him off at work, he had a good feeling about the coming days. But it seemed that Murphy's Law was playing out in every aspect of his life. And with the weekend upon him, he wasn't sure how he was going to handle being back at Thornton's place after the week he'd had.

He'd finished his work without any more mishaps and had revved himself up for Thornton to arrive. So when Daddy's sleek new BMW SUV slid into the parking space that had just emptied up in front of The Glasshouse, he pushed through the double doors, a smile on his face, ready for some Daddy time, some playtime, and some sexy time.

Things had to get better, right?

He slid into the passenger seat and leaned across the console to kiss Thornton. "Hi, Daddy."

Thornton clasped the side of his face and gazed into his eyes. "Hey, baby boy. I missed you this week. You ready for the weekend?"

He nodded because he was. He really was. Maybe he'd be able to get some decent sleep, and playtime would get him back on track. Thornton sat back and clasped his hand, and Asher closed his eyes as they idled, Enya's "Watermark" already playing. They sat as he silently did his deep breathing exercises and repeated his mantra in his head.

It was the ritual he'd always gone through for himself, and when Thornton had asked to know what he did to keep the panic at bay when he was in a car, he'd told him exactly what. From that point forward, Enya had been available, and Thornton had told him they'd sit and wait as the car idled, holding hands. And when Asher was ready, all he had to do was squeeze Thornton's hand and they'd be on their way.

It was the first car ride he'd taken with Thornton during his recuperation. Or rather, it was the day he'd agreed to take a ride, but his panic had been so awful, he'd lost it in the garage, and then they'd only made it to the car before another one hit. Thornton had promised him they wouldn't be driving anywhere; they'd just sit in the car. That was when he'd asked what Asher did to get by, and pretty soon Thornton had opened the garage bay and turned the car on, queuing Enya immediately. And they'd sat there, doing nothing but holding hands and listening to Enya.

Thinking back, he realized that was the moment he'd fallen in love with Thornton. He hadn't known it at the time. It hadn't clicked until the night he'd lost his virginity, but when he thought on it long and hard, that had been the moment it had happened. Just about at the two-week mark after they'd met. Jesus, talk about falling fast. It was ridiculous. But he realized he wouldn't change it for the world.

Squeezing Thornton's hand, they backed slowly out of the parking space and were on their way home. Or, rather, to Thornton's home. He kept his eyes closed most of the way, and Thornton didn't say a word, allowing him to focus on his mantra, music, and breathing. When they got there, Thornton grabbed Asher's backpack and led him inside. Beauty and Beast were there to greet him. He got down on his knees in front of the dogs and hugged them, getting several licks on his face as a result. Asher's heart swelled in his chest when he realized how much he'd missed them since he'd left.

He felt a warmth at his back and realized Thornton had squatted down behind him. He gave his pups some scratches and then placed his hands on Asher's shoulders, giving the side of his neck a kiss, his voice a near-whisper when he said, "They missed you. Daddy missed you, too."

He nearly broke right then but held himself together by the skin of his teeth.

He leaned back into Thornton's embrace and managed to keep his voice steady when he said, "I missed you all, too."

They stayed like that for several minutes, petting the puppies, Thornton's strong presence behind him. He needed that time to settle himself before he could meet Thornton's gaze, or his emotional turmoil would show. When they finally made it into the kitchen, Thornton asked, "Have you had any lunch?"

He shook his head. "I was too busy. But I can just have a snack. You don't have to go to any trouble."

Thornton met his gaze then, and the look he gave Asher made him uneasy for the conversations he was sure would be forthcoming during his weekend stay. Daddy saw through him. He'd known he would. All Asher could do was play down the trouble he'd had while he'd been on his own. There were no rules he had to tell Daddy everything, and Asher wanted to keep a bit of pride.

"Go on up and change. Get comfortable. By the time you come down, I'll have your lunch ready. I want you to be in your little space as much as possible this weekend. I think you need it, and I want you relaxed. Daddy wants his boy here with him. But I'm happy if you'd like to save that until tomorrow and Sunday. What would you prefer?"

He could tell Thornton hadn't wanted to give him a choice. He'd wanted to demand, and honestly, he'd have preferred it that way. He didn't want to make decisions. He wanted to sink into regression and let it take him away from himself. Away from the week, away from the feelings and emotions of everything he'd had running through his head every day since he'd left Thornton's house to go home.

"I'd like to be little, Daddy."

Thornton approached, arms outstretched, and gathered him in, rocking him back and forth and rubbing his back. "That's my good boy. Go on then. Come back down when you're ready."

He'd made quick work of shucking off the remnants of his adult self as he pulled on some Star Wars pajamas with baby Yodas on them. He'd gone down to a train sandwich on his plate, baby carrots, and hummus. He'd never been so happy to see his place setting in his life. He felt himself settle for the first time in five days, and it felt like he'd lost a heavy burden when the weight of the week slipped off his shoulders.

Thornton sat down kitty-corner to him, with his own sandwich.

Asher beamed up at him, bouncing in his seat. "Thank you, Daddy. It looks yummy." He took a sip from his cup, wondering what he'd find in it, and beamed when he tasted grape juice. "Mmm." He gasped and stood up. "Did you leave my track out?"

He started to turn towards the front of the house, wanting to get a glimpse of the huge track he'd made and never taken down. It was too perfect. He knew he'd eventually want to rebuild something different, but—

"Asher, I promised I'd leave your track just exactly as it was, and I did. But you need to eat your lunch like a good boy before you get to play."

He sighed, knowing he wouldn't be able to talk Daddy out of his decision. "Okay. Thank you for leaving it up."

"You're welcome. You can play with it this afternoon, and then I thought we could play Go Fish, or you could color. I got those new coloring books we ordered last weekend, and I might have gotten you some pretty gel pens to use as well."

He gasped and bounced in his chair. "Are they sparkly? Remember I said I liked sparkly gel pens, and mine were running out? Did you get me new sparklies?" When Daddy just chuckled, Asher patted him on the arm. "Can I see them?"

"You can see them after you've eaten."

Oh my gosh, it's going to be such a good weekend.

He hurried through his lunch, finishing every last bite and soaking in Daddy's praise when he took his dishes to the sink. Daddy showed him his new sparkly gel pens, and he drew a couple of doodles but couldn't hold back anymore and practically ran to the playroom, Beauty and Beast on his heels. When he saw the room had in fact been left as he'd requested, he squealed and got down on his knees to play.

***

When Asher had seen that his place setting for dinner on Sunday matched Thornton's, he knew little time was over. He'd had the best weekend and had been little throughout. He'd finally started feeling like he'd felt the week before, and he knew he'd flourished under Daddy's care. He knew adult time was coming, but he'd been happy to ignore it and continue as his little self for as long as Daddy would allow.

But after he'd washed up for dinner, he'd walked in the kitchen and seen the adult place setting, and it had been like a record player coming to a screeching halt. It almost felt like a physical blow; he'd stumbled a bit when he'd seen it. He glanced over at Thornton, who was getting them both some milk to drink with dinner. He met Thornton's gaze and saw a deep well of understanding there, tinged with sadness.

He turned away to keep Thornton from seeing all of his emotions written so clearly on his face and got himself under control before Thornton brought their drinks over. They ate together and chatted about Thornton's week and the conversation Asher and Madi had with Jenn about buying The Glasshouse.

She was still five months out from leaving, so they had time, but she'd begun to show each of them some things here and there that she did as the owner. She wanted to spread out their training so they could decide how they were going to handle the managerial tasks and didn't want to push while Asher was still only working part-time, but they'd agreed as soon as he was back full-time, they'd start to sort out the particulars.

He was both excited about that and scared to death. Being a co-owner of The Glasshouse had been all in his mind until he'd gotten back to work. Suddenly, it had become very, very real, and while he hadn't changed his mind, it had overwhelmed him and, Asher could admit to himself, had probably prompted some of his anxiety during the week.

When dinner was over, he brought his plate to the sink and began to clean up, but Thornton stayed his hand. "I want you to go take a relaxing bath while I finish up down here and lock up for the night. I'll help you finish once I get up there, and then I think we need to talk, all right?"

Asher drew in a deep breath and let it out slowly. "Okay. Thank you for dinner, Daddy."

"You're welcome, sweet boy. Go on, go relax for a bit. I'll be up soon."

He'd put in his favorite bath bomb and soaked until he was nearly pruney. Thornton, true to his word, came up and washed his body from head to toe. He'd grown hard while Thornton's soapy bath mitt was running over his body, but Thornton hadn't done anything but clean him. Once he was dried, he brushed his teeth and packed all his toiletries in his bag, bringing it into the bedroom with him. He pulled on some fresh pajamas, began gathering his things, and putting them in his bag.

"What did you want to talk about?"

He figured he could play dumb and keep busy, so he never even looked at Thornton, who was in his lounge chair, his own pajamas on, watching his every move like a hawk. But when Thornton didn't respond, he couldn't help but look up. Daddy's steely gaze was on Asher, and his expression was not happy. That sent a jolt of anxiety singing through every synapse in his body, and he stilled, caught in the trap of those eyes.

His heart rate ratcheted up, and he looked down, folding the clothes painstakingly to avoid the scrutiny he knew was absolutely unavoidable. "Asher, put your clothes down and come sit with me."

"I'm almost do—"

"Now, boy."

He shivered in some kind of weird "scared to death and yet turned on by that commanding tone" sort of reaction before he finally got his feet moving. "Yes, Daddy."

When he stood in front of Thornton, not knowing what he was supposed to do, Thornton tipped Asher gently into his arms and onto his lap. "That's better. I'd like you to tell me about your week—"

"I already told—"

Thornton clasped his chin in his hand. "Boy, you will not interrupt me when I'm speaking. Is that understood?"

Again, with his body's weird reaction to Thornton's tone. "Yes, Daddy."

"As I was saying, I'd like you to tell me the *truth* about your week. I want to know what you haven't told me. I want to know what's put the dark circles under your eyes, and the unhappiness there as well, and the tension and wariness in your shoulders. You were a mess on Friday, boy, and you looked so unhappy at dinner. It's killing me."

Asher didn't think he'd be able to hold back any longer. He wanted to unload his burdens, and he wanted to tell Daddy everything, but he didn't want to be weak, and he didn't want Daddy to think less of him. Thornton leaned down to bring their foreheads together. "Asher, have you been happy this week? And please, for god's sake, tell the truth."

Asher could only shake his head.

"Me either."

That got Asher's attention. "You haven't been happy?"

"Fuck no. I've been miserable. Just ask Beauty and Beast. Hell, ask Trent. He called me a grumpy bear, a pain in his ass, and an asshole."

Asher could hear Trent calling him all those things, and he couldn't help but smile at the thought of asking Beauty and Beast if Daddy had been miserable. His voice was hoarse when he whispered, "You're not an asshole, Daddy."

Thornton kissed his forehead and then gazed into his eyes. "Asher, I've thought of nothing but you this week. I hardly got any work done; the meetings I was in will have to be repeated because I was useless. I hate not being able to come home to you. I hate eating alone at my table with only the dogs watching me."

Asher pulled his lips between his teeth to keep a grin from splitting his face as Thornton continued his gentle tirade. "I hate taking showers alone and not giving you a bath. I hate not falling asleep with you lying next to me and waking up with you wrapped around me like a limpet. And I swear to god, if I have to keep walking by that playroom door with your train track set up but no boy there to play with it, I'm gonna lose my mind."

He couldn't help but picture Thornton looking in the room every day and not seeing him there. All week he'd been thinking about trying to prove—god, he didn't even know what. But one thing was for sure: he hadn't thought about how it was making Thornton feel, and that realization, like nothing else, made him feel awful, and sick, and so angry at himself.

"Asher, I don't want the man I love to live across town. I want him with me, every day. I get that it's quick. I know we've moved faster than what people consider normal, but fuck normal. I need you by my side. You've given me a taste of what my life could be like, and then you left and took it with you."

Thornton clasped Asher's face in both of his hands. "Please, please, baby, stop punishing yourself because you think you should be able to do it on your own. Of *course* you can do it on your own. You've been doing it your whole life. Let Daddy take care of you. Let Daddy be your strength when you need it. Jesus, just... let Daddy love you. Please."

Love. Love. Love. Love.

"You love me?"

"Sweet boy, I am so head over heels, cupid's arrow through the heart, over-the-top in love with you, it consumes me."

And just like that, every emotion, all the turmoil, every bit of the stress, and all his anxiety was released, tremors wracking his frame as Daddy's arms wrapped around him and held him tight. It was a long time before his body could catch up with his mind and calm down, the tension had been so all consuming it was like his muscles were twitching as they released the burden of his fears.

CHAPTER TWENTY-TWO

Thornton

W hen Asher's body trembled in his arms, he wrapped himself around his boy and just held on through the storm of emotions Asher had clearly been holding in. Thornton had been miserable without him that week, but every time he'd seen him, he'd put on a smiling face and done his best to support Asher's need for independence. But as the week wore on, he saw signs of things going downhill.

Goddamn, watching his boy suffer every single day he'd picked him up, having Asher deny anything was wrong, and having to drop him off at his apartment had been torture. He'd asked Asher to call every night before bed. He'd also asked him to call if he was having a panic attack and needed help, even if it was just to hear his voice over the phone line. But other than the nightly calls, Asher hadn't reached out.

The fact that Asher had immersed himself so deeply into little time that weekend brought home like nothing would that Asher needed that time like he needed air to breathe and food to eat. Every bit of stress just floated away for his boy when Asher allowed himself to let go and be the little he was meant to be. This boy needed him, and not just on weekends. Asher needed him every day, and he needed Asher just as much.

He could admit that it hurt when Asher had wanted to step away from them to be able to think clearly, and in the end, he'd needed to give that much to his boy so Asher didn't have doubts later on. But in only a week, Asher seemed like a shell of the man he'd been the night they'd made love.

It was obvious thinking clearly hadn't been what had been going on. And the fact Thornton didn't even *know* what had been going on had frustration churning in his gut. Asher was exhausted, that much Thornton could tell, but there was so much going on under the surface, and he was bound and determined to get at it and fix it.

It wasn't going to be easy, but he'd have to wear Asher down. He'd given him the weekend to relax, get some rest, eat well, and just be: no panic, no outside stimulation, no visitors. But he wasn't about to put it off anymore. Asher was going back to work the next day, and damned if he was going to let the boy continue to torture himself.

He started speaking softly. "I realized I was in love with you the day before you went back to work. It happened gradually, before that, but when you were showing me your train track and everything it could do, you were so excited, proud, and happy, I realized I wanted to spend the rest of my life making that smile, happiness, and radiance show on that beautiful face of yours."

Asher blinked, emotions written all over his face. "I love you too."

He smiled at that, knowing and feeling the truth of it. He'd known when they'd made love that night. It had been in his boy's eyes, written so clearly. "Yeah?"

Asher swallowed and nodded, his earnest gaze making Thornton smile. "I realized it that same day. It overwhelmed me, scared me. Suddenly, I had so much to lose, and I got scared I was going to be too much for you."

He shook his head, his heart breaking at Asher's doubts, in himself and in Thornton. "Never."

Asher hunched in on himself. "You can't know that."

"I can. Asher, I'm in love with you, and I'm a Daddy, a true caregiver, and it's all I know how to be. The fact that you need my care, and thrive under my care, makes us a perfect match. I may not know the extent of your anxiety. I'm sure I'll see that as time goes by, but it doesn't matter what you need; I will always move mountains to help you get it."

"But you can't fix me. And you can't do everything for me. I don't want that."

"Oh, baby. I won't be doing everything for you. *You'll* be doing the work, I'll just be a safe place to run to; I'll catch you if you fall, or I'll bandage your knees if I don't get there in time. And I'm not trying to fix you."

Doubt shone in Asher's gaze. "Are you sure?"

"I'm positive. I know you feel broken—you've said as much—but you're not, Asher. You're banged up, and you're bruised, but it's nothing a little time, attention, and a helping hand or two can't fix as long as you're putting in the work. And you know how I feel about the importance of therapy."

Asher nodded, looking down at his hands in his lap. "I know. I haven't cancelled the appointment. Maybe..." Asher glanced up at him, eyes hopeful. "Maybe you could take me and go in with me?"

"I wouldn't miss it for the world, baby. I already had Jason block off my calendar."

Asher drew in a deep breath that faltered with shaky emotion and nodded. "I'd like that. Thank you."

He leaned down and kissed Asher's nose, which earned him a little smile, and then those sweet kissable lips called to him, and he answered with a kiss. "You're welcome. Now, I know you're hoping I've forgotten, but I really do want to know everything you've gone through this week. I think it's important for you to tell me what went wrong. It will help me know how to help, and it will help you learn to let your guard down and trust that Daddy can take care of you and your needs."

This time, the sigh Asher heaved out was frustrated but resigned. "I didn't think it was going to be as hard as it was. You dropped me off at work on Monday, and I just felt untethered. Madi and Jenn were there waiting, and we had a quick meeting about the business. But then I had to fill out some paperwork about my medical leave, and I don't know why, but it stressed me out."

Asher's voice was taking on a frantic edge as he continued. "And then later that day, a customer approached me, and they wanted help and guidance on planting in their own gardens. I had to excuse myself because I felt a panic attack coming on. I got myself under control and eventually went back and helped them, but that isn't usually something that would set me off. One-on-one discussions are usually okay. It's crowds or too many people trying to talk to me at once that set me off."

"I hate that you had to deal with that, baby."

Asher shrugged. "After you dropped me off at home, I realized everything fresh in my refrigerator had gone bad. I had no fresh produce. And even though I had enough frozen meals and dry goods to get me through, I still felt panic clawing at me. Then I worked out pretty hard that night, but when I went to go shower, the shower curtain was still gone, obviously, and I had a flashback of that night, sitting on the floor of the shower with the freezing cold water pouring over me. I couldn't hold a panic attack back, and when I finally got myself under control, I couldn't sleep for hours."

He knew Asher needed to get it all out, so he didn't interrupt. His boy took a fortifying breath and continued. "The next morning, I woke up late because I'd finally fallen asleep at four in the morning, and I kept hitting snooze. So then I made my coffee, but it was too sweet, so I made it again and added too much creamer. I made coffee four times for myself that morning. And I don't know how, but I managed to get through most of the day on Tuesday without much incident, but after you dropped me off, I was getting calls from your car insurance company about my doctor appointments and my medical leave provider about my return to work. And it just seemed like it was all too much. I was panicking trying to get the information they needed.

"On Wednesday—well, you remember Wednesday. It took me twenty minutes sitting in your car, doing my exercises, for me to be able to allow you to drive me to work. I had low-level anxiety all day that day and was so scatterbrained. I kept forgetting stuff. And you came and picked me up to drive me home, and I did okay, but when I got to my door, I realized I'd left my keys at work. I kept myself under control and contacted the landlord, but I had to leave a message."

Thornton pulled him closer, hugged him tighter, and murmured, "Baby, why didn't you call me? I would've turned around immediately."

"I know, but that's just the thing. I wasn't thinking logically, and honestly, I wouldn't have wanted you to see me panicking over something so stupid. I just sat, waiting in the hallway outside of my door. I was about to order a Lyft ride to take me back to work, but the landlord finally called me back. He had to come over anyway for maintenance on another apartment, so he let me in with his master key."

"How long were you waiting on your own, baby?"

Asher scrubbed his face, his frustration mounting. "An hour and a half."

Thornton wanted to ask again why he didn't call; he wanted to point out he could've taken Asher home, and they could've had a nice dinner together, or he could have taken Asher directly back to The Glasshouse to get his keys. Either of those things would have worked as long as Asher called him. And it fucking killed him that Asher didn't.

"Thursday went pretty well. No big incidents. Just the low-level anxiety as my constant shadow. That and forgetfulness. My concentration wasn't there. I was frustrated with myself. Jenn was so patient and kind, and so was Madi. But I just felt so out of control. Friday was pretty miserable. There was a big sale at The Glasshouse, which drew a lot of people. In the past, that would have made me uneasy, but I would've handled it better. And for some reason, it didn't occur to me to get done with all of my work in the public areas so that when it got to be really busy, I would be working in the part of the greenhouse that is closed off to customers."

All Thornton could do was rub his boy's back and let him get it all out. "I lost my shit, practically ran through the store, and locked myself in the supply closet in the stockroom. Madi eventually came back and helped me, told me I should have called you. Told me everything I already knew. And I wanted to. I so badly wanted to call you so many fucking times, but I swear to god, Thornton, we would've been on the phone every goddamn day, all day long."

He wanted to interject—he wanted to shake the boy for not calling him—but Asher was already down on himself enough. "I barely slept all week. I went home and tried every night to color in my coloring books, but I just couldn't regress on my own, no matter what I tried to do. And when that happened the first night I was home alone, I think things just started to spiral out of control for me. Somehow, I felt like now that I had had a taste of life with you, I couldn't function without you. But that just made me more determined to do so, and things just kept getting worse and worse. I felt weak, stupid, and so pathetic."

Thornton wanted to tell him to stop with the negative self-talk, but Asher was talking about his feelings during the week, and Thornton wouldn't downplay those emotions. Asher's body had begun to relax the more he purged. But it was Asher's self-confidence he needed to work on. "I'm sorry, baby. It sounds like you had a really rough week."

Asher huffed out an incredulous noise. "That's quite the understatement. I was a fucking basket case. I mean, god, I can't even consider myself a fully functional adult. At one point, I didn't know whether to be grateful to you or angry at you for showing me how good life could be. I know it wasn't your fault; I know I brought last week on myself. Whether I manifested it like a domino effect or if it was just one piece of bad luck after another, I was fucking worthless."

Thornton couldn't take anymore and let his frustration show. "That's enough."

Asher's deep sigh hurt his heart. "But that's the truth. I felt worthless."

He hugged Asher tight and rocked them both back and forth for a bit before he dove in to try and help. Taking a deep sigh, he asked, "Is that all of it? The worst of it?"

Asher nodded against his chest and murmured, "Yes."

"Okay. First, let me say: you are not worthless. You are the farthest thing from worthless. And you went through a lot, so please know I'm not diminishing how you feel. You have the right to feel what you're going to feel. And even if I wanted you to stop feeling negatively about yourself, especially about last week, it's not like I can reach into your head and change your thoughts. But as of now, you're done castigating yourself for it. You've purged it, and now it's out of your system. Understood?"

"Yes, Daddy."

He couldn't help but admonish him a bit because much of this week could have been avoided. "I know you know this, but you should have called me. Every time you panicked or felt out of control, I could have talked you down or come to help. It doesn't matter what I'm doing, I will drop everything for you if you truly need me. I love you, Ash. It kills me you didn't reach out to me."

Asher sucked in a breath and nodded. "I know. I'm angry with myself. I should have. I just... I couldn't, and I don't fully understand the reasons why."

He sighed. "Moving forward, I'm going to need you to promise you will call when you're feeling like that. I can't do my job if I don't know when I'm needed."

Asher nodded and threw his arms around Thornton's neck, hugging him tight. Thornton ran his hands up and down Asher's back. "I promise, Daddy. I'm sorry."

"I know. I know, baby. Let's talk about the rest of it, okay?"

Asher shrugged like he wasn't sure he wanted to, but he eventually nodded.

"Good boy. So what I think we should do is look at all of this from a different perspective. Let's break things down into bite-size chunks. I'll ask you some questions, and all you have to do is answer with the facts, not your feelings about them. Okay?" Asher merely nodded, not looking up at him but keeping his head against Thornton's chest. "Let's talk about the groceries, the shower curtain, and the coffee. Did you eat dry and canned goods or frozen food all week?"

"No."

"What did you do?"

Asher's brows furrowed when he answered. "I ordered groceries and had them delivered."

"Did you shower all week without a curtain?"

"No. I ordered one on Amazon, and it came the next day."

"And how about that coffee? You said you made it four times. Was the fourth one to your liking?"

Asher nodded. "Yes, it was perfect."

"So, what about all of the insurance issues? Did you figure out what they needed for your medical leave of absence? And were you able to answer the questions from my insurance company as well?"

"Yeah, it was just a bunch of questions and some paperwork they needed me to get from my doctor's office."

"And did you get the paperwork they needed?"

"Yeah, Syed helped me."

"And what about when you panicked at work? Did you treat the customers with respect and excuse yourself properly, or did you treat them rudely and possibly lose their business?"

Asher pulled back, insult written all over his features. "I'd never do that. A few times I was able to leave before I had to deal with customers at all. The one time I had to deal with the customer and I was panicking, I excused myself, got myself back under control, and then came back and helped her. She seemed really happy when she left."

He clasped his boy's chin, drawing Asher's eyes up to his. "So, from an outsider's perspective, it looks like you hit a few bumps in the road, but you dealt with every single one of them as they came along. Maybe doing so stressed you out more than normal. Maybe you panicked more often. But in the end, everything was dealt with. Do you understand what I'm getting at here?" Asher didn't respond but met his gaze. "You absolutely are not worthless."

Asher shook his head. "But… Why did it feel so big, so awful, so out of control?"

Asher tucked his head under Thornton's chin, and Thornton kissed the top. "I don't really have all the answers for you. I have some theories, though, if you want to hear them."

Asher didn't move, but Thornton heard his soft whisper: "Please, Daddy."

Feeling awful for his boy, he squeezed him tight. "I think you're a bit of a perfectionist. And I think you hold yourself to a higher standard than you hold others to. So, when you feel like you've done something wrong, it's ten times worse because of the lens you're looking through."

When Asher didn't respond, he continued, "And I think that lens has gotten more and more distorted as time goes on. You set unrealistic expectations of perfection for yourself, and when you don't reach those unrealistic goals you've set, you feel like a failure. Does any of that resonate with you?"

Asher's whole body moved with his sigh. "Maybe."

He smiled to himself and continued to talk, knowing Asher needed to hear it. "So I think you built this week up to be this huge deal in your head. Right?"

"Yeah."

Thornton nodded and rubbed Asher's back. "It was going to be the week you were going to figure everything out and prove to yourself you could do it all alone, which might then give you permission to accept my offer to move in with me because you'd proven to yourself you don't *need* to, but you *want* to." Asher cuddled deeper into his arms. "That's a pretty big week to live up to. A pretty big week to determine a really important decision in your life all on your own. Don't you think?"

"I guess." Asher's sullen response made him smile.

"I think maybe all of that snowballed and got bigger and bigger and bigger, until it was so big in your mind that all of the little things that happened during your everyday seemed too much. What do you think?"

"But why does everything always seem so hard when I'm alone, but when I'm with you, it doesn't? How are you making it all better?"

"Sweetheart, I'm not making it all better. You panicked with me three or four times, and they weren't little panic attacks, either, right?" Asher nodded and hummed in agreement. "It's not like your time here was without any problems. I'm just helping you get out of your own way a little, out of your own head. And maybe see a side of yourself you didn't know was there. Regression helps you slip out of the real world where nothing matters but the trains, the crayons, the stuffies, and the cookies."

Asher's body shook in silent laughter, and he kissed the top of his boy's head. "Maybe I'm helping because I'm someone you can rely on, someone you know you can trust, deep down. You haven't had much of that in your life, and my guess is it's something you really needed. And you know what?"

Asher leaned back and met his gaze. "What?"

"It's something I really needed, too. And I don't think I've told you how much. I was lonely before you, really lonely. I dated, but never found the right one. *You* are the right one. And, Asher, I don't care how fast it is. My mom said she knew my dad was the one the first day they met. It can happen like that sometimes. So, maybe it's just as simple as we are the right match for each other and found each other at the right time. Puzzle pieces fitting together to make a whole."

"You really need me? You're not just saying that?" The emotion in Asher's eyes and in his voice melted Thornton's heart.

"I really do. You allowed me to see I was taking my life and my work too seriously. And even though I knew Jimmy and I would never work, you helped me see I need to be needed more than I even realized. And that I'm a twenty-four-seven Daddy who needs a twenty-four-seven boy."

Confusion marred Asher's brow. "I can't regress all the time."

Thornton chuckled. "I know that, baby. But I realized I love it when you call me Daddy when you're not regressing, maybe especially then. I love hearing it when we're making love. I know I'm gonna love it when I'm fucking you into the mattress and making you scream it out loud."

Asher's sweet blush made him smile and chuckle when his boy ducked his head under Thornton's chin again. "And maybe when things settle down a bit, you and I can talk more about the aspect of control, and how much of it you want to hand over to me. It might help to know I'm the one tasked with making your decisions. If you don't have to worry about things like that, it's less anxiety for you to deal with."

That got Asher's attention. "You'd want that?"

"If you didn't, I'd be happy without it. But yeah, I'd really want that, if you allowed it. God, the things you do to me, Asher. I just want to take you over, own you, be the one that leads so you can follow."

Asher's eyes grew wide, his cheeks pinked up, and his pupils blew wide. "Um... I think I'd like that, Daddy."

Thornton smiled and booped Asher's nose. "I thought you might. But that's not going to solve everything. My guess is you have some form of PTSD from the abuse you suffered when you were a child."

Asher shook his head. "I wasn't—"

Thornton interrupted, unwilling to let Asher deny the truth. "You were. Neglect and child endangerment are both forms of abuse, Asher. And you had more of both than any child should be forced to withstand. That's where the therapist is going to be able to help you where I cannot. But I'll be there every step of the way; I'll support you and make sure you're getting what you need. How does that sound?"

Asher took a deep breath. "It sounds really good."

"Good. Now, about the issue of you moving in. What my instincts are telling me to do versus what I'm going to do are very different."

Asher sat up straight and met his gaze. "What are your instincts telling you to do, Daddy?"

He sighed, not sure he should admit it but unwilling to lie. "My instincts are telling me to make the decision for you. To tell you you're moving in with me immediately, and we'll make arrangements to get your things packed up and moved over as soon as possible. I'd like to take the stress of making such a big decision off your shoulders and place it upon my own. But—"

Asher clasped Thornton's cheeks in his hands. "That. I want that. Don't make me choose. It got all jumbled up in my head, and I second-guessed myself so much I could barely function. Please."

Thornton's heart rate shot through the roof at what that could mean for them in the future, but for right that moment, all it did was make him happier than he'd ever been. He grinned, kissed Asher on the lips, and rested his forehead against Asher's. "Then I'll schedule the movers once we discuss our schedules, and we'll sort out the details later."

"Yes, please, Daddy."

"That's Daddy's good boy."

CHAPTER TWENTY-THREE

Asher

He twirled and twirled the spaghetti on his plate until his little fork had an enormous bite on it. Stuffing the whole thing in his mouth, he met Thornton's gaze. He wasn't exactly in little space. He was eating with one of his little place settings, but they'd both realized the comfort of it being used, even when he wasn't in that headspace, helped him. It was a strange line he walked sometimes, bisecting the two parts of himself.

Daddy's eyebrows raised in what Asher knew was admonishment, but all he could do was shrug with a sheepish smile on his face. It was *good*. "Sorry, Daddy. So yum."

Thornton shook his head, leaned forward, an amused smirk on his face, and wiped Asher's mouth with his own napkin. "So, has Madi decided what she wants to do?"

They sat, finishing their dinner, their conversation straying back to what seemed to be the only topic they talked about since he'd returned to work three weeks prior, two since he'd moved in with Daddy. It had been the best two weeks of his life. He'd never felt as at home anywhere as he did living in their home together. And Daddy had made it very clear it was *their* home, not Thornton's.

Thornton sat back and waited for Asher's response. Trying to remember what they'd been talking about. *Oh, Madi, but...* Confused, Asher's brows furrowed. "What do you mean?"

Asher took a sip of his milk and speared his last meatball, closing his eyes in ecstasy. When he opened his eyes, the look of hunger on Thornton's face as he watched Asher lick his lips had a grin spreading over Asher's lips. "Daddy?"

Thornton raised his gaze to Asher's once more. "Hmm?"

Smirking, Asher asked again, "What do you mean what Madi wants to do?"

Thornton moved his plate back a bit from the edge of the table, turned in his chair, crossed his long legs, and leaned back. He stretched his arm across the table and placed his hand on Asher's, fiddling with his fingers. "I mean, you were just talking to me about starting a search for a manager to handle a lot or most of what Jenn does on a daily basis."

Asher didn't understand. "Okay?"

"Does Madi want to hire someone for the position, or does she want to do it herself?"

Asher frowned. "What? She's the floor manager."

Asher wondered how Thornton's shrug could somehow look elegant and blasé all at the same time. "She is now, but does she want to remain so?"

He was about to say yes when he realized he had absolutely no idea. "I... don't even know. I thought so. She hasn't said anything."

Thornton continued to play with Asher's hand; having turned it over, he trailed his fingers lightly over Asher's palm in a lazy caress that had the potential to completely distract him from their conversation. "And you haven't asked if she'd like to do it?"

Feeling somehow like he'd missed something vital, he shrugged. "I didn't know I was supposed to. I guess I just assumed she didn't because *I* don't want to, or, if she did, she'd tell me."

Thornton tipped his head to the side, as if weighing his words. "Maybe she hasn't thought of it herself, or she doesn't feel confident enough to suggest it, or maybe she *doesn't* want to, and your assumption is correct. You might want to ask her, though, just to be sure, before you look into hiring someone for the job."

Asher nodded, not liking the idea Madi might not feel confident enough to suggest a change like that if it was what she truly wanted. However, he also knew she was pretty straightforward, and he hoped she'd ask for what she wanted. But the truth was, they were both out of their depth with this new venture they were going into together, so maybe she wouldn't ask or hadn't thought about it.

"Do you think she'd want to?"

Thornton shrugged. "You know her better than I do, but from what I've observed about her, she's got a great head on her shoulders, she knows the ins and outs of the business, and from what you told me, she's covered for Jenn several times when she was sick or on vacation. And isn't she going to school for her business degree?"

"Dang, I forgot about that."

"Can't hurt to ask, especially if she hasn't thought about it herself."

Asher nodded. "Yeah, I guess you're right. Do you think she'd do well in that role? She's just so outgoing, so I guess I've always seen her position of floor manager to be suited to her personality."

"Yes, I think she'd do well, and it would make sense from a strategic standpoint. She knows the business, and she'll be part owner, so having her in that position would make sense."

Asher nodded, nibbling on his lip in thought. "It probably would."

Thornton continued. "Not to mention it's easier to hire and train a floor manager than a business manager you don't know, who doesn't have any stake in the success of the business itself. Not that you can't find a perfectly suitable candidate who will care about their job and the business, but having one of the owners in that role is a smart business move."

"I just don't want to pressure her to do something she doesn't want to do. I'd feel awful if she did it because of some sense of obligation and then ended up hating it. Let me just..." Asher pulled out his phone. "... text and see if she can come over tomorrow to talk."

He looked up, asking with his eyes if that was okay. "Good idea. Have her bring Gigi. The dogs miss her."

Warmed by Daddy's response, he nodded, typing out his message. Madi responded and planned to join them for brunch. Thornton squeezed Asher's hand in his. "Either way, one of you will need to be fully trained to take on that role, should you be unable to find the perfect person to fill the position before Jenn leaves, or if the new hire quits or gets sick or anything else that would leave you in the lurch if they aren't there."

Asher smirked. "So, like, this is why you're so successful, I take it?"

Asher grinned when Thornton snorted out a laugh at that and shrugged. "I do okay."

He narrowed his eyes. "Mmm hmm. You do more than just okay."

Thornton nodded, gaze turning serious. "I do. I also have a knack for knowing when a business venture is a smart investment, which I think The Glasshouse is, which is why I want to back both you and Madi financially."

"*Daddy...*"

"This is what I do, Asher. I've built my entire career around it. Why won't you let me help you?"

Asher's shoulders sagged, hearing Thornton's frustration. "You *are* helping me. Thornton, you've spent countless hours working with us regarding marketing, business, and staffing strategies. You've done a shit-ton of research on what's successful in this industry."

"Watch your language, Ash."

He couldn't help but smile at that. "Okay, Daddy." He leaned forward and clasped Thornton's face. "Look, you've been amazing. I can't even believe how much time you've taken—away from your own businesses, I might add—to learn about ours in the hopes you can help us grow. You know more about cannabis than I do, and I grow it, for god's sake."

"I want to do this for you, baby."

"I won't have you buying the business for me and Madi."

"You act like I'm just throwing millions of dollars at you—"

Asher raised his eyebrows and couldn't help but ask, "Aren't you?"

"Boy." Thornton narrowed his eyes at Asher, who frankly shouldn't have been turned on by Thornton's dominance but kinda was.

Asher drew in a deep breath and let it out. "I'm sorry for interrupting."

"I would be offering you financial backing in the form of business loans."

Asher huffed out an incredulous breath. "With ridiculous returns... basically no financial gain for yourself. If we get financing from the banks like we plan, we won't feel like we're price-gouging you or whatever. Don't laugh."

Thornton smirked and rubbed his hand over his mouth as if to wipe it away. Asher continued before Thornton could argue again. "I know that's not the right term. I don't know what the heck it's called. All I know is you're getting the short end of the stick while we're walking away with basically free money and a free business."

"What would you have me do—offer you the same terms as all my other clients?"

Asher's eyes popped wide because really, was he serious? "*Yes!*"

Thornton sighed and pinched the bridge of his nose in exasperation. But Asher wasn't going to change his mind. He wasn't about to take advantage of Thornton like that. He and Madi were in agreement there as well. But he could see the hurt lying underneath the frustration, and it was breaking his heart.

He knew how much Thornton wanted to help them both realize what had recently become their dream. It was never something he would have even imagined was possible, but now that they were in the middle of the process, it had quickly come to mean everything to them both.

He could see Thornton's mind working things out, turning things over, trying to figure out a way to make it work for all of them. He wasn't against going into business with Thornton. Hell, he had a feeling it was a smart business move, and he and Madi would really do well with his guidance, but the fact was Thornton would give them his guidance regardless. But he wouldn't have Thornton basically giving away a huge sum of money just so he and Madi didn't have much interest to speak of. It wasn't smart business for Thornton, and the only reason he was offering it was because of who Asher was to him.

It wasn't right, but he hated telling Daddy no all the same. He watched as a sad acceptance fell over Thornton, and he got up to grab their dishes. "All right, I'll let it go for now. I'm going to get things cleaned up. Why don't you go have some little time in your playroom or color in the family room? I'll be out in a bit."

Asher's shoulders slumped as he stood up. "Daddy, don't be mad. Please. I'm just trying to make the best decision I can."

Thornton drew in a deep breath and let it out; the gentle smile that followed wasn't fake and gave Asher a bit of a boost. "I'm not mad, baby boy. I understand your reasons. I just don't like them. But I'm not done yet. I'll try to come up with better terms for all of us once I talk to Trent and get his input."

Asher raised his brows. "You haven't talked to your brother about this yet?" Thornton's sheepish expression had Asher chuckling. "Daddy, you're gonna be in so much trouble! He's gonna lecture you all day and night about it tomorrow."

Thornton grumbled. "He's not the boss of me."

Asher guffawed. "I'll make sure he knows you said that. And while technically *you're* the boss of *him*, he's your financial advisor for a reason."

Thornton narrowed his gaze at Asher and pointed out of the kitchen. "Go, brat, before I give you a spanking for your impertinence."

He sucked in a startled breath before he could catch himself. But if that didn't clue Thornton into the fact he liked that idea more than he should, the pink he felt warming his cheeks would have given him away. And from the way Thornton was looking in his eyes, he figured his pupils might have blown. Which, according to Daddy, was something that turned him on like mad. He bit his lip and then gave Thornton a flirty little wave.

As Asher skipped out of the kitchen, he called back, "Maybe we can try that later and see how much we like it, Daddy."

He couldn't keep a giggle in when he heard Thornton cursing his hard-on. As he sat down at the coffee table and turned the TV on, he couldn't help but think about it. And think about it some more. And as he began to color, it was still right there, front and center in his mind, and his own hard-on didn't seem to want to go away either.

***

The next morning, they slept in after having tested out the spanking theory with much success. That was going to become a favorite thing to do together, that was for sure. Asher had to laugh, thinking about his life just a couple of months back. If he'd have told his past self where he'd be in two months, he'd never have believed it in a million years.

They worked together taking out ingredients for the quiche Daddy was going to make for brunch. He pulled out the potatoes for the hash browns they planned on making. "Baby boy, let me take care of brunch. I want you to have some playtime before company arrives."

He turned to Thornton. "Are you sure, Daddy?"

Thornton leaned down for a soft kiss that lasted longer than he'd expected. His dazed eyes met Daddy's when he finally pulled back. "They could be here for hours, and I want to make sure you're in a good headspace when they arrive. Go on, do as I say now."

"Okay, Daddy. Thank you." Grinning, he leaned in for one more kiss before he skipped from the room. "Come on, Beauty and Beast, you can be the monsters coming to invade the town!"

In reality, all Beauty and Beast would do was keep him company as they lounged around on their enormous dog bed together. He heard Daddy's chuckle before he was out of earshot and found himself doing the same. Maybe he'd move their bed in the middle of the room and build the train track around them.

Excited to do just that, he dragged their bed where he wanted it, and the dogs hopped on, ready to be part of the fun as they lazed about. He'd put away all his track the last several times he'd played, so he was going to start from scratch, which he loved to do. He'd gotten several new pieces since he'd moved in as well, so as soon as he pulled out everything he'd need, he got lost in his own creativity.

He had no idea how much time had passed when he heard a knock on the playroom doorjamb. "Knock, knock. You want some company?"

He grinned. "Hi, Trent! Sure, come in." He made kissy noises. "Guinness, come join the puppy pile."

They'd gotten several of the biggest dog beds they could find to put throughout the house just for this purpose. As Guinness joined Beauty and Beast on the bed, Trent joined him on the floor. The first time he'd joined Asher in his playroom to play, Asher had been worried Trent would judge him, but then they'd just started playing and building mega tracks, and he'd ended up looking forward to doing it again.

They played for a while, working together to surround the puppy bed with track as their canine audience looked on, vaguely interested in what they were doing but more entertained by the inside of their own eyelids. Trent, focused on building track with him, asked, "So, how were your first couple of appointments with your therapist?"

Asher sighed and paused what he was doing, trestle bridge in his hand, thinking about his appointments with his new therapist, Mark Miller. "It was hard. But I think it's going well?"

Why he said that as a question, he didn't know, but when Trent only nodded, waiting for more, Asher continued. "Both times Thorn came in with me. So that was good. And Mark said he could come in whenever I wanted him with me. But he's suggesting hypnotherapy, and that makes me nervous. I dunno."

"Why does that make you nervous?" Trent continued to put track together rather than focusing on him, making it easier for Asher to talk about everything.

"I guess because I know there's a lot I've kind of blocked out, and I don't know if I'm ready to remember it all."

Trent hummed as he started setting up the town. "Yeah. That would be scary."

Trent's understanding allowed him to show a bit more of his vulnerability. "I guess I just don't understand how remembering will help. But he said he could focus more on my anxiety symptoms at first to help me when I'm around too many people or have to ride in a car. If Daddy can't drive me, Madi usually can—"

"I can too." Trent's voice sounded timid and perhaps a bit like Asher's when he was in little space.

Asher's gaze slid up to meet his, and he smiled. "Thank you."

Asher had kind of gotten the feeling his new friend had really enjoyed playing with him whenever he came over, that maybe it was *more* than just Trent hanging out with him. Perhaps Trent needed to be little sometimes too. That made him happy. He liked having someone to play with that understood him and didn't judge, and if he could be a part of making Trent feel less anxiety, all the better. They could help each other.

Trent smiled a shy smile that had Asher shaking his head. They might not have been related by blood, but both Hayes brothers were ridiculously handsome. They got back to building, all talk of therapy forgotten. It wasn't long before they heard a squeal and the pitter-pattering of little feet down the hallway. The puppies' ears perked up, turning towards the door, definitely interested in that familiar sound. "Puppies!"

Gigi ran in the room and gasped. "Oh my gosh, it's puppy island! I wanna do that."

Asher grinned. "Do what?"

Gigi bounced on the balls of her feet. "Be a prisoner on the island!"

Trent laughed and stood up, holding his arms out for Gigi, who looked at him with narrowed eyes. "You're a stranger. I have to know your name before you're allowed to pick me up."

Asher snorted as Trent got down on one knee and held out his hand. "My name is Trenton Hayes, but you can call me Trent. Thornton is my older brother. And who might you be?"

Gigi grinned and clasped his hand. "I'm Gianna Girand, but you can call me Gigi. Madi Girand is my mother."

"I've heard great things about you both. You wanna join the puppy pile now?" Trent stood and held out his hands.

Gigi nodded and practically jumped into Trent's arms. He lifted her over all the track and added her to the huge dog bed. The dogs adjusted so she was in the middle, and she sat and petted them, chattering away about how much she'd missed them.

"Well, what do we have here?"

Asher turned to smile at his closest friend. She leaned against the doorjamb, arms crossed over her chest, a wide smile on her face as she took in the scene before her. Trent stood like he'd been prodded with a hot poker. Wiping his palms on his pants, he approached Madi, who was dwarfed by his large size, yet somehow looked the more dominant of the two as she stepped forward.

"Hello, I'm Trent, Thorn's brother. You must be Madi, Gigi's mom." As they shook hands, Asher noticed the blush on Trent's face and couldn't help but smile.

"It's nice to meet you." When Trent pulled away, he put both of his hands in his pockets, suddenly bashful. Madi reached up, patting his shoulder. "Don't let me interrupt playtime."

"Oh, I wasn't..." Trent lowered his gaze to the floor, obviously embarrassed.

Madi stepped towards him, her hand still on his shoulder. "Oh, I'd hoped you were. I like that my friend has a playmate."

Trent's head snapped up, surprise written all over his face. "You do?"

"Yeah. I really do. Why don't you guys play for a bit longer while Thornton and I finish up with brunch? We'll call you when it's time to eat, and maybe we can get to know each other better." The motherly smile Madi had on her face made Asher grin. Oh, he couldn't wait for this to play out.

"Oh, y-yeah. I-I'd like that." Trent's endearing stammer had Asher grinning at Madi as she glanced his way and winked. Trent turned back towards the toys, enthusiasm renewed as he sat on the floor again and started to play.

They continued as they were for another twenty minutes before Madi came to get them. "Okay, kids. Time to eat."

They all got up, including the dogs, and headed towards the kitchen: Gigi running after the dogs; Asher following the smell of bacon; and Trent and Madi bringing up the rear, murmuring to each other. They all ate brunch together, talking over each other and laughing when Gigi kept feeding the dogs people food.

"Gigi, stop that. We don't know what the dogs can eat without getting sick."

Trent leaned closer to Madi. "She's okay. She hasn't given them anything they can't have."

"Okay." Madi smiled at him, causing Trent to blush.

Everyone continued to talk as they ate, Trent and Madi getting along with ease as they got to know each other a bit. Talk inevitably turned towards The Glasshouse and Madi and Asher's plans.

"Mama, I'm done. Can I go play with the dogs outside?"

"Sure, as long as that's okay with Thorn and Trent."

When both Hayes men said they were happy for her to go out and play with the pups, Madi and Asher excused themselves to chat business. Asher knew Thornton and Trent had a discussion they needed to have as well, so he was happy Gigi had something to occupy herself with. They headed into the family room and sat on the sofa, which reminded him of the time he sat with her there weeks ago, when he'd admitted Thornton was a Daddy and he was a little.

"Okay, so what's up? You wanted to talk about work stuff?"

Asher sighed and nodded. "Yeah. So Thorn, being Thorn, realized that maybe you'd actually enjoy being business manager instead of floor manager. And me, being me, didn't even think about it. So he suggested I ask you and we talk about it, so here we are."

She laughed and poked his arm. "You know, we lucked out that Thorn, being Thorn, fell in love with you, being you. Because your Daddy is pretty smart."

Asher sighed, all heart eyes. "He is, isn't he?"

Madi rolled her eyes. "Lord save me from besotted boys."

"Pfft. Says the 'Mommy' with a besotted boy blushing all through brunch at the attention she was lavishing on him."

At Madi's narrow-eyed glare, he shrugged. "I'm not *that* type of Mommy."

Crossing his arms over his chest, he raised his brows. "You sure about that? Because it sure seemed like it earlier. And he's like *perfect* for you."

"What makes you say that?"

"He'd obviously let you lead. He's *very* gainfully employed. He's become a really great friend to me. He's loyal and funny and charming and is so gentle with

Guinness and Beauty and Beast and was really sweet with Gigi today. I just think you should give it a chance."

She met his gaze for several moments and then shrugged. "We'll see. And about the business manager position, I'd thought about it and figured with everything we're taking on, it might be best for us to stay in the roles we are in now because there's going to be so many other things that are new. I'm not against it. I just didn't know if it was the right time."

"Well, think about it. I won't pressure you either way. I want *you* to be happy, and if being the floor manager is what makes you happy, that's what I want for you. It's not something I have any interest in, personally. The thought of it gives me high blood pressure."

She shook her head and placed her hand on his knee. "That's not for you. The whole reason this works is because you know one side of the business and I know the other. You need to work with the plants. It's what you're passionate about."

"Yeah. I want you to do what you're passionate about too. Thornton said you'd be great at it. He also reminded me you've covered for Jenn when she's been on vacation and know what you're doing already, so it actually wouldn't be that new for you. But, if it's not something you think you'd really enjoy, then that's that."

"He thinks I should do it?"

"He wants both of us to be happy and for our business to thrive."

"But?"

"No buts. He said it would be a smart business decision. Having one of the owners managing the business itself would make sense because we'd have a very personal stake in making things successful. But he also said we could find someone that would take it seriously if that's what needed to happen, and he'd help us."

Madi leaned her arm on the back of the sofa, head in her hand. "I mean, he's *not* wrong. It *would* be a smart business decision. And I've done it before several times. I haven't had to take care of everything because Jenn's always taken care of a lot of things before she's left on vacation. But I'm confident I can learn it. I love being the floor manager, but it would definitely be easier to fill that position."

"Why don't you think about it over the rest of the weekend, and we can chat about it on Monday? Don't make any rash decisions. I really want you to make the best decision for you. Your happiness and my happiness in our chosen roles will make a difference in how we run the business."

Madi smiled. "Okay. I'll think it over. I'm so glad we're doing this together. I think we're going to kick some ass."

Laughing, Asher admitted, "I'm scared to death we're gonna fuck everything up. But once I get past that paranoia, I get pretty excited about it."

"So is Thorn still pushing us to take his money?"

He grumbled. "Yeah. But I think he finally understands we don't want him throwing money at us. But now it seems he's bound and determined to talk to Trent about coming up with a better financial offer for all of us. So I don't know. He wants to help us so bad, and I hate saying no to him."

"So don't."

"What do you *mean* don't? I thought we agreed—"

"We do agree. We can't do it as he first suggested. It has to be profitable for all of us, not just you and me. But, if Trent, being the accountant type, will make sure Thorn isn't using his Daddy brain but his *business* brain, maybe the offer will work this time. I'm happy to go with a bank loan, but I also know having a more personal touch, and having Thorn's vested interest, will only help us in the long run. If he wants to help, and the terms are right, we should at least think about it."

Asher's heart sped up at the thought of being in business with Daddy. If Thornton was truly willing to give them an offer that worked for everyone, maybe it *could* work for all of them. "Okay, we'll think about it. Let's see what they come up with and go from there."

"Sounds good. Let's go check on the boys and track down my wayward daughter."

Asher laughed, knowing Gigi was having the time of her life with the puppies. They walked into the kitchen and found it empty. Heading outside, they both stood shocked, watching Gigi sitting astride Trent's back like he was a horse, the puppies running around, barking and cavorting around the two of them.

"Onward, my noble steed!" Gigi cried as she pointed ahead of them, then proceeded to clap two dog bones together to make clopping sounds.

Thornton approached them from behind, more dog toys in his hands, head tilted to the side in consternation. "Madi?"

Asher turned to Madi and saw her charmed grin. "Uh-huh?"

Thornton looked her way. "Has Gigi watched *Monty Python and the Holy Grail*?"

Madi grinned and was about to answer when Gigi hopped off her noble steed and fell over as if she was dead when Guinness jumped up and grabbed one of the bones from her. She hopped back up and, as she chased after Guinness, yelled, "It's merely a flesh wound!"

Trent, having watched it all from his hands and knees, fell over on his side laughing while Asher, Madi, and Thornton were dying from the sidelines. Gigi, completely oblivious she'd caused such a reaction, started rolling around on the ground with all three dogs.

Asher chanced a glance at Madi and saw her making her way towards Trent, holding out a hand to help him up. "I'm sorry she used you as a horse."

He climbed to his feet, a huge grin on his face. "I'll be her noble steed any day. She's awesome."

Asher watched as Madi's smile turned to a wide grin, pride shining in her eyes. "She is, isn't she?"

They stood and watched for several more minutes until Gigi ran out of steam and asked for a drink. Once inside, they chatted while Gigi drank one of Asher's juice boxes. When she was done, Madi pulled on Gigi's braids. "Come on, peach. Let's get going."

They all made their way to the front door, and Madi turned to Trent. "Guinness is great. Thanks for letting her play with him. She loves dogs. Maybe soon we'll be able to get a house with a backyard so she can have one of her own."

Trent, looking like he was trying to get up the courage to speak, finally rushed to say, "You can bring her over to my house anytime. Guinness loves to play."

Asher felt bad for Trent as he continued to blush, but when Madi placed her hand on his arm, Asher could see his friend relax under her attention. "She'd really love that. Thank you. Maybe I could bring dinner over sometime this week."

"Really?" The surprised happiness on Trent's face made Asher's heart swell.

"Really. What are your favorite comfort foods?"

Trent rubbed his stomach. "I love meatloaf and macaroni and cheese."

Gigi jumped up and down. "Mama's loaf n' cheese is the best!"

Trent tipped his head in confusion. "Is that, like, some kind of meatloaf mac and cheese combo? Because that would be awesome."

Madi laughed. "No. Although... Hmm, I'll think on that. She just mashes it all together, so that's what it becomes on her plate."

Trent laughed and turned to Gigi. "I bet it's good like that."

"It is! You should try it."

Trent turned to Madi, all heart eyes, and said, "I'd love to."

Madi nodded. "Then it's settled. I'll get your number from Asher and text you later."

After Trent agreed, Madi and Gigi left, and Asher turned towards Trent. "You two could seriously be adorable together." Trent blushed and stammered, but Asher didn't want to embarrass him anymore and turned to Thornton. "Daddy, can I go play with my track some more?"

"Sure, baby. Trent and I still have some things to discuss. I'll come get you when he's ready to head out."

"Okay." Asher skipped to his playroom, dogs following happily in his wake.

As he continued building his mega track, he thought over the last several hours. But even after all the shop talk and everything else, the thing that hit him most was the fact he'd somehow found a family in the midst of everything crazy going on in his life.

He'd never felt like he belonged anywhere, nor did he think he'd ever have what had essentially fallen into his lap. He was happier than he'd ever been and more comfortable in his skin than he ever thought he would be. And he couldn't have been more grateful.

CHAPTER TWENTY-FOUR

Thornton

The following Monday when Thornton pulled up to The Glasshouse, Asher leaned forward, turned off Enya in Thornton's car, and leaned close to kiss him goodbye. "Have a good day, Daddy, and say hi to Trent."

"I will. Tell Jenn and Madi hello."

They kissed again and grinned at each other, equally ridiculously besotted. "What do you want for dinner?"

They played this game every time Thornton dropped him off for work. Anything to lengthen the time they had together, even if only for another minute. Asher's eyes grew wide. "Can we get food from Mama's Chimichangas?"

Thornton chuckled. "You're ruining my schedule. That's on *Tuesdays*."

His boy's big doe eyes and pouting lips had him smirking. Asher knew how to pull all his strings; he didn't just have him wrapped around his little finger—he had Thornton wrapped around every finger and every toe. "Please, Daddy? We can call it Mulitas Mondays, and we can still have it again for Taco Tuesday."

Thornton snorted. "Mama Hernandez doesn't even make mulitas in her food truck."

Asher grinned. "I bet she would for me. She loves me."

Thornton smirked and nodded. "She does," and it was true. When Mama had learned they were together, she'd been so happy for them. She didn't know Asher, but they'd waved to each other often enough when Madi swung by to grab food from Mama's truck. The fact he had always stayed in the car had made him memorable and she'd always thought his shyness was adorable. Now she doted on him every time they visited there. "And so do I, so Mama's for dinner it is. Now go, before I start talking about business."

Asher smirked. "We can talk about it tonight. I promise. Love you."

"Love you, too, baby. Be good." Asher leaned in for another kiss, and then he was gone, leaving Thornton to go about his own workday.

Once he got back at home, he and Trent were ensconced in his kitchen for their breakfast meeting. At the end of their night on Saturday, he'd talked with Trent about everything he'd proposed to Asher and Madi regarding The Glasshouse. His brother had given him a ton of shit for the offer he'd given his boy, but after they'd talked, he'd felt pretty good about their final decision.

The fact that Trent had immediately understood, and even agreed with, his need to help provide an offer for Asher and Madi that gave them a distinct advantage over other financial backers had calmed his defensive instincts. He hadn't gotten any pushback regarding his desire to help, just the way he'd originally gone about it, which he admitted to himself had been foolhardy. Asher and Madi's refusal to sign on to such a deal had also gone a long way in soothing Trent's slightly ruffled feathers.

Sunday, with Trent's advice still in his thoughts, he'd worked up a new proposal. They ate breakfast as he detailed out his full offer for Asher and Madi. "Do you see any issues needing to be addressed before Asher and Madi get a look?"

"No. I think it's good for everyone involved. I'll need to move some money around for this as well, so let me know when they've signed. It's a huge investment, Thorn, but a smart one."

"I think so too. Why don't you come over for dinner tonight? Asher talked me into Mama's, so I'll get your favorites. Madi will be there as well, which reminds me…"

He took out his phone to text Asher to be sure he remembered to ask Madi what she wanted, only to find Madi had texted him herself with an order for her and Gigi. He grinned, knowing that would please his brother.

"Looks like we'll see Gigi as well." He watched closely and saw the telltale signs of pleasure, nerves, and anticipation his little brother had just thinking about seeing Madi and her daughter again. The blush got deeper, but there was hope in his eyes.

"Do you think she'll still want to come over to my place with Gigi later this week if she's seeing me tonight?"

God, he hoped it worked out with Madi. They could be so good together, but if it ended badly, things could get a bit uncomfortable for everyone. "From what I've learned from Asher, and my own observations, she follows through on her promises, and I think that's what she'd consider your conversation Saturday."

Trent nodded and stood. "Okay. I'm gonna get back to work. I'll head over around six-ish?"

"Sounds good."

***

After breakfast, Thornton had gotten busy with the rest of his workday and had to haul ass to get back to The Glasshouse at the end of Asher's day to pick his boy up. Once Asher was in the car, they'd been on their way. With Asher's calming music on, his boy was finally able to chat about his day. His excitement was palpable as he explained Madi had decided she wanted to be the business manager and how excited they both were to talk about the proposal later at dinner.

Ten minutes later, they stopped not only to get food but to chat with Mama, so six-ish came sooner than they'd expected. They passed Trent's car on the driveway and pulled into the garage five minutes before the hour, two huge bags of Mama's best foods making the car smell like heaven.

Trent and all three dogs met them in the mudroom, his brother relieving Asher of his bag of food and leading the way back towards the kitchen. They began to unpack dinner and divvy it up when the doorbell rang. Thornton glanced up and saw Asher grinning at Trent, saying, "Why don't you go let them in, and Daddy and I will finish up?"

Trent blushed, unable to hide his excitement and nerves. "Okay."

Asher met Thorn's gaze, and they both grinned at each other. "I hope things work out for both of them. They'd be really good together, and I think they need just what the other can give them."

Thornton tugged Asher's belt loop, drawing his boy near. "Me too, baby."

He kissed Asher, and they brought the food to the kitchen table just as Gigi ran in. "Hi, Asher, hi, Thorn. Mommy said I get flautas tonight! They're my favorite."

Thornton raised the plate he had in his hand. "They're right here, sweetheart. Do you want some juice, milk, or water with it?"

She hopped up and down before she took her seat. "Juice please. Thank you."

Asher went to grab the juice, and Thornton watched as Madi and Trent walked towards the kitchen. Madi, a tiny little thing, was looking up at Trent, a smile on her face as she reached up to touch his shoulder. He replied to whatever she said, and she tipped her head back and laughed.

The grin his brother had on his face, not to mention the pride at having made her laugh, warmed Thornton's heart. His brother could use someone that put a smile like that on his face. Trent smiled often, but never were his smiles that full of unbridled happiness. He mentally crossed his fingers they'd fit together perfectly.

They all sat down and dug into their meals with gusto, holding work discussions until later. When Gigi was done eating, she asked to go with the dogs to color and watch TV. Trent stood when Gigi did, placing a hand on Madi's shoulder. "I'll get her set up. Be right back."

Madi smiled and patted his hand. "Thanks."

When Trent and Gigi left the room, Asher turned to Madi and just stared at her and grinned. Madi pointed at him, narrowing her eyes. "Knock it off. I told you I'd give it a chance, and I will, but quit giving me those looks."

Asher sucked his lips between his teeth and nodded, all mock serious. "You got it."

Trent came back in, and they finished their meals. Thornton couldn't wait any longer. "So, after talking with Trent, I have a new proposal."

He watched as Asher glanced at Madi and received a nod. Asher looked back at him and grinned. "Can you hold that thought?" Thornton sat back in his chair in surprise; he'd been so ready to give them the proposal he assumed they couldn't refuse that the wind went out of his sails, but the excitement on their faces had him nodding and gesturing for them to go on. "So *we* have a new proposal for *you*."

That surprised him, and he couldn't help but grin. "Well, aren't you two tricky. It's a good thing Trent is here to help me make a decision then. Let's hear it."

Madi reached down into her bag and handed over a file. His brows rose, and he looked between all three people at the table. Trent shrugged, obviously as in the dark as he was, while Madi and Asher looked equal parts enthusiastic and nervous. He opened the file, and his eyes popped wide at what he saw.

He pushed his plate back and set the file down, flipping through page after page of a very thorough, very professional business plan, much like the one he had sitting on the counter across the room, but with a few surprises thrown in. When he reached the last page, he glanced between them again as he passed the file to Trent. Trent pushed back his chair and brought an ankle to his knee, resting the file in his lap as he opened it. After seeing the first couple pages, he looked up at Thornton, grinning.

"You both want me to be part owner? Twenty percent share is huge. Are you sure you're comfortable with that?" Thornton asked.

Both of them nodded, Asher speaking up. "We are. We've been talking about it, and while we want to go with you for the loan, we also want you to have a stake in the business. It's a good business move. Jenn was enthusiastic about it when we talked to her, and we spent all day drawing up the proposal."

Everyone sat at the table in silence as he took it all in. Trent leafed through the pages, brows high, smile wide. That was all he needed. "Why don't we adjust the interest to the numbers Trent and I were going to propose, which is just a bit lower than the ones you're proposing here, and we'll add a clause that you can buy me out when you're ready?"

They both shook their heads, and Madi spoke up. "Both Jenn and I have done a *lot* of research on you and your company since Asher first mentioned you were interested in backing us." She looked down at her lap and blushed, the first he'd ever seen on her since they'd met, and he grinned when she looked up again, meeting his gaze. "Sorry, but—"

"Don't apologize," he interrupted. He couldn't help himself; he wasn't going to have her doubting her good sense for a second longer. "It's smart, and it makes me feel relieved you aren't going into this blind. I know Jenn would have done a thorough check as well for both your sakes and hers."

Madi let out a breath, and her shoulders relaxed. "Good. Thank you. Like I was saying, we did our research, and the companies you invest in that you also have a stake in flourish with your involvement in the day-to-day operations. This is all new for us, and we won't be able to fall back on Jenn because she wants to be done with it. We're smart enough to know we're going to need help, and yeah, we know you'd help us if we needed it, but we want you to be a part of our success as well."

When she was done, she kept eye contact, and when he grinned, she grinned too. He glanced at Trent and got the official nod before he interjected, "I'll take a closer look at this and fiddle with the numbers, make sure they work for everyone. Once you all sign off on it, I'll send it to our lawyers to write up an official contract, and then we'll be good to go."

He glanced at Asher, and the beatific smile on his boy's face sent a thrill racing through his body. He pushed back from the table, making room for his excited boy, who bounced up and hopped in his lap, kissing him for all he was worth. He heard Trent and Madi laughing, prompting Asher to pull away and blush. Thornton leaned down and whispered for only his boy to hear, "We'll continue that later, baby."

As Asher, pink cheeked with arousal coupled with embarrassment, was moving back to his own chair, Madi leaned over again and pulled out a bottle, sending a jolt through Thornton's system. He was shaking his head, hoping to avoid a panic attack from Asher, when she held up a finger to hold him off. "So I brought a little bubbly with me, of the non-alcoholic variety, of course. How about we have a toast?"

Relieved and annoyed he'd jumped to the conclusion she'd bring alcohol into their home, he grinned. "Let me get the glasses. Can Gigi have some?"

Madi laughed. "She loves this stuff. We only have it on special occasions, but she saw the bottle tonight and was excited."

He opened the bottle, poured some into one of Asher's straw cups, and took it out to Gigi, who was engrossed in her coloring and her movie. When he came back, they each had some sparkling cider and were raising their glasses in a toast to celebrate.

After a few sips, they all began to chat about their ideas, talking over each other in their excitement. He'd been excited for Asher and Madi to take on this new adventure, but the excitement he felt at being directly involved in the venture thrilled him. He couldn't wait to help them navigate their way in their new business.

***

Later that evening, he approached the playroom, juice box, coffee, and iPad in hand. He'd known Asher had needed some downtime after all the excitement of the evening, so he'd sent his boy to put on his favorite pajamas and then play in the playroom for a bit while he cleaned up after their dinner. Asher had chosen the baby Yoda pajamas for his little self.

Stepping into the room, he had to chuckle at the dog bed still in the center of Asher's monstrous train track and village scape he'd left up since Saturday. Asher jumped at the noise, hand to his heart as he turned, eyes wide. "Daddy! Oh my gosh, you scared me."

"Sorry, baby." He walked towards the side table by his large, leather chair and ottoman and set his coffee and tablet down. He grinned and approached his boy, squatting down for a kiss. "Here, I brought you some juice."

Asher took it with a grin, ripped the straw off the back, and stuck out his tongue in concentration as he put it through the hole in the top of the box. Sticking the straw in his mouth, Asher turned his gaze back up to him, causing Thornton's cock to harden in his pants. How was it an innocent, slightly demure upturn of those beautiful eyes nearly made him come? Couple that with those plump, juicy lips sipping from the straw, and he was a goner.

His boy sucked and swallowed, sucked and swallowed until the tiny juice box was empty. Thornton raised a brow as Asher set the juice box down on the floor without losing eye contact. "Thirsty, sweetheart?"

With a little bob of his head, Asher murmured, "Mmm hmm."

He booped his boy on the nose. "Don't look at Daddy that way."

False innocence bled into Asher's features, a pout topping it all off. "What do you mean?"

Narrowing his eyes, he gripped Asher's chin. "You know exactly what I mean. Don't pretend you don't."

Asher crawled closer, invading his space. With Thornton's knees spread wide in his crouch, Asher slotted his small body right between his legs. Asher lifted his butt off his heels, leaning in close to Thornton's ear. "Am I being a naughty little boy, Daddy?"

A rumble filled Thornton's chest, and he let his knees meet the carpet, nudging their bodies together. "You are. And I think you like being my naughty boy, don't you?"

Asher bit his lip, a move he *knew* drove Thornton wild. Asher nodded and licked his lips. "I do." As Asher gazed down at his own cock and then back up to Thornton, his boy's whisper was seductive. "Daddy, my penis is hard."

Oh yeah, his boy was being such a wicked little minx. "It is? Does my baby boy want special touches?"

Asher's eyes were wide as saucers, pupils blown. His pink, plump lips were wet, and Thornton wanted to shove his dick between them. Asher's voice was still a breathy whisper. "Yes, please."

Thornton sat back on his heels, gripped Asher's ass in his hands, and lifted him so Asher was straddling his lap. Asher immediately started to grind his hard cock against Thornton's, the mewling noises almost more than Thornton could take. Thornton knew, grinding or no grinding, if his boy was making breathy, sweet little whimpers, whines, and moans, it wouldn't take long before Thornton came.

He gripped Asher's hips in his hands, stilling his movements. "Daddy didn't say you could rub yourself on me. What did Daddy tell you about that?"

The soft little catch in Asher's throat, followed by a needy little whine, had Thornton's cock leaking in his pants. "You said only bad little boys try to make their penises feel good without Daddy's permission."

Goddamn, that sweet little voice. He cleared his throat, trying to gain back a little of his own control. "That's right. And you were rubbing that sweet cock of yours all over Daddy. What do bad boys deserve when they're naughty?"

Asher's sweet whimper did a number on his libido. "Daddy…"

Thornton's voice was a deep rumble, his hands gripping Asher's hips hard to keep himself under control. "What do they deserve?" He nudged his nose under Asher's chin so his sweet boy would lean his head back, and Thornton bit along the column of his throat, reveling in the small frame shuddering in his arms. "Hmm? Tell Daddy."

"I deserve spanks for being bad, Daddy." Asher gripped Thornton's head, digging his nails into the back of his neck, holding Thornton's mouth to his throat. Thornton obliged, sucking and nipping at Asher's sensitive skin. Asher's hips tried to move again, and Thornton gave his boy exactly what he'd just admitted he deserved.

He growled and spanked Asher's pert little ass again. "That's right. You deserve spanks."

He gripped Asher's ass cheeks and stood with him in his arms, and then a wicked idea popped in his head. He unhooked Asher's legs from his waist and let him down, Asher's pout drawing a smirk to Thornton's lips. He looked around at the floor of the playroom. "Looks like there's quite a mess for Daddy's naughty little boy to clean up."

Asher gasped. "Daddy!"

Thornton raised a brow, a warning gleam in his eyes. "Do as I say, boy, or you won't enjoy those spanks you were just begging for."

Asher got to his knees, resignation in his eyes, a sad little pout on his lips, as he went about cleaning up the spare track that littered the floor. When everything was cleaned up, Asher grabbed the empty juice box and tossed it in the bin by the door. Instead of walking towards him when he was done, Asher crawled, allowing his hips to sway seductively.

Thornton smirked, nudged the ottoman aside so his boy could kneel between his legs, and leaned forward, elbows on his knees. Clasping Asher's face, he tilted it up so their gazes met. "Good boy."

Asher shuddered at that. "Thank you, Daddy."

"Does my little boy deserve a spanking?"

"Yes, Daddy."

He leaned forward, nuzzling Asher's neck, nibbling up to his ear and biting on his lobe. "Yeah. I think so too. I think my naughty boy needs to be taught a lesson."

He leaned down, gripped the edge of Asher's shirt, and pulled it off. "Stand up, baby."

Asher stood, his cock making a tent of his pajama pants. Thornton finished undressing his boy until he was completely naked, standing before him. Thornton sat on the ottoman, the arms of the chair too high for his boy's comfort. He tugged Asher down and draped him over his lap.

The fact his boy had taken to his first spanking and had asked for more made Thornton so happy. He'd always loved spanking his boys, and not all of them had liked it. He looked forward to exploring some more impact play, which he had a feeling he and Asher were going to love.

He rubbed Asher's ass, squeezed his cheeks, and spread them, loving the way Asher's hole contracted when exposed. He rubbed a finger down his crease and over his boy's sweet pucker several times, his boy's moans music to his ears.

"Your pink little hole is so pretty, Asher. Daddy can't wait to sink his cock into it."

"Mmm, please, Daddy."

"You want that, sweet boy? You want Daddy's cock in your little hole, spreading it wide?"

"Yes, yes, yes."

"Your hole is so greedy for Daddy's cock."

Asher bucked his hips back onto Thornton's fingers at his words, doing his best to get some friction to his hard cock and against his tight pucker. Thornton drew his hand up and brought it down in a reverberating slap on his boy's ass. The groan had him doing it a second time, and Asher's nails biting into his shin as he gripped Thornton's leg tight had him doing it a third.

"Naughty, naughty boy."

He continued with his spanking, making sure to cover every inch of Asher's sweet ass and upper thighs, his boy enjoying it so much he was humping Thornton's leg. When Asher's ass was nice and red, and the boy was moaning and begging him to be allowed to come, Thornton stopped all movement, leaning his weight on his forearm, which was across Asher's lower back to slow his movements.

"You don't seem to be learning your lesson. What should Daddy do about that, hmm?"

"Daddy, please. I need to come."

"Daddy's dirty little minx. You'd come all over my leg if I even caressed your pucker, wouldn't you? Yeah, you would. Maybe I need to fuck some good manners into you. See if that works. What do you think?"

Asher gasped and gripped his leg tighter. "Please, please fuck me, Daddy."

Thornton slapped his ass once more, hard, eliciting a cry of surprise followed by a breathy moan. "Up you get."

He helped Asher up on wobbly legs, crowded in behind him, and leaned down to nip at his neck as he reached around and clasped Asher's cock in a loose grip. When Asher's hips pumped forward, greedy for more, Thornton let go. Whimpers followed, and Asher's hips stilled as he whispered, "Daddy, please, more."

"You want more of Daddy's special touches?"

"Oh, god, please, Daddy. I'll be good, I promise."

"Yeah? Gonna be my good little boy?"

"Yes, yes. I swear."

"Mmhmm. Why don't you climb up on Daddy's chair? Knees on the edge, forearms on the back of the chair."

He watched as Asher climbed up and assumed the position, but his legs were together. "No, no, no. That simply won't do. Spread your legs as wide as you can. That's it. Look how pretty."

Asher's sweet, reddened ass was there for the taking, his pink pucker clenching and releasing, just begging to be filled. He pulled a lube packet out of his pocket, unzipped his jeans, and pulled his hard, aching cock out of the confines of his boxer briefs, nearly moaning in relief at finally being able to free it. He quietly ripped the corner off the lube packet, but when Asher turned to see what he was doing, he gave the boy a hard swat directly onto his hole.

"Daddy! Oh, god. I'm so close. Please, I need you inside of me."

"Liked that, did you? Such a little slut for Daddy's cock, aren't you?"

"Yes."

"Say it."

"I'm a greedy little slut for your big, fat cock, Daddy."

Jesus, his boy had a filthy mouth. The more comfortable Asher got with his sexuality and their Daddy/boy dynamic, the better he felt about being himself and letting his preferences come out. They often surprised Thornton in their naughtiness, but it only prompted Thornton to come up with new ways to pleasure his boy and new things for him to introduce Asher to.

He gripped Asher's hair at the crown of his head and drew his head back for a kiss. Pulling back, he slicked his fingers up and began to prep his sweet little boy's hole and then his own cock. "Beg me for it."

He enjoyed seeing Asher's body shudder at his words, enjoyed even more the words pouring forth from his boy's lips. "Please. Please, Daddy. I need your cock so bad. Fill me up. Make me yours. I need to feel you inside of me."

"Such sweet begging, baby."

He lined himself up and slid in to the hilt. They both moaned, Asher at the intrusion, Thornton at the tight heat enveloping his shaft. He reached behind himself and gripped his shirt, pulling it off. He needed to feel his skin against Asher's. Leaning down, he blanketed his boy's back with his body and wrapped one arm around him, hand holding Asher's throat in a gentle grip, his other snaking down between Asher's spread legs to clasp his cock in another barely there grip.

He began to pump slowly in and out of his boy until Asher was begging, "Harder. Please, Daddy."

"Shh, shh. You'll take what Daddy wants to give you."

"Oh, god. Daddy. It hurts."

"Mmm, hurts so good, though, doesn't it?"

"Fuck, yes. So good."

He sped up a bit, but his loose grip around Asher's cock didn't tighten, and if Asher's hips pistoned too hard into his fist, he let go, reveling in the power he felt as Asher whined at the loss of his touch. "How does my naughty little boy feel?"

"So good, so good, Daddy."

"You like being punished, and I love punishing you. I have a new soft spot for naughty little boys."

"Fuck. Daddy, god. Please. Please. Please."

"What does my dirty little slut need?"

Asher's hips slammed back into him at those words, mewling in desperation. "I need more. Please, more."

"More of what, baby?"

"Everything. God, everything."

He let go of Asher's cock and throat, slowing his fucking to a snail's pace. "Be specific, baby, or Daddy won't know what you need."

Asher turned his head to face him, and Thornton nearly shot his load at the need in Asher's eyes. "Hold me tighter, fuck me harder. Please. Please, I'll be good, I promise."

"You are good. So damn good for Daddy." He wrapped himself tighter around Asher and slammed into him. He gripped Asher's cock again, harder this time, as he slid out and slammed back in again. His grip tightened on Asher's throat as well, but not enough to cut off air, just enough to exert his dominance, which they'd found Asher couldn't get enough of. "Is this better? Is this what you need from Daddy?"

Asher sucked in a breath, nodding. "Yes. Oh, god, Daddy. More."

So Thornton gave him more, and more still, until their breaths were sawing in and out of their chests, and Asher was shaking so bad Thornton thought he'd fly apart. "Daddy, please... Can I?"

"Come for me, baby boy."

Asher came on a scream, his ass clamping down on Thornton's cock, prompting Thornton's own release that seemed to last forever. Hot jets of cum pumped deep into his boy, marking him as Daddy's. Always Daddy's. "God, Ash, so good, baby."

"Daddy."

"Shh, shh. I've got you. You were so good for Daddy. Such a good boy."

He pulled Asher up from his kneeling position. Thornton sat on the ottoman and pulled Asher down to straddle his lap. "I love you, so much," he heard his boy whisper.

Asher snuggled into him, gripping him tighter, making Thornton's heart melt. "I love you too, baby. More than I can ever express. I'm so damn lucky I found you."

Asher snickered. "Ran me over you mean?"

Thornton chuckled. "Exactly."

EPILOGUE

Asher
Six Months Later

Asher tugged on his shirt sleeves, fiddled with his collar, and smoothed down the fabric of his button-down shirt as he stared at himself in the mirror, giving himself a pep talk. He'd been equally excited and scared to death for this day since the moment he'd come up with the idea months ago.

Thornton's parents, Gwendolyn and Jasper, had been in town for one week of their two-week stay. Both he and Thornton had tried their best to get his parents to stay with them during their visit from their home in San Diego, but they'd refused, saying they wanted them to have their space and wanted to be pampered by hotel waitstaff. In the end, Daddy said he wouldn't push them because he hadn't wanted Asher to have more anxiety than he already had meeting them for the first time.

But he needn't have worried; Thornton and Trent came by their kindness and generosity naturally. Both Gwen and Jasper had hugged him when they'd first arrived, and Asher had immediately felt comfortable with them. Obviously, it had helped that Asher and Thornton had talked on the phone and FaceTimed with them many times. A couple of months after Asher had agreed to move in with Thornton, he had finally had the confidence to say hello.

His mom had even taken to texting him randomly after their first phone call to tell him funny stories about Thornton and to send snapshots of old photographs of Thornton as a child, much to Thornton's chagrin. As a result of that, he'd only had a couple of mini panic attacks leading up to their arrival that first day, and none since.

He'd been welcomed into their family with open arms and had finally discovered what being part of a family was supposed to feel like. He felt the love, connection, and care that he'd only seen and heard of, and what he'd always hoped to find with a family of his own but never thought would truly happen. He was sad their trip was half over. He'd taken several days off to spend time with them while they'd been there and had even braved one of the local coffee shops close to Thornton's house with Gwen.

Over the last several months, with the help of Thornton, Asher's therapist, his medication, and his new sense of confidence, he'd begun to venture out in public more often. It had been slow going, and he'd had a lot of mental and emotional obstacles in his way, but after a few failed attempts, they'd gotten coffee at the shop closest to them. Then the next week they'd eaten lunch at a tiny little hole-in-the-wall sandwich joint close by.

He hadn't really been able to go anywhere with big crowds yet, but the fact he could go out with Thornton to several local places, and even take walks with Thornton and the pups at their local park that was never really busy, had felt monumental to him, and seeing the pride on Thornton's face every time he tackled something new and scary was a reward in itself.

But dinner that night was special. He'd planned everything meticulously, knowing it had to be perfect. He'd arranged everything with Gwen's help and even some input from Jasper, Trent, and Madi. Regardless of his preparations, he was a nervous wreck. If things didn't go as he hoped, he didn't know what the hell he was going to do.

The doorbell sounded, and, heart in his throat, he left the downstairs bathroom to answer the door, making it there at the same time as Thornton. They grinned at each other, and Daddy leaned down to kiss him silly before opening the door. Gigi ran inside, Guinness at her heels, calling for Beauty and Beast.

Trent, handing over a bottle of sparkling cider, greeted them, his other hand holding Madi's much smaller one. "Hey, guys. Thanks for having us."

They all hugged each other, and by the time they were done, Syed and

Damon arrived, another bottle of sparkling cider—grape this time. It was a good thing Asher loved sparkling cider because everyone seemed to think that since they couldn't bring wine over for dinner, they had to bring cider. But there was never any leftover after their guests headed home, so he figured nobody was that broken up about not drinking around him.

He'd gotten better about it. He and Daddy had visited Syed and Damon's house once, and they'd arrived earlier than expected, so the men hadn't put away the alcohol before they got there. He'd had a momentary panic, but as they'd put the bottles away, Thornton had blocked his view and rubbed his arms, whispering calming words to keep him from losing it. He was thankful it worked and hoped he'd be able to get over it altogether.

He'd never be a drinker, but he wanted to be okay with others drinking around him. It would take a while, but his therapist always reminded him it was a marathon, not a sprint, and these things would take time. He knew it was true; he'd come a long way since the day Thornton ran over him with his car.

They were chatting in the kitchen when the doorbell rang, and he told Thornton to stay where he was, that he'd let Thornton's parents in. He opened the door, and Gwen looked behind him, a grin on her face when she didn't see Thornton. She walked through the door and hugged the stuffing out of him, and he hugged her back just as fiercely. When she pulled back, Jasper hugged him, giving him a gentle pat on the back.

Gwen grabbed his hand, a little bounce in her step as she moved closer. "Are you ready? Jasper and I are so excited for you both."

He shook his head, anxiety hitting him. "I don't know that I'll ever be ready, but tonight is the night, so we'll see what he says."

She gave a tinkling laugh as they walked towards the back of the house to join the rest of the group in the kitchen. "You have nothing to worry about."

He didn't know if that was true. He was stepping out of their usual roles and taking the lead that night. He was so nervous he wasn't sure he was even going to be able to eat. When they walked into the kitchen, the others greeted Gwen and Jasper, and they chatted for a while, eating hors d'oeuvres and drinking a couple of the mocktails he'd been fiddling with lately, trying to come up with better options to offer people than water, juice, and coffee.

Dinner was a loud, boisterous affair, people talking over one another and having fun. There was a lot of laughter, a lot of storytelling, and a lot of good food. When it was done, they all migrated to the family room to hang out and talk some more, and as they were just about to get situated, Gwen stopped them. "Hang on. Let's get a group picture. Let me go get my camera."

Thornton took his phone out of his pocket, a confused look on his face. "Mom, here. Just use my phone."

Shitshitshitshitshit.

Gwen, bless her heart, rolled her eyes and waved him away as she left to get her camera. "I don't want some picture where we're all huddled together trying to fit in the shot while you hold the phone over your head, for Pete's sake. I have a real camera. You *do* remember what a real camera looks like, don't you?"

Trent snorted. "Thorn, when are you gonna learn? Mom does things her way. Just roll with it."

Thornton laughed, nodding. "Yeah. I should know this by now."

Gwen returned, waving her camera with a mini tripod attached, in her hand like a prize, and went about setting up on the console table behind the sofa. "Here, stand in front of the fireplace, Asher and Thornton in the middle."

Folks shuffled around, but this only got a frown from Gwen. "No, Thorn, pull the side table over, and you can sit on it so you're a little lower and everyone else is around you."

"We don't have to be in the center, Mom."

Trent scoffed. "We *just* went over this, Thorn. She's got something in her head, and she won't be happy until it's just the way she wants it."

Thornton rolled his eyes and threw up his hands. "Okay, okay. Here."

He put the lamp on the floor and pulled the side table in front of the fireplace. He sat down on it and tugged Asher down beside him, laughing. "Come on, might as well humor her."

Asher chuckled and snuggled into Thornton's side, his heart beating a mile a minute. They watched as Gwen told the others where to stand and then set up the shot, running around the sofa to join them in the photo before the camera took the delayed picture. "Smile big, guys!"

Asher was shaking when the camera went off, knowing the others were holding up their surprise signs, each with a single word, asking Thornton the scariest question ever. Gwen went to check on the photo. She glanced at it and then walked around the couch. "Here, Thornton, I don't know if it's good enough. Should we take another?"

Thornton, probably responding to the uncertainty in her voice, stood to check the photo, which was his cue. Getting down on one knee while Thornton checked the photo, he pulled out the ring box, hands shaking and palms sweating.

Asher waited with bated breath as Daddy checked the photo, Thornton's voice confused as he stared at it. "Wait. What are you guys holding? 'Thornton, will you…'"

Thornton gasped and turned around as Asher held up the ring. "Thornton, eight months ago, you ran over me with your car…" The others chuckled and Asher's tremulous smile grew when he saw the happy disbelief on Thornton's face. "And then you proceeded to steal my heart. Will you do me the honor of becoming my husband?"

"Baby…" Thornton's eyes filled as he got down on his knees in front of Asher, ignoring the ring and clasping his cheeks. "God, I love you. Hold that thought, though, and come with me."

Shocked Thornton hadn't said yes right away, Asher clasped his hand and allowed Thornton to pull him up. Then he proceeded to hold his hand and lead them out of the family room, down the hall, into the foyer, and down the other hall, stopping at the closed door of Asher's playroom.

His heart started to beat even faster. Gwen and Jasper knew about their lifestyle, but they hadn't ever seen his playroom or seen him as a little because that was something he only shared with, well, Thornton and occasionally their friends. It felt strange to be walking in there now, the sound of the other's footsteps behind them as they followed.

Thornton opened the door and ushered him in. It was then Asher saw his dad's old Lionel train set, lovingly restored and looking like new on a track table that looked professionally built, a little town in the center of the track, with grass, animals, and people. He got down on his knees, shocked at how new the train looked.

"How did you do this?"

"It took you a while to feel comfortable enough to get the train set out and show it to me, and you were so disappointed when it didn't work. I told you I'd figure something out and not to worry about it. So I found a local guy that specializes in this kind of thing. He restored everything, baby. It works. Try it."

His hands were shaking when he reached forward and flipped the switch. The train started chugging along the track. It went all the way around and then headed back towards him. When it was right in front of him, Thornton reached out, stopped it, and murmured, "Hmm, what's that?"

Confused, Asher leaned forward and looked at the coal car, only then noticing something sitting on top of the coal. It was his turn to gasp as he realized it was a black, Tungsten band, much like the one he'd gotten Thornton. He watched as Thornton leaned forward, picked the ring up, and faced him, on bended knee. "Asher, my answer to your question is yes. I would be honored to be your husband, and I'm hoping you'll say yes to being mine."

On a gasp, he threw himself into Thornton's arms, his whole body shaking. Thornton gathered him close, rubbing his back in soothing circles. He couldn't believe they'd both planned proposals on the same night. So overcome with emotion, all he could do was whisper, "Daddy..."

Thornton's arms gripped him tighter as he whispered back, "I love you, baby boy."

Only noticing everyone was gone when the door snicked shut, he let out a sigh and pulled Thornton's ring from the box. They exchanged them, slipping them on each other's fingers, tears clouding his sight, unable to see the details of his own ring. Asher threw himself back into Thornton's arms. "I love you. I love you. I love you. I love you. I love you."

Thornton gripped his hips and pulled him flush against him, so he was straddling his hips. Once he was ensconced on Daddy's lap, Thornton pulled away enough to clasp Asher's cheeks. "My sweet boy. I've never been so happy to run someone over in my life."

His watery laughter mixed with Thornton's as they gazed at each other. "I love you, Asher Simmons, and I can't wait until I officially make you my *real* husband, even though I've been your husband since the day we met."

They both chuckled at the long-running joke, and Thornton sobered. "I couldn't have dreamed of a better man for me. You are the extra piece of my puzzle, the perfect fit, and I can't wait to grow old with you, baby boy."

Asher let out a soft, happy sigh. "I love you so much. I never thought I'd find anyone who would want me to be theirs. But you became my accidental Daddy. You started taking care of me the second you laid eyes on me, and I know you'll never stop. You've helped me so much. I'm the man I am today because of you."

Thornton shook his head. "No, baby—"

"It's true. I know I did the work, but I'd have never taken the steps on my own, or if I had, the results wouldn't have been the same. You are my everything, and I'm so grateful I'm your perfect fit."

Thornton rocked them back and forth as Asher gathered his emotions enough to call their family back in. When they all made their way in, giving congratulations, along with hugs and well wishes, he knew there was nothing on earth better than family, and he was so grateful he'd found his.

The End

BONUS SCENE!

If you want a kinky little bonus scene of Asher's first spanking, join my reader group
Luna's Lunatics

Also, don't forget to sign up for my newsletter, so you don't miss any new releases, updates on book signings, giveaways, and much more.
Luna David's Newsletter

Check out my entire collection on Amazon
Luna's Amazon Author Page

Find me on the interwebs
Luna's Social Media Links

ALSO BY LUNA DAVID

Custos Securities Series

Trusting Cade

Protecting Braden

Saving Sebastian

Finding Ky

Custos Securities/Catharsis Novel

Saving Sebastian

The Boys Club Series

Let Me In

Kink Chronicles

Open Mind

A Kink Chronicles Short

Open Encounters

Open Play

Ace's Wild Series

Caged In (Ace's Wild Book 12)